BLOOD DRAW
GABRIELLE JARRETT

Are the events in here true? Most likely not. Are they real? Perhaps.

What is truth?

P. Pilate

John 18:38

The Christian Bible

GabrielleJarrett.com

To my adult children,

Keli, Heidi, Kirk, and Meghan,

for whom my love and pride are boundless.

WHAT ONE MUST FEAR, MOREOVER, IS NOT SO MUCH THE SIGHT OF THE
IMMORALITY OF THE GREATS AS THAT OF IMMORALITY LEADING TO
GREATNESS.

ALEXIS DE TOCQUEVILLE

IF ONLY IT WERE SO SIMPLE! IF ONLY THERE WERE EVIL PEOPLE
SOMEWHERE INSIDIOUSLY COMMITTING EVIL DEEDS, AND IT WERE
NECESSARY ONLY TO SEPARATE THEM FROM THE REST OF US AND
DESTROY THEM. BUT THE LINE DIVIDING GOOD AND EVIL CUTS
THROUGH THE HEART OF EVERY HUMAN BEING.

AND WHO IS WILLING TO DESTROY HIS OWN HEART?

PETER MATTHIESSEN

CHAPTER ONE
PAUL/TOM: MINNEAPOLIS, 1963

"You must sit on the house, on the eaves," the father owl instructed. "They need to know to prepare for death."

"I don't like it," stated the young owl. "I hate death."

"It is part of life, all of our lives, my child. It's part of the baby's life who will soon enter the house with his parents. I will never lie to you, loss is pervasive. But sometimes, just sometimes, the lost can be found."

The young owl thought about it all, as it perched on the bungalow in Chicago in folds of sadness. *Was it true?*

Paul's memory of his last days in Chicago moved in and out of awareness. He called his only relative, Maggie, a pediatrician in Minneapolis. In eight hours, she was at his door, hugging him for as long as he needed. Her shock and disbelief at the tragedy were oddly comforting to Paul. She could share the earthquake that had shaken his world. She held Aron close as well, declaring him beautiful and healthy.

After Paul told her as much as he could about the morning, she gave him a sleep aid and announced she would stay in the day bed in Aron's room so Paul could try to sleep. Paul chose the guest room, after giving Maggie permission to tell Bruno, her partner of many years, the entire story. Bruno worked for the FBI, but he would do nothing until he spoke with Paul in person.

Maggie phoned Bruno after Paul had gone to sleep. It was only with Bruno she could let herself sob uncontrollably. He reassured her that he would do everything he possibly could, which was quite a bit. He would get the guest rooms at their house ready. No, she shouldn't tell Paul that an owl on a house once meant an imminent death.

Paul and Maggie spent the next days getting rid of furniture, packing the essentials, and selling the house to a home broker. The three of them would go to Minneapolis. Paul and Aron would stay for as long as they needed. Maggie nearly demanded therapy for Paul before he searched for a job.

"A far away job," responded Paul. "Far away from the Midwest and those men. As soon as I can."

"I understand." Maggie attempted to soothe him. "But you must stay with us until you are ready to begin your new life. We'll get a plan. Bruno has some suggestions. Paul, I don't think you should drive."

Paul agreed and sold his car. They started on their trip north.

He was eternally grateful for Maggie and Bruno taking him and Aron in and making them part of their family. Bruno's suggestion was to immediately take new identities so that Paul could throw off the murderers and begin a fresh life. Paul repeated the story of the horrible morning several times. Bruno held off his full opinion for weeks, while confirming that events like unreported murders do happen, and his compassion for Paul was deeper than could be expressed.

Six weeks had passed. Maggie knew Paul was waiting to be accepted and hired at a school in Portland, Oregon. She advised him to tell them he couldn't be there until the third week of September. He would only miss one week of school and they would surely understand with his extraordinary circumstances. Paul needed the time to begin his process of healing as well as bond with Aron, his new son, now his birth son, no longer adopted.

Paul stood in the guest room, staring at the three pieces of paper in front of him. One read *Elizabeth Freborne: born July 6, 1939. Died August 10, 1963. Cause: complications of childbirth.*

Paul hated the lie. He wanted to tear the paper into shreds. He had a sharp intake of breath, remembering the last paper he ripped into tiny pieces. It lay on the top of his wife's body. He read the name Elizabeth Freborne once again. That was not her name! She was Suzanne Miller. His wife. His name. She wasn't born on July 6, but on July 14. The final lie was the cause of death. It was an abomination of the truth.

Paul read the second document, a birth certificate for his son, newly renamed Derek. He questioned Maggie somewhat incredulously about Derek's birth date being changed by five weeks, "How can a baby suddenly lose five weeks of development?" Maggie explained the development markers have a wide range in the early months. She also explained that Aron was small and would pass as "bright for his age." She told Paul not to go to a pediatrician until mid-October. She would take care of his immediate medical needs, and by then he'd clearly pass as a two-month-old.

The third certificate was his own. Thomas Freborne. Birth date changed by one year and two months. His birth place was listed as Minneapolis, not Chicago. He could not care less. He didn't want to be found, by anyone. Bruno explained the new identities were essential for him and his son. They could not trust that the men only wanted Suzanne. Paul would give his life if needed for the life of his son. He would never try to find who killed Suzanne or to find her family. He would believe the story he created. He would become Thomas Freborne. He and his son would be born free.

T om walked to Maggie's backyard. It bordered on one of the many lakes in Minneapolis. Derek was asleep inside, under the teddy bear mobile. Tom couldn't leave the teddy bears behind; it was his only continuity. It didn't make sense, but he needed the bears. Maybe for the future. Right now, they caused tremendous pain but then again, almost everything did. Seeing the teddy bears reminded Tom of the fact that the men did not take his son. As crazy as it seemed, Tom saw the bears almost as angels, though he told no one of his teddy bear angel thoughts.

Tom sat on the wicker rocker looking at the three certificates, close enough to Derek to hear him awaken. How, how could such events have crashed into his life in forty-six days? He and Derek had been living with Maggie for forty-two days. He kept thinking in terms of days.

Somehow, he could not get his mind into weeks or months. Tom makes a vow: once he hears from his first choice of jobs, the Open Heart Open Mind Academy in Portland, he will think in terms of weeks, months, then years. Tom and Derek Freborne will be as natural to say as...their old names.

Disappearing and new identities. He had read of such things in a novel series. When he read the novels, he thought, "Unbelievable! Fiction is so...well, fiction. Untrue." Now fiction was fact. Tom and Derek Freborne were facts. Bruno told him things in Chicago were "taken care of," and he wasn't to worry. He was safe. Tom knew he could never tell the story of his wife's death after he left Maggie and Bruno's. He would bury within as much as he could, even though he was now in therapy. Tom knew about burying pain. His parents were killed in a car accident when he was a senior in high school. That memory could not be exhumed or he would lose his mind. Deaths of loved ones were in an impenetrable memory box inside of Tom.

But, right now, rocking gently, Tom had to go over the days and the weeks since the day he would never forget. Even though he was no longer Paul Miller, he had to remember as much as he could. Going to therapy three days a week had already begun the healing process within him. Part of his therapy was writing. Almost every day for an hour, Tom sat and wrote the events that brought him and his son to be Freborne, living in Minneapolis without Suzanne, and awaiting an acceptance letter from OHOM Academy, where he would create a new life.

Tom knew he had to accept the events in order to heal so he could be the best dad ever for Derek. After writing the pages, he ripped them out and carried them down to the lake. He burned them and let the water carry the ashes away. With each burning, he believed he would lessen his grief a tiny bit. He also knew the grieving would never be over.

Bruno walked down to the lake after he saw Tom burn the afternoon's writings. "Are you up for talking?"

Tom stopped breathing and said, "Sure, Bruno. Go ahead."

Bruno sat on the bench. "Tom, you are aware the men who took Suzanne from you are in a cult, right?"

Tom was startled, first by the use of his new name, and secondly by the use of the word cult.

"Bruno, there really aren't cults." He turned to look at Bruno. "Are there?"

"Yes, Tom, there are and always have been cults. Suzanne's father was a minister in a small town in Indiana, right? Reverend Oscar Schmidt? Smotelyville? Did she ever tell you anything about her father? His church?" Suddenly Tom was plunged back into his memory. Two memories. His proposal to Suzanne and her murder.

CHAPTER TWO
PAUL AND SUZANNE: CHICAGO, 1963

T*he sun escapes from the clouds as I hold Aron for the first time. I take him from the arms of my wife, Suzanne. She is aglow with love. I cannot help but see the Madonna, albeit with a single long dark blonde braid down her back, cradling our newborn son.*

"Paul, now he is our son. Hold him. He looks so very much like you: dark hair, green eyes, brow in a furrow. How is that possible?"

As we sign the adoption papers. we stare at our miracle and drive home dazzled, in love with our new family. "Look, Suzanne. An owl on our house!" We go in feeling a special blessing.

Paul stopped writing. The pain in his chest crashed against his ribs. He stared at the lake and continued to put his pen to paper, hating the owl.

Our first night with Aron is magical. He sleeps six hours. We don't, because we take turns checking on him to see if he is still breathing. Then we make love, exquisitely, while the teddy bears dancing on the mobile keep watch over our son.

In the morning, I kiss her. "Happy twenty-fourth birthday, my love." Her eyes glisten as our hug is deeper than ever. "I must go out, sweetheart. I'll be back in less than an hour. Do you need anything?"

She smiles, shakes her head no. "Just you and Aron."

I kiss her on the lips and drive to buy a double gift. I know exactly what will make the perfect birthday and new mommy gift. On the way home, I smile at the wrapped package on the seat next to me.

After passing a black van parked down the street, I pull into our drive, notice the same owl, and feel a cold shiver in my spine. I go in, bounding up the stairs.

6

"I'm home, birthday girl!" No response. Maybe she fell asleep after our wakeful night. Quietly, I open our bedroom door.

My heart stops beating. My head pounds. I fall to my knees at the side of the bed. "No! My God! No!" I shout in a strangled cry. Suzanne is cold and white. She's turning blue. No breath.

There is a sheet of parchment paper on her unmoving chest. I see red writing. "No!" I shout again. "No! Not blood!" I drop the sheet on the floor as if burned, and read:

Now she is ours.
Our promised one.
One score and four.
Yet, the vow ne'er done.
The prophecy is fulfilled.
The sacrifice now holy.

Silence must reign.
Or your son will be slain.
Yet. The vow ne'er done.
Mother and son. Daughters and sons.
Our vows in blood.
We live on and on and on.

"Aron! I've forgotten about Aron." I rush unsteadily to his room and open the door without a sound. He's intensely watching the dancing bears. He doesn't see me and I close the door. I return to our bedroom to reread the parchment. "Silence must reign or your son will be slain."

I struggle. The papers are evidence. Of what? That I did not kill her. Police? What do I do? My helpless tears begin to mix with her blood in our last union. I touch the words with my finger, bringing it to my lips. I rip the words into tiny pieces to flush down the toilet. Then I vomit.

Paul grabbed his stomach, feeling the same nausea as his eyes flooded. He tasted the salt and the blood. "I've got to go on." He gripped the pen so hard and didn't care if it broke. Everything has been broken.

I hear footsteps on the stairs. My stomach drops again. My heart pounds out of my chest. I know who is coming. Four men in dark suits and black fedoras reach the landing, one by one.

The killers. Did they come back for Aron? For me? Sweat seeps from every pore in my body.

They keep their faces averted, speak little.

One looks at me pointedly, briefly. "Go. We'll take her. No police." He looks to Aron's room and commands me. "Your son."

I get the message. I stagger to Aron's room and sit in front of his closed door. I hear Aron begin to cry. I watch Suzanne being carried down the stairs on a stretcher. They are very careful with her. I move to the top of the stairs and watch the black van pull away. They left the front door open so I could see them take my life away. My wife. My sobs will never stop, will they. Aron begins to cry louder. My son. I'm his only parent. I drag myself up, walk to his door, open it, and hold him close. We rock for the next hour, or perhaps days.

Paul could write no more.

CHAPTER THREE
OSCAR: SMOTELYVILLE, 1984

Oscar grew up with the Rituals. They were as natural and predictable as the orange juice and coffee Oscar had every morning. He asked no questions of his father, which was also natural.

What does a five-year-old know? A ten-year-old? mused Oscar in his later years. *They adapt. They believe. They obey. Or they are punished. I did what any five-year-old would do.* The unspoken end of his limited and recurring introspection was: *I kept believing. I kept my promise. I kept believing whatever my father did was not wrong.*

Oscar is sitting in his study attempting to write a sermon. His thoughts of the past slide in and out of his brain, casting long narrow shadows on his ability to concentrate on the sermon.

Oscar has embraced a blank stare, his response to unwanted thoughts from five years of age. When Oscar remembers to blink, he returns to the present. Now even that seems confusing.

He has little access to his own memories. Sometimes Oscar is five. Then he is thirteen. Or he is twenty-two. The phrase "one score and four" keeps intruding into his mind. The time it takes Oscar to write his sermons is longer and longer because of the intrusive thoughts.

He continues to muse. *It wasn't wrong then, so it couldn't be wrong now. Truth is eternal. Truth does not change. Never.* Oscar writes into his sermon the words, "Truth does not change." He dozes once again.

Later Oscar's wife Bernice finds him in his vacant gaze. She writes it down in the small notebook she keeps for the neurologist. Oscar knows nothing about the notebook.

nside Oscar, he is ten. *He begins to feel afraid. He doesn't know how to look inside. His capacity for introspection never developed. With every "Sir" he uttered to his father, one more seed of inner knowledge dried and died. Oscar did not know about the seed murder, but he did know his insides reeked of original sin.*

Four of Oscar's friends and their fathers also joined in the Rituals. All of them attended his father's church.

During one particular Ritual, Oscar feels the familiar fear arise in his bowels. He scans the room and sees the faces of men he knows. Although they are wearing dark robes with hoods up, their familiar faces are in familiar places during the Ritual. Oscar sees the chief of police, the mayor, his dentist, and other members of his father's church. He talks to himself: I see good men. Good Christian men. Honored and respected in their jobs and in my father's church with positions of power.

f course, Oscar would not have used those words at ten or even thirteen. Only in his retrospective questioning did he create such sentences to describe his ten-year-old self. He called each one Sir. The older Oscar and the younger ones fade in and out of each other. His shadowy memories relentlessly attack his present self. His seven decades of living fight each memory's clash with current time. At times, Oscar loses the onslaught. It is during these losses that sharp knives wrack his stomach.

"I find no abnormality," stated the gastroenterologist. "Take this prescription. Come back in three months. Don't worry about the side effects; they'll go away. If not, I'll give you another prescription for the side effects. Give it time."

Whatever happened in those rooms with those men is a secret. Secret means never ever to be told, even now. The members in the rooms did not discuss it with each other. The "Sirs" would know immediately if he ever breathed a word. They would know even if he wrote a word. Now Oscar fears even thinking a word.

The boys never talked to each other. Somehow Oscar felt safer, even these many decades later, knowing no one ever told. He could count on secrecy. Or he would die. Oscar does not now know the secret is the cause of his dying, his dying mind. He does know one boy left to go who knows where. Perhaps he died. He knows one committed suicide and another died in a car accident. The others stayed in Smotelyville.

O nce Oscar's father tried to trick him. *Oscar is lying on his bed. "What did you think of what you saw tonight, Oscar?" asks his father, who still wore his black robe. It was like the one he wore every Sunday morning, except this robe had a hood. He also wore it in the Rituals. The hooded robe adds to Oscar's increasing fear. The fear drills his bowels mercilessly.*

Oscar's father looked right into Oscar's eyes, boring a permanent auger of terror into Oscar's brain. The tip of the auger went right into Oscar's stomach.

"I'm not sure what you are talking about, Sir. I was in my room all night." The blue eyes above the unsmiling mouth began to shine with pride as a slow half-smile emerged from the hooded face.

"Why, Oscar, I see you are the smartest boy I know! Tell the Truth. Always tell the Truth. Just like now. Just like tonight. Remember your Promise and Special Vow to be given to you at thirteen years of age. Your initiation will be special because you are my son and will carry on our lineage of many centuries." His father's half-smile disappears as he leaves the room.

Oscar runs to the bathroom to throw up. Over and over and over.

After the terror was spewed out, Oscar begins to feel the specialness that can only come with a father's love and pride. The secrets added to his feeling of being special. Oscar is different than the other boys in his group, his school, and his Sunday school. Oscar is very special because he goes to a Lutheran school. He wants to be a Lutheran minister, just like his father, the Reverend Adolf Schmidt. Just like his grandpa. Oscar knows for certain that the Lutherans have replaced the Jews as God's Chosen People.

Oscar knows he is Chosen. The men told him so tonight.

"Dear, dear, you fell asleep." Bernice repeats the same words to him every time she awakens him. She continues to spare his pride as he continues to lose his mind. "Tonight, the Deacons are coming for a visit. We best eat now. "

Oscar and Bernice walk into the kitchen. Her thoughts are filled with the anticipation of the meeting. She knows the Deacons are determined to tell Oscar he must retire as soon as possible, even though he is very part-time in their small, remote church, a few counties north of Smotelyville.

Oscar's thoughts are filled with trying to remember why he was so special. He wishes he could remember his Special Promise. *One score and four.* The words float into his mind. He blinks and they retreat into their demented prison.

CHAPTER FOUR
JEMMA AND AZURE: SEATTLE, 1992

Azure sat in her office, a suite of two rooms in an updated mansion in the Queen Anne neighborhood of Seattle. Her office boasted a gas vertical heating grill in the small fireplace. The walls were paneled in beautifully polished walnut. The leaded glass windows were open to let in the warm autumn breeze.

The sign on Azure's door read *Azure Manjursi, Storytelling Therapy.* She knew it raised a few eyebrows, which mattered little to her. Storytelling was her preferred mode of therapy. It brought a centuries-old form of healing to many people.

Azure watched the gathering grey of twilight that El Niño season, which arrived in Seattle the autumn she met Jemma. El Niño and El Niña spoke of related opposites. While Azure preferred to see fate as destiny, she could not sever that two-faced god of related opposites that comprised mystery. In a deep mood of wonder and welcome, she looked forward to meeting her new client and opened the door to the waiting room.

Jemma was forty-six when Azure met her. Her features, black hair, and blue eyes clearly put her in the category of beautiful. Like some beautiful women, she was unaware of her physical gifts. Azure could see that she carried a broken heart beneath its walls, and a restless spirit, yearning to be free.

"I'm not sure I'm in the right place," Jemma began immediately as Azure opened the office door. "I was referred to you by Charles Dirgence at the university. He gave me three names of therapists. I'm working in the Adoption Project. I thought you were a therapist, but I don't understand the storytelling part." Jemma looked puzzled as she rapidly spoke.

"It's confusing, I realize. Come inside. I'll explain." Azure reached out her hand and introduced herself.

Jemma sat in one of the large overstuffed purple chairs. Azure sat in the other.

"I start with a chime, Jemma. It's meant to help us both get centered and present. I'll chime and while it's ringing, we close our eyes and breathe into our hearts." She looked at Jemma with a questioning nod and Jemma nodded back. Azure chimed.

The chime tones faded. "I like that. It makes me a little more relaxed. But, I still need to hear about storytelling." Jemma waited.

Azure explained that storytelling was the client's task. "There are many modes, techniques, and philosophies of therapy. I have been trained in many and have found when we approach our lives as stories, the healing is deeper and our insights clearer. Often a natural sort of wisdom emerges. You can research storytelling, of course, and may prefer something more traditional. I prefer storytelling to neurosis and diagnosis. You don't have a pathology; you have a story that needs understanding, a story that needs to be told."

"Well, that makes me anxious. I feel like I have to perform somehow. Alone and on a stage, judged by how well I do, rather than who I am." Jemma sat up straighter in her chair. Azure could see the walls around her heart were being threatened. "Jemma, it's not something you do alone. I am with you, just like regular therapy. You'll see, if we continue to meet, that the process is not so different. When is the last time you told any of your stories and experienced that the listener was really listening?"

Jemma glanced to the window. "It's been a very long time. Maybe that's why I am here. I told you I work with the Adoption Project. I'm on sabbatical from Macalester College where I teach English Lit." She stopped and smiled. "Stories, right? I'm a collator in the Project, gathering stories...jeez, there it is again, the story idea." Jemma shook her head and seemed to relax. "The Project focuses on adoptees, those who adopted, and the moms who were unable to raise their babies, giving them up for adoption."

She stopped and exhaled. "The collators collect the information from the interviewers who are working with the subjects. I do not have direct contact with the subjects, but already I feel emotionally off-center. That is why I am here. You see, I had a baby at seventeen and had to put her up for adoption."

"You have a story, Jemma, perhaps one of the most significant ones in your life. I want to hear it. Are you okay with telling me?"

Jemma nodded slightly. "Twenty-nine years ago, I gave up my newborn daughter for adoption. I was seventeen. Back then, of course, I saw no therapist. I delivered in a home run by nuns. They told me giving up my daughter was for the best, as they took her from me. I couldn't even hold her. My conflict is whether to accept I will never meet my daughter nor know anything about her, or if I should try to find her. Obviously working with adoptees is bringing my story to the surface."

"Who knew of your pregnancy, Jemma?"

"My parents, of course. They sent me to the home. After college, I was married for six years and divorced ten years ago. I told my husband about the pregnancy and adoption, though I wish I hadn't. He brushed it off quickly and offered no consolation, and I felt alone again. Like when I gave birth."

"You are not alone now, Jemma. You have begun several stories. Your pregnancy, the birth, not holding your daughter, and your divorce as well. How are you doing?"

"There's so much more to say. I'm not used to talking about myself so much."

"You're doing a very good job. But how are you feeling about it? Do you want to continue?"

"Where do I start?" questioned Jemma as she closed her eyes and exhaled.

"You already have..."

Jemma made another appointment with Azure for therapy. She would be a storyteller with an experienced and compassionate witness. Her daughter was one of the most important stories of her life and she would not stay silent.

CHAPTER FIVE
JEMMA AND PETER: SEATTLE, 1992

I n her small university office, Jemma was overwhelmed. All she had to do was organize the findings of the interviewers. Fortunately, she didn't have to interpret the findings. She picked up The Adoption Project Manual for Level One Research Assistants as she changed the position of her chair in an effort to clear her mind, hoping for a new perspective.

She was aware that she had read and reread the manual far more than she would have thought necessary given her background and profession. She also noted that she was being judgmental of herself, sighed, and drank her Darjeeling tea that had cooled beyond enjoyable as she opened the manual yet again.

Someone knocked lightly and almost hesitantly on her open door jamb as a shadow fell over her manual. She looked up to see a tall man in a topaz sweater, blue jeans, and very worn hiking boots standing in her doorway. He asked if he was disturbing her.

She smiled. It was the researcher she had described to her close friends, Cindi and LouLeary, the night before. They had spent some time discussing his potential as a boyfriend. Jemma did not usually date movie star types, but Cindi said to go for it. And here he was! She felt a most pleasant surprise and prayed that she was not blushing. *Disturbing? Hell, no!*

"No need to apologize. I'm Jemma." She smiled and introduced herself, extending her hand while rising.

"I'm Peter. Nice to meet you." His eyes seemed to agree with his words, she noted with relief. "I see we are on the same project. The Adoption Project for the social work department? I'm not convinced I know anything at this point." Peter looked directly into her eyes.

"Yes, and yes. I'm not getting this either." She picked up the manual, returned his direct look, and sat down.

"Ah, so glad I'm not the only one!" Peter's face broke into a sunlight of relief.

"Not at all. I was about to read the manual for the twentieth time to determine if it's my lack of social work background or if I want to apply to rewrite it."

"You, Jemma, have made my day! My field is computers. I just decided I made a very poor choice to sign onto the Project. It sounded so straightforward in the job description, the interview, and the first group meeting. Now? I can't even get through the manual, much less understand it."

Jemma smiled in agreement as she flipped through the manual, holding it as a fan. "You are not alone." She knew she was flirting and loved it.

Peter flashed a conspiratorial smile and whispered, "We are not alone."

She wondered to herself how a whole face could smile. Out loud she responded, "I didn't think the Project would be so complex. Here, this is what I understand. The ten collectors we supervise go out to get ten interviews. Then they pass them to us, requiring us to read and organize the one hundred stories in nine months. That part is certainly doable. The manual is overflowing with statistical analysis. So, what's up? You must know more about this than I do."

"Don't count on that at all! I can't make any sense of it." He shook his head as if he were on the wrong bus.

She realized she was enjoying his confusion with a light peace from the innate need to console. She exhaled, feeling freedom.

"What are you smiling about?" Peter's face turned serious.

She told him she didn't know, but that finding a familiar in this place of chaos was an unexpected surprise.

The shades in his eyes began to lower as he suggested, "We are only two and perhaps everyone else is getting it?"

Jemma noticed the shades in his eyes continuing their descent, erasing any emotional expression. She had never experienced such an immediate and definite change in anyone's emotions. The glass veneer in his eyes was nearly opaque.

"Hey, don't go away. I wasn't laughing at you. Honest! It's the relief of knowing a computer guy and a literature major can't read a manual written for us. I was sitting here, all alone with my critic and I'm happy I can share the frustration." *And enjoy your company*, she said to herself.

As the shades in Peter's eyes raised, he asked her if she would like to leave the building and get some coffee, adding that a fresh start together might be helpful.

Jemma switched off the light and dropped the manual into her messenger bag. "I'd love to. Let's take this just in case we come up with some kind of rare insight."

"I'll drive, if that's okay with you?" He raised his eyebrows. She nodded. "Have you ever been to Paradox? It's new and owned by two doctors. Get it?" She took a second, then laughed as they walked out.

"My car is right out front. I just stopped for some papers."

Neither talked as they walked down the marble stairs - each in their own thoughts about the other and the unknown.

Jemma put on her seat belt in the navy-blue Jeep Wrangler that was not at all in the new category. Peter drove easily as he asked her reasons for accepting the research position. "Are you from Seattle, Jemma?"

"No, I live in St. Paul, Minnesota. I teach English lit in a small college."

"Is that the Midwest?"

Jemma smiled. "Well, I think of it as the mid-north. But that's just me, being from the Midwest and adverse to it."

Peter winked. "A geographic elitist?"

She sighed resignedly. "I guess I am and not so proud of it."

"Well, why not be proud of it? Owning my own beliefs is something I work at and find admirable in others. Even if I don't like my own beliefs."

"Not like your own beliefs?" Jemma turned to him, puzzled.

"Yeah. If you truly believe something, it's one thing. If you had an unpopular belief, I would admire your courage to believe in whatever it is, even if you are uncomfortable with it or others complain about it."

"Well, if I had a belief I no longer liked, I would drop it. So, courageous beliefs of neo-Nazis, Satanists, and terrorists earn your admiration?"

Silence. Peter murmured that the question was if he could admire a person owning their beliefs, even if he did not especially admire their beliefs or even held such beliefs in contempt.

She waited in supreme confusion, knowing that was not what he said, while examining his fascinating face.

"Nope. Can't. Yes, maybe. Maybe my effort to construct an unshakable and logical worldview will be toted to the trash. Maybe not. Maybe I have beliefs you think unlikeable, but I offer you the chance to hear and understand them." He parked in front of Paradox and looked at her. "Never have I had such a strange conversation while driving to a coffee shop with someone I met twenty minutes ago."

"Nor have I. Where did all this come from? What are you talking about, Peter?"

"More to be revealed." Peter responded mysteriously in a most engaging manner.

Her chemistry began to buzz.

Later Jemma remembered that he never really answered her question about the Neo-Nazis, Satanists, and terrorists. *Was he one of those?* She smiled at herself. Right...

CHAPTER SIX
AZURE AND DEREK: SEATTLE, 1992

Azure opened the door to her waiting room with anticipation. She enjoyed meeting new clients. "Hello Derek? I'm Azure. Please come in. Thank you for filling out the intake sheet." She extended her hand warmly.

Derek handed her the paperwork and settled into the deep purple overstuffed chair while gazing around the office. He explained he received the referral from Charles Dirgence.

"Please thank him for me," Azure smiled.

"Your name is Azure Manjursi?" he asked, with a somewhat suspicious look. He continued in a commanding voice, "What's a storytelling therapist?"

"I will explain, but first I'd like to begin with a chime." She told him the purpose of the chime. When the tones stopped, she began again, "The idea of storytelling can be confusing."

He interrupted with, "Which is, of course, why I called. My whole life has been in a state of confusion. I wasn't prepared for more of it on your door. *More on the Door*, a great book title," he smiled sardonically.

She returned the smile and continued. "My way of doing therapy is within the framework of storytelling. Mine and yours. You tell your story. In time, with my questions and observations, your story will most likely change, certainly evolve, and often evoke deep healing."

"This is one of the most off-the-wall therapies I've ever heard." Derek spoke with soft finality. He shook his head and fixed Azure with an unrelenting gaze.

"I realize it may seem 'off the wall' to you, yet it does serve the purpose of healing and resolution. We live the stories we have created about ourselves. Some are based in truth, some in lies. Maybe what was true for us at ten is very different when we are twenty or thirty. When you hear your own story, you become a witness to your life in a different and more effective way than focusing on the problems. You mentioned your life being in a state of confusion. What's the story of your confusion?"

Derek began. "I don't believe my story has anything to do with my confusion, but I will start at the beginning. My mother died a few hours after I was born, in August of 1963. The cause was undetermined post-delivery infection.

"It took me a long time to believe I was not the undetermined cause. In fact, on occasion, I still wonder. I think I memorized her death certificate before my birth certificate. Then I think I forgot her. Because I never knew her."

Azure saw the flicker of sadness in his eyes. It seemed he was unaware of the sadness.

He continued. "My dad is a great guy. His dream was to create the family he lost growing up. He answered every question I ever asked about my birth mom. About my step-mom, Terese? He married her on my first birthday, the very day she adopted me. We lived in Minneapolis where I was born. Six weeks later, my dad and I moved to Portland Oregon where he took a job teaching. He was a high school history teacher at Willamette Academy. Now he is the dean of students. The school was begun as Open Heart, Open Mind by Quakers, hippies, and educators. During his first year of teaching, my dad met Terese, who taught art and literature. I have two half-sisters who are my real sisters," Derek stated with emphasis. "So, you see, I had a very good childhood with no confusion."

"I've heard of the Academy. Did you go to school there as well?"

"Yes. I loved it. And I understand why my dad had to leave Minnesota and get as far away as possible from the memories. I'm here because of my career. Well, and something else. After my high school graduation, I wanted to go to school back East, but ended up choosing Reed College in Portland, due to a scholarship and the continued philosophy of OHOM. After Reed, I did go back East to the University of Chicago where I earned a law degree. It was the only thing in my life that my dad ever opposed. He didn't want me to go to school in Chicago. However, in the end, he agreed. After passing the Illinois bar, I moved to Seattle to study for and pass the Washington bar. On the day I passed, I signed up for the MCATs and pre-med classes. Well, I've signed up for both several times, and was unable to do it. Something stops me from completing the task."

Derek stopped. "I'm pouring out way too much. I just want to get to the answers."

Azure took a minute to add some space. "Your story told and retold will give us the answers. Go at your own pace. I will ask you to repeat some of it. I'm curious about your feelings. The ones you haven't mentioned." She knew her eyes held a twinkle. "Why medicine?"

"The most obvious answer for my choice, is my mother's unexplained death so young. I also wonder if the little bit of therapy I had as a child enters into my thinking. Maybe I want to be a child psychiatrist. The years of training exhaust me. More confusion keeps me in my job at Elliot Bay Bookstore. I know I need to resolve all of this confusion, though, grow up and get a real job."

"I've always considered being a bookseller a real job," she told him with a smile. "How did you choose law?"

Derek stared out the window. "I think it was a search for a truth to get me out of the confusion that began at Reed." He stopped and mused, "Maybe it was in high school. I'm not going to that place right now." He cleared his throat. "I wanted a black and white, clear and unchangeable truth. I thought I would find it in law. But all of this is not the only reason I'm here. It's about the woman I love."

The change in Derek was patent. His breathing changed and his body tensed. His eyes actually changed from blue to green. He talked about Tabitha, with whom he had an eighteen-month relationship. He knew the next step would be to live together but wanted to be engaged first.

"When I enter a jewelry store, I freeze. Just like the MCATs," he explained. "The indecision is paralyzing. Tibs, my nickname for Tabitha, has a fellowship opportunity in Denver. She told me she needs some kind of direction of where our love is going and that she needs distance to heal if we do break it off. I need to make a decision very soon." His eyes wavered.

Silence filled the room. Derek spoke.

"I need to return here. With my story, as you call it. I need to know. Both where I am going and why I can't get going. And maybe even possibly, where I came from. Whatever that means." Derek walked out with Azure's card, shoulders squared, but not yet ready to make an appointment.

Azure had a sense Derek held many stories, some of which he had no idea existed. He puzzled her with his confidence, even as a sad and wandering look often appeared in his eyes. After writing her notes, she decided to phone her friend, Charles to thank him for his recent referrals.

She needed their connection.

CHAPTER SEVEN
DEREK: SEATTLE, 1992

Derek was hesitant as he walked closer to Peter's office at the university. Was he being controlled by confusion once again? He knocked softly on the half-opened door. Peter answered in a loud voice, "Come in!"

"I'm Derek Freborne and I'm not sure I really belong in this Project. As a subject." Derek pushed the door open and stood in the doorway with his arms crossed. "I'm only half-adopted." Peter looked up. "Half-adopted? Please come in. Sit down and tell me more." He looked curious and softened his voice.

Derek entered and sat down. He explained that his father was his biological father, and that his mother had died shortly after Derek's birth. His dad remarried the following year to Terese. She adopted him on his first birthday, so maybe he did belong in the Project, or maybe he really didn't fit. Derek quickly glanced away, but not before Peter noticed the anxiety clouding in Derek's eyes.

"I'm pretty sure 'half-adopted' fits the criteria. In fact, I would think the researchers might really like the variable. I'm sorry about your mom," he added.

"Thank you, although that is not the reason for my emotions. It's the not-fitting-in thing."

Peter nodded, all too willing to give advice to a young man in trouble. He was especially gleeful to give it to the one in front of him. Peter knew Derek, but Derek did not know Peter. "Derek, I think..."

Derek interrupted with a "designed-to-make-the-other-feel-better" smile. "No worries, mate. I know this isn't a therapy session. It's a factual interview. I just didn't want to waste your time if I am...um, not appropriate."

"I'm sure you are very appropriate. I will double-check to be sure so you feel comfortable." Peter was very accommodating.

They continued and after an hour, Derek left. Peter took out his vellum book and made some notes with a satisfied smile.

Derek walked down the hall in the social work department after closing Peter's door. "Where is that storytelling therapist's card?" Derek mumbled as he went through his wallet. *God, I couldn't just tear up in a stranger's office because he used the phrase "not fitting in." Maybe Peter didn't notice.* He went to the parking lot and got into his car, feeling grateful for his new mobile phone. He left a message with Azure, asking for an appointment. Then he called Tibs to see if she was free for dinner that evening.

T
ibs and Derek sat at their regular table in Paradox. She began, "Sweetheart, I really don't know if this research project is the thing for you right now. You've got so much going on: MCATs, the bookstore, and..." she hesitated, "us." She glanced back to the menu to avoid Derek's eyes.

So much going on, I always have so much going on. He continued to think as he read the menu - always so much going on. Since birth, it had been that way. *Had it ever really let up? After my sisters were born and in school? Perhaps.* He remembered being thirteen immediately. Thirteen was awful. All those thoughts. The thoughts he still ignored. Yet, they kept a steady shadow with every turn he took.

"Derek? Where are you?"

"Sorry, the menu caught me up."

"It's the same menu we have read for over a year." Tibs replied crisply, feeling her irritation rise. *Why wait until after ordering? After eating?* "Derek, I don't know how much longer I can be an 'us.' The professors who offered me the fellowship in Denver are understandably pressuring me for an answer."

"It's not the job, Tibs, I know that. I'm not easy, especially now with the Adoption Project. Maybe I should drop out."

"It's not your Project, your work, or your MCATs, Derek. You know that. It's my feeling of disconnect with you. You're with me, yet not with me. I'm with your ghost that you leave behind from wherever it is that you go when we're together. What's happened? I know better, but I have to ask. Is it me?"

He could not stop the tears welling up, once again. Her pain and his pain were too much. *God, I must need an antidepressant.* "It's never been you. I'm not complete, Tibs. Not complete. Not present. Not enough. Not worthy. No! Don't say it. I can't be here for me, much less you, especially not us. Being worthy means you deserve a full partner. Not empty, not half-empty."

"What happened? For a year we were so perfect. You were present. Strong. Not half. Not gone." She spoke softly.

"It's the pattern, Tibs. The one I warned you about when we met. I fall in love quickly, easily. Then something happens in me. I don't know what it is. I space out and begin that empty feeling. Then my security ebbs slowly. How can I offer you emptiness? I won't. You're worth so much more."

After a silence, she offered, "I thought you were in therapy." Her irritation returned, bringing impatience with it. Then she saw her self-recrimination trailing behind. He HAD told her. She saw him thriving in the glow and magic of their new love. It made her believe she was different so their relationship would be different than his other relationships. She could and would help him. They could do this together.

She quickly remembered her best friend's advice that she had discarded in the magic glow. It was what every momma raccoon told her babies: when you see something sick along the side of the road, keep traveling. Tibs had forgotten to keep traveling. She knew she could make a difference. Derek wasn't really sick, either. He was immature. Maybe he was depressed. He seemed to lose sexual interest after three months. She continued to believe in him. He was searching. Twenty-nine and still searching. No real career that brought out his passion. He was too insecure and too young. Time to follow the mama raccoon with her broken heart.

She took a deep breath. "Derek, I am going to Denver." She had to keep talking or she would never say what she had promised herself she would say. "I'll continue my career path and take the fellowship. You can find yours. We can meet in a year and see where or who we are. We leave as free people. I say all this in the midst of loving you. It's my gift to both of us."

People turned their heads as Tibs and Derek stood together, gathering their sadness, their lives, and their bruised hearts. They walked out of the restaurant, silently holding hands.

CHAPTER EIGHT
TOM: MINNEAPOLIS, 1992; PAUL: CHICAGO, 1963

t was the last chapter Tom would write about Paul. He hated the writing exercise but could see some positive effects. He took a breath, closed his eyes, and willed himself to go back to yet one more beginning.

I learned the truth of Suzanne's life (well, some of the truth) after I asked her to marry me. We sat on the terrace of a century-old restaurant overlooking the Chicago River. As I lowered to my knee, Suzanne's eyes brimmed with tears. I thought it was because of love and joy but now I know I was dead wrong. Her tears were from fear and nearly terror.

"I shouldn't have let it go this far. I'm devastated. It was so wrong of me," she whispered. I could feel the color leave my face as I rose and pulled my chair in front of her, sitting to stare at the woman I loved. Who was she? Who was this woman I have known and loved for two years? I knew I loved her, but did I know her? I knew her laughter. I knew her heart that held compassion for every living being. I knew her body as well as my own, even better. I didn't know she could speak the words she just whispered.

We had talked of marriage, children, dreams, vulnerable experiences, sexual needs and desires. Suddenly, an almost buried memory crept out of its grave. Suzanne had told me she couldn't have children. At the time, I asked if it was a medical reason. She said yes, unwilling to add any more information. I silenced myself with the perpetually optimistic thought that "it would all work out." Was that exchange rising from its burial ground and demanding to be continued right now?

"Because you can't have children?" I asked quietly. "It's okay, it's really okay. We can adopt or not adopt. We can talk about it. Now or after we are married."

Tears coursed down her face. She was seemingly unaware of them as she shook her head and closed her eyes. To what? I wondered. To me? To the future with me? To something I should've known?

Suzanne began to speak. "Paul, the talk we never had? We need to have it now. It's already too late. It's way too late." She began without beginning, it seemed to me. Her voice was rote, monotone, emotionless. It seemed like a recitation a child had memorized. She said that when she was seventeen, her father, Oscar, came up to her boarding school. It was the first and last time he ever visited her. Sister Michael and her father took her to a doctor who told her she should never have children. Her father agreed and told her it would be a horrible disaster. He couldn't tell her why she must obey him. She saw the fear in his eyes, which only grew when he repeated the words, "they are very powerful." Then she heard him be sick in the bathroom, not uncommon in her experience of him.

"Who?" I asked incredulously. "What are you talking about? Who is very powerful? What doctor? You never talk about your parents. Tell me about Sister Michael. I want to know you. More and more of you. I love you."

Suzanne stared over the river, watching the currents bearing twigs, branches of leaves, and other debris from the past. I watched her watch the water, without a clue. We were at our favorite restaurant, Yorkshire on the River. The perfect table. The perfect rich burgundy. I had created the perfect setting for our betrothal. The ring was still in my pocket, feeling like it was vibrating.

"Paul, my father was involved in a group of all men. No women. A few of the boys stayed in until they were thirteen. They met every Thursday night at the church. My grandfather, who is also a minister, came along with some men from his congregation as well. They were secret meetings. No one ever spoke of them." Suzanne could not look at me.

"Your father's a minister." I stated the obvious. "But secret meetings? In church groups? In Smotelyville, Indiana? What are you saying?"

29

Suzanne sighed deeply as she brought her eyes to meet mine. She seemed to understand my confusion and denial.

"I don't know. I didn't know my father. He was always gone. Then I left at fourteen, when my mother sent me to her alma mater for high school. I learned what was true and what was not. It wasn't until I was a junior that I spoke with Sister Michael. I cried with her. It was my therapy, my healing. My second experience of loving and trusting."

I had no family left except for my cousin Maggie, as my parents were killed in a car accident when I was eighteen. I never met Suzanne's parents. I knew that she had not seen her mother since her high school graduation by her choice. Why did her mother honor that choice? Suzanne always tensed up and became teary-eyed when she spoke of her mother. I hadn't pushed any further. "But, secret meetings? Going to a therapist so young?"

"I told you early on it wasn't important. It's not, exactly. What was important was my new life at boarding school and college. Smotelyville is over. Eight years ago, Chicago became my birth place, my rebirth place. The last two years have been the happiest in my life. My heart was nearly healed by Sister Michael, and you finished the rest of the healing. I'm getting closer to talking to my mother. Our love sealed the healing. I found me, then you."

I interrupted. "And now? Now you will lose it all? Lose our healing love?"

"I can't bring you into it. The past isn't gone. I was so stupid to think anything could be different. Those fourteen years did exist. And now, the person I love most in the world is in danger."

It seemed her heart was breaking again, slowly and steadily. I moved my chair closer to her, took her hands, and began to speak. She interrupted me by placing her finger over my lips, but I took her finger away and tightened my hold on her hands. I said that we would get through the pain and memories together. As well as I knew pain, I also knew love could heal. Suzanne had healed me.

"We met for a reason, and healing is part of that reason - why we fell in love, why we are getting married. I'll never leave you. Will you be my partner, my wife, my forever beloved?"

Two years ago. Now murdered. He would never write about Paul again.

CHAPTER NINE
SUZANNE AND MICHAEL: CHICAGO, 1955

Suzanne sat in the window seat in her room, writing.

February 18. 1955.

Hard to believe I'm already a junior in boarding school – Rosemont School for Girls. I feel happy for the very first time in my life. Well, not the very first time, but the first time in a long time. I've spent two years getting used to the differences. Chicago, Illinois is certainly not Smotelyville, Indiana. Being in a Catholic school for girls is not anywhere close to my Lutheran grade school with boys and girls. The biggest difference is being gone from home and somehow feeling safer and happier, even though I cried myself to sleep so many nights. I know it was homesickness, but not for home, just for Mom. Or maybe for home before the Horrible Night. So, happy is a start. I know there's a wall between me and love, safety, trust. The good feelings.

Maybe the wall will go away? Not yet, I need it.

How did my mom ever convince my father to allow me to attend a Catholic high school?

Especially because he's a Lutheran minister. Maybe because Rosemont is my mom's alma mater.

No one ever said Mom was a Catholic before she met my father and gave up her faith for him.

That's what she did, didn't she?

Did Mom really fall in love with Father? What happened? How could her love be so distant? Cool, but kind. Wordless. Yet so warm for me. Now I feel like I'm growing a little closer to Mom again, even though I am gone. I miss her.

Pretty odd, isn't it? To get closer as I move away? Maybe because it's her school, her religion, and her hometown? Chicago doesn't fit "hometown" at all. Home city is much better. I remember leaving home at fourteen, never to return if I could help it. The town, my father's church, and sadly, my parents. The feeling of love was sparse. Intermittent. Confusing. Who loved who? Who didn't? Who loved me? I want to believe Mom loved me. Way long ago. Before the Horrible Night.

How did I know love was missing if I didn't know love? Books. All the books I took out of the library and believed. My first library visit - a wonderful gift Mom gave to me. I DID know love from my mom. It just feels so long ago. It makes me cry. When is she coming up again? I'll look later.

She gave me another gift: how not to be a wife, especially a House Wife. Who marries a house? I'll never ever give up who I am to please a man, even the man I might love. To make him happy every time he is moody or frowns. To take care of his every need. To give so little to my child. Maybe that's why I felt orphaned at times. All she did for my father, the Empty Robe.

She gave me so much love. I know she did.

I've done so much writing, thinking and deciding since I left home. I turned Catholic, for one. The Lutherans I know are almost all cold, mostly fake, and very secretive. My mom isn't, but then again, she wasn't born Lutheran. She couldn't accept the secretive part. Father always went to the secret Thursday meetings he attended since he was a child. The huge change in my life happened when I crept down the church basement stairs right before my eighth-grade graduation. I peeked through a window whose shade wasn't all the way down. After seconds, I fled, thinking I would be killed if they saw me. Even now I am shivering, remembering while I write it down. It was real, and not one of the Gothic novels I read. I remember counting twelve men plus the one in front, my Grandpa Adolf. Everyone in black robes with hoods over their heads.

I want to stop writing! It hurts so much. But Sister said I have to write it in order to right it. They were in a U-shape, thankfully with their backs to me. They all looked the same with their hoods up and their hands raised. But I knew my grandpa and father. They chanted in a language I've never heard. There was a large raised table in front of them with thirteen black candles burning. There was something on it. I moved my head a tiny bit and saw something Horrible. It made me turn and run. There was blood flowing into the Communion chalice that sat on the floor under the altar. From where? Whatever was on the altar had to be alive. An animal? My heart starts to race with the memory.

Suzanne threw the pen across the room. She ran down the hall and knocked on Sister Michael's door. Suzanne didn't know what she would do without Sister Michael.

"Come in, my child. My dear! What is wrong? Did you see them again?" She took Suzanne into her arms and held her as she sobbed. Michael cried, too.

Silence and being held while she wept always gave Suzanne the feeling of love she was so confused about. Yet she seemed to be remembering her mother's love as Michael held her. After fifteen minutes or so, the compassionate nun started to speak softly. "It's been at least four months since the last time you saw them. You are healing, my child. You are healing. Yes, it was real. Yes, it was wrong. I say evil. Yes, I think we should tell someone but no, I'll never betray your secret. Not even to the priest who hears confessions. I will tell no one."

"Because I asked you to keep the secret?" Suzanne sounded like a puppy whimpering.

"Yes. Because you came to me in trust. Because I believe even more evil will result if we told anyone. Because of Love, we have to leave it to God, who is Love."

Suzanne, though she loved Sister Michael, strongly doubted God was Love. Not in her lifetime.

"Every time the memory comes back, two things happen. I feel so much pain in my lower belly. My periods are so heavy, even heavier after the memories. Second, I seem to remember my mother holding me. It's so confusing. I can't remember much at all about my mother back then. I remember sitting in her lap, sobbing, choking, vomiting. She kept asking me, 'What did you see? What happened? Tell me. Show me.' Never. I couldn't tell her.

"I also remember her hugging me so tight when she brought me here. She told me how much she loved me and had ever since I was in her womb. She pleaded with me to talk to you, Sister. What happened? Who were my parents? Did my mother love me? I know my father never did."

"You suffered extreme shock, Suzanne. You had to forget in order to survive. I know your memories of your mother loving you will come back. Because I know she does, so deeply. That is why she took you out of Smotelyville. You must see a doctor, Suzanne: a gynecologist. Soon. You can't keep losing so much blood. Will you be okay if I make that appointment?"

Suzanne nodded. Her eyes filled. Like the Communion chalice.

CHAPTER TEN
AZURE AND JEMMA: SEATTLE, 1992

Jemma settled into a different chair than her first visit. Azure sat in the rocker and chimed. At the end of the sound, Jemma began. "Despite the story-telling piece, I feel somewhat okay here. I appreciate that. Sometimes those not-okay feelings come from outside of me. Other times I feel they come from inside. I guess I'm sounding not so sane already. Inside, outside. Do you get it?" Her eyes were pleading.

"I think I understand. Not to contradict you, but feelings always come from inside, though often the catalyst is outside you. First, we feel something, then we look around to see what is causing it. An outside cause? Or an inside catalyst? Maybe a memory, a premonition, a warning, a distraction from another feeling, or myriad other catalysts. It's why we build awareness, almost a constant vigilance, to be in the moment. It takes a lifetime, I might add. At least for me." Azure smiled. "Go on."

The chime reminded Jemma about her meditation experience of the past and told Azure she might resume meditating. She also mentioned beginning to write again. Azure suggested waiting to see what came her way.

"But, today, Jemma, what is on your heart?"

Jemma continued her story from the first session. She recounted the sadness of her pregnancy and having no choice. Her story nearly filled the hour. She spoke of her judgments against herself, her fears of never resolving her confusion, and her wishes to see her daughter's placement as a gain for the baby. She wanted to be free of the obsession, let go, and forgive herself. "I want my heart to be unblocked and open to a different life, maybe a long-term relationship. It has to be a successful one. And, yes, I know my heart is blocked."

Azure nodded, noting to herself that Jemma quickly resorted to a cynical stance. "Do you ever dream of your baby?"

"I've dreamed of babies and can't tell if they're boys or girls. It's been awhile since I had those dreams maybe once or twice a year. At one point, I had a dream and knew the baby was a girl, but I think that was because it was during a time I was convinced one of my students was my daughter. About three years ago there was a twenty-six-year-old woman in my class from Wichita. The home run by nuns where I had my baby was in Wichita, where I had my baby. I thought she looked like me and immediately lost all sense of emotional boundaries. Of course, I kept my boundaries on the outside.

"I wasn't inappropriate but did feel very close to her. Naturally, being my student and favored, she also felt close to me. That was the second time I went to therapy. I feel a huge responsibility to my students. Once a male professor came onto me in undergraduate school. The main thing I took from the experience was to be very clear about my role as teacher." Jemma shifted her eyes to the window.

Azure waited, then asked, "Do you feel you have anything left over from that undergraduate experience? Anything you want to talk about?"

"No. It wasn't scary; if that's what you mean. Actually, it did quite a bit for my self-esteem at the time, even though I was falling in love with someone else at that time. It never progressed to anything physical. It was before that kind of thing was seen as wrong and as an abuse of power. Fortunately, there's no sexual abuse in my life."

"You are extremely fortunate with one less loss to heal. How did it work out with your student?"

Jemma told Azure that the parents came for a weekend with two younger sisters who looked exactly like her student. She told Azure that her therapist at the time used new healing techniques with her. Jemma felt very resolved about the student experience but not about her daughter or where her life was going. "I think the two are intertwined. I want to know and choose where I am going and who I am becoming. And I'm embarrassed I am not there yet. I want to be a whole person without conflict."

"It's a rather abrupt leap from three decades of sadness and confusion to becoming. I do suspect you already know you continued to become even with unresolved emotions and conflicts, and more likely, because of them." Azure knew conflict is the root of all growth.

"The story I hear, Jemma, is that you gave birth to a daughter at sixteen; no one knew but your parents; people thought you took time off from school to take care of a dying aunt in Philadelphia. In reality, you were in Kansas in a home for unwed mothers, run by nuns who wouldn't let you hold your newborn. The father of the baby never knew about the pregnancy that was caused because he didn't know how to fit the condom the first time you had sex." Jemma nodded, blushing.

"Your first marriage ended in betrayal. Now being a researcher in the Adoption Project has reawakened all the unhealed pain and questions of past. That's quite a great deal to carry, Jemma. It's a great deal." Azure knew her compassionate reaction was warming to Jemma. Not that she would ever make up a reaction. Azure knew honesty and what it felt like to be seen and heard. She knew it was an honor to listen to someone's story.

Jemma was silent. "I was almost seventeen." She took a breath, "I guess it is quite a bit when you put it all together."

For a moment, Azure let the quiet be, as if it were absorbing the heaviness. Silences can do that. "Did you ever wish it had happened ten years later when *Roe v. Wade* would have given you a different option?"

Jemma breathed deeply. "I couldn't end a pregnancy with abortion, even though I agree with Ram Dass when he suggested that an abortion is an agreement between three souls. I wonder if maybe an adoption is an agreement between four souls."

"Perhaps. It's a comforting thought. Did you ever try to find your daughter? I don't think there are many resources, but Charles might know."

"I can't do that. I'm afraid if I ever found her, she would reject me as I once rejected her."

"You didn't reject her, Jemma. You are still carrying her in your heart."

Jemma left the office, took a bus, and stopped at the B&O Espresso on Capitol Hill on her way home. Post-therapy – even and especially if it was storytelling – demanded that she write. She did not want to forget what she had learned, paid for, and needed to understand. What was becoming? Becoming what? Happy? *More at peace,* she decided.

October 14 1992

I am so sick of going back to my place of loss and pain. Of no control. Of shame and exclusion. Loneliness. The kind of loneliness that seeps into my every inner space as I walk in the winter evening twilight. Or drive. Or read. The searing brambles reminding me of a time long before the pregnancy. Perhaps I am ten years old, walking home from swimming lessons. November cold. November dark. Then I take a bus home with my friend Sandra. Our hair is wet. No portable hair dryers.

When we get off the bus, she goes one way; I go the other way to Southwood Circle. It's safe outside the home. It's the 1950s. The fifties of many horrors disguised in "Father Knows Best" and good church fathers. The fathers of the fifties...

I have five blocks to walk. The cold twilight is turning to an even colder darkness that takes the chill of my damp hair into the center of my bones. My heart. I look into the houses with their lights on and kids moving around. They are happy, I determine. There is Love. Warmth. Maybe even laughter. I so want to walk up to one of those driveways, open the back door, go in, and be enwombed with all the missing parts of my family, my house, my life. I knew they were missing in my heart; yet in my head, things looked okay. Maybe that was my first conflict.

The repeated longing that sometimes arises during the evening twilight must have its roots in those winter walks home with damp hair and so many unrealized wishes and dreams. While the experience is not as frequent now, it still surprises me in its intensity. The manifestation of my wishes still eludes me even as it draws me with its whispered, "find me, find me."

Is that my search? My goal? To find the missing parts of my childhood? Possibly. It's what the self-help books, psychology, and most literary works promise. Is that why I chose literature as my career? To immerse myself in other peoples' lives via literature? Safe lives. Printed lives. Not my life. Make-believe lives? No. Their lives are just as real as mine: not flesh and blood real to the exact detail, but all too real feelings. Yet, it's not the kind of real where I am responsible for their happiness, or lack thereof.

Is that what has kept me from writing? That, somehow, I would be responsible for my own characters' lives and emotions? Stupid. How stupid. Useless. Very effective writers' block! The truth is that I am only responsible for midwifing them into existence while watching their choices and emotions create their own lives.

Is that why I chose a passive role researching in the Adoption Project rather than an active plan of writing a novel for my sabbatical?

Something about the deep regret that I couldn't be responsible for my baby, my child. I was unable and had no choice. Stop. Maybe I really WAS responsible?

Jemma looked up and out the window at the cars, the bikes, and the walkers. *They all have their own lives, choices, molds. Maybe I'm not on a path to find the missing ingredients of my childhood and lost baby. Maybe I have to create them.*

I now write with a new sense of resolution. A sense of hope. There is a strong chance that the extreme loneliness was not because of my pregnancy and birthing but had already been rooted and embedded in my womb before my daughter even entered it. I wonder if she felt and took the loneliness upon herself.

Tears spring to my eyes with the declaration of NO! I loved her so much and still do. I wrote to her every day. Before I even knew she was a girl, I wrote to my unborn child. It's all I could give. A distant part of me realizes I am weeping in a coffee shop and do not even care. It is the first time I have ever even thought that adopting her out was the best choice. Not right, not wrong, but best. Coming to Seattle was possibly the right choice as well, with finding Azure. Have I signed onto a project that will complete my unfinished life? Could Charles provide information to find my daughter? Or the other co-researcher? I'll file that in my Magical Thoughts folder.

The Project. It draws my curiosity, especially now that Peter and I have decided we don't need to understand the project nor rewrite the manual. We figured out the steps we need to do and found the proscribed unified grid to put in our data. I'm not nearly as overwhelmed as yesterday. Whew. I smile as I write. It's a gift to meet Peter and another to see him tonight! What's his story? Is he curious about mine? He appears to be open and present and has asked about my life. I know it's only been one coffee. Even though it was a three-hour coffee. We do work right down the hall from each other and I did enjoy being with him. It seemed mutual. So far, no ego to coddle. Very rare. How long will that last? He seems so kind and gentle. We'll see.

Jemma packed up, got a refill of coffee, and walked the two blocks to her apartment, noting her loneliness dissolved with her troubled memories. She had a newfound sense of peace. She suspected it was from her recent resolutions and choices, and maybe a little from telling her story.

CHAPTER ELEVEN
OSCAR: SMOTELYVILLE, 1915/1939

Oscar lay on the twin bed his father had built for him in the attic of their parsonage. He had learned that if he was very still and did not breathe very much, his headache wouldn't come in full force. Maybe it would even go away. *One score and four.* Why was that Oscar's special promise? What did it mean? Is he the only boy to have a special promise or did the other boys have one also? Different ones? Maybe not as special as his?

Maharba continues for generations.

Our sacrifices continue for generations.

We assure our special place in the Plan.

Abraham. Isaac. Abraham. Isaac. Father. Son.

Oscar blinks. Who spoke the words? No one is in his room. He feels the familiar twinge of fear. The voices fade. He blinks several times. Oscar has discovered blinking will turn the tide of terror. He also stops breathing. Two steps: blink and don't breathe. The panic subsides as he looks at his new Confirmation suit. It is black and itchy. He wore it with pride last Sunday. He is thirteen years old and will continue to go to the Meetings with his father and the Deacons, but only when he is not at school. Since he was five, Oscar and often four, five, or six other boys would be at the Meetings. After their Confirmation, only a few of the boys, the special ones, would return. They would each have a separate initiation designed especially for them and would return only for certain Meetings.

Oscar tells no one how he becomes terrified of the meetings and rituals, and never will. The previous night was his first Meeting and Ritual as an initiate. He was allowed to hold the Sacred Knife of Abraham and was given his special promise of *one score and four*. He refused to see the blood on the knife as he blinked. Then and now again the blood disappears and he repeats, "One score and four."

He remembers his Confirmation. Oscar is the sixth son in his family of ministers. He was confirmed by his own father, the Reverend Adolf, just as Adolf was confirmed by his father. Some confirmations were in Germany, the later ones in America. Of course, the Rituals also emphasize that Oscar too will become a Lutheran minister. He hears how the tradition is sacred and special and rare. He will go to an all-boys high school and only come home one weekend a month. Oscar is afraid. He has heard the term "hazing." He blinks and stops breathing. Maybe some of the older boys at his new school will attend the Meetings also. Do they also throw up from the pain of terrible headaches and stomachaches? Will they protect him at the new school?

Even with blinking and not breathing, Oscar knows the headache has shifted. His left leg begins to twitch as he waits for the vivid and terrible pictures.

"No! No! No!" whispers Oscar. He tries to get up. The pain pushes him down. He puts the pillow over his head and goes into a trance. He senses someone pulling it away. "You must watch, Oscar, you are special. Take the knife, Oscar."

Oscar prays as he moves in and out of trance and memory. *O Father, remove this cup from me. Please, please, please, O God. Make it go away.*

God does not comply.

Oscar sees the men enter his pulsating head. The black robes. The altar. The sacred knife of Abraham. He feels the band tightening around his eyes as the blindfold is pulled tighter. The knife is placed in his hand and he is led into blackness.

O scar grew up and graduated from the Lutheran seminary in 1937, when he was twenty-two years old. Two years earlier he met Bernice, who was nineteen and in her first year of a Catholic teachers' college. She converted to the Lutheran faith and they were married the week after his graduation. The more important event was his ordination, when his father placed the stole over Oscar's black ministerial robe to consecrate him to God and the Church forevermore. His father whispered, "Never forget *one score and four,* your special promise and blessing."

God called Oscar to be the minister in Smotelyville, Indiana, a rural town twenty miles east of his father's church. Most ministers would be called or asked to lead different churches during their careers. Oscar looked forward to moving away from his father. However, Oscar was never called to another town, though his father arranged for him to move to a different church not very far away when things got bad. On occasion, he was visited by certain men from his father's new church in Illinois. They praised him for sticking close to home and keeping the home fires burning. Oscar always had a terrible headache and vomited as soon as they left. He didn't know why. He wondered if he did not receive another call or job offer because of those men. Maybe it was because of his father. Was it his headaches and increasing bouts of depression and anxiety?

As Oscar approached his twenty-fourth birthday, the special promise kept repeating itself in his mind. *One score and four.* Twenty-four. He grew excited, but his birthday passed without anything special.

However, Bernice did deliver their first and only child, their daughter Suzanne, when she was twenty-two and he was twenty-four. Was she his special blessing? Oscar hid his disappointment that she was not a boy to carry on the ministerial tradition. He comforted himself with the notion that there was plenty of time for more pregnancies and more children. Surely one would be a boy.

A few days after Suzanne's birth, his father Adolf and several of the deacons came to Smotelyville to congratulate Oscar. "Let's go out for a shot and a beer to celebrate," invited one of the deacons. They walked to a local pub.

After Oscar's second shot, while drinking his second beer, he began to feel very uncomfortable. He emotionally separated from the men in the pub, watching as if from a distance. Even when the men visited his church, they never arrived in a group. He realizes he hasn't seen the deacons in a single group since he was thirteen. Wait. He did see them at the Meetings. He becomes confused. At that very moment of realization, one of the deacons locks his eyes with Oscar's in unyielding tenacity. "What do you remember from the Meetings, Oscar?" he asks.

Immediately Oscar's stomach begins to hurt. The effect of the alcohol reforms into stone-cold sobriety.

"Which meetings?" parries Oscar, unsure if he is still being tested to see if he had kept the sacred secrets.

Individually, each of the five men at the table lock into Oscar's eyes as did the first deacon. As a group, they speak, "Maharba grants you permission to remember, Oscar. You have permission to tell the truth."

Doubt and fear create a barrier of silence in Oscar. His gut knots the two forces together. The men join the silence until one whispers, "One score and four."

"It is my special promise." whispers Oscar back to the deacon in a very small-boy voice. "Good boy, Oscar. You have answered correctly. Your father is very proud of you," intoned another deacon. Rev. Adolf nodded without a smile.

"What does it mean?" Oscar's voice becomes prepubescent as he enters his thirteen-year-old self.

The deacons smile with satisfaction and success as one spoke. "Oscar, listen very closely. We will speak only once of your sacred promise. Once it was special. Now it has become sacred. You will ask no questions. You will only obey. Of course, as always, you will tell no one. Nor will you write it down. Your promise is giving your firstborn daughter to Maharba. You will give her to us in death. We will receive her blood when she gives birth to her first child. She, like you, will do so at twenty-four-years of age. She is your ultimate gift to God in gratitude for all your years of Meetings and participating in the Rituals. You will accept and perform the ultimate gift of sacrifice as symbolized by the sacred knife of Abraham. Do you remember using the sacred knife, Oscar?"

He can only nod as the knot in his stomach pulls tighter.

"You will return to the Meetings on a regular basis if you wish. It is always your choice. You will begin Meetings in your own church with your own deacons. Your earthly father blesses you as does your Heavenly Father. It is known that the daughters chosen for sacred sacrifice are extremely joyous and willing, as are the sons. We remember Isaac following his father Abraham joyous to be his little lamb. We have been asked by God to complete the work begun by Abraham, which has remained unfinished for many centuries.

"There is one very sacred sacrifice every twenty-four years in our Maharba, held in different towns. The others are simply special sacrifices. Because of your many generations of special calling into the Meetings and the ministry, you have been given the sacred redemption of your daughter's child, your grandson, being spared so he can join the Meetings. He will become a leader in Maharba. Your family is deeply blessed. One score plus four."

Oscar said the words simultaneously as the deacons repeated his promise. Inside Oscar, the thirteen-year-old boy whose mind was in the Meetings as he spoke felt the honor of being chosen, though he doesn't know what he is actually promising. The mind of a twenty-four-year-old who has just become a father is absent. He no longer feels any fear or doubts. The trance protects him from himself as he senses his sacred specialness.

Again, the deacon across from Oscar locks eyes with him. "As you do not remember your participation at thirteen, and as you return to the present time, you will not remember your renewal promise which will be manifested in twenty-four years. In twenty-four years, all will be revealed to you. Meanwhile, you will see but darkly through the sacred glass of your life. As your mind continues to forget, your heart will close. You will make no emotional connection to your daughter Suzanne in order to keep future pain from your life."

The deacons do not tell him that just as his heart continues to close, so will his mind. He will slowly forget as he grew older. He will forget many, many things.

46

The final deacon speaks. "You will now return to your adult self with no conscious memory of our words in the past thirty minutes. You will remember that you, Oscar, a pastor, are special and honored as you continue to serve the Meetings, the Church, and God in your body and in your soul."

Oscar began to enter the pub again. Each deacon did an odd configuration with his hands and fingers. It looked like the same sort of benediction sign that Oscar made after each church service. However, the deacons were using different signs. He could not understand their words, even though both were vaguely familiar. Oscar drank his now-warm beer with an expression of bewildered distraction as his knot multiplied rapidly into a twisted mass.

"Drink up, Oscar! Another child for God! Congratulations to you!" the deacons shouted with avuncular cheers.

Oscar completely rejoined his knotted doubts, fears, and confusion. He did not tell Bernice of the deacons' visit when he went to visit her and his new daughter that evening. He did not hold Suzanne ever again.

CHAPTER TWELVE
JEMMA AND PETER: SEATTLE, 1992

Peter met Jemma at the Spiderweb Cafe in Capitol Hill. She was often early when meeting someone, preferring to choose the table and wait. Their chemistry was immediate and vibrant as Peter spotted her waiting in the corner booth near the door.

"You found me easily?" she began.

At the same time, he joined in with, "I found you!"

Both laughed and touched fingertips. Jemma felt confident and centered, even while being excited. She credited her composure to her session with Azure and her realization at the coffee shop that her daughter was the adoptee of another mother. She was starting to believe it was okay and most likely the best decision for a just-turned-seventeen-year-old mom. Jemma had a difficult time letting go of her relentless critic. *My life is beginning right now, with freedom and no confusion*, she told herself. She smiled.

"So, have you been here before, Jemma? Nice choice!"

"It's become one of my favorites in the short time I've been in Seattle. I can walk here. Although, in truth, it's the bumbleberry pie."

Peter smiled and asked if red wine went with bumbleberry pie. She assured him a cabernet would make the perfect pairing. He ordered the wine. They ordered appetizers and again, began to speak at the same time.

"You go first." Peter covered his mouth to stop talking and opened his eyes wide.

"Well. What's your story?" Jemma could at times, cut to the chase with ease. "Are you from Seattle? When's your birthday?" Then she covered her mouth and widened her eyes, mirroring his efforts to listen. The bottle of wine came, was

48

uncorked, and poured. She slipped off her shoes, crossed her legs yoga-style, and waited for his answers.

"Easy one first. November 1, 1951. I am about to be fifty-one. The beginning of my story? I'm from Montana and have lived in Seattle since I came to UW at eighteen. So, I've lived here five years longer than my birth state. I majored in world religions and minored in theatre. No, I didn't plan to become a minister, as I grew up religion-less. The theatre part of being a minister fascinated me. I love to be a leader and experience people engaged within a community, following me. I needed to discover a group with a common purpose."

"Religion and theatre? An odd mix, no?" Jemma looked into his eyes.

"Not really. Aren't most ministers actors? Anyhow, after graduation, I wandered a bit. The eternal quest of 'what do I do' never left my mind. Soon a good friend of mine who studied computer science told me about a small company that was hiring and would train newcomers in computer programming. It was a match made in heaven. As you recall, I'm still in the computer world. Not a geek." Peter hesitated and smiled. "Well, maybe not a geek."

Jemma asked whatever happened to his original interests in theatre. Did he give it up? Weren't they his dreams? Peter told her he had been in community theatre at times and had found an offbeat group that answered his religious curiosity. He asked her if she "did" religion, forming quotation marks with his fingers.

"Not really. I'm looking for a meditation group, which is not at all difficult in Seattle, as you know. There's even a meditation group for people who have been abducted by aliens. Do you believe in aliens? Outer-space aliens, that is."

Peter put his fork down, poured more wine, and ordered another bottle. He told her, "not exactly," and, "certainly not like the abductees report. Personally, I think they are off their medication. I do believe beings different than humans live in other dimensions that are generally inaccessible to us."

What in God's name is he talking about? thought Jemma as she nodded. *Maybe this potential relationship is going nowhere.* Disappointment began its upward climb.

Peter continued, "Right now, for instance, I became aware you are startled and skeptical and even doubt my sanity. Your thoughts add more doubt that we could even have a close friendship. Right?"

Jemma blushed lightly. "Close."

"So, because of my training in meditation and concentration, I was able to read your mind, as it were, although we use different terms. Entering another dimension is the next step in..."

"Mind control?" she interrupted. That did not feel good at all.

Now Peter stopped and cocked his head to one side as she could see the previously noted shades go down in his eyes. She didn't know what the change in his eyes meant but decided to keep her own eye on it. *Was he hurt? Displeased? Confused? Whatever he's feeling, he is stepping back emotionally.*

"Peter, I'm so sorry for interrupting and jumping to conclusions. Really, I am interested, although in all honesty, I was thrown off a bit by your seeing and knowing my thoughts. I can and will be very open-minded about your path. I really don't know where my anxiety about all that comes from but will work at finding out. Someone reading my mind is a good start on that discovery, though. Meanwhile, truce?" She wondered why she capitulated so easily.

"Of course." The Peter she sat with before he mentally left, reentered the conversation and took her hand. "I have a very difficult time if I sense someone is mocking me, especially about my spiritual path. I started a most important group here in Seattle called Unconditional Love, Inc. It gave my life greater purpose and meaning, more than I have ever had. So many of the participants who attend tell me their spirituality grows by leaps and bounds due to the meeting. But I won't proselytize. If you ever want to visit our group, you are most welcome. In fact, would you come to the next meeting?"

"Thank you. I'll think about it. I would like to know more. Does it fit in with you joining the staff of the Adoption Project?"

He stared at her, hesitating. "No. Not at all. The Project is an opportunity to meet people and flesh out my life in new directions. I was divorced five years ago and have put my life into work and my spiritual group. I want to add socializing and meeting someone outside of my world. Invite them in, like you." He took her hand and waited while searching her eyes.

Jemma could feel parts of her body awaken that had been hibernating for too long. Was this the chemistry she longed for? The person? The body? She lingered on each part of him starting with his hiking boots. Could he see the pictures in her mind right now? She had nothing to hide. Her body's opinion of him had drastically changed.

The server came with dessert menus.

"One bumbleberry pie with two forks," requested Peter without taking his eyes from hers. "And the check."

Jemma was grateful she had changed her sheets that morning.

The following morning Jemma could not believe that she had shared her body with Peter and that she had agreed to go to the meeting, much less have him pick her up. She phoned him to say she couldn't attend that evening. She did plan to go the following week even though she had lost most of her interest in Peter. The lovemaking was less than she had imagined during their time at Spiderweb. She couldn't put her finger on it. Somehow the magic had ground to a definite halt. *Magic usually does,* reflected Jemma. *Yet, never so quickly.* What had appeared to be a raging bonfire during dinner turned out to be a small match with a quick flame in bed. His flame was quickly extinguished, leaving her unfulfilled. Plus, Peter had left in the middle of the night. Clearly, not okay. Going back over the night, Jemma felt he had left emotionally during their lovemaking. It was a new experience for her. Now it was a topic for Azure. She did not like the way she felt. It could only be described as skeeved.

CHAPTER THIRTEEN
PETER AND DEREK: SEATTLE, 1992

Derek wandered through the social work building at the university, hating the confusion he wore like a second skin. *What if I can never shed this? Why am I looking for Peter?* He had Azure, whom he liked and was beginning to trust, even with the odd storytelling option. He had visited Peter already at the start of the Project and worried about being bothersome. He admired the ancient mahogany wainscoting and sat on one of the side benches. *Breathe and look at your surroundings.* He used his anxiety-lowering technique and studied the beautiful wood, the marble floors, and the tall windows letting in the autumn sunlight. With a little more peace, Derek got up to find his way to Peter's office.

Derek knocked on Peter's open door lightly, re-introducing himself. "Hi, Peter, I know you don't remember me. I'm Derek, the half-adopted subject in your sub-research group."

"Ah, yes, I do remember. You are the only half-adopted person of my one hundred subjects in the Project, by the way. How are you doing? Can I help you somehow?"

Derek warmed again to the tall man with the scuffed hiking boots and green eyes that would not retreat. The intensity of his gaze was both inviting and off-putting at the same time. How could that be? Could he trust Peter with his confusion? Why add another person to his confessional when he had Azure? Without knowing why, he was drawn to Peter to reveal himself and to seek comfort. He craved answers as he decided to experiment and be direct.

"Peter, I am not exactly sure why I'm here. The interviews in the Project have stirred my emotional pot, so to speak. I do see a therapist. Maybe it's more appropriate to talk with her?"

Peter held back a smile as he pulled his chair from behind the desk and placed it next to the other chair in the sparse institutional yellow cinder-block room. "Really, come in. Sit down. It's most appropriate. It's part of my role as data collator. Adoption is a very emotional issue. I apologize for the shabby un-chic office," as he waved his hand around in a deprecating way. "We could go out for coffee, but it looks like you need some privacy right now. Do you mind if I close the door?" He briefly put his hand over Derek's. "I certainly don't want to intrude on your therapy. I've been through therapy myself and admire those who are courageous and open enough to do it. My path was very different from yours, I suspect, as it was done within a group rather than with a therapist. In fact, I'm the group leader and I invite you to join us. There happens to be a meeting tonight. Will you come?"

"A group therapy session?" Immediately Derek's anxiety set in. "Tonight?"

"Well, not exactly. We're a metaphysical group, a spiritual group seeking inner peace and our own truth. Do you know your own truth, Derek?"

It seemed that Peter's green eyes were dancing while at the same time appearing still as stone. Did Peter always evoke such opposites or was it just Derek who saw it? "Sure, I always have known my own truth. Well, not always. Sometimes. I used to." He took a deep breath, knowing his eyes were clouding. "No, Peter, I don't know my own truth, like you put it. Sometimes I doubt everything about me."

"What a great opening, Derek! Pilate had it right, 'what is truth?' I believe truth has an ever-changing center. All of your doubts are gateways to your own truth."

Derek felt mesmerized. Peter's agate eyes, his words, the intensity: all meant especially and only for Derek. "What time do you meet? Where? I'll be there. Wait, I don't even know the name of the group I'm going to find."

"We call it Unconditional Love, Inc. We meet at 7:45 in the Unitarian Universalist church at the corner of East Harrison and Capitol. The pews are quite comfortable. See you tonight."

Again, Peter put his hand over Derek's. "It is exactly what you need."

Derek opened the office door and walked down the hall with a smile on his face.

Jemma decided to scope out Peter's meeting. She found the meeting place easily. It was within walking distance of her apartment. The UU church was home to many different groups, twelve-step groups in particular. The signs said those meetings were held downstairs and Unconditional Love, Inc. was held in the main chapel.

"Welcome. Welcome." Two smiling greeters held out their hands to usher her into the chapel. They handed her a glossy sheet with Peter's picture in the center. "Peter is our leader," chirped one of them. "You'll love him!"

Don't think so, Jemma's mind responded as she sat on the right side near the end of the last pew, her goal to observe. Plus, it was one of the last available seats open. She was surprised at the large crowd, guessing over three hundred people. *How many in Jonestown,* she mused.

When Peter stood up in front of the altar and raised his hands, applause thundered. His light blue oxford shirt tucked into faded jeans above hiking boots were last seen on the floor of her bedroom a week ago. *For some reason, I should feel flattered,* reflected Jemma, putting together the applause, the good-looking guy, and their coupling. Those warm feelings were nowhere to be found among the ashes of regret. Curiosity was foremost. Skepticism grabbed its hand.

"Thank you all for coming. You won't regret a minute of your time together here with our members of Unconditional Love, Inc. My heart opens to our visitors as well as new members. I know most of the guests will join us! You won't be able to help it. You will choose Love. Right now, will everyone choosing Love, please stand and say 'Yes! We choose Love!'"

Jemma grimaced as she observed the group from her position. *Seriously. Really?* She began to study the people around her, recognizing several from the Adoption Project. *That's odd, why would they be here? Did Peter tell them? Is he proselytizing?* Ethics sprung into her mind, first as a criticism of Peter, next as a concern for the people in the Project, knowing they were often vulnerable during the research process. Looking more carefully, it was more than just a few; she saw many from the Project.

"Choosing Love," Peter continued in his oration, "is what we do each time we come to find joy and peace in our meetings. Our principles are not religious, but spiritual. Join with me in invoking the spiritual.

"Dear Father, Mother, Brother, Sister, God, Goddess, and all Beings of Spirit. Enter our hearts and minds with your Essence of Love. We do not ask for Light, as we are Light. We ask to remember that we are Love. Each one of us is a flow-er of Love, in and out, flowing out Love, taking in Love, being Love."

Jemma noticed several people swaying slightly, eyes closed, smiling. Slowly, they began to link arms and chant as they continued their movement.

"We are Love. Only Love. Flowing out. Flowing in. Unconditional. Forever free. Love for you. Love for me."

She began to feel creeped out, noticing one subject from the Project across the aisle and very close to the front who seemed to be completely mesmerized. Now she remembered seeing him in the hallway of Peter's office several times. He looked so innocent to her. Jemma felt powerless.

Unaware of Jemma's gaze, Derek was blissed out. Never had he felt so free, so unconfused, so clear. He now knew Love was the only way. He knew it was this particular Love, in this place and with these people. It was the Unconditional Love flowing out of his heart and to his neighbors, as their Love flowed into him. All his. More love than he had with Tibs, more than his step-mom Terese, even more than his dad. The tears in his eyes reflected the deep colors in the stained-glass windows. Tears of joy, for the first time ever. All because of Peter. All because Derek made the decision to be bold and walk into Peter's office. He opened up the depths of his soul to the man in the front, who smiled and chanted the Love Chant in a hypnotic voice with arms raised. Derek trusted these people of love. He wanted to hold the arms of his neighbors and stay in these feelings forever. He looked up at Peter, who was smiling just for him. Derek had come home.

The next afternoon found Derek back in Peter's office. "Jeez, Peter, I can't thank you enough! What an experience! I haven't felt so accepted, so understood, so supported since... since my days at OHOM over ten years ago."

"What's OHOM?"

Derek inwardly flinched. *Why was Peter frowning? Why was his voice so staccato?* "It's the school I went to for fourteen years in Portland. It stands for Open Heart, Open Mind. It's now called Willamette Academy."

"Oh." Silence. "Did you know the truth then?"

"I thought I did. Now I don't. Is something wrong?"

"No, no, not at all. Often our group is the first time that people experience unconditional love. I see you are more evolved than I first thought. I watched you sponging up the joy. Have you been depressed, Derek? You seem to be on the verge of tears quite often."

"Maybe. Tibs, my girlfriend just left me, I guess because I couldn't commit to a deeper relationship."

"What's your family background? This OHOM?"

"Actually, my father taught at OHOM. He met my stepmother there and they married on my first birthday. My birth mother, died shortly after I was born. I told you."

Peter expressed sympathies before he asked casually, "Derek, how old was your mother when she died?"

"Actually, she died on her twenty-fourth birthday." Derek's stance weakened. He sat down.

A barely audible sigh escaped from Peter. His green eyes began to dance as his mouth turned ever so slightly upward. In his mind's eye, Derek had a flash of a big black cat with yellow canary feathers on the sides of its mouth. He blinked as the image faded. It was gone in a second. He let it go. Just more of his crazy thoughts..

"I'm really sorry, Derek. It must have been so hard on your father. Where were you born? Back East? Do you have any memories?"

"Memories of being born? Peter, I'm just like everyone else. I have none. Why?" The familiar surge of sadness in his chest began to swell. It was the wave he connected with the mother he never knew. The next wave was loneliness, followed by abject sorrow and the bottomless pit of despair. Tears followed the flood of emotions. "See, Peter, I can't do this. I can't be in the Project. I'm too confused. My moods are out of control. I can't be tearing up after each feeling. How could I be so filled with joy a few minutes ago and now unable to fathom even small happiness? I can't commit. I can't connect. I never could and I never will. I have to leave." He got up and headed toward the door.

"Wait, Derek. Really, wait. Sit down." He took Derek by the shoulder and led him back to the chair. "Just sit for a moment. You are able to commit. I know it. You spent fourteen years in one school, not to mention one with a name like OHOM. You committed to two degrees and are thinking of a third. You are committing to our group. I know being part of our group will help with the Adoption Project's interviewing process that's so upsetting to you. In fact, I have a brilliant idea. I'll make this one exception for you and I'll be your interviewer. Then you can feel safe with the questions that are sensitive about your unknown mother and Terese, your adoptive mom. I want to help you, Derek, and I know I can. Unconditional Love, Inc. has opened you up. Don't give up. Your truth will set you free, Derek. I know that in my heart from personal experience." He put his hand on Derek's, keeping it there longer than before.

Peter got up and closed the door. "I have a special invitation for you, one I haven't extended in the last five years. But I must have your utmost pledge not to share what I am about to tell you. It's not secret. It's sacred. Your pledge, Derek, to hold my sacred invitation only in your heart - telling no one - is the first step in creating and knowing your own truth. Beginning to feel confident and secure, and, of course, beginning to feel loved. More loved than you have ever felt. More connected than you can even dream of!"

"What are you talking about?"

"Unconditional Love, Inc. is a great organization. I want you to continue those meetings. And..."

"And?" Derek swam in a deluge of feelings, his old and new fears.

"And, there is another group that is more exclusive due to their higher spiritual evolution."

"It's not for me, then. My spiritual anything is not evolved."

"Ah, Derek, one of the signs of being so evolved is forgetting you are evolved. It is a natural part of you."

"I have to go."

"Derek. Please. You're upset, confused, hurting, and depressed. Afraid of your own truth. You don't need to live this way. You can feel what you felt last night most of the time."

"Most?" Derek's hand was on the doorknob.

"I say most because the members in our group do feel compassion. It is a component of the Love you felt. We learn compassion through feeling one another's pain and sadness, which I am feeling for you right now. Once I was there, surrounded by sorrow and confusion. Now I am here living my truth and encouraging you to do the same. You don't have to suffer. You can learn compassion for Derek first. You can feel the Love again.

"I'm inviting you to the subgroup meeting. Just come to one. The meeting of the Evolved Ones. I cannot tell you the name of the sacred meeting until you are initiated. Only if you choose. You will begin to remember who you truly are, more than the legacy of adoption or the teachings of your father and OHOM. These were, of course, important, but not the whole truth. It's not your truth. Come with us. One meeting and you can stop if you want. You have time to think about it. Meanwhile, keep coming to Unconditional Love, Inc. Your heart will be filled. I won't bring it up for a few weeks. No problem."

Derek's head was spinning. *One meeting.* "When?"

"In two Thursdays? We always meet on Thursdays. I'll call you soon. Maybe coffee before then? I like you, Derek."

CHAPTER FOURTEEN
DEREK AND TOM: PORTLAND

Tom embraced Derek in the winding driveway of their family home. Derek left for Chicago seven years ago; now living in Seattle, he returned home often. "Derek, it's so good to see you!" Tom closed his eyes during the long hug.

"Dad, what's up? Is something wrong?" Derek returned the embrace with a slight hesitation. "Wrong? No, of course not! It's been four months since we've seen you. I always miss you and want to hear about your life. You know, just dad things. How are you? Tibs? MCATs?"

Derek pulled his small canvas carryall out of the back seat. "There is a lot to talk about, Dad. For starters, Tibs and I ended our relationship." He turned so Tom could not see his eyes, understanding that his dad would know anyhow.

"Oh, Derek, I'm so sorry." Tom wanted to ask how his son was doing but had learned from experience that too many questions shut Derek down and Tom out.

"I think it's for the best. I was unwilling to move to Colorado for her fellowship and long-distance relationships are too difficult. I've got some new stuff going on. Is Mom home?"

"Not yet. She's at your sister's, helping with Seth, your new nephew. She'll be home for dinner. I'm making manicotti, spinach, of course. Hope it's still one of your favorites. Derek, how long have you been vegetarian? Since you were in kindergarten?"

"Yes, Dad, since kindergarten. You know that," Derek said with an eye-roll. "Do you have any vodka and tonic?"

"Sure. Coming right up. Get settled and I'll meet you on the patio."

Tom and Derek sat and drank companionably watching the shades of dark pines and lighter laurel hedges. The explosion of purple and red flowers was set off by the many greens behind them. The emotion elicited by nature's exquisite beauty brought to mind Derek's last exchange with Peter. He had such a strong visceral response to the memory that he rested his open palm on his stomach.

"Derek, is something wrong?"

Derek smiled. "Within forty minutes, we have asked each other if something was wrong. What's that about?"

"I don't know. You seem a tad different, somehow."

"Well, you do too, Dad. Like, the way you hugged me when I got out of the car."

Tom sighed inaudibly. *Is my son growing away from me? Again?* Periodically, they went through the "distancing time," as Tom called it. *Was the origin Suzanne's death? Or being adopted? Or being "half-adopted," as Derek liked to describe himself?* Every time Tom heard the term, his heart cringed. *I lied to Derek about Suzanne's death. I lied about his birth. Who wouldn't? I never told him about the name changes. Who would? Or about his birthdate change. I couldn't. Bigger yet, Derek thinks I am his bio dad. He doesn't know he has lost two mothers.*

The murder? Never would Tom reveal the murder. His pulse started racing. The murder took more than his wife and Derek's mother. It had taken his life. He, an upstanding father, husband, and an educator who won awards for developing and living the Open Heart, Open Mind principles, had taught his son a pack of lies. *I tried to save Derek's life,* reasoned Tom. The vision of Suzanne's bloodless body and the teddy bear mobile turning in the breeze while his son slept escaped from its prison of decades. *Were the memories coming out more often?*

Derek was unaware of Tom's inner fears and memories. He was consumed with his own conflict. "Nothing new," he replied absently. "Dad, let me run this by you. You know I'm involved in research at the Adoption Project?"

"Sure. How's it going?"

"Well, it's a problem of sorts. Ever since being in the Project, I've become pretty depressed. You know that's my go-to response. It's more than Tibs, more than MCATs, which, by the way, I have postponed. It's a deep and bottomless lonely feeling. I've seen a therapist named Azure several times. I like her. She asked if I would be okay with asking you if I ever experienced trauma early on? Other than my mother's death or our move from Minnesota."

Tom almost broke the vodka and tonic glass he was holding. He drained the glass and did not answer.

Derek told his dad that he still loved being a bookseller, and one of the data collators had taken him to a metaphysical group where he felt some hours of joy the previous week.

Any mention of a group, especially a spiritual group, set Tom's teeth on edge. "Oh? What's the name of it?" He faked warmth.

"Unconditional Love, Inc."

"ULI?"

"What?"

"The initials spell out YOU LIE. Like, y-o-u l-i-e."

"Dad, life is not a Boggle game. They are just initials. That's all. The leader is Peter from the Adoption Project."

"Okay. I'm sorry. It just struck me. What do they do?" The "you lie" stuck in Tom's craw. *It was deception and lies all over again. They are outside and within me. Now another organization? A group with love and lie in the same name?* He felt sickened. He felt despair. All he ever wanted was to recreate the perfect family that was killed with his parents when he was eighteen. It was his single mission in life. He overcame Suzanne's reluctance to marry, only to discover her murdered. Then he became the master of deception.

"This special subgroup that I'm not allowed to discuss..."

"What? What did you say? I'm sorry Derek, I was lost on a different train. Subgroup what?" Tom's voice was distracted, rapid.

"Dad. Easy. I didn't yet agree to join. But I am going to a meeting on Thursday."

Thursday. Tom flashed to his forced engagement. *Suzanne used the words, "Deacon's Meetings on Thursdays." Of course not! Coincidence. Stupid coincidence.* "Derek, don't go. Please don't go."

Derek had only seen his father this upset once before, when he had chosen the University of Chicago for law school. Tom thought all of Chicago was filled with mobsters. He said the city was too far, too big. There were so many bizarre reasons that had made Derek think something else was going on with his dad and Chicago. No matter, he went anyway. His first and only act of outright defiance. Was it time for the second? "Dad, I'm a grown man. I will go to a meeting if I want to. You know nothing about it. You haven't even asked."

At that moment, Tom reversed his decision of thirty years ago. He would no longer lie to save his son's life. He could no longer bury anything connected with Suzanne and her murder. Now he would go back East and discover all he could about Suzanne, her family, the secret group, the four men, especially the murder. He would ask Bruno to tell him everything. He would tell it all to Derek. He knew he had to do the hardest thing he could ever imagine.

"Derek, could you wait a month? I can explain it all then. My fears, Chicago, my craziness."

Derek looked into Tom's eyes, saw his father's desperation, and heard his pleading from fear and love.

"No, Dad. I can't."

CHAPTER FIFTEEN
AZURE AND JEMMA: SEATTLE

A zure sensed something different in Jemma as she entered the office. After the chime tones diffused, it was Jemma who began the session.

"Two stories for today. One about Peter. The other is my decision to find my daughter." Jemma noticed a candle burning. "Do you light a candle every time?"

"I do. It absorbs any difficult energy. Jemma, your decision is pretty major. Tell me about it," Azure invited.

"First, Peter. We are not dating even though, at one point, I thought it was a possibility. We met for dinner at Spiderweb. It was magical. Our chemistry was intense. We went to my apartment after dinner." Jemma blushed slightly, "I did sleep with him rather quickly, which is generally not my style. It's not often I share my body like that, Azure. I'm still wondering and confused. In the morning he was gone, taking the magic with him, although it had already disappeared while we were having sex. He left a note saying he would pick me up that evening for a meeting he runs.

"I phoned him that day and told him not to get me, that I would try it some other time. We hung up as strangers. A week later, I went and, Azure, his meeting turned me off totally. The night at Spiderweb was wine, magic, and chemistry. Later, at the meeting, I saw his huge ego, his almost hypnotic leadership. Is it possible to enthrall an entire group of people? Even the name is spellbinding: Unconditional Love, Inc. Who would really buy that?"

"While not buying the meeting, it does sound like you did buy his magic, Jemma."

Silence.

"You're right, Azure. I did." Jemma eyes closed briefly as she sighed deeply. "What I called magic and chemistry is Peter's whole being. It wasn't special just for me. He's intense and captivating. How did I let myself be drawn in? I've been around the block, so what happened? I shared my body with a guy who is now creeping me out."

"Have you ever slept with someone who, as you say, creeped you out before Peter?" Azure questioned thoughtfully. "Or is he the first?"

"The first and the last! How could I have been so naive? I have been with men who I saw as spiritual. They were true men who lived what they believed. I've been that route. I studied Wicca, which taught me "harm towards none.' The Pleiadians taught me about purpose and meaning on our planet. Buddhism, above all, teaches me compassion and impermanence. I've been with Christians who actually live the message of Jesus. I'm not naive."

Noting Jemma's distress, Azure knew she was on sensitive ground. "Doesn't Buddhism teach compassion for yourself? Forgiveness of self?"

"Yes, it does." More silence. "I get it. I had compassion for the people I saw at his meeting, but I don't for me."

Azure held off with the Socratic method, feeling her own sympathies for Jemma.

"Sometimes it just takes time to learn to be kind to ourselves. That's why it's called a practice."

"I'll work at it." Jemma stared out the window. She needed relief from eye contact.

"Even if the night with Peter and then his meeting served only the purpose of learning self-forgiveness, which is a valuable lesson, I sense there is more going on for you. As to your other question; Jemma, I do believe group hypnosis is possible. Some even believe the Crucifixion was mass hypnosis in order to begin a religion that opposed established Judaism. I don't hold an opinion on that theory, but who knows? I do suspect Peter used a variation of hypnosis with you, maybe at the meeting as well. The wine and chemistry at Spiderweb certainly added to the smoke and mirrors Peter produced. You did mention he has a theater background... But I have to ask you more about the meeting. You seem to have concerns. What are they?"

"At the meeting, I saw several people who are in Peter's group in the Adoption Project. We have a hundred cohorts, so he has a large supply of would-be followers"

"I thought you only collated, not interacted."

"So did I. The interviews come to us and we read them. They are coded and anonymous, but even so the ten interviewers get to know their subjects pretty well. A collator could talk with the interviewer and gain a lot more information than is necessary. Ethically, I have a difficult time with that just like I have a difficult time seeing many of his Project subjects at the meeting. He is influencing vulnerable people. Now my own experience of him leads me to mistrust."

Azure realized that Jemma's concern was for the subjects in the Project based on her vulnerability with Peter. "Tell me more about being vulnerable."

Again, Jemma found the window. She explained her lack of eye contact. "It helps me to organize my thoughts. The staring away," she clarified.

Azure waited with patience and thought that Jemma was expressing her own vulnerability in therapy, bringing up feelings and thoughts from years ago. *She lost total control of her body, her choices, and her baby. She told me that not holding her daughter and only seeing her from afar was the worst of all. "All that labor and pain with no prize," was the way she put it. The seventeen-year-old was reflected in her tears. The wound was not healed. We were gently removing the bandage. Vulnerability always lies under the emotional bandage. Sometimes it is lifelong.*

Jemma continued, "I feel so open and exposed with my conflict. It hasn't been lessened by all this time. Instead, it has become demanding of resolution. If I feel so anxious about being open, some of the subjects must as well. The moms who 'gave their babies away' or 'up for adoption' - however you say it - it's a deep loss laden with guilt and feelings of abandoning a part of you. Of me." She stopped abruptly.

"Back to my original subject. Peter's influence is powerful, especially for people who are sensitive and have been opened to private feelings of long ago. I suspect he is aware of what he is doing. I saw it at Spiderweb. I saw his intense probing. I'm concerned that he is wielding too much power over naive and innocent people who are not aware nor protected. They trust him."

"It sounds very unbalanced, like Peter does have a large amount of control. He uses his charisma to get what he wants. But what is that, exactly?"

"I don't know. I just see big power, all on one side of the equation: within Peter. The other side of the equation holds many fragile people. It scares me. I keep remembering what he told me about mind control and his expertise in it. I don't trust him to use his power in the right way. It's all my intuition, though it is influenced by my interaction with him."

Azure thought much the same way as Jemma. She saw real concern about real people meeting in the sphere of real power. "What can you do about it the Project subjects and Peter? I agree with your ethical concern about the misuse of power. Can you talk with Charles?"

"Yes. Of course. That's the perfect answer. He would know if I am being too...whatever. I don't have to tell him about our date, just the meeting and what I saw. I will make the appointment tomorrow. Thank you."

Silence. They were each in their own thoughts and memories.

Azure opened the next topic. "You had two stories, Jemma. You've decided something about your daughter?"

"Yes. I've decided I will no longer live with my conflict. After our last session, I journaled in the coffee shop. I wrote and wrote." She stopped talking and swallowed.

Azure waited as she internally marveled again about the power our stories hold and give back to us when shared.

"For the first time, Azure, I could see that I had no choice when I was sixteen. Now I do have one and I choose to find my daughter. I've met the contact for a small group of moms who adopted out their babies right after birth. Their name is The First Moms Group. They now want to find their children and see if the children, now grown up, are open to meeting their birth moms. Currently there are only two states to have open birth records so the whole process will take a lot of time and effort." Here Jemma's excitement shone in her eyes. "One of the two is Kansas, where I delivered!"

Azure's eyes glistened. "What a miracle your aunt lived in Kansas!"

"Ah, my aunt did not live in Kansas. She lived in Philadelphia and was not ill at all. It was all part of the lie. I actually went to the Catholic Orphan Asylum. Yeah, terrible name. It was connected with the Infant Home run by the Sisters of Compassion, I think. It was in Wichita, Kansas. What a stroke of luck!"

Jemma took a deep breath. "I'm going to my first meeting with the moms tomorrow night. A meeting that will truly help me, unlike the last meeting I attended."

Azure was pleased and excited about Jemma's journey. "You're making a major commitment. I applaud you, Jemma. Already you have an energy in your voice, your eyes, and your spirit that I haven't seen before. All the 'what-ifs' we can discuss next time. You told me your two choices were to search as best you could or accept and close your mind. It's very difficult to stop a mind, to suppress conflict, or to dam a rushing river. You have decided to follow the river rather than try to build a dam to fight it, because you would only block your spirit, your happiness. The river is your life source. You may not find your daughter. Then again, you may find her, by following that source, the one that birthed your baby."

CHAPTER SIXTEEN
TOM AND TERESE: PORTLAND, 1992

After dinner, Derek left Portland while Tom and Terese sat on the patio, each in their own thoughts. "Did Derek seem different to you tonight, Tom?" Terese closed her book, using a fallen leaf as a bookmark. She looked directly at Tom. "You've been staring for an extra-long time. Are you merging with the sky or the pines?"

Tom turned to her with a rueful smile. They locked eyes in a familiar and loving silence. He knew it was now or never. Could he trust her? Their twenty-eight-year relationship? He had betrayed his longer relationship with Derek. Would this one disintegrate if he told her?

"Tom?"

"I'm sorry. My head is filled with tree frogs."

"Tree frogs, sweetheart?"

"Their songs, their thrumming. They seem especially loud tonight. It's not pleasant. As if... they are competing with my thoughts, each side increasing in tension. Terese, there's something I have to tell you." He shook his head. "No, there is no one else."

"I know that, Tom. I know you. I love you. What is it?"

He took a deep breath, his stomach reacting, his fear growing. He was about to betray a decades-old promise to himself, his son, and them. He could no longer deny the murder. He felt simultaneous relief and fear. Coupled with the denial was yet another lie, that he was not Derek's biological father. The fear outweighed any relief. "Derek is not my biological son. Nor Suzanne's. We adopted him in Chicago the day before her twenty-fourth birthday."

"Oh, Tom. He's not your son? You've lived with the secret for his whole life? He's lived with it." Terese was clearly shocked and not hiding it very well. She took his hand. "No one knows?"

"My cousin in Minnesota does, and her husband. But," he hesitated and looked away. "It's far worse than Derek being adopted and not knowing."

Terese put her other hand over his and moved her chair closer. "Go on. I'm here to stay. It's okay."

"Terese, stop! It's not okay. It's not okay at all. Suzanne was murdered." He disengaged his hand and abruptly stood up.

Panic filled her eyes. "Murdered?"

Tom could see her stop breathing and that she had no idea what to do or say. He sat back down and moved his chair to face her, taking hold of her hand. His love for her in his quickening heart seemed uncontainable, but immediately his fear blocked it. The reawakened image of Suzanne, bloodless with the parchment on her cold and lifeless body would not go away. Remembering his love for Suzanne, Tom closed his eyes as despair seeped out into his close-shaven beard. Drawing his hand back and covering his eyes, he yearned to remain in the lie, not see, and send it all away.

Terese tightened her mouth, working incredibly hard to keep silent and let him talk. Interlocking his fingers, stretching his arms, and sighing deeply, Tom whispered. "You don't know. It's worse than murder and lying to my son. I didn't hear Suzanne as she tried to tell me the truth of her life. I forced my will on her. I urged her to marry me and discarded her history. By not listening and not hearing, I wronged her. She gave her life for my blindness and deafness."

There was a long silence. "Tom, go on. I'm here without judgment. You know that."

Tom took his handkerchief, folded and ironed, out of his pocket, wiped his face, and blew his nose. *Terese always smiles when she sees me ironing them. Jeez, how could such an inane thought come to me now?* Tom continued to judge and hate himself for all his thoughts, actions, lies and determination. He cursed himself for the deaths of Suzanne, Paul, and Aron. All the lies, legal and illegal, were demanding their voice.

Now was the time. Sitting up straight, Tom spoke in a low voice. "Okay. The story. The one I never told you." He remembered those were Suzanne's exact words, the ones he did not hear on the long-ago night they became engaged.

Tom put his elbows on his knees as his eyes pierced hers. "Let me talk. Don't ask any questions. Please. I feel like I'm unwrapping a desiccated mummy and must be extremely careful."

Terese nodded. She was sitting on crossed legs. He knew she was listening with every fiber.

He sensed her opening her heart to him, or was that a wish?

"I'm here. Now more than ever before." she whispered.

How could she still love me, seeing my fear, exhaustion, and grief? Hearing my lies, deceptions, and betrayals? "Where do I even begin?" Tom questioned.

Terese waited.

"I met Suzanne in 1959. She was twenty and had one more year of college to finish. I was twenty-one, beginning my Master's Degree. We were married the next year. She started working in a lab while looking into a Master's program; I began teaching. We lived in Chicago, not Minneapolis. I know you know all that, except for the Chicago part. It was our engagement night and she started to tell me why she could not marry me, nor have children. I stopped her by saying our love would carry us through anything. I just did not listen. I disbelieved, ignored her story. I never even heard all of it." He stopped talking. Several moments passed.

He felt so unworthy as she listened and prompted. "Her story..."

Again, he was flooded with the memories of not listening, not hearing, not seeing. *I will no longer be blind again to another's truth, no matter whose, and especially my own,* he vowed.

72

"Yes. I'm ashamed to tell you how willful I was. The blind and deaf Don Quixote of Love. Here is Suzanne's story. Her father was a minister in Smotelyville, Indiana and she had almost no relationship with him. Suzanne was very close with her mother, until she left home to go to a boarding school in Chicago, her mother's alma mater. I never knew why. The relationship with her mom began to grow distant. It was at the high school that she began to have nightmares. Suzanne began to remember that her father met in secret with the deacons at his church on Thursdays. I had no idea what that meant. She did."

Terese held her chin in her palm, first two fingers over her lips. He saw her working to stop her questions.

"She only told me and one other person about the meetings. Or rather, tried to tell me. She told one of the nuns at her school, whom she began to trust. The nun did listen but I wouldn't believe her. I said her father was a minister: how could he be doing something wrong? She stopped telling me. She took care of me because I couldn't hear her. I needed to listen and take care of her. I did not."

Tom's pain was unbearable. Terese sat. She touched his shoulder, then stopped when he shrugged her off.

"Before I silenced her, she told me it was a group of church and community leaders with really bad men in it. It sounded absurd: Stephen King in the middle of podunk Smotelyville? I was grateful she stopped telling me her story. My God. For my selfishness, my blindness and deafness, she suffered alone.

"Suzanne couldn't have children as she had surgery during high school. I didn't really hear what she said when I asked her to marry me. I easily suggested adoption and she told me we'd have to think about it. After we married, we both agreed adoption was our next step. She found the agency."

Tom was silent and staring. Terese was silent and waiting.

"The day after we adopted Derek, I went out for thirty minutes to get her a birthday and new mommy gift. She was resting on our bed and Derek was sleeping in his room, in his crib. God, Derek isn't even his real name! We named him

Aron... All these lies! I came home and went right to our bedroom, excited about what I bought for her."

There was silence as Terese began to process what Tom was saying.

"Go on, Tom. Tell me."

"Suzanne was dead. She was lying on our bed. Lifeless and bloodless."

"Oh, my God, Tom. My God." Terese got up and went towards him.

He stopped her. "Sit down. Please. I have to tell you what I remember. There was a sheet of parchment on her body telling me the promise was kept. It sounded religious and said the sacrifice was holy. It said twenty-four. It was written in red, I thought her blood, and they threatened to kill Aron if I kept the paper or told anyone. I started to tremble but ran to Aron's room. He was still sleeping. I'll always see his teddy bear mobile circling slowly in the breeze. I went back to our room, got the paper, ripped it into pieces and flushed it down the toilet.

"I did not even think to call an ambulance and especially not the police. I was frozen and terrified. Within minutes, four men showed up in a van. They wore dark suits, dark glasses, and fedoras pulled down low. They walked right into the house with a stretcher. Horrified, I realized they were the murderers. They told me they were there for her body. No one was to be told. Clearly, no police. One pointedly looked over to Aron's door and cocked his head. I said nothing. I couldn't speak. I only shook. 'Please, oh please,' I prayed over and over, 'don't go near Aron.' They took her body. That's the last time I saw Suzanne."

Tom's head was down, eyes closed, his body wretched and immobile.

Terese's face was wet. She moved in front of him and knelt. "Tom, look at me."

He raised his head slightly.

"Tom. It's not your fault."

An hour later they sat in the kitchen drinking tea, but neither could eat. Tom didn't even know how he could sit, only wanting to curl up in darkness and make it all go away.

"Why now, Tom? Why today did it come up? Is it because of Derek's visit?"

"Terese, he has been invited to join a secret group. It petrifies me, not least because it meets on Thursdays."

"No, Tom. It's a coincidence. It's not possible."

"It is possible. It's the most possible thing in the world. He has no idea of evil. Not this kind of evil. Most people don't. I didn't. What did the parchment say? 'The vow is never done.' Secret societies are generational, I know that much. Now I know, why not before? I was blind, deaf, and mute. I was buried alive. Terese, I'm so scared. What if they are coming for Derek? My fear is just as it was when I saw her bloodless body. I thought the fear was gone. Eradicated. But it's not just as it was, it's worse. But I'm not worse. Now I will handle what I have to do. No more lies. I am going to fix it. I have to find the truth. I couldn't save his mother, but I have to save my son."

CHAPTER SEVENTEEN
BERNICE AND MICHAEL: CHICAGO

Bernice Schmidt sat in front of the Rosemont School for Girls, somewhat spaced out. She remembered her years of high school at Rosemont. She remembered bringing Suzanne there for her freshman year. It was as if the past fifty years never happened. It was before Oscar had influenced her to leave Normal School. It was before the cobwebbed town of Smotelyville and before Suzanne's birth brought unbelievable joy into her life. The night of Suzanne's untold horror had not yet stolen her daughter from her. Bernice kept believing Sister Michael would have the answers, even a small one.

Unlike her, Rosemont School for Girls had changed little in the half-century since Bernice attended. There were fewer old trees and more young ones. The shrubbery was dense, and the stone buildings strong as ever. The familiar peace filled Bernice as she opened the well-oiled oak door. *Would that I could breathe the peace in and keep it forever.* Feeling memories of love and belongingness opened a window in her heart that had been locked tightly for too long. The unwelcome feelings of loss and hope followed. She asked the young novice behind the desk in the great open entry if she could see the Mother Superior.

"Of course, you phoned yesterday. She's expecting you. Let me take you to her."

Bernice gently refused. "No, I remember the way. Thank you." She followed the darkened cherry paneling as her heart continued to open.

"Mother Superior," began Bernice as she walked in the open door.

"Please, Bernice, you knew me as Sister Michael - how many years ago? I was twenty-three and had just taken my final vows. You were in your senior year."

They looked at each other. The memories flooded each of them. Unspoken feelings imbued the soft hug.

"I'm seeming to remember - weren't you called Bernie?"

Bernice smiled, meeting Sister Michael's eyes with gratitude, connection, and confidence. *I can trust you,* she thought. "I haven't heard that name in forever. Was that really me? Before I became not really me? Down the road, I may become Bernie again, but not until I can understand and accept what happened. And, perhaps not even then." They both sat down.

Sister Michael's brow gathered, but she kept her voice even. "I haven't seen you since Suzanne's graduation. How is she? I was so surprised not to hear from her. It's been over thirty years."

Instantly, Bernice's face changed. She spoke haltingly as her words rushed out with no plan, only emotion bursting its bonds. "I was hoping you might know, Sister Michael. But in my heart, I knew that was a false hope. You were close with her in her years here, closer than I was to her. I felt a distance growing between us when Suzanne left home to live here, but thought it was normal. Since she was not close with her father, I didn't think she would turn from me.

"I am certain it started when she came running back from something she saw in the church basement at the end of eighth grade. Whatever caused her such fear prompted me to bring her here to your care. I don't know what she saw, but it was horrible. Where was I? Where was her protective mother? So many things I didn't know, and still don't." Bernice pressed her palm on her forehead and dropped her face, eyes closed. "Before you ask, forgiving myself is not even a remote possibility."

Neither woman smiled anymore. *The room is thick with unexpressed heaviness and confusion that needs to be spoken,* thought Michael. "Bernice, you're going back thirty years. I have to catch up with you. You haven't seen Suzanne either? Tell me. I'll tell you. Maybe we can tell..."

Bernice interrupted her. "Sister Michael. I think Suzanne is dead." The Sister's eyes filled with tears. Bernice forced herself to go on. "I don't know how or when, but there is no legal information about her after 1963. I hired a private investigator two years ago. She could find nothing after '63. Suzanne would have been twenty-three or four. The investigator did find an application for a marriage license in 1960 with a Paul Miller in Chicago. In 1961, she was accepted to the University of Chicago graduate program. They lived in Park Ridge in an apartment. There was very little about Paul Miller. Apparently, he taught in a high school in Oak Park. The only thing she could discover was that he left with very little notice.

"What happened? In August of 1963, every other record of Suzanne or Paul Miller stopped, as if it were erased and they were both killed. Gone. The investigator had never seen anything like it. She used every possible government agency. Nothing but silence."

As Bernice dried her eyes, the redness remained. Her face was creviced in grief. Sister Michael felt her own pulsating anxiety. She moved to take Bernice's hand and sat beside her. "My heart breaks for you. For me. Yes, her death feels pretty definite to me as well. I don't have a feeling about Paul Miller. I never met him. Suzanne left me at her graduation with the deepest hug, saying 'I've got to live my life. I'll come to see you in seven years. I'll be a real person then. All because of you.' I asked her why seven years? She said, 'I don't know. It just came to me. After I'm twenty-four.' I never saw her again. It is time, Bernice, to share what we do know. I know some things about Suzanne and her experiences in Smotelyville. You know of Oscar and your life with Suzanne."

"I need tea, Sister. Do you have any? I knew coming here would be hard. I didn't know this hard. I did not expect the flood of despair." She got up and began to pace.

"Of course, we have tea. Let me ring for some." While they waited for the tea, the nun asked Bernice if she still lived in Smotelyville.

"Oh, no! No! We moved from there in 1963 to a town a few hours north. Oscar had a nervous breakdown and couldn't work like he once did. He died two years ago and I moved back here. I'm still friends with Elena from here and Maureen from college. Do you remember Maureen?"

Sister Michael laughed. "I do. I do. Who could ever forget Maureen? Do you live together?"

"A few blocks apart. It's perfect. We have our own space, which I desperately need. Yet easy proximity, which we all want. I began coming up after Oscar entered the Dementia Unit over six years ago, gradually bringing my things up and found the best apartment ever. I officially moved here the day after his funeral." She chuckled in remembering.

The nun's eyes opened wide at the chuckle. "And never looked back?"

"Not to him. Not to Smotelyville. I wanted to find Suzanne. She had cut off contact with me as well right after graduation; like you, I haven't seen her since. She did call to tell me she was married and going to graduate school. Still she was not ready to see me. Before that, though, she never even called. I had to let her lead the way. I loved her too much to do anything else. I also thought I didn't deserve her time. She never knew how much I loved her. Because I believe her dead, I have to find out whatever I can. I feel her death was from something..." She wavered, "Something very terrible."

A novice brought the tea. The conversation paused as the young woman placed the tea service and wordlessly left.

"Bernice, I struggled with calling you during Suzanne's years here. I met with her whenever she needed me. Sometimes when her memories overwhelmed her, we met daily."

Bernice's face became ashen. "Why didn't you call? I don't understand."

"I'm not sure. I have never been that close with a student. I'm sorry. That's not true. You and I were the closest. Nor have I ever heard..." Sister Michael's voice faltered, "anything like the story she told me."

Both women sat in their own remorse and bravery. The nun was slightly shaking her head.

Bernice rubbed her forehead, eyes crystalline with unshed tears, as she listened to Sister Michael.

"I need to hear it," Bernice said quietly. "I need to hear why."

"She trusted me to keep her secret." The Sister sighed softly. "Bernice, I was afraid for her life if I talked to you. Now I wonder if her life was in danger because I kept silent. At that point, Suzanne had to trust herself, develop her strength, and ultimately recover. Bernice, please call me Michael. Our bond is growing. We don't need formality."

"Sister, I mean Michael, we have to tell each other now what we know, and what we knew. The men I have come to suspect as dangerous - the church men - are all gone now. I have no idea where they moved and I don't care. I never sensed Oscar was dangerous. I knew he was horribly weak and feared the influence the deacons and his father had over him. The church is literally gone, burnt to a crisp.

"But my fear and grief remain. The fear I felt, when Suzanne was fourteen and I sent her here, is beginning again. My guilt grows. Something was terribly wrong with my husband, his Thursday meetings, his minister father, and the deacons. His dementia symptoms were not sudden. I saw his mind leave in little pieces since the day Suzanne was born. The man I married was not the man I lived with after her birth. Is it safe now, Michael? I feel so scared."

"I don't know, Bernice. I don't know how safe we are or aren't. I have come to respect the power of evil. There is no other word for what happened. I do not believe in a personified devil, a Satan, but I do believe evil is a very powerful and real force. It always seeks the Light."

Bernice was silent for a moment, her face drawn and weary. Then she spoke clearly, "Does the Light seek the evil as well?"

CHAPTER EIGHTEEN
DEREK AND AZURE: SEATTLE, 1992

A zure opened the door to the waiting room. "Come in, Derek. It's good to see you again." They entered and took their chairs. She began after the usual opening chime, without taking her eyes from his. "How are you? What brought you back? Tell me."

He glanced to the window. "Wow. Cut to the chase. I've been away. I know I cancelled twice. If you're still willing to see me..." his voice trailed off.

"Derek, of course I want to see you. I wasn't scolding you and I'm sorry if it sounded that way. I really want to hear how your life is going. How you are doing with your career, your Adoption Project, Tibs, MCATs?" Azure looked sincerely curious.

"I'll tell you. The Project has brought up so many issues and opportunities. I've met a wonderful spiritual teacher. I've attended several of the meetings he leads." Big smile. "I think it's because of the meetings. It seems like I'm getting more sensitive, thinner skin, and actually more confused, if that is possible! When I am at the meetings, though, I feel strong and whole and happy. There I don't have to make decisions. I have no confusion. It's called Unconditional Love, Inc."

Azure quickly thought, *It's Peter's group that Jemma described. Maybe not. I have to wait. I haven't seen Derek so alive. His body seems to exude dancing colors.* Suddenly his face fell. The colors dissipated.

"Out of the meetings, I'm actually more confused, and about more things." His gaze studied the turquoise rug as if he were memorizing the patterns.

"Well, I'm glad you returned. You have so much going on. Where do you want to start?" She reflected on his confusion. *Some people get energized from chaos. Some get immobilized. Derek looks as if he wants to jump out of his skin.* "What's confusion like for you, Derek?" In one movement, his eyes went from the rug to

Azure, where they focused. She felt the connection like a coupling between two train cars.

"It's a long story about confusion and not confusion. So much has happened in a month." He leaned his head back on the chair. She waited. "Okay, here goes," as he sat up and crossed his leg. She noted he crossed them differently than previous visits. Before, he had crossed ankle over knee; now it was knee over knee. *Perhaps nothing, maybe something. It bears noting.*

"My dad's upset with me. I've stopped the MCAT course. I've been invited to a special subgroup of Unconditional Love, Inc. Tibs and I have no contact; she's moved to Boulder. I miss her a little, but not like I thought I would. Peter, the leader, has been great." He stopped, looked down and back up. "Umm. Well, that's the reason I've not been here in a while. I still feel mixed coming in today. Peter's not a fan of therapy, or storytelling. He doesn't know I'm here. I'm sorry."

"Derek, why are you sorry? It's always your choice to be here or not here. You have a story to tell. You are living and creating your story when you're not here as well, even more so. You can continue to make your appointments as you need to or want to. Really. Tell me about Peter." *It must be the same Peter that Jemma referred to, the researcher she slept with, fell out of lust with quickly, and saw his manipulative side at the meeting. Jemma wondered if he was preying on the vulnerable subjects in the Adoption Project. How could it not be him? I must remember to be careful. Boundaries. I see two other subjects in the Project and neither of them mentioned the meetings.*

"Azure, I'm not sure. There's always something to be sorry about. But Peter? He's so engaging." Derek exhaled. "He's an amazing leader. Incredible. He's all about love and openness, which is why I'm confused about why he doesn't believe in my coming to see you. He's clearly not a fake. I know that. He just believes the Love Meetings can heal everything. He wants us to come and talk to him if we have any questions or doubts. I think he's afraid I will tell you about the sub-group. There. I've said it." He breathed what Azure took as a sigh of relief.

"Was that a sigh of relief?" she asked, needing to double-check her impression.

"It was. I'm not telling him. I'm not telling my dad either, although he believes in therapy, because I'm not talking to him right now. Because he was so..." Derek went silent, reflecting out the window. "Actually, he seemed scared. My dad, who is always strong and reliable, was scared. I've never seen him like that."

"Do you want to say more about Peter? Or go to your dad?"

Five seconds passed. "After my first Unconditional Love, Inc. meeting with Peter, I went home to Portland. I wanted to tell my dad about it and how it felt so good for me. He started out by saying 'Unconditional Love, Inc.? It spells U L-i-e.' Like the Boggle addict that he is."

"Boggle addict?" *I don't play Boggle, but immediately see the meaning in the initials. No need to share that.*

"Well, not an addict, although he does love Boggle. Just sometimes he has to make meaning out of every little thing. It seems to be his nature. I probably got defensive when he said that. Peter would never lie. He's all about Love! Then, when I told Dad about the sub-group, he freaked."

"Freaked," Azure repeated.

"Yeah. Totally freaked. He has only done that one other time, when I told him I was going to law school at the University of Chicago. He said he wanted to finance it and I could go anywhere – Yale, Stanford, Georgetown – anywhere but where I wanted to go."

"I'm curious about your decision to go to Chicago."

"I don't know. It just felt right. For some reason, I wanted the Midwest and a challenge. I also thought about Case Western Reserve in Cleveland. Once he was so riled up against Chicago, I dug my heels in. Told him I chose it and would pay for it. I went. He adjusted and I loved my time there. Azure, this was even bigger than that."

"Is that why you're not talking to him?"

"I guess so, except, now I miss him. We were so close. Are so close. Were so close. I could count on him to be interested in me. I called to talk to him and Terese said he was on a road trip. A road trip!" Derek rolled his eyes. "He's never gone on a 'road trip.' Now I really miss him. I feel guilty. Like I caused a big deal. Road trip?"

Azure saw so much going on in Derek. She had never seen him so animated. He was a popcorn machine at full tilt. "I'm curious about your guilt. I don't understand your feeling guilty about your dad taking a road trip."

"The last time I saw him, I was firm about me living my life and not him doing it for me. Then he left. Like if I live my life, he leaves me alone." He almost whispered the last word. Then he squinted. "Actually Azure, now that I am talking about it, it could be your fault." Azure stopped her almost-smile, not wanting him to think she was being patronizing or discounting. "Now, how did it come to be my fault? Not that I mind, you know. Or agree."

"You asked if there was early-on trauma for me, more than my mom dying. So, I asked him. Then the freak-out and him leaving me all began with that question." Derek wiped his tears with the cuff of his shirt.

She sat for a moment, her finger over her lips. It was her "just wait, let it sit" reminder.

He began again. "It is, you know. Your fault. Maybe Peter's right. I don't need therapy. I just need love. Plus, extra love from the sub-group."

"Derek, it sounds like so many changes are happening all at once. You broke up with Tibs?" Azure questioned.

"She broke up with me," he interrupted.

"You're right, you did say that. Tibs broke up with you. You entered the Adoption Project to find out more about being adopted by your step-mother and your confusion. You met Peter and joined a meaningful group. You came here for therapy and found a storytelling gig as well. Plus, you were in the midst of your career searching. That's a lot to deal with.

"I don't agree with Peter. Sometimes individual work is necessary as well as group work. Both are useful and work together: a catalyst for each other. Now you see a strong connection between your time here and your dad leaving. I do understand the confusion you first mentioned. I see it more than confusion, though; it feels to me like an emotional earthquake."

"It is. Perfectly said. An emotional earthquake." Derek went back to the turquoise rug patterns. "Okay," he started, looking patently at Azure. "You're right. I'm an emotional disaster. In truth, which I no longer know, I feel like I have always been in an emotional earthquake. I know you did not say disaster. My words."

She waited, inwardly urging him to stay engaged in the session.

"Can you help me?" his voice tremulous.

"Yes, Derek. I can. We can. I commit to my truth and listening to yours. Can you do the same?"

He pressed his thumb and finger on the bridge of his nose in an effort to dam the rivers of tears. "A truth journey?"

Azure permitted herself to hear hope. "Yes, Derek. A truth journey: yours."

CHAPTER NINETEEN
PETER: SEATTLE, 1992

Peter sat in the second suite of his penthouse condominium, which operated as the headquarters for the Northwest Quadrant of Maharba. The suites were joined by one door that only Peter used. Members entered through the front door of the Maharba suite. Peter demanded and received his privacy. The penthouse suited him well, no one above him. He sat at the Arbus-designed desk, back straight, ready. He dialed his father in Sedona.

"Martin, sit down. We have him." Peter informed his father, with whom he rarely spoke.

"You mean Suzanne's kid? Peter. You know not to joke about this. I'm sorry, you don't joke. I know that. I'm just astounded. After twenty-nine, thirty years. Son, I'm, um, proud of you. Give me the details! It was so wise of me to decide to keep him to fill the line of Rev. Adolf. Even though he is not a true blood Schmidt, he became a blood Schmidt and completes our circle of sacrifice. Adolf's great-grandson will become our next leader, despite being adopted."

Peter picked up his legal pad and fountain pen. He wrote down the word: Proud. He wrote Derek Next Leader and drew a large X through it. He reviewed with Martin that the idea to lure Derek into Maharba came to him in California. After getting his Bachelor's degree in Computer Science, he spent seven years studying with club leaders and with the powerful Church of Satan, skilled in the art of selling power, greed, and satisfying desires. The seven years finished Peter's vicarage, as it were.

Peter created Unconditional Love, Inc. when he moved to California. He planned it to look like just another New Age group, although it would be their front and feeder, out of the attention of the federal government. ULI would be innocuous and open, preaching Love, on the outside, of course. Within subgroups, studies of the ancient occult, Aleister Crowley, and modern Satanism permeated the minds and consciousness of the disciples. When Derek moved to Seattle, Peter was thrilled. He would use ULI to succeed in completing the circle, where Martin and the whole of Maharba had failed.

"So, Martin, using my college studies and the tremendous resources of the Church, I learned how to infiltrate many of the national organizations and their agendas for their future."

"All to our own advantage. Our thirty-year plan. Thank you, Peter."

Peter smiled. Getting a compliment from his father was extremely rare. Getting two? Peter could hear the pride in his father's voice. All his work, his studies, his years of training were worth it. He remembered calling Martin after he knew how to hack the organizations with the declaration, "Martin, I have found us a gold mine."

Peter realized again he no longer needed his father's pride nor gratitude now that he felt competent and knew his IQ was in the top 1% of the population. It was too little, and too late. Peter had made it on his own. He cleared his throat to continue.

"In California, I searched for any adoption research that might be in the planning stages. I figured something like that might draw out our boy. I found one that was starting in 1992 in Seattle, five years out. When I found he had moved to Seattle, I moved here immediately to create the perfect milieu, the web that would beckon to him. I could only intend that our chosen one would show up at the Adoption Project that was being organized by the social work department at the university. I sent him an official-looking notice announcing the Project, hopefully drawing him to it. I set up the Unconditional Love, Inc. forum as a magnet for the vulnerable subjects in the Project. Now we had a pool for possible Maharba members. I established the Northwestern Quadrant of Maharba with several of the leaders from the other Quadrants. Uniting us with the Church of Satan was brilliant." Peter was loving his list of successes.

Martin interrupted. "Why are you telling me things I already know?"

Peter ignored him. "I signed on to be a collator for the Project, which gave me total access to all the names and information about each of the one thousand participants. His name was on the list. I was easily able to put him in my group to oversee. He walked into my office with the best lost and confused look of all. Little did he know he was walking into the elaborate web of my creation. We have him, Martin: Suzanne's adopted son, Derek. Soon he will be with us. The circle is nearly complete."

Silence. Peter waited. He knew his father could not know the future.

"I'm coming up to Seattle, Peter. I'll bring Wolfgang K. We cannot discuss any more over the phone."

Peter had not seen his father in a long time. How would it be to talk with him in person? Peter felt nothing but distaste. "Sure, Martin. When are you arriving?" The pleasure he felt in Martin's pride was short-lived. He held no love, no memories of love, regarding his father.

"Tomorrow evening. I will phone you with the details as soon as I have them."

"No, Martin. Not yet. Give me a few weeks to cultivate Derek's friendship and trust in me. We also need a Lesser Ritual before his initiation. I need to prime him. We need to observe him and his emotional receptivity. He should be ready to initiate during the most sacred full moon in the sign of Scorpio on November 10. I will get back to you with progress. Plan on coming up for the Seven Windings on the Thursday before the full moon. Better yet, wait until we come down to Sedona on the full moon."

"You have thought of everything. I'm...ah...impressed. G'bye Peter. I love you."

Peter stared at the phone in his hand. *I love you?* Those words had never crossed his father's lips. Never. Fortunately, Peter had learned long ago to suppress or to invoke tears when he needed or willed either. He also was excised of any love or yearning for love that he may have had for Martin as a young boy. No need for sentimentality. He needed no one's approval, no one's love. What was love anyhow to Peter, but the honeyed glue on his web? Dying flies are far more interesting in a web than on fly paper. He knew how to get blind admiration. For Peter, admiration meant submission to his will, his needs.

He left the Maharba suite and locked the door as he entered his own rooms. He drew in deep satisfaction from the elegant and extravagant decor. Moving into his study, Peter reflected on his father's forthcoming visit. The tide had turned. Martin was now coming to him. Sitting on his burgundy leather tufted chair, Peter pulled out a glass pipe – a commissioned work by the best glass blower in Seattle – and a small pouch of ganja, his one indulgence. He lit his pipe, drew in the pleasure, and began to reflect on his life.

Peter always started his reflections with his thirteenth birthday gift in Smotelyville. He was called Hans then. Hans Peter. He dropped the Hans on his eighteenth birthday in Montana. He found his purpose in life, his gifts of courage and control, his lust for power and his pleasure during his thirteenth birthday celebration.

His father told him his initiation into Maharba, and into his manhood, would be more special than any other boy's. Very few ever had the privilege that would be given to Hans Peter. He did not know what his father meant, but he looked forward to that day.

"Hans, you are the only boy in twenty-four years to be invited to our most sacred Ritual." He could actually hear Mr. K. now, feeling the empowering excitement of his initiation.

He stands in the circle of men, in his choir robe without clothes underneath, as his father had instructed him. "Your thirteenth birthday gift will be unveiled after you make your Pledge and your Abrahamic Vow." There are twelve men in hooded robes. Hans had seen in previous rituals that sometimes the robes were brown and sometimes black. Today they wear the latter. Hans is the thirteenth member. He repeats what his father had taught him.

"I, Hans Peter, proclaim to this sacred circle of men, complete and total submission to the Abrahamic Order of Maharba. I trust the power of sacrifice. I honor true blood sacrifice." He focuses on each man as he speaks. "I will never reveal any members' names to anyone. I vow to live my life for the purposes and continuation of the Abrahamic Precepts I now embrace. I will drink the Blood. I will satisfy the pleasures of the flesh. I will hold sacred the Power given to me. Abraham. Isaac. Father. Son."

He remembers his father saying, "Hans, take off your choirboy robe and receive the hood and cloak of a man." He drops his robe with confidence and pride. Martin puts the cloak and hood on him. Each man walks before him and fingers the Symbol on Hans's open chest. They chant in low flowing voices, "As the thirteenth and youngest member of this Abrahamic Order, we welcome you and the power which is now given to you."

One man steps out of the circle, puts his hand on Hans's shoulder, and walks him to the drawn curtains. "Open the curtains, Hans. Receive your gift of initiation."

Hans swallows his gasp and stands very still as he feels his arousal while looking at the naked motionless woman on the altar in front of him. Blood is in the crystal chalice next to her.

Somehow, he knows it is the woman's blood. He does not know what to do.

"Watch each man, Hans," whispers Mr. K. "Watch carefully and when we are done, you will follow. You will follow us. Then you will follow your blood instincts."

Each man drinks from the chalice, dips their middle finger into the blood, and draws a figure on her body. Hans is next.

Peter deeply inhales from the pipe as the memory demands he follow.

Hans is sweating with excitement and fear of doing the wrong thing, which only excites him more. Walking forward to the body, he forgets he is in a room of men, his self-consciousness transforming into desire. After sipping from the chalice, Hans moves in slow motion to the altar, and with slow deliberation, drips the rest of the contents of the chalice down her neck, torso, and legs. He moves over and then in her, feeling the ecstatic release of life uniting with death, transcendent in the sacred. His initiation is complete. The men applaud.

Thirty years later, Peter breathed in the smoke, continuing to visualize, using his first sacred sexual experience as he pleasured himself.

CHAPTER TWENTY
TOM: SMOTELYVILLE, 1992

Tom drove through stark deserts, endless mountains, and wide and narrow rivers before crossing into Indiana. He was driving, needing time to think and something familiar to stop his tectonic plates from shifting so rapidly. *I need to be alone, to try to get some perspective. The movie frames of my life move at warp speed. I am glad to have Terese to love, be loved, and talk with every night. But I know I have to handle my life, my journey by myself. None of it belongs to her.*

Suddenly Tom broke out in a sweat, his chest pounding, and pulled into a rest area. He fell on his crossed arms over the steering wheel. *What was going on?* He tried deep breaths to no avail. *I've got to get out of here. Walk.* He remembered the billboard a few miles back with four or five bears dancing under an umbrella. "Get more than bare protection. Call Hillside Insurance for home and auto coverage."

The bears. Umbrella. Derek's mobile. Aron's mobile. He sat on a bench and let the fear come. *I can't do this foolhardy journey. How could I know it would be filled with ripping flashbacks? Of course, it would. The reason I am here is to find out the truth about Suzanne's death. No, I am here to protect Derek because they threatened his life. I fear "they" are back. I can't endure the terror again. The fear. The pictures. The deluge of feelings drowning me. Recrimination. Sorrow. Hopelessness. Shame. Grief. Betrayal. Stop! Stop! Stop!*

He decided to call Maggie. He had to talk to someone who knew the tragedy of Suzanne's murder. They spoke occasionally, at least once a year, each hesitant to bring up the summer of 1963. *She is practical. I know she will tell me to go back to Portland. Let sleeping dogs, memories, and parchment lie. LIE. There it was again! Lie. Lies. This is why I started this impulsive journey in the first place.*

Derek. I left Portland to save Derek. My purpose. I have to get control of my mind, my feelings. My life. I can't continue this looping and colliding. Where to go? What to do? I'll phone Maggie tonight, after I find a place near Smotelyville. Yes, I have a plan.

Tom felt somewhat better after his plan. Smotelyville. One of the few details he knew about Suzanne's life was that she was born in Smotelyville to a Lutheran minister, left at fourteen, never to return. He tried to remember where she went. *Of course! Chicago, where we met and fell in love.* Tom knew he must go to Chicago, find her boarding school. *What was its name? God, where is my memory? Maybe the ... what's she called? Ah! Sister. Mary, Marie? Maybe she is still there. Maybe Suzanne's parents are still in this little town. Do I really want to meet them? No. I only want to settle everything and get back to my family: my wife, son, daughters, and grandson. My life. Smotelyville will soon be over, Chicago next, then Minneapolis to see Maggie. Finally, at last, home! Everything will resolve and my fears for Derek will vanish.*

He could see a problem developing that cut deeply. As he crossed the country to travel back East, he realized he was thinking more of Suzanne than of Terese. He was remembering his first love while he feeling unfaithful to his second.

Tom turned into the parking lot of "Richardsons' Bed and Breakfast." *Perfect. I want a home, not a cold concrete motel. Not that there was any motel anywhere near Smotelyville. Probably one night. A quick answer.* Tom felt a distant thrumming in his head which he quickly suppressed.

"Hi. I'm Tom Freborne. Do you have a room?" *Damn, I wish I could do the French accent.*

The robust woman behind the small antique counter smiled. "You're in luck. We are only taking Toms tonight."

Tom blinked. "Please?" cocking his head.

"Oh, now I'm just pulling your leg. All our rooms are open. It's midweek. Is there just you?"

"Yes. Thank you. I apologize for the blank stare. I've been on the road for several days, alone and not talking to many people. I promise I'll do better tomorrow. I just need some sleep."

"Oh, Tom. You're fine just the way you are. I should just keep a lid on it sometimes." She turned to the wall with assorted keys on hooks, muttering that was what her husband always told her. "You have your choice of rooms, Tom. I'll show you the biggest and best first. Problem being it's on the third floor. But you look healthy. You look fit, as they say. No knee troubles like myself here. I'm Lily Mae. That's M-a-e. Not like the month. Howdy do," as she pumped his hand. "My husband, Ferdie," her eyes twinkled, "is in the barn. Few goats, pigs, chickens. You'll be glad of them in the morning, supplying you breakfast for a king and all."

He was exhausted by so many things: solitude, travel, thoughts, questions, emergent feelings, and memories. Lily Mae was certainly welcoming. He just couldn't take her big personality right now. Sometimes he hated his inability to have an open heart and open mind every minute of the day. "You know, Lily, the third floor sounds great. You don't need to go up all those stairs. I'll just take the key and my bag to the top floor."

"Oh, you are the sweet one, Tommy. I do so appreciate it. The hall lights are on, so you'll be finding it quite easy. You can shut the hall light when you want to sleep. Now I know I may be chattering too much. My Ferdie always tells me that. You look starved. I'll be fixin' you a plate. Come down in fifteen minutes or so. No, you don't need to eat down here. Take it up with you. You look in need of sleep and food. I know travelin' takes the spit outta your shine."

"Lily Mae, thank you. Thank you." He went up to the room, was pleased, and sat on the bed to phone Maggie.

Tom hung up with Maggie, feeling grounded and lost at the same time. She told him of course to visit, especially now. She looked forward to seeing him. Bruno and she had gotten married in the past two years. "After living together for nearly thirty-five years, we decided to take the plunge." He heard her smile. He went down for his dinner, thanked Lily Mae once again, and carried the tray up the two flights.

The memories of Suzanne's twenty-fourth birthday and the murder would not stay down. He stared at the water-stained papered ceiling as he laid stretched out on the high bed, appreciating the new mattress, food, and a jelly glass of red wine. He felt safe, centered, and stronger. Lily Mae. Who did she remind him of... Sleep gently cradled him as he thought of his grandmother and remembered her warm love.

Tom awakened damp with sweat, feeling something on his chest. He sat up, swatted the parchment off as if it were on fire, and stared, finally seeing it was only the map he had been reading as he fell asleep. He closed his eyes, saw the real parchment on Suzanne, terror in her opened dead eyes. Tom turned on his stomach, eyes burning and memories bursting out of control. Did he sleep at all? Or did he merely remember sleep from before his journey?

The next morning found Tom downstairs meeting Lily Mae's Ferdie. "Name's Ferdinand, but everyone calls me Ferdie. Appreciate you doin' the same."

Tom sat at the table, eating his kingly breakfast generously given by the farm animals. Ferdie swayed in a rocker close to the fireplace, reading the newspaper. "Ferdie, this is the best breakfast I have had in years. Your Lily Mae is some cook!"

Ferdie smiled as he looked up. "Yep. I love her dearly, chatter and all. Forty years now. Of course, we were kids when we married. High school sweethearts. Lily Mae says you been travelin' quite a bit?"

"Yes, I left Portland three days ago. Oregon. It feels like forever."

"Don't know no one who would leave that coast for Smotelyville, Indiana. You got folks here? Family?"

Tom picked up his coffee mug scrambling for an answer. *Damn, why did he not think people would ask his reasons for being two thousand miles from home?* "Well, Ferdie, that's a good question."

He sipped more coffee. *Truth or lie? Surely, I can't say that I'm looking for a secret group of men that murdered my wife thirty years ago.* His stomach lurched. The reasons for his trip back East became clear. First, it was for Derek. Next, it was just as much for Suzanne, to find the truth and give her murder some kind of meaning.

"I'm here for a cousin in Portland who is researching her family's history. I told her I planned a trip to my hometown in Michigan. She asked if I was going near Indiana and could check on some birth and death certificates for her in Smotelyville." *Where is this coming from?* "Sure, I told her. I can stop to see what I can find. Not that I know anything about genealogy."

Ferdie laid the newspaper on his lap. "Sure. Lotsa folks doin' that nowadays. I bet I can help you. Born and raised right here in Smotelyville."

Breathe. "I would really appreciate that. I don't know where to begin."

"We can start with a few names. What times you lookin' at?"

Gulp. This is real. Keep talking. Discuss. Put your jumpy heart in brackets. Don't think of Suzanne. Just her parents and what you know. "Let me see, she wanted information from the forties and fifties, I believe. I have her notes upstairs, but I know it was that time period. Let me run up and get them. Do you think Lily Mae has more coffee?" *This will give me ten minutes to think of something.*

"Sure, Tom. I'll go check and brew a pot if she's not around. By the way, where is she?" His voice trailed off as he walked into the kitchen.

Tom walked slowly up the stairs, realizing he had lied again. *How did I not have a plan? What did I think would happen? People magically telling me about a murderous group of men within a church?! Get real.* He opened the door to his room. *Okay. Plan. Quickly. Make up some names. Places. Do I write Suzanne's name? Do I actually mention my wife, my other wife, by name? I have no choice. Stay cool.*

Coming into the cozy dining room with the smell of fresh coffee, nearly roaring fire, and Ferdie and Lily Mae welcoming him back, Tom felt some sense of resolution giving him strength. "Thank you, Lily Mae. I haven't had such a grand breakfast in years. The coffee is delicious."

"Oh, Ferdie made this pot. And he's the one slaughtered the pig..." She stopped, noticing Ferdie's look.

"Lily Mae, Tom don't want to hear that right now." He turned to Tom. "Did you bring the notes?"

"I did. Right here. I'll give you some names and what I have. I'm sure Lily Mae might remember some of the people as well?" Lily Mae nodded solemnly, quiet as a mouse.

"Oscar Schmidt. His wife Bernice. Their daughter Suzanne. I think he's a minister?"

Silence thundered in the room. Ferdie and his wife exchanged a lightning look. The fire spat sounding like a split tree. Looking to the fire, then at Ferdie in his rocking chair, Tom ventured, "Not a great start, I fear?"

Lily looked to her husband who began to speak. "I'm supposin' the only way to do this is to be honest." he said with determination.

Tom took out a pen as he flinched inside. *There it was again. Honesty versus lies.* "Have you heard of them? Is he a minister?"

"Oh, yes. In a way, I know more than I oughta. There's a chance you've come to the right spot. Another chance, I don't cotton to tellin' that story again. The last time I told it was mid-seventies, after most people had left young Rev. Oscar Schmidt's church. You see, Tom, I was the janitor for Wittenberg Lutheran Church, called Wuttenberg when Oscar's grandpa was the preacher. Oscar's grandpa and father preached in German. So did Oscar until he had troubles remembering the language. Summing up, I was here from 1930 right after the

97

Depression up 'til, well, 1975. Most of them years was under the Rev. Adolf Schmidt as main preacher. His son came in the late thirties, but his mind wadn't quite right. Did okay for some years when his daddy left, but the Rev. Adolf had to come back when Oscar had a breakdown, loony crazy. I took another church, my own Methodist church in the seventies, as Wittenberg had near to none comin' by then."

"Wow. I did come to the right spot. Do you mind saying more? I won't reveal your name if that would be more comfortable. My cousin will be thrilled."

"Yes, you ain't gonna reveal my name. Lily Mae and me want to walk to our graves in peace." He chuckled a little. "And alive. I'll be right quick about this and then answer more if I can. Oscar was the third Rev. Schmidt to run that church, 'ceptin' he wasn't the man his pappy and granpappy was. Oscar was gentle, soft-like, you know. Quiet. No fire and brim. Always gazing off to the faraway. He'd only look to you if you cleared your throat or said 'Pastor?' softly. His wife was real smart."

"A little hoity toity," Lily Mae interrupted.

"Well, yes, maybe. Her being from Chicago and all. Plus convertin' from Catholic to Lutheran. Maybe a bit aloof, you could say. Boy, did she take care of her hubby though, rain or shine. Especially when his health began to go. Served her man, she did." Lily Mae glared, but remained silent.

"Suzanne?" asked Tom softly, memories and emotions beginning to swell.

"Now that were a pretty gal. She left Smotelyville when she was just fourteen."

"Went to that uppity boarding school her mother went to in Chicago," chirped Lily Mae, her arms folded over her ample breasts. "What was it called? Rosewood? RoseHill?"

Her husband watched the burning logs intently. He glanced up at his wife, "Rosemont. Rosemont School for Girls." His focus went back to the fire. "Now, here's somethin' Lily Mae don't know. The last time I saw Suzanne, she was runnin' as fast as she could go. A Thursday night. Runnin' cross the parking lot from the church to the parsonage. I do know it was Thursday cuz that was the deacons' sacred meeting night. I called out to Suzanne. She looked back at me with open mouth, eyes big and bulging. 'Go away, I'm fine. Don't tell anyone you saw me. Please, Mr. Richardson.' 'Of course, honey,' I said. "You need anything?' 'No, no. Just don't tell! Please?' 'Never tellin', sweetheart. Never. Trust me.' Never saw her again. Off to Chicago." He looked to Lily Mae. "That's why I never tol' you, dear wife. I always keep a promise."

Tom blanched as he heard, "We never forget a promise," from the parchment. His love and grief for Suzanne seeped through the tightly nailed coffin where it had been confined for so many years. The nails were loosened.

"You okay, Tom?" asked Ferdie. "You look pretty peaked. You know her?"

"No, no. I'm fine. I have a younger sister who was really scared once. I still remember her fright. It stays with you."

Ferdie just rocked and nodded slowly. He gave Lily Mae his look that meant something was wrong, maybe not the truth. He continued. "After she left for boarding school, we never saw her again. Her mama did go up to see her. In fact, stayed up there for the holidays and the summers. Rev. Oscar was on his own."

"Not so servin' him then." exclaimed Lily Mae. "But those women in that church took to him. Brought him casseroles and pies. Even me, although I was Methodist."

"The Thursday night deacons' meeting, Ferdie? Did you ever go to them? What was that all about? Did Suzanne go to one?"

Ferdie squinted his eye a bit as he turned the rocker more directly to Tom. "Oh, no, Tom, nobody ever went to those but the twelve deacons and the minister. Or two when Rev. Adolf was still around. Well, that's not exactly true. Sometimes, a few of the boys went once when they come up to thirteen. I had to set up more chairs then, be double sure all the blinds were shut. In fact, I remember one of those years, maybe 1963? One of those boys was joinin' the meetings. Never left them 'til he moved for college.

"To sum it all up, bad things was goin' on there. I felt it in my bones, creepy-like. Next morning, I find they cleaned up everything. Bathroom and all. Except for one time. I found blood they must've missed. That was the morning after that boy went. The one who stayed with the Meetings. I seem to remember his dad was one of the deacons. A big shot.

"But now I'm kinda tired of talkin', my friend Tom. I don't mess with evil spirits. Don't ask, I just know. And Smotelyville's a much better place with those men gone and the church closed. By the way, big fire in 1975. All burnt. Church records and all. Volunteer firemen couldn't stop it. Arson. Rev. Oscar was up the road apiece, fifty mile or so at a small church. He really couldn't do much anymore. Rev. Adolf? I don't know where's he at. That's all I got to say. Hope that's enough for your cousin?"

Tom had a flash that Ferdie was not buying the cousin and genealogy story. "Oh, I'm sure. Thank you for sharing so much. I need a bit of time to take it all in, write it down. I think I may go for a walk. See where the church was and look at the cemetery. I appreciate your time and going through the story once again. Thank you." Tom could not wait to leave the house and walk before his emotions were visible.

Tom walked to the empty church lot. No church. No parsonage. Only blackened earth. *Why don't they clean that up? Why don't I clean myself up, is the better question? Just be honest. It's the easier route by far. Yet. Why do I see all the dominoes falling down once I confess the first lie? To whom do I confess? Terese? Derek? Ferdie, for starters? Maybe Ferdie since I'm here.* The scarred land turned his stomach. *What had happened to his beloved wife? What did she see that Thursday night?* He continued on his walk. Maybe he would find her grave? Nope. No information except her father's tombstone. Next to Oscar's grandpa. Weird little symbols on both of the stones. No Suzanne. Did he really expect a tombstone for his murdered wife?

Tom decided to see if anyone else in town had information. *The small-town post office is the center of gossip and information, if I believe the novels I've read. I'll look for someone older.* He left the post office. *Nope. nothing from the post office.* The woman he did ask crinkled her nose as from a noxious smell and reported, "I don't think so. Sorry, busy now."

He opened the creaky door to The General Store, aptly named with wooden floors and musty odors. He spotted an older man and introduced himself. Tom grew excited with the response.

"I'm William. I've owned The General Store for decades, Tom. Yes, I knew the Reverend and Mrs. Oscar Schmidt. Also knew his dad, the Rev. Adolf Schmidt." He took a deep pull on his pipe, exhaling cherry tobacco aroma.

"Would you mind telling me anything you know about them?"

"Why?" William riveted into Tom's eyes.

"Well, I'm looking for a friend."

"Looking for what." William kept his gaze steady.

Tom was emotionally spent. He hadn't slept well nor long enough. Hearing the story that morning drained him. He couldn't lie at that moment and he made a snap decision to disclose his marriage. "Because, William, I married their daughter Suzanne thirty years ago. I came to Smotelyville to find out some details."

"Little late, isn't it? Did you divorce her? Looking for money? Why don't you know details about your own wife?"

Tom's anger came up as his guard went down. "No, I'm not divorced. She was murdered two years after we were married and I want to know why."

William kept inhaling and exhaling. He looked at Tom with unreadable eyes and one eyebrow raised.

Tom was sick of being judged. "William, the murderers threatened to kill our son if I were to breathe a word. I took our son and moved across the country. What would you have done?" Tom couldn't believe he was disclosing the old secret to a complete stranger, especially one who was cold and judgmental. He lost all composure and common sense.

"So, you've come back to find the cult?"

Tom blinked. "The cult? A cult? What do you know about...a cult?"

"Well, I knew of it after they left town. People felt safer to talk about it then. Me? Out of sight, out of mind. I'm sorry your wife was a victim. I've got no more to say." William walked to the creaky door, opened it for Tom, and ushered him out. "I'd let that go, son. No sense dredging up old stuff. Let it be."

Another closed door. Literally. Why had William suddenly opened up to him? Tom couldn't believe he heard the word cult. He still did not believe there could ever have been a cult in Smotelyville, or anywhere, for that matter. Were the Richardsons the only ones who knew or would talk about the church? The library and drugstore brought no news. *I've got to get out of here. I feel so creeped out. Tomorrow morning. Let me get to that Sister Nun at Rosemont.* He suddenly felt exposed as he whispered his thoughts. The ghoulish feeling increased.

At breakfast the next morning Ferdie and Tom took their respective seats. Ferdie put his paper down and turned his rocker to face Tom. "Gettin' an early start? Did you get what you come for? Where to next?" He sounded friendly and kind, not sarcastic and aloof, thought Tom. He deserved to know the truth. After all, he had told William. Both men believed the church men, the deacons, were gone, never to be heard from again.

"Yes, Ferdie. Thank you. But, I have to be honest. I'm here for me, not my cousin. I was married to Suzanne Schmidt and two years later, she was murdered. We lived in Chicago. I fled to Portland." *I will not bring Derek's name into Smotelyville.* "Now I must know the truth about her murder. I know you won't mention me to anyone. Of course, I won't mention you or anything you said to anyone. Risky business, wondering about evil people."

"Not surprisin'. Your look yesterday told me somethin' different than your words. God bless you, son, and guide you to your truth, as hard as it might be. Call me if you need me. By the way, Lily Mae's out gardening. She won't hear a word what you told me. I'll bid her goodbye for you."

They shook hands somewhat awkwardly. Tom paid in cash and walked out to his car with his host. He started the car and opened the window. "I have one more question, Ferdie. You mentioned telling your story one other time. To whom?"

Tom grimaced. "1975. The FBI."

"Thank you, Tom. I'll keep that to myself. Peace." He drove north, to the city of memories.

Ferdie checked on Lily Mae before he walked to the private phone line in the barn and dialed. "Hello? Peter? Got us some news."

CHAPTER TWENTY-ONE
JEMMA: SEATTLE, 1992

Aromatic roasted beans, echoing espresso machine exhalations, and books on warping shelves in all directions gave Jemma a deep sense of pleasure. Books and Brews was the best. It was her favorite Friday or Saturday night date with herself. The weekend music was folk, blues, or instrumental, all acoustic. She possessively guarded her best find tonight, the two-top on the side of the room. Finding any seat on a Saturday night in the university district was a coup, much less the perfect table.

The coffee machines were far enough away to hear the soft voice of the performer singing to his guitar. He looked familiar, yet Jemma knew very few people in Seattle. For which she was grateful. Could he be from the Adoption Project? She began to look through the books she had brought from the shelves to peruse.

Current fiction was mixed with Nobel laureates, and personality disorders next to Antonio Machado. Jemma rued the absence of Finding Your Baby books, although she was thrilled with her new resource of The First Moms group. Her first meeting was an informational night, but the next in two weeks would be a discussion group. Jemma was excited. Returning to her cinnamon cappuccino, she began to sort the books into buyable and those to remain in the store.

"Mind if I sit with you?" asked a fairly attractive man with lapis-blue eyes.

"Actually, I'm not up to company right now. Better luck next time."

He left, posturing a, "Who do you think you are anyway?" walk.

"That was easy. No, I don't want company. I have my own, thank you. And my writers," as she thumbed through José Saramago.

The singer sang, and the lights dimmed while leaving enough light to read. Jemma began to stare mindlessly and found tears adding to her blurred vision. She blinked and looked to the guitarist singing softly.

O Sometimes I feel like a motherless child,
Sometimes I feel like a motherless child,
O my Lore, sometimes I feel like a motherless child:
Den I gi'down on my knees and pray, *prays*
Gi'down on my knees and pray.

Jemma dabbed her dripping eyes with her hankie, lowered it, and blew her nose as softly as she could. She opened a book only to see blurred words. She made the mistake of looking up at the singer and saw his eyes on her. *Was that the man from the Adoption Project? One of the co-researchers? God, I hope he doesn't recall me. More tears. This is not helping. Don't look up.* She got out her journal and began to write. Anything to dispel the emotional upsurge. Thank God she knew so few people in Seattle. Also, grateful Posturing Blue Eyes had left the vicinity.

Twenty minutes later she felt the singer next to her and heard him asking to join her. Somehow, she knew the only way out was through. "Sure." She moved her book stacks. *Now what?* Jemma thought, being at sixes and sevens due to her immediate attraction, her just recovering emotional fest, and his leveling gaze.

"I wanted to check on you. I have never seen such a soul-filled reaction to my singing. Sorry. I am Giles Wright. Thank you for letting me barge into your quiet."

"Oh." stumbled Jemma. "Not at all. I think I'm back in the present now. I'm Jemma. Jemma Gran. This may sound random, but do you happen to be related to the author Richard Wright?"

A luminescence grew in his eyes. "Actually, I am. My father's cousin. Very few people have ever asked me that. I see you are a reader." He looked to her books. "Antonio Machado. I love him. Saramago as well? Do you know Murakami? He is one of my most favorites. What's this? Personality disorders? I'd better watch out." The steady light in his eyes scattered into twinkling.

Relieved to be away from her flooding response to his song, Jemma genuinely grinned, now in her book discourse mode. She was totally unprepared for his immediate one-eighty.

"Do you mind going back to the 'Motherless Child' song? In addition to being concerned about you and your well-being, which I hope you receive as my most sincere offering, I have to say I'm honored by your response. Being a singer, it is a huge compliment. Thank you. But at what cost to you?" Concern seemed to be showing while he unabashedly built a bridge to Jemma.

God, he is direct. I wish I had a Scotch rather than the espresso caffeine. How to respond to his emotional bridge. Walk across? Nope. Too unsafe especially after Peter several weeks ago. Meet in the middle? Peter. Was Giles another Peter? Maybe not even step onto the bridge.

Giles waited in kindness. "Unless, of course, it's totally none of my business. I can be fine without knowing."

Hearing she had a choice eased Jemma a bit, even though she was nonplussed by his interest. "Well, I'm on sabbatical from Minnesota as a collator for this Adoption Project at the university."

He grinned with glee. "The social work department's Adoption Project? Sorry to interrupt. Go ahead."

"Yes. Do you know it?"

"Do I know it? Jemma, I have lived with it these past years. I wrote the proposal for the grant. I'm one of the two lead researchers. I sing on the side, for my soul. I've been singing 'Motherless Child' recently because I can't get it out of my head." His excitement softened.

Jemma stopped herself from gulping. "I apologize for not recognizing you. You must have been in the opening meetings."

"Not me. No apologies even if I were there. I keep a very low profile in most of what I do. Performing here, while quiet, uses up my extrovert allotment. Otherwise, I'm most comfortable on the sidelines. Please go on. The coincidence of being in the same project overtook my good manners."

His slow smile made Jemma more relaxed. She even felt comforted. Comforted? How could that be? She ingested the Project surprise he produced almost as a gift. She needed to keep him off the cause of her tears. "Have you always been a musician? Always solo or were you ever in a group? I did notice you sang as if to your guitar, with closed eyes," she ventured.

Big laughter. "Guilty as charged. The aforementioned introvert thing asks for closed eyes. I sing solo now." His eyes sparkled. "In high school, however, I played with The Little Brothers and Clock Wirk. Have you heard of them?" He laughed at her head shaking. "Back to you, is it being among all the subjects in the Project that evoked your tears?"

Surrendering to his persistent gentle probing, Jemma crossed half of the bridge, although she took her guard with her. "No, Giles, it's far more personal." *Silence. Do I say more? Is it safe?* "I gave up a baby for adoption many years ago. I think my choice of sabbatical was subconscious. I've begun an active search for my daughter. I usually keep those old feelings at bay. Your song, however, and your passion rendered me helpless. There you have it."

"Jemma, I'm sorry for all your difficulty. It must have been lonely."

"Thank you. It was and the memories still are. The memories, the Project, and a commitment to heal the past has found me in therapy. Well, a kind of therapy. If you were going to ask that, being a social worker and all." Her guard stood close to her, taking the offense. How could she have revealed she was in therapy to a complete stranger, especially one she was attracted to?

"Research social work. Not a social worker. So you know, I wasn't thinking that a passionate response to an emotional song is grounds for therapy. Sounds perfectly normal and healthy to me. I respect therapy, naturally. It's just that sometimes it's overused. Jemma, I'm sorry. You don't need to hear my jaundiced reaction to therapy. In my case it is a reaction to an inept therapist after my divorce. I gave him three sessions and no-go. He nearly fell asleep in the last session. I am sure yours is good. Charles, my co-researcher, often sends people to a woman whose name I don't remember. Seems competent. Maybe Buddhist?"

"If it's Azure Manjursi, she's very competent. Charles actually did refer me to her. She is a little different than a traditional therapist. I like her. But enough of therapy talk! Especially my personal therapy."

"My apologies, Jemma. I'm glad you have someone to be with you during your journey, inner and outer. Being on sabbatical with a midwestern accent means far from home. Yet you are here, plumbing the depths of your own life experience. Forgive me, Jemma, for my therapist views. It's stupid of me to generalize based on one experience. That's a researcher for you! Do you need to leave? I would love to talk with you: books, music, the Project, and all. Can you stay?" implored Giles with naked pleading.

Few men can beg while still retaining their strength, thought Jemma. *Yet this man does. Strength seems to ooze from Giles. Besides, he feels like a social worker, even though he claims researcher. Aren't social workers supposed to have compassion and understanding? He certainly appears to be compassionate. He's a researcher and a grant writer. Smart. Open. Gentle. He reads what I read. Most of all, he sees me.* She sent the guard away but asked it to stay near. "Sure, Giles, I'd love to stay."

CHAPTER TWENTY-TWO
TOM AND SISTER MICHAEL: CHICAGO, 1992

Tom gratefully checked Smotelyville off his list. As he drove northwest to Chicago, he was amazed again at the flat land. He had grown up in Michigan with more lakes and a greener, more interesting terrain. Tom knew he could never live in the Midwest again. Where was Mount Hood? Where were the blue skies? The high cloud cover when it did rain? Perhaps he was tired of his journey. What had he discovered? Not enough. Suzanne lived in Smotelyville for fourteen years. Nothing much else. Well, yes, there appeared to be suspicious activities in the church, but it seemed to be gone now. The town still felt creepy to him. Even its name ran shivers through him. But Lily Mae and Ferdie weren't frightening. They were warm, friendly, and willing to help him. Plus, they jarred his memory about Suzanne attending Rosemont High School.

He mentally organized his finds. *1) No church records. 2) The Richardsons seemed to be the only and last people in town to know anything about the Reverends Schmidt, other than unforthcoming William. 3) Suzanne left for Rosemont when she was fourteen. 4) She saw something horrific at the deacons' Thursday night meeting. 5) There could've been a cult, according to William. Well, to be honest, he said there actually was a cult. Maybe William just read too many horror books.*

"Why didn't I listen to Suzanne on our engagement night?" He chastised himself once again. "Did she use the word cult? No, she said secret meetings." He didn't care that he was speaking only to himself in the car. The doorway to his heart quickly opened ever since Derek's visit, a now well-worn path had been cleared for remorse and many of its companions to join the rush. Guilt. Self-hatred. Despair. Shame. Tom distracted himself in an attempt to shut that door.

"Well, I do remember something Suzanne told me. While at her boarding school, she relied on some nun to help her. Of course, it was Rosemont. How could

I have been so unaware of her? To not even remember the name of her high school. Lucky for me that Ferdie reminded me." He was on his way, remembering a very uplifting song by an artist named Brian Lee. "I've got the green light. I'm on my way!" He began to sing aloud. The crisp autumn blue sky bolstered him.

Oak Park was the next exit and he hoped to the God he did not believe in that this nun was still alive and in reasonably good health. The remorse would never go away but he succeeded in putting it aside for now. He felt somewhat balanced. He pulled over to a side street and consulted his map. Bingo! Oak Park was three blocks away. He located Rosemont. *Ah, if she is alive, well and available, our time should only take thirty minutes.*

Forever the optimist, Tom fortified himself with imaginary hope. He parked and walked toward the largest building. He admired the great architecture, loved the traditional landscape design. The bells began to ring their comforting sound as the smell of the fallen leaves eased his heart. Suddenly he remembered a poem he read about autumn, titled *Pregnant with Death.*

Tom had to wait almost an hour before he was led to the elegant office. He learned the nun was now retired, but still active. Her title was Mother Superior. During that time, he alternated between despair (*she must be eighty*) and hope (*she was alive and working*). He knocked on the half-opened door. She got up, invited him in, and offered her hand.

"Hello, Tom. Please come in. I'm sorry you had to wait. Sometimes I'm not so retired around here. How can I help you?"

She appeared to be healthy and very much alive. He began to feel awkward. "I'm sorry to arrive without an appointment, Mother Superior. I wasn't thinking."

Her smile was gentle and rose to her eyes. "It's okay, Tom. What brings you here?" She sat in the upholstered chair next to him.

Clearly, he was many miles removed from the Richardsons, their pigs, and their farmhouse. He took a moment to remember his professional role as Dean of Students at Willamette Academy. Taking a hidden deep breath, "I appreciate you seeing me. I'm here because my wife - over thirty years ago - told me you saved her life. Her name was Suzanne Schmidt."

The Mother Superior widened her eyes as they began to glisten. She gripped the arms of the chair until her knuckles turned white. "She's alive? My Suzanne's alive?"

Tom immediately stood up and gently touched her shoulder. "No, she is not alive. I am so sorry I wasn't clearer. She was my wife. She died thirty years ago." Helplessly, he walked to the window, rubbing his temples. "Can I get you something? Water? Do something? I'm sorry for being so tactless. I don't know how to continue. The story is gruesome and tragic. I know I'm going to be upsetting you more." He turned and saw her unmoving deep golden eyes, seeming to go through him.

"Sit down, Tom. I'll be okay. Last week I sensed almost for certain she was dead. So many memories came to me when you said her name. I think I really had not given up all hope. My heart goes out to you. I can see your suffering is still with you. I need to hear the tragic story. How did she die?"

"She was murdered on her twenty-fourth birthday. We adopted our son Derek the day before. I almost succeeded in burying my memory of her murder. No one but my second wife Terese knows." He remembered he told the Richardsons and William. "Except three people in her hometown, who I told yesterday. It seemed to be the right thing to do. I'm so exhausted carrying this all alone. They knew Suzanne before she came up here." He stared out to the slightly bare trees and dying leaves. Clouds were closing in on the sun.

"Tom, I loved her too, although differently than you. I loved her like a daughter. You have a son, maybe more children. You know how deep that connection is and how long it lasts."

"I do, Mother Superior. I have two daughters also and one grandson. My heart won't stop aching. My mind won't stop castigating me, especially now talking with you. The reality and memory of her death rise up like vampires."

"Tom, you can call me Sister Michael. You don't need to use my title."

"Michael?" Tom looked completely befuddled. "Sister Michael?"

"In the Roman Catholic clergy, nuns take a saint's name at the time of our consecration. We take the name of a saint who is meaningful for us. Often, we take male names as there are far more male saints than female." Her mouth twitched for a second. "The Archangel Michael has been in my heart since childhood. I have no need for formality, so please call me Sister Michael. Please sit down. There is one other piece of information I need to tell you."

"Yes? Sister Michael, I am so discombobulated. I need some time to think. I didn't know how unprepared I was for this, mentally or emotionally."

"Tom, Suzanne's mother lives in Chicago. We knew each other when she was a student here. We both saw Suzanne for the last time at her graduation. We reconnected on occasion in the past three years, but only on the surface. Last week she came in and we had the conversation we both had been avoiding: the one about Suzanne. Was she alive? Where? Her mother felt strongly that she had died."

Tom shook his head imperceptibly. "Her mom? Alive? In Chicago?"

"Yes, and I would like your permission to invite her here, if she is available, to hear your story. Is that okay with you?"

Tom's sigh was palpable. "Sister Michael, I'm lost at sea. Both of you in one day? Today? After Smotelyville this morning? Why did I ever think meeting you would tie things up quickly? I know my naiveté has caused so much harm, death, lies, and betrayal. I'm not the man I see in the mirror. Now to meet her mother for the first time?"

"No rush, Tom. I know talking about Suzanne and her death has to be very difficult, especially now being flooded with memories on your journey and. I'll have someone bring us tea. Is black okay? Cream, sugar, or lemon? Or do you prefer herbal? Or coffee?"

He nodded. "Tea. Black. Lemon. Two pots. I need it."

Sister Michael nodded. "As do I! I'll be back shortly. There is a restroom for visitors down the hall to your right." She left the room quietly.

Restroom? He said to himself. *If only it were so easy. Go to the restroom and out the door. Why did I think Suzanne's mother was dead? How can I meet her after being a fool with her daughter and with her daughter's life? More than a fool! A useless ass. Even a murderer. It's my fault Suzanne is dead. I buried the knowledge. How can I tell her?* He got up and went to the window to join with the emptiness of the nearly naked trees. He was with the dying leaves in their expanding graveyard. They weren't even pregnant with death; they were dead. *I have to do it. I have to meet Suzanne's mother and learn the story. I'll do it for Suzanne, for Derek, and for me. I will make meaning out of her death and her life. Somehow.*

He was seated in a new place when the Mother Superior returned. "Our tea will arrive in a few minutes. How are you doing? Different chair. Different perspective? Tom, could you please move that table over here for me?" She pointed to a coffee table on the side of the room.

Tom barely smiled as he did so. "I've decided, Sister Michael. Please call her. The vampires of fear and secrets are draining me. Nothing about Suzanne's death is easy. I'm now suspecting nothing about her life was easy. It'll be better to tell the two of you together. Does she live close?"

A young novice knocked and brought in an exquisite silver tea set with two pots, three cups, lemons, and madeleines. She placed them on the glass table. A plate of fruit finished the picture-perfect service. She left without a word.

Sister Michael continued, "Closer rather than farther. Let me phone. Would you bring me a cup, Tom? No lemon or sugar, thank you." She dialed the phone and waited. "Hello, Bernice? Are you busy? I have someone here on a matter of importance to all three of us. Is there any way you could be here within the half-hour? I apologize for the short notice." Silence. "Yes, it is about Suzanne. Your intuition was correct. She is no longer alive. Her husband Tom is here in my office." A puzzled look drew her eyebrows together. "No, he said Tom. Of course, I am sure. Let me check." She put her hand over the mouthpiece. "Tom, right? Berenice said she married a Paul Miller."

"She's right. She did marry Paul Miller. I am Paul Miller. I mean, I was Paul Miller. I changed my name." Tom kept his focus on the nun, drawing on her strength. "Can I speak with her?"

He stood up, straightened his shoulders, and breathed deeply as he took the phone. "Mrs. Schmidt? This is Paul Miller. I am here with Suzanne's story. I am terribly sorry to spring this all on you and Sister Michael. I should've done it differently. I hate being the messenger of more grief for you. Yet, of course you need to know. She was your daughter. Thank you. I look forward to meeting you. I apologize again for everything." He put the phone back on the cradle. "She'll be here in twenty minutes." Now the three cups made sense. He knew to move the third chair into place.

CHAPTER TWENTY-THREE
DEREK AND PETER: SEATTLE, 1992

D erek stepped out of the elevator on the twenty-fourth floor. The polished inlaid wood in the walls, deep carpeting, and low lighting stopped him in his tracks. *Jeez, o man. If it's like this out here, what's it like inside?* He wished he had worn his khakis rather than jeans. He saw two doors. One had a bronzed plaque with ornate symbols embossed on it. Below in elegant script was a No Entrance: Private sign. The light above the door was darker, dimmer. The other door was brighter in a soft, subtle way. The name on the engraved plaque read Peter Gehman, Ph.D. Startled, Derek realized he didn't even know Peter's last name, much less that he had a Ph.D. He always called him Peter. Should he call him Dr. Gehman?

No time to think or knock. Peter opened the door. *Whew, he had on jeans too.* "I heard the elevator and knew it must be you. Come in, Derek." Peter flourished an *enter please, mi casa es tu casa* arm sweep, welcoming Derek into his home.

Derek had never seen such digs in his life, not even in *Architectural Digest.* He hoped he wasn't gawping. "Thanks Peter." *Damn, I'm glad I left the $5.99 bottle of wine in the car.* "This is so gorgeous. Very different than your university office." He winked at Peter, tending to joke when he was emotionally overwhelmed.

Peter smiled, observing most men did not use the word "gorgeous" unless referring to a woman. "Yes, Derek, my life is very separate from the Adoption Project or Unconditional Love, Inc. My home is for me. It expresses me. It's very much in keeping with the subgroup you've come here to discuss and explore. Then you can make a decision about our invitation."

"Yes, I know. I've been really excited all week."

Peter became the Cheshire Cat as Derek oozed anticipation. He purred, "Do you want to take a quick tour, my friend? I would love to show you. Then we can have a drink and talk by the fire." *And see how you do with the pipe.* He zoned in to Derek's attempts to mask his awed admiration and inwardly chuckled.

"Peter, I don't know where this is coming from, but I keep remembering some Bible verse about 'In my Father's house are many mansions.' I'm not religious."

"And if it were not so, I would have told you. I go to prepare a place for you," responded Peter, ending the quote. "I'm not religious, either, but it does fit." *At this point, my young friend, you have no idea just how well.* They were stopped at the bedroom in front of several portraits that set a completely provocative mood. The paintings were of men with strong jaws and intense features. Fascinated, Derek watched as the lighting wavered ever so slightly, causing a seeming disappearance of the men's clothing as breathtaking bodies came into view. Derek felt warmth in his chest. His heart beat faster. He could not speak. The clothing slowly appeared again. A surprised sense of pleasure coursed through his body, awakening him. Not a word was said. Music infused the ambiance.

Peter watched the entranced Derek. *Not yet. Patience. We're on the right track. How splendid the anticipation.* He licked his Cheshire lips. "Do you like Mahler, Derek? The one you are listening to is a combination, a union of pain and joy. I believe it's his Third Symphony. The sound system in here is state-of-the-art."

Derek felt hesitant. "I don't really know Mahler. I'm familiar with Bach and Beethoven. In high school, I had the honor of being the principal dancer in a quartet of Debussy's ballet pieces."

"Well, Derek, I did not know you were a dancer. I'd love to see you dance sometime."

Derek's face turned pink. "It's been years, Peter. I danced a bit at Reed but haven't in the past seven years."

"Why did you stop?"

Silence. *Why did I stop?* Memories emerged within a tsunami of emotions. "I don't know, Peter. I'll look into it." The rush he was now feeling was the same rush he felt back then when he looked at the male dancers. *My confusion of emotions stopped my dancing. Well, I'm not telling Peter that! He's so male, he'll think me a queer. Am I a queer? So what if I am? I've squelched my feelings for years. Now they are squelching me. Men's bodies are so, so beautiful!*

Derek's entire body suddenly filled with freedom.

"What are you going to look into? Old yearbooks?" chuckled Peter.

"Great idea. I'll keep you posted." Derek stuffed his shirt into his jeans to quiet things.

Peter led him out of the bedroom and down the hall, passing a bathroom overgrown with black and deep red marble. It seemed bigger than Derek's whole apartment.

They ended up in a leather study. "Let's talk in here, Derek. I'll light us a fire. What do you drink? Scotch? Bourbon? Wine? Coke?"

"There aren't many condos with working fireplaces, are there? Bourbon's good. With ice."

The previously-laid fire flamed into glory. "No, most don't. It's one of the advantages of owning the whole top floor. Privacy. There is also a fireplace outside on the patio." Peter stepped back and stretched his Cheshire paws. "Bourbon it is." He opened the leaded glass doors above the leather counter. Derek had never seen nor even imagined a leather counter.

Peter handed Derek one of the two etched glasses. "Cheers." He raised his glass and the two clinked softly. Suddenly and for the first time, Derek felt he was a grown-up and did not feel prepared. Could he be at peace with himself? Now he got it when others used the term "coming home," and managed a "Cheers!" He remembered another feeling of coming home with Peter. He looked at Peter's eyes and again warmth expanded his body.

"Sit, Derek," as Peter pointed to one of the two oversized burgundy chairs.

"I've never felt such soft leather. Is it Italian?"

"Actually, no. It's from Cordova in Southern Spain."

Derek was never a fan of leather but put aside his values and enjoyed the moment of surging warmth. He was free. *What would Peter think? Maybe Peter was gay? Those pictures! Not what a normal man would have. Could Peter feel his attraction? How did it all work in the gay world?*

The thought that the attraction could be mutual increased his temperature.

"About the subgroup, Derek. First, it's paramount that you tell no one about what you see, learn, hear, or experience."

Derek thought he really hadn't told his dad anything. He only said he was invited to a subgroup. He wouldn't tell him anything else. "Yes, Peter, you have my pledge. Tell me what it's all about."

"Well, Derek, pledge is a good word. It's what I hope we can do tonight. The lineage is generations – even centuries – old, passing from father to son to their sons. The power grows with each passing of the pledge. We've come a very long way from our German beginnings. I'm the leader of the American Northwest Quadrant of the group. There is so much to tell. I cannot possibly do it in one sitting. We invite you to observe one meeting first to see if it agrees with you. We meet next Thursday, in six days. Are you free?"

"I've got to check my work schedule at Elliot Bay. But I think I can manage it."

Peter glanced at Derek. So far, so good. "I'll tell you a little before you observe. Then we can discuss the second meeting." Peter talked and Derek listened. He learned about power, both good and bad, and about its transmission. Peter shared the importance of blood.

Derek interrupted him. "You've mentioned blood before. Do you have children? Sons?"

Peter stared into the fire. "No, Derek, I have no sons." *He's confusing blood with bloodline. He reeks of innocence. I'll be his first. My sweet virgin boy.*

"Well, then, how will you pass your power on?"

"Derek, we are reversing the cart and horse. Because my bloodline would stop, we have altered the doctrine to include adopted sons and even grandsons. How old are you, Derek?"

"I'm twenty-nine. Actually, sometimes I feel just born."

"And I am fifty-two. I'm drawn to you: your depths, your intelligence, your trust and curiosity, and your willingness and commitment to Unconditional Love, Inc. You even came here to talk with me about the subgroup. Down the road we'll speak more about everything. Now, it's important to pledge your commitment to silence. Everything must be secret. It is the core of our power. It can be yours."

"Yes, of course!" *Peter, at this point, I would do anything for you.* Derek felt every nerve in his body come alive with warmth to near implosion. *Was this surrendering? Was this falling in love?* He had never felt like he did now. Derek surrendered to the man he had always been, awakened for the first time.

"Have you ever smoked marijuana, Derek?"

"A little."

"If you don't object, I'd like to bind your pledge with a ritual of smoke. Do you see that elaborate glass water pipe over there? Would you bring it here?" Peter got down on the floor, removing the two seat cushions to serve as back supports. He added more logs to the fire.

Derek brought the piece. "Is this a bong?" he asked in wonder.

"I call it a water pipe or a hookah. It's a commissioned work of art. Before you sit, can you get that pouch?" Derek picked it up and held it to his face. "I have never felt anything so soft, so warm."

Not the time to tell him it's from the skin of a fetal pony. "Only the best pouch for the best hash. Only the best for you, Derek."

Derek threw everything he ever thought to the wind, as he drew in the smoke ritual. Peter began to make symbols on Derek's leg. Each movement released more adrenaline into Derek's already pulsating blood. His heart started to pound to nearly bursting. They returned to the magnificent bedroom with Mahler's soft movements of pain and joy. Derek was awake and free, like never before.

CHAPTER TWENTY-FOUR
JEMMA / FIRST MOMS / AZURE: SEATTLE, 1992

Jemma nearly skipped to the second meeting of First Moms. She knew it was the discussion night, making her sing, "Follow the yellow brick road," in her head. She was in a great space. First, her baby was born in Kansas with open birth records, a four percent possibility in America. Tonight, she would learn how to secure a way to see and copy them.

Second, she and Peter rarely passed each other at the university. If they did, each politely smiled and continued walking. Jemma had not returned to the ULI group and never would. She was still troubled by his obvious preying on vulnerable subjects in the Project, which led her to realize that now she could speak to Giles about it. He was another reason for joy. The attraction and friendship with Giles was growing rapidly and mutually. She felt a safety and security previously unknown to her. Truly, life was good.

An arrow under the First Moms meeting sign inside the old school building pointed down the hall. Entering the room, she saw Heidi, who came up to her immediately, having been introduced at the previous meeting. Jemma counted six women, a few looking nervous and expectant, the rest seeming to know each other. They were welcoming and seemed comfortable.

Heidi, the leader of First Moms, began the meeting with a brief overview of the mission of First Moms. The grassroots organization's mission was to help all mothers who have given up their babies for adoption and signed off their rights to any further contact, most many years ago. Tonight, the discussion topic would be centered around birthing lies, the most significant of which was the baby's gender.

Jemma blanched. "Pardon me, what?"

"Yes, it's an important fact to know as you begin your search."

Jemma couldn't believe what she heard. "Are you saying they may have lied to us about the gender of our baby? Even if we were in a home for unwed mothers that was run by nuns? They wouldn't have lied." She felt her anger rising, her eyes tearing, and her face getting hot and flushed as she remembered.

Heidi had a wry expression. "Yes, Jemma. Many of them lied. I was heart-stricken myself when I first heard the possibility and, later, found it to be true in many cases. Sometimes the nuns seemed to lie more than the other agencies. I grew up Roman Catholic. It took me some time and tremendous struggling to accept the reality of their lies, though I have never thought it was okay. Before you ask, yes, I left the church."

"Even though the adoption records in some states are open, how could they change the gender on all the legal records?" Jemma was stunned with disbelief.

"No, they wrote nothing illegal. They TOLD us wrong."

"I don't understand." Jemma spoke slowly, blowing her nose and sinking into despair.

She always teared up when anger overtook her.

Another woman spoke, "I didn't either, Jemma. I thought it was no big deal. We found out about it so we can just look for the baby with the right gender. However, there was a big exception. In some states, you can read the birth certificate and it's all true. You then go to the adoption papers and some, not all, are jumbled and of no help. Hard to read and decipher. By the way, I'm Cynthia." She smiled. "We met last month. I know it's hard to remember everyone."

"I hate to ask, Cynthia, but how many moms actually find their child, given so many lies?" Jemma was spiritless. She heard a shifting of seats, audible sighs, and some throats clearing.

"Jemma, I don't have encouraging news." Heidi spoke quietly. "In the past year, only one of our moms found her child's name and adopted parents."

"Out of how many women?"

"Twenty or so. Our group meetings average from six to eight women. Over a year, moms stay for four or five meetings, then leave." Heidi watched Jemma. "I apologize. I don't know when to give out this information. I don't want it to be at the first meeting; that's why I suggest the speakers' meeting first. It can be discouraging."

Jemma held herself back from saying, "Duh," and instead stated, "Yes, it's very discouraging, especially as my hopes were high. I got so excited about the Kansas open records at the last meeting. Now, my daughter may be a son? And that's all I'll ever know?"

"Your search could be different. It is for everyone. Someone has to be the one this year. I know it sounds lame, but it is possible," she attempted to console Jemma.

"Tell me more about the woman who did find her child. Or, how did you say it? 'Found her child's name?' Did she find her child? How did she do it?" Jemma's hope, in which she thought she did not believe, started to climb out of the pit. *Who said it? Nietzsche? Hope is the greatest evil of humankind? I get it.*

More shuffling.

"Okay, just tell me everything I need to know so I can be realistic about the possibilities." Her hope-filled anticipation was rapidly disintegrating back into anger.

Heidi took the floor. "Jemma, the woman found her baby's name because, well, her husband had connections. He lived in the computer world and could tell no one what he was doing. We don't know how it happened. He couldn't help us. Maybe someday we'll all have access to computers, making the search much easier. But for now, we don't."

"I see. What about the other part? Did she see her child?"

Cynthia spoke. "Heidi, I'll tell it this time. Jemma, the woman found her daughter but the outcome wasn't good. The birth mother wrote a letter to the adopted parents; they passed it on to their daughter, who wrote back stating, 'I won't meet you. You didn't want me then and I don't want you now.' I'm sorry, Jemma, it's a risk we all take. We're a grassroots group and doing our best. I continue to say 'don't give up.' But many do and, unfortunately, it's understandable."

Jemma spoke in a loud voice. "That's awful. Terrible. Already my search is a roller coaster. No, my emotions are. Actually, you know what? Right now, it's the whole huge amusement park, although amusement is the furthest thing from me. I appreciate the bunch of you continuing to hope and believe. I just don't know if I can do it. I'm already feeling the loss of my daughter again because what if she was not my daughter, but my son? I began to accept my loss recently, now it's beginning all over again. I know it doesn't make sense. I grew so attached to her for all these years, to my image of her. Finding out she could be a boy is so shattering. I don't know why. I don't know what to do." Jemma sat with her elbow on her leg and her hand over her mouth, eyes wet. "I don't know what to do."

"Maybe just think about it. Think about the fact that the Kansas birth records are open: a rarity. What if your child was a boy? Would you stop the search? We're here as a strong support group. Please call me or Cynthia when you want or need to. I'm so sorry for your pain." Heidi walked over to hug Jemma. Cynthia did, too.

It felt like a funeral.

Walking to her appointment the next day, Jemma was glad she could discuss it with Azure. Another dream shattered. The whole sabbatical was a huge mistake. Thinking positively was another. Believing in the clergy of the church was yet another. There were plenty more. She sat in the waiting room.

Azure opened the door and saw things were off. Jemma started talking as she walked to the overstuffed purple chair she had appointed as hers. "Azure, it was horrible. I left the Moms' meeting so discouraged. Deflated is a better word. Burst balloon is even more perfect. There's a strong possibility that I may have a son and not a daughter!"

"Jemma, let's take a minute. Sit down. Breathe. I'm going to chime." The two sat in silence, each in her own thoughts. Azure began. "You were so encouraged last time. What happened?"

"Azure, this whole venture is more than I can do. I didn't really think I would fly to Wichita, copy papers, and find my daughter quickly, did I? Some part of me pictured exactly that. I learned that thirty years ago some agencies told the mom that her baby was the opposite gender. The baby was whisked away as some of us were told a lie. We were judged for getting pregnant, being promiscuous, then for giving up our babies. Apparently not all of us deserved the truth."

"Wait, Jemma. Are you saying you could have been lied to as to the gender of your baby? You've come so far in your decision to search. It's clearly a setback. Tell me more. Do you could express it in a story after we talk?"

"Of course. After each session, I've been writing a story of what we discussed and what it brought up for me."

"So, you have the birth written in a story?" Azure blinked. "Could you bring it next time?"

"Actually, I have it here. Should I read it now?" She cocked her head in a question mark.

"Yes. Please. Thank you, Jemma."

HELL IS GREY

The walls are grey. No windows. The room is empty and yet filled with my pain. We receive no instruction or information about what will happen when our babies will be born. There is girl talk in the dorm, but it is sketchy. The oft-repeated word is pain. I am doing laundry in the hot steam-filled room when my pains begin. I hold my stomach and bending over see the puddle between my feet splashed on my brown oxfords. Am I in hell? My two friends come to me, take me to a chair and tell me it will be okay, soon my baby will be born. But it isn't and I will ever be okay again.

I hate these brown oxford shoes. I'm sixteen, almost seventeen. I am president of my junior class, in the National Honor Society, assistant editor of the school newspaper. I never worn oxfords in my life. Where am I? Working in a laundry ten hours a day. Beginning to have a baby that I have to give away. They tell us we can hold our baby for a few minutes. No choice. No God. No parents. No hope. No love.

I'm taken to the delivery room and left alone for hours. Days?

Two nuns float in on grey habits and one's mouth wears a smile, but her eyes do not. The other sports a shadow of a mustache, squints into my eyes, and grimly tells me to open my legs. She says she must check to see when my baby will be born. She doesn't tell me she is going to put her finger into me. It's hurting. She is cold, cold, cold. She demands that I relax as she raises her voice. How can I? I start to cry.

"Tears won't help," scolds the other one. "Too bad you didn't think of this nine months ago. Right?" The other says it will be awhile. It's already been awhile. Timeless forever. They turn to leave. "Please. Can I have something for the pain? An aspirin?" "Later," they chorus as they close the door. Devils.

I can't stop crying, except when the pains hit me. I try to get up. The pain cripples me. I thought hell was hot, but I'm so cold. I'm shivering, shaking. The thin wool blanket does nothing but scratch. The more I move, the more it scratches. Sandpaper. Steel wool. Why doesn't my mother come? They visited me once. My mother never smiled. My father was fake-friendly.

All for show. "You'll be home soon. Come up with a story for your friends about Aunt Lillian. Don't breathe a word of this place." "I hate it here, Mother. I'm working too hard. Doing laundry in the steam." "You should have thought of that five months ago," she tosses out as the door closes. Bitch. Bitch. Bitch. I say in my head.

The pain brings me back to my room. I have to use the bathroom. The table is up so high. The pain cripples me. I can't get down. I have no strength. No balance. The dank smell of urine fills the room. Pain. Whimpering. Where is the fire? I thought there would be burning. The devil and flames.

How long have I been here? *I keep asking myself. I can't see outside. Hell has no windows. Is the sun up or down? Is there still a sun? Who did this to me? He doesn't know how to use a rubber. He's a virgin too. I tell him to wait, it doesn't look right. Then it hurts. The full rubber pools under me, and it isn't right. Now I am here.*

A different nun opens the door. "How are you, my dear?" *Her kindness brings flooding of tears. Will I ever stop crying? Hurting? Can I ever leave?* "I can't do it. Pain won't stop." *Tears come to the nun.* "Jemma, you can do it. It's not forever, although I know it feels like it. I've brought you pain meds. Don't tell the others."

She lifts my shoulders and head with a gentle arm and gives me the pills and water.

Another pain. I whisper, "How much longer?" *She checks me like the other nun, except gentle. Easy. My angel nun is holding my hardened stomach. Tells me soon. She changes my sheets and puts pads under me.*

"Stay. Stay" *I implore her.* "I don't know what's happening. They told me I would go to hell. They're right. I'm already there."

"No, no, Jemma. Yes, there is pain. But it will end. Your pains are closer. The baby's head is right there. Closer. I'll stay with you. I'll hold you. Push when I tell you." Push? "Yes, push like you're having a bowel movement. Just push the baby out."

The other two clump into the room. They wash, put rubber gloves on. "She's close," *my angel reports. The stomping devils bring a small baby bed over with a light on it. A baby blanket. It's mine. I can hold it. I can hold my baby. They promised. Soon.*

"Put your feet in the stirrups." They swing up cold metal cups for my bare feet. I am so cold. Exposed. Humiliated. Another pain stops me. "Hurry up!" they say. "We want the baby alive."

Panic. Pain. Terror. Alive? My angel rubs my shoulders. Whispers to me, "It's okay. The baby is alive." The devils glare at her. One says she sees the head. "Quick, come here!" she tells the other. "Push," says my angel. "That's it. Push again." I feel ripping and tearing and searing. I smell blood.

"It's a girl," the devils say. My angel begins to cry. She flares at the two. The baby is wrapped. One of the demons holds her four feet away from me. "See. See your daughter." Her smile is evil. I want to hold my baby. They promised. I reach out.

"No, missy. She's not yours to hold. She's ours, until her real mother comes to get her. That's the way it is." They push the baby bed out of the room. The door closes hard.

My heart is breaking. Ripping. Tearing. Searing. Worse than the pain in my lower portal. The angel gives me more pills. She holds me. She rocks me. "A few stitches," she tells me. "Just a few. I'm so sorry, Jemma. It's not your fault."

I didn't know angels could lie. I fall into black oblivion. No more grey hell.

CHAPTER TWENTY-FIVE
TOM, SISTER MICHAEL, AND BERNICE: CHICAGO, 1992

Tom stood up when Bernice entered the door. His heart almost stopped as he saw his wife in her mother's features. He stumbled in his introduction, "Hello, Mrs. Schmidt. I am the Paul Miller your daughter married." His hand shook as he took hers. Long-held tears appeared in everyone's eyes. Bernice took a slight step toward him but stopped herself. "Hello, Paul. Or should I say Tom?" Bernice spoke softly, her slight smile disarming him again.

"Tom. I prefer Tom. I've been Tom longer than I've been Paul. I buried Paul when Suzanne died, not that I did a very good job of that." He murmured the last part to himself. Both women heard.

Everyone walked to a chair, innately knowing what to do in the present while preparing for the unknown to come. Sister Michael began, "I doubt any of us care to endure the small talk. We're here to understand the death and the life of Suzanne, whom we all loved." Nods confirmed the need to continue. "We all carry pieces of Suzanne's puzzle within us, both joyous and mournful. If we can resurrect them from our hearts and lay them out, I believe we can finish the puzzle and restore Suzanne to the place of knowledge, honor, and remembrance she truly deserves. I'm not sure where to begin." She looked to each of them.

"If it's okay, I'll start. She's my daughter."

Bernice's voice was stronger than Tom expected. *I should have learned long ago that little is as expected. That has been true since I was a senior in high school. But, isn't that surrender? It doesn't seem to be a good thing.*

Sister Michael nodded. "Thank you, Bernice, I agree with you."

"Yes, Mrs. Schmidt. Suzanne told me very little about her growing up."

"Tom. It's Bernice, okay?" Again, that smile, so like Suzanne's.

"Sure. Thank you," his heart quieted.

Sister Michael poured the tea.

"I was almost twenty-two when Suzanne was born. I have never felt such immediate love, before or after." Bernice drew a sharp intake of breath. "Forgive me, I see this won't be easy. Not that I ever thought it would. I'm a visual woman, making everything I tell you come up in pictures. My mental photo album is a blessing and a curse. I know I will have to stop every now and then."

"Of course, Bernice. Of course. I know that feeling. Thank you for going first. This is the most, one of the most difficult things I've ever done." Tom added.

The nun looked at each of them. "I suspect for all of us. It's your story, Bernice. It's your time to decide what you want. Let us know whatever you need."

"I'll highlight the events, the memories that have troubled me. We all have the good events, her beauty inside and out, and how we love her. I think the missing pieces are the trying times. The first troubling memory is right after her birth, when the deepest joy in my life was darkened. My husband, Oscar, came into the hospital room after my delivery. He held her with instant pride and love. He kissed her downy face. I heard him whisper, 'I will never hurt you.' I thought it was an odd comment but put it aside.

"That day he had to leave quickly as his father and four of the deacons were coming to congratulate him with celebratory shots and beers. The following evening holds my second troubling memory. Oscar returned that evening, late. I'll never forget it. In looking back, I now see that was the beginning of a lifelong change in him. He would not hold Suzanne. His face was vacant. 'What's wrong?' I asked. 'Nothing. Nothing. Everything's fine. I'll see you tomorrow.'

"He left without a kiss. He left us. Even while loving Suzanne and being very close with her, I was lonely. I lost my husband without knowing why. It wasn't even bit by bit. It was one fell swoop. I gave Suzanne so much love, yet I often felt it was not enough. My heart was broken. Parts never returned. I began to believe grief and love would always walk hand in hand." Tom put his hand on Bernice's arm. She gave him a thankful smile.

Bernice shared the difficulties in a voice that seemed fragile to Tom, even though he knew she wasn't. "At the end of her eighth-grade year, Suzanne came running into the parsonage. It was May 28, 1953, a Thursday evening. I will never forget. There was a full moon. I've never seen such fear, terror. I held her. She told me between sobs that she wanted to leave home, to go to my alma mater in Chicago. "You can,' I told her, 'but tell me what happened.' 'I can't, Mom. I have to go away.'

"I kept asking her what she saw, who she saw. She kept throwing up, backing away, and covering her eyes. I drew her near, with the foreboding sense Suzanne and I would never be as close again. I saw her shutting down and remembered her father checking out after her birth. Again, I was helpless.

"I brought her here. I felt safe leaving her with Sister Michael, who I knew from my own high school years. Truth be told, I thought Sister Michael would be better than me. She was a new young nun when I met her. However, she was an old soul. I suspected twenty years later, she would be more experienced and perfect for Suzanne to overcome whatever it was that terrorized her."

"You were in such pain when you brought her here, Bernice," the nun recalled with wrought compassion.

"I know, Sister Michael. Smotelyville was suddenly unsafe. Oscar's distance from his daughter always cut me to the quick. Who did I choose for her father? My husband? He replaced his family with the church, the deacons, and his father. He rarely saw or spoke with us, nor did his father. His mother was dead. We had members of the congregation who were friends, but I was never really accepted. I was not a Lutheran originally, having converted from Catholicism.

"Suzanne was a quiet girl, usually reading or spending nights with friends. We were close in those years, cooking, laughing, sewing, coming up to Chicago to shop and go to the theatre, concerts, museums." Bernice was out of breath and stopped.

A minute later, she continued. "What happened to our family? The family that never was. I knew Suzanne needed to leave Smotelyville. I could see her father's developing mental illness. She needed to be away from it.

"I came up for summers, we did our Chicago things, but we really never got close again." She looked to the window, the threatening clouds, the dismal grey. Silence. "Oscar saw her once. He came up here by himself for three days. That was the last time he saw her. Suzanne became quite ill after that visit, but she would not let me come to see her. She never told me what happened."

Sister Michael poured more tea, looking downwards.

Bernice sat straighter in her chair. "Oscar had an important meeting the Thursday night Suzanne graduated from Rosemont, and that was the last time I saw her. She did phone to say she was getting married and perhaps I could meet her husband down the road. I had no idea it would be thirty years later." She reflected ruefully. "Nor that it would be without Suzanne. That's all I know." Bernice stared out the window, aware of autumn being a season of death.

The nun dabbed her eyes. "I can fill in some of the missing pieces of her high school years. But I need a break and suspect you both do, too. I've got to walk a bit to relieve my distress."

They all agreed and left to walk in silence, in different directions.

The two women returned first. "Sister Michael, I'm so afraid to hear your story, and Tom's."

"Bernice, I understand. I'm not so much afraid as sad, weary. He told me some before I phoned you. I'm here with you." She touched Bernice's cheek with the back of her hand.

Tom walked into the room, apologizing for being late.

"You're not late, Tom, and there is no need for such regrets. What we are doing has no timeline. You warned us that Suzanne's death was a tragedy. Tom, do you think you could tell your story next? Are you ready to hear of her death,

132

Bernice? Tom, are you ready to talk? Or should we meet tomorrow?" Sister Michael looked to both of them.

Bernice was adamant in her response. "I'm not leaving here until I know much more."

"I'll share my time with Suzanne after Tom. It seems to make the most sense for him to resurrect his pieces next. Perhaps mine can fill in more of the puzzle."

"I believe hearing both of your memories will be difficult. I prefer Tom to go next. I want to get to know my daughter's husband. I have to learn of her death and some of who she was before she died."

Tom shifted in his chair. He stood up to remove his cardigan sweater, putting it on the back of his chair. He unbuttoned and folded his cuffs over his sleeves, put his arms on his thighs, and combed his hair with his fingers. Finally raising his head, he began. "Of course, I'll go next. It has to be said. Michael knows part. Bernice, it's much harder telling you. First, I never knew I would meet you. Second, I didn't know it would be today. I..." He faltered. "I didn't think I would ever see Suzanne again. Yet I do: in your smile, in your expressions. I'm seeing two women I never thought I would see, ever. Suzanne's smile. You, Bernice, her mother." He ground the heels of his palms into his temples.

Bernice rested her fingers on his knee. "I suspect you won't believe it, Tom, but you have given me the second greatest gift of my life: to meet Suzanne's husband and to hear how she left our world." Tom looked at her in wonder. "Now that I have met you, I am beginning to see how Suzanne fell in love with you."

Tom's amazement turned to shock and embarrassment. He got up and walked to the long stained-glass windows. "Bernice, I don't deserve your words. It's because of me Suzanne is dead. She tried to tell me to leave on the night I proposed, that she couldn't have children and that too much had happened that was too much beyond her control. I discounted, even discarded her concerns. I insisted that her – our – love would conquer all, even her father's secret meetings. I was wrong. The secret meetings conquered us. Maybe it was a cult." He didn't see the

Bernice's startled look. "I've never said it until now. I've never admitted the possibility of that word applying to me: *cult*. How much is my fault? I did not honor or protect your daughter, Bernice." He looked at her. "I feel so responsible for her death."

Now Bernice was in shock. Her face went ashen. Her hands began to shake. "Cult? Secret meetings? I don't understand. What do you mean by cult? What do you mean she couldn't have children? Cults are aligned with evil. Are you saying her father was in one? How, how could I not know about all of this!?" Her face showed disbelief and fear.

The silence held her suffering.

Bernice began again. "How could that happen? I'm her mother. He was my husband. How could I not know? Is that what happened on that Thursday night? Did she see them doing something wrong? There couldn't have been a cult. I've got to know now. How could I not know?" Tears poured down her drawn cheeks. "That's why she left me. She saw something horrible and unbelievable in our church."

Sister Michael attempted consolation. "We are not trained to look at our husbands as cult members or suspect them of anything untoward to our children. You certainly were not trained to think evil of a minister."

"No, Michael, I should have known. Stop telling me why or what I didn't know! Did you know about this? I will never forgive myself. Never."

"I know this may look highly irregular. I have a bottle of excellent brandy. I don't think the tea is helping." She got up to go to the armoire in the corner of the room.

Both nodded. No one spoke.

The nun put the snifters on the table and filled them halfway. She spoke as she poured. "I knew of the cult. Suzanne told me. I'll tell you later, in my story. I was deeply wrong in the decision I made for confidentiality, to make her world safe so she could talk, and because of my own fear of evil. I have so many regrets that

134

Suzanne's life ended as and when it did. I apologize to both of you for not protecting her by revealing the existence of the cult to whomever deals with such horrors. I, also, am partially responsible for her death. There are no words."

"Both of you are blaming yourselves. Perhaps that is true. As her mother, I am most to blame, especially while we lived together in the parsonage. I did not know. I never knew. But now I must. I need to know what both of you know. Please tell me, Tom." Bernice beseeched him. *Was it a plea or a demand?*

Sister Michael observed the intensity of their gazes meeting each other with emotions she could not contain. She deflected. "Tom. Are you able to continue?"

Tom turned to her. "Yes." He settled in his chair, completely tense. "After I pushed Suzanne to get engaged, knowing she could not have children but knowing how much we loved each other, we were married. We lived in joy for two years. She was finishing her Master's Degree in biology. I had just accepted a position in the history department of a community college. We applied for adoption in our first year of marriage, knowing it usually takes a while. The unexpected phone call came. We were told we could pick up our son on July thirteenth, the day before Suzanne's twenty-fourth birthday."

"We were ecstatic. What a beautiful birthday gift for Suzanne. For both of us! We raced around with so many details to be completed. Bernice, we had two days of joy. Actually, just about thirty hours. Suzanne died on her twenty-fourth birthday. She was murdered by what I am beginning to suspect was a cult, as she had foretold." His voice was bitter.

"No. Tom, no." Bernice reached for Michael, who clasped her hand. "It can't be true." She covered her face with her hands. "Murdered. What about the police? No arrests? Tom. What are you saying? As foretold?"

The silence was a bittersweet balm. It lasted for a helpless and resigned moment.

"How, Tom? Tell me everything. I need to know. Is the...your son...still..."

"Yes, Bernice. Derek is close to thirty and lives in Seattle. He is alive. He is fine. He believes his mom died of childbirth complications. He believes my wife and I are his biological parents. I know that's not right. It just felt like too much to tell him growing up. Now it feels too late."

Bernice took her hand back. "I'm ready, Tom. Go ahead. I haven't yet heard the details, but I don't know how you went through it. Go on."

Tom was warming his brandy. He put the glass down. He rubbed the back of his neck and closed his eyes briefly. "I left the house for thirty minutes that day to get Suzanne a new mommy gift and a birthday gift. She was resting on our bed and Aron asleep in his crib, under the dancing teddy bears." His mind wandered off, remembering Derek wasn't Derek yet. "We called the baby Aron then."

Bernice and Michael nodded with expressions of compassion and listened.

"I came home to Suzanne's lifeless body on our bed. There was a parchment on her body that stated the foretold prophecy was now fulfilled. If I ever told anyone, anyone, they would take our son instantly. I believed them. I ran to check on Aron. He was sleeping peacefully. He was breathing. The window was open. The bears on his mobile were dancing, ever so slowly. I ripped the paper into shreds and flushed it.

"I don't remember much of what happened in the next few hours, days. My last memory is of sobbing on her cold chest. You see, they had drained her blood. A van pulled up within ten minutes of my coming home. No bell, no knocking. They just walked in, four men with fedoras pulled over their foreheads, and told me they came for her body. I watched as four black suits took her away on a stretcher."

Bernice's tears slowly rolled onto her cheeks. Michael's tears dropped to her lap. Tom fell to the floor sobbing and curled up on the carpet. The two women looked at each other, got down next to him, covered him with a blanket, and wept with him as he shuddered.

CHAPTER TWENTY-SIX
PETER AND MARTIN; DEREK; SEATTLE, 1992

Deeply enjoying his first real experience of power over his father, Peter lounged in his chair, facing the fire, bourbon in hand and speaker on low. *Let him get out of this one. The tables are turning, Martin. Please notice that I am turning them.* Peter liked the speaker on low for his father, making Martin often ask, "What?" Plus, having enough of Martin's booming voice for most of his lifetime, Peter enjoyed being able to control it. "What I don't understand, Martin, is how you lost track of Aron and Paul, or, rather, Derek and Tom."

"Peter, we've been over this topic."

"I guess I need to hear it again. Go on, Martin."

"They left in July of '63 and dashed to Minneapolis. They went to stay with Paul's, I mean Tom's, cousin whose husband is named Bruno. He holds a high position in the FBI. One of our men, Reinholdt, worked for Bruno. You may not remember Reinholdt, but he was at your initiation."

"I remember Reinholdt. I remember everything."

Martin stopped abruptly with the interruption and took an audible breath. He continued, "We thought Reinholdt was well-placed for Maharba and trusted he would be an excellent mole. He could keep them off of us, plus give us their information. He turned out to be untrustworthy. Knowing what we wanted and the power of blackmail he now had, he asked how much it was worth to us to get the information from Bruno's file, including their destination."

"Wait, Martin, if he was your man, and an upstanding member of Maharba, why did you have to pay him?"

"You know the answer to that, Peter. Didn't I mention blackmail?" He responded in dangerously low tones.

"Tell me again." Peter enjoyed his trek on the limb, each question moving him further into growing pleasure and excitement.

"Peter, I'm not at all pleased with the way this is going. Have some respect!"

"Sure, Martin. Go on."

"Because he was a member of Maharba and worked for the FBI, if we did not pay him, he would give Bruno all he knew. Yes, I know it was blackmail. He had what we wanted. Our plan was backfiring."

"He had you by the nuts."

"Peter, there's no need to be vulgar. We gave him the money."

"How much again?"

Martin exploded. "Why are we doing this? What's your agenda? Are you blackmailing me?!"

"Whoa, Martin. No need for rage. I just want to be sure I have it all correct, especially now that I, or we, are so close to the denouement, as it were. We are almost done." Short pause. "I think I have it straight. You paid the mole quite a bit of money. And he gave you?"

"Do you recall, Peter? The extra sacrifice added to our twenty-four-year ritual offering? Surely you remember your ordination."

"Of course, I remember my ordination and my initiation, Martin. Reinholdt gave his life to Maharba, not that he had much choice. How could he have predicted a fatal car accident? He gave you nothing. Ah, but did he give the FBI information? Continue, Martin. I'm writing it all down so you won't have to go over it all again." Peter smirked when he heard his father rattled. His thoughts drifted to Derek in bed. *The boy was in heaven. Who would have thought Derek would be so willing to enter the web? Become intoxicated with my honey?* Peter loved his two current successes. The first was Derek and the second was Martin, who was clearly losing his cool.

"Would you be more comfortable if I reviewed it with you, Martin? I certainly don't want you to feel you are answering to me." Peter's cruel and sensual lips curved upwards as he thought of a vaudeville villain in a silent movie stroking his mustache and muttering, "Heh. Heh. Heh." He loved his mental imagery. In fact, he loved everything about himself. Peter stroked his imaginary mustache and poured another bourbon.

"No, Peter. I'm telling you. You listen to me. We knew they went west. Reinholdt gave us that much. He would not give us more information until we coughed up more money. In 1975, we demanded more facts. The transaction of information, the game, had gone on long enough. Where were they? Next thing we knew, the FBI was down in Smotelyville. We burned the church down and got the hell out. Sorry. We got out."

Peter shook his head slowly in disbelief. *He doesn't even want to say "hell?" Maybe I could teach him "H-E-double hockey sticks" for hell.* "Then?"

"He prepared all the paperwork, including where they went. We waited."

"A hundred grand for no info or paperwork?" Silence. "I mean, you must have been furious!" Peter was so grateful for the conversation being held on the phone so Martin could not see his slithering grin.

"We did the best we could. He died for his sins. We had to be extremely careful or the FBI would be on us again. The convenient car crash gave us time. It gave us our sacrifice. Then the raid in Montana, after Smotelyville. They seemed to be on a cult chase for not just Maharba, but the many cults in Montana. You know. You studied with them. I'll tell it straight, Peter, we were scared. So were you! You left Montana and moved to San Francisco to join with the Church of Satan. The FBI was so hooked into discovering their workings that Maharba was put on the back burner. You know the rest. I applaud you studying with the Church. I supported you moving to Seattle and starting U.L.I. Because of you, we will soon have Derek joining us. He will be our leader, the Grand Kapitan, in good time. Good job, Peter."

Was he really trying for my good favor? Go, Martin! "You're right about the good job. But you are wrong about me being scared. I saw an opportunity and went for it. I have an appointment with Derek soon, so I have to close. I'll let you know about his first blood ritual. If you cannot make it, you'll meet him at his initiation during the full moon on November 10 in Sedona. Call me when you need me." Peter slowly placed the phone on the receiver, feeling victorious after the exchange and recalling his triumph as a little boy after slowly pulling legs off of ants with tweezers. He graduated to a BB gun to shoot birds. Next the cats, dogs. Peter wished he had been the one to kill the mole, not just drink his blood.

Hearing knocking, Peter knew Derek would be eagerly on the other side of his door. It was such a joke about Derek becoming a leader. Derek would never surpass Peter. No one would. Peter continued to portray soft Derek as the completion of the thirty-year plan to his father in red herring form. Peter would be the Grand Kapitan, not Derek.

Knowing his lust for the young man outside the door would only increase, Peter opened the door. Derek stood with dinner in his hands.

"Hey, Peter." The guileless young man awaited with eyes of love, holding deep scarlet roses. "I thought these might go with our dinner."

"Derek, come in. Beautiful blood roses. Aren't they called that? I'm so glad to see you." He touched Peter's face tenderly. "So glad."

He could tell Derek's insides were melting when he spoke softly, "I am too, Peter." Derek stooped for a brightly colored plastic reusable bag, "And here's the salad and a really great raw food casserole. I've only made it once before but I know you'll love it!"

Peter blinked. "Raw food casserole? Great. Let me see if I have a couple of steaks we can grill outside."

"Not for me. I'm a vegetarian, moving towards vegan. I've been a vegetarian for most of my life. I seem to have been born loving animals and protecting them. It doesn't bother me if you consume animal protein, though."

Peter closed his eyes accompanied by a deep sigh, muttering, "Mother..."

"Peter, what's wrong?" Derek sounded concerned, and Peter saw his face paling.

Now is not the time to mention anything about blood sacrifices. We'll cover up the lamb. We'll do something. Damnation. "Oh, nothing, Derek. I didn't remember you being a vegetarian. Because of your health? You mentioned the animals?"

"Oh, the animals! You don't know the cruelty forced on ..."

Peter interrupted. "Of course, Derek. I understand. I was a vegetarian once, for quite a while."

"Really? Why'd you stop?"

"Ummm. Let me recall. Yes. A naturopath I was seeing told me it wasn't good for my blood type. He told me to eat meat, I mean, animal protein for my health. Not often, just sometimes." Lying was an art form for Peter, which he continually perfected. "Well, let's go eat. The dining room is set for you. For us. I know I'll want your recipe for the raw food casserole." He took the bag into the kitchen and returned to light the candles.

Derek beamed. "Wait 'til you try it, Peter."

Peter pulled out the upholstered side chair for Derek. "And then, I have something new for you to try." He massaged Derek's shoulders and softly kissed his hair, inhaling the aroma of fresh shampoo.

"I can't wait, Peter. I mean, really, I can't wait." Derek spoke as his body stirred in anticipation. Peter noted his tented chinos.

"Well, since this meal's raw and cold, let me serve a hot appetizer first. I hope my meat is acceptable?" He pointed with a flourish to the bedroom.

Derek's breathing increased as he stood and led the way noticing the dimmed lights, hearing the deep music, and seeing the bed turned down to reveal black satin sheets. "Very acceptable. Desired. Yearned for." He turned to put his arms around Peter and kissed him fully.

CHAPTER TWENTY-SEVEN
DEREK AND AZURE: SEATTLE, 1992

Azure opened the door to the waiting room, welcoming Derek into her office and noting he looked quite different. "It's good to see you again, Derek."

"Good to be here. Are the purple chairs new?" He looked around Azure's office. "The candle new?"

"No, Derek. Same as always. Actually, I can't help but notice that you, not the chairs, are looking very different. New hair style? Taller? That can't be. Your smile is even different." Azure looked quizzically at him, luminous crystals in her eyes. *He has an adult smile.*

"I hope it's a good different!"

She nodded in affirmation. She also couldn't help smiling back at him.

"I've so much to tell you. I might even need an extra half-hour."

"That's doable, Derek. Take all the time you need. What's happened?" They both settled into a companionable quiet as the chime heralded a sense of peace for the moment. Both opened their eyes within seconds of each other, two solitudes joined. The candles seemed especially bright.

"Remember I told you about Unconditional Love, Inc., the group my dad freaked out about?"

"I do. Wasn't it something about the sub-group that upset him?"

"Good memory. He was upset about both. He didn't trust the Love group and seemed really scared of the sub-group. Scared enough to take a road trip, remember?" She nodded. "What can be wrong with a group focused on love? I haven't heard from him since he went back East." Derek's eyes glistened for a small moment, but he wiped them with the back of his hand and brought papers out of his leather folder. "Azure, I brought a story to read to you, a real story like you mentioned when we met and I was so rude?"

Azure shifted in her chair and took a sip of tea. "You weren't rude, Derek. Storytelling is a different concept and it was new to you. So, begin your story. Once upon a time..." Derek read:

THE DANCE

Once upon a time, there was a baby boy who was sad because his real mom died.

Then he was happy because his dad gave him a new mommy who loved him very much.

He knew he shouldn't be sad anymore, but sometimes he was. He never told anyone. Who would think a baby could be or remember being sad? He got two sisters whom he loved, too. It was a very happy family, except the boy couldn't get rid of the sad feelings. When he was alone, or reading, or walking in the Oregon woods, or just before he fell asleep, holding his scruffy bear, whose name actually was Scruffy, then the sadness showed up.

The boy loved school, especially high school. He loved dancing. His parents gave him lessons and he was in several musical revues of all classical music with modern dance. Even though the boy was an introvert, when he danced, he felt no anxiety, no fear of crowds, no confusion or sadness. His only feeling was pure joy. After high school, he stopped dancing. His confusion grew. Who was he? A student? A dancer? Often, he felt he was an orphan or perhaps he was in the wrong body, the wrong family. He was only certain of three things. He carried sadness, felt confusion, and knew that he did not fit.

The three emotions always took the form of three bears, constantly dancing in his head. After college, the boy who was now a man, although he did not feel like one, decided to go to law school. There he would discover truth. Law was the one true thing: black and white, right and wrong. He thought it would dissemble his

143

confusion, except it did not. In fact, the older the young man grew, the more he felt he did not fit. He passed the Bar in two states, but he was still sad and confused. Was there no truth? He decided he would be a doctor, a psychiatrist who would help the sad and confused little ones who didn't fit.

The man now worked in a bookstore and studied to go to medical school. He fell in love with a woman but failed at both love and his studies as well. One day he received a personal letter about an Adoption Project, inviting him to join if he was suitable. They were looking for participants who had given babies to adoption, been an adoptee, or adopted a baby. He knew his mom adopted him when she married his dad. So, since he was half-adopted, he would check it out. A few weeks later, he saw a sign in his bookstore for the same Project and signed up. Maybe the man would find many adopted people who felt like him.

It was there that the man met a very special friend who worked in the Project. The special friend took the sad man to a meeting about love: unconditional love, whatever that meant. The sad man began to feel happy and almost free, like when he was dancing. Because the special friend was the leader filled with light and love, he asked the now-not-so-sad man to come to his home and talk about trying out another more special group. The sad man now became a special man: special and chosen. Two bears stopped dancing and left his head. Sad walked away with not fitting. But he was still confused. He was happy because he was special to the leader and fit into the love group. So why did the one bear of confusion remain in his head?

One night the leader invited the special man to come to his home and the man's life changed forever. Confusion finally danced happily out of his head. The leader opened up his heart to the special man, who opened his in return. He fell in love with the leader, and gave his body to him, who treated it with loving care. As confusion left, peace flowed in, having waited at the door a very long time.

THE END

Silence filled the room. They sat with it for a few minutes.

"Except it's not, Azure, it's not the end. I made a choice. I love Peter, the teacher of Love. I love a man. Our relationship may not last, but it's real now. I know I'll always be attracted to men. My feelings are real and I'm happy. Free. For the first time ever."

Azure took a deep breath, dried her tears, and spoke. "You found your self, your truth. I celebrate you, Derek. You didn't find it at law school, but in your risking and knowing. There will be more truths, as you know. But you will meet them as a whole person. Thank you for your beautiful story, Derek."

"Do we still have time?"

"Yes, we do. But I need a break to take in your story, get some tea, and breathe. Would fifteen minutes be okay with you? We'll still have the thirty."

"More than okay. I'm going outside to walk. I'll see you in fifteen. And Azure?" She nodded. "Thank you."

Azure needed time to process his news. She now knew Peter was the Peter Jemma slept with once and who was concerned for the vulnerable participants in the Project, the ones he invited to his Love Meetings. Azure also knew Derek to be one of the defenseless ones, although he appeared very strong now. The confidentiality issue had come up once or twice in her practice, but the issue was not as complicated as this one. Had damage already been done with Derek? Certainly, some good had been. His sexuality was resolved. But, who *was* Peter?

Azure could see Derek was at peace with himself for the first time. *He is no longer confused. But*, she wondered, *at what price? Jemma is the only source of my information. Peter was older, very smart, and clearly seduced Derek. What about the subgroup that made Derek's dad panic?* Azure decided there was nothing to do at this point but continue to treat Derek's story as a celebration, while staying aware that Peter was a questionable character. She would talk to Charles and see what he had to say about Peter.

Both returned with renewed energy and silently held each other's eyes with intention.

"Derek, I want to understand more about your decision to become gay."

He interrupted her. "Azure, it's not a decision to become gay. It's a decision to become my real self. I have always been gay. Now I own and celebrate it! It's me."

"Thank you, Derek. I do apologize that I used the wrong word and I believe you. It's certainly consistent with your story and what you've told me about you. My only concern is Peter's part in your change. I want to be certain it's your choice in timing and manner. It must be a huge relief to be at peace and finally feel comfortable in your own body and life."

"Oh, it is, Azure! I know part of my falling in love could be fantasy or infatuation. It doesn't matter. I'll trust my feelings until they no longer feel the same. Then I will trust my new feelings. Peter gave me my true self and for that, I'll be forever grateful. Yes, I do look different. He took me to his hair stylist and bought me gorgeous new clothes. He gets me high. I have never been so relaxed while at the same time so excited about life." Derek closed his eyes and breathed deeply with a smile on his face.

Azure felt her stomach churn. Peter was making him over. He was redesigning Derek as he broke through Derek's inhibitions and boundaries. Yet she felt at peace with Derek accepting his gayness. It did fit with her intuition early on given his whole story.

"What concerns me, Azure, is that I notice Peter being different at Love, Inc. than when he talks to me about the sub-group."

"What do you mean?"

Derek took some time to answer. "He seems to change his personality, his persona. He's all light and love at Love, Inc., then he becomes darker when he speaks of the sub-group. There's an almost scary intensity. I can feel it. When we are together, it's a combination of the light and dark. It's incredibly exciting. I don't have all the words: it's just a sense I get. He is the most tender, romantic lover I have ever had, at the same time being the darkest and most aggressive. He certainly is the most expressive. By the way, he laughs when I say 'make love.' He tells me it's raw sex, nothing more. Whatever."

"Derek, I hear more words, more feeling from you than ever before. I think I get the sense of light and dark you are describing. Does it bring back confusion?"

"No, not really. Nothing will bring back that constant confusion. The darkness is an intuitive thing, a seductive energy. It's how he gets when he talks about the sub-group. His eyes even darken. It doesn't scare me, it excites me. That's all I know. It's something I feel in my gut."

"I'm watching. I'll watch at the sub-group also. I'm really looking forward to visiting to experience the special man coming into his own. I know nothing about the group except that it's the first step in my possible invitation to join if I like them and they like me. The meeting is Thursday. I'll let you know next week."

Derek stood up and so did Azure. She stepped over to give him a hug and he thanked her, "for being here for me." He closed the door softly.

Azure sat at her desk, writing notes and staring out at the gathering dark clouds bringing evening. She started doodling and, coming out of her reverie, noticed that she had drawn an intricate spider web. She held herself back from taking her red pen and adding drops of blood. *Something is wrong, very wrong...* She phoned Charles.

CHAPTER TWENTY-EIGHT
TOM, BERNICE, AND SISTER MICHAEL: CHICAGO, 1992

Tom lay shivering on the Persian rug. Bernice and Sister Michael covered him with another soft blanket, putting a pillow under his head. He slept, spent from emotions that revolted against their decades-long burial. When his heart broke into pieces long ago, they were held within by makeshift wrappings. They slowly decayed over time dampened by the tears he forced into their wrapped chambers. Now it all exploded from the memory of sudden and tragic deaths of those he loved. The women sat in silence, each in her own world of memories, regrets, and loss.

Tom stirred. He sat up, leaning against a large chair, pulling the blanket around him. Bernice sat on the floor and Michael brought cushions from the couch to sit on.

"How are you, Tom? What do you need?" the women asked delicately as Bernice took his hand.

Tom told the story to the rug. "A long time ago, I was strong. I could go through anything. I was young and thought myself invincible. I think the shock held me together so I could bury my grief. Eight years later, I buried more grief, moving across the country with my infant son. I had to save him, nurture him, and give him every ounce of love I could find." He shook his head. "I don't know how I did it. We had new names, birth certificates, Suzanne's forged death certificate." His head fell to his knees, tears dripping. "I'm sorry. I must be confusing you." He looked up to the women.

Bernice raised her eyebrow. "You had to be strong eight years before the murder? What do you mean? What ages are you talking about? I don't understand, Tom."

He sat up straighter, but still could not look at them. His eyes glazed. "I'm back in high school my senior year. It's 11:00 on a Friday night. I walk in my front door and see my grandparents. I don't understand them being there, much less how they look. 'What's wrong? Where are mom and dad?' I'm scared. I stop breathing. My grandpa stands up and tells me to sit down, it's not good news. He sits on the couch next to me. My heart is racing. I begin to whisper 'no' as he tells me my parents were in a very bad car accident. They were killed immediately. He puts his arm around me, tells me he is so sorry and that we have to be strong. My grandma comes to my other side, weeping into my shoulder. She is breaking down. I break down with her. I fall to the floor. I can't move. I can't cry." He looks up and reenters the room at last.

"My grandparents were good to me. I moved in with them. They were kind enough not to clear out or sell my parents' house until after I graduated, although it was no longer a home, just a house with a death shroud. They gave me a bedroom in their home. It was my mom's bedroom growing up. I wanted that room. Maybe she was still there, somewhere. I kept dreaming of her telling me she and dad were okay, that she loved me and would always be with me. My dad did not come to me very much. He had always been the reserved parent although I felt his love as much as I did my mom's. You know, I never told Suzanne all these feelings. She knew my parents were killed in my senior year, but I more or less reported it. I can't believe I'm sitting here, broken, with her mother and her therapist."

Bernice looked to him with her open heart, offering love. "I'm here, Tom. I don't want to lose you. You are my connection to Suzanne. Plus, I really like you." Bernice looked to him with eyes of compassion and love. "It's been so long." She brushed his hair back.

Sister Michael spoke softly. "I really wasn't her therapist, Tom. I was her guidance counselor. She had to talk. I listened and believed her. I loved Suzanne like a daughter and always will. You're a good man, Tom, and incredibly strong. You were then and you are now. Few people would be able to take your journey:

three deaths of the ones you loved most in all the world. None of it is your fault, Tom. Destiny, fate, chance – however you see it – then the intrusion of the real force of evil into your life. Of course, Suzanne would fall in love with you. It was your healing as well as hers. Then it ruptured by the forces of evil, not because of you. You did hold it together, Tom. I don't know how."

"My cousin Maggie and her husband Bruno were a godsend. A year later, Terese entered my life, followed by my two daughters and recently my new grandson. Derek has always been the greatest gift of my life. We've been together through it all. Without him, I would've joined Suzanne. But now it feels like all of them are gone." He looked down. "This was to be about Suzanne, not me. I've taken all the attention."

"Tom, you must stop. Now." Bernice's voice was strong and clear. "You had to open. People who don't feel and accept the past, people who don't grieve, often get sick and slowly die. We're here to share Suzanne's life as well as her death. The death of your parents would have to come up. Please, Tom."

He closed his eyes tightly, then opened them. "Thank you. I'm working on accepting. I strive over and over. I'm shocked to meet my first mother-in-law decades after I married Suzanne." He stopped as he looked at Bernice. "Your smile..."

"Not to be flip, Tom, but get used to it." Bernice touched his cheek and announced they all had to go home so Sister Michael could tell her story on the next day. "Where are you staying, Tom?"

"Staying? I didn't dream I'd be here this long! I thought it would be short and I'd be on my way to Minneapolis, to Maggie's. I never thought of booking a hotel."

The nun smiled. "Tom, we have rooms, but it is a girls' school and not nearly as private as the hotel three blocks away. Our guests often stay there. I know they'll have space. Give me a minute." She walked to the phone. "Yes, one gentleman. He'll be there in ten minutes." She looked at Tom. "Keep going in the direction of your parked car. Three blocks down, turn right on Acorn Road. You can't miss it. The Oakes has room service and excellent food."

Bernice looked thoughtful. "Tom, I would invite you to my home, but I can't. I'm too raw. I need to repair, alone."

"I understand. We all need to refuel." He hugged both women. He picked up the blanket with a questioning nod to Sister Michael. She smiled. He took the blanket and folded it, putting it under his arm. "I know I can't be here before noon."

"Neither can we. Let's make it one."

The two women watched him go and wordlessly held each other's eyes for a moment before Bernice followed Tom out of Rosemont School for Girls.

The Mother Superior sat at her desk, lit a candle, and reached inward to remember as much as she possibly could about Suzanne. She reflected on the decades-old file. The memories held so much conflict. How much would she reveal? Tomorrow would come soon enough. She opened the safe, took out the yellowed file, and began to read.

CHAPTER TWENTY-NINE
JEMMA, AZURE, AND GILES: SEATTLE, 1992

"*I didn't know angels could lie. I fall into black oblivion. No more grey hell.*"

Jemma put the story down. There was a very long silence. Azure could not speak. She dried her face. "Jemma, your grey hell. You were so judged, scorned, punished, alone. You had no choice except to endure. You made that choice and survived. You are here, alive, successful, a good writer, and searching. My head rages and my heart breaks for you."

"Thank you, Azure. The system still exists, you must know that. At times, my inner sixteen-year-old comes to me, huddled and grasping her knees, her head hidden in her arms." Jemma unknowingly sat that very way.

"Jemma, we've got to rescue her from the grey hell. We need to hold her, comfort her, and heal her. Bring her out of your memory and into your heart. We'll leave the system until later. But we'll return to it. That's my promise."

"Yes." Jemma's whisper was husky. "I'll be right back. I need to use the restroom." She left and shut the door.

Azure pondered. *Where were her parents? She stated in our first session she wasn't going to speak of her parents. Later I'll understand another whole chapter of grieving. I'll take directions and leave her daughter's birth for now. She shared and trusted deeply. She expressed her feelings so beautifully, so poignantly, through writing. I'll continue to honor her process, her timing. What else can I do...*

Jemma returned, looking exhausted but resolved. "I don't see the point of going to Wichita anymore. They've certainly burned all those records by now. Yes, it's an open birth record state, but I can't imagine the asylum did anything in truth. It seems useless. I would only be seeking more disappointment. It's easier simply mourning my daughter while coming to terms with her loss and with the betrayal of the nuns. I'll move on."

Azure nodded. "Is that really enough for you now? Knowing what you know? The possibility of knowing more about her?"

"What I know now could be enough." Jemma changed her position in the chair. "I can accept the healing process and let the chapter be done. Move on with the book closed. Why start another chapter called Girl or Boy?"

"Jemma, you don't look too enthused about your tidy solution. Can you really do it? You know, there's often no quick fix in matters of the heart. We have to sit with the unknown. What's your experience of sitting and not knowing? Personally, I think fear of the unknown is the number one fear – not public speaking."

"Unknowns? Well, of course my pregnancy and delivery come up first. Returning to my senior year in the same high school. What will they say? I told no one the truth. My sick aunt in Philadelphia is the story. Another unknown was my marriage. I never told him I knew he was having an affair. I quietly got divorced. Coming out here and knowing no one was a huge unknown. Ah, and coming to therapy." She half-smiled.

"So, what did you do? Were you aware those events were unknown? At the time."

Jemma tucked her hair behind her ears, seemingly annoyed. "Actually, no. Sitting and not solving a problem is not my cuppa. I get things done."

"Is that working now?"

A flash of irritation shadowed her face. "Obviously it's not working. I need a new plan. That's why I'm here."

"Can we create one together?"

"I know where you're going, Azure. I've read enough novels and talked to my friends to recognize that more feelings and emotional stuff are next in this therapy process."

Azure raised her eyebrows and quelled her instinct to smile. "Many times, I'm amazed at the elaborate ways we avoid emotion. Most systems are non-conscious.

Jemma, it takes so much energy to avoid feeling. Simply experiencing feeling gives you energy, not depletes it. Plus, having feelings available to you gives you a much richer life. It gives your heart a reason to beat. You write them beautifully but you don't often speak them."

"I think fear of feeling is number one," mumbled Jemma, her face downcast. "You know it's not safe to feel the things from long ago. If I go there, there's bound to be a nun to hurt me. Or a parent."

"Jemma, I'm not your parent, nor a nun of the past. Remember, there was an angel nun present also. I have to comment, this is the first session you've clearly let yourself be free. What do you know about that?"

"First, I don't know if it's true. Second, it feels like I am giving up. Giving in."

"Giving up what? Into what?"

"I really want to end this. Azure, I DO feel. I'm having feelings for Giles, who I told you about. I feel in reading and in films. I just don't want to feel about the past, nor talk more about it right now."

"Okay. We can be done. I'm glad to hear you and Giles are still seeing each other. Growing in like." Her eyes twinkled. "What's your thinking about Wichita now?"

"Discouraged is down. Curiosity is rising."

Azure gave her the thumbs-up. "Do you have someone to go with you since it's one of the major unknown crossroads in your life?"

Jemma looked thoughtful. "Actually, I do. I'll ask Giles when I see him in fifteen minutes." She got up, smiled at Azure, and left with a spark in her step, leaving the grey hell behind.

J emma loved Lakeview Cemetery. The fountains, ponds, and monuments brought her to her heart. She chose it for their first date. Now she was nervous and excited to see Giles and give him her story. She saw him coming toward her, knowing his walk. "How did it go, Jemma?" Giles handed her a large Earl Grey tea. "Looks like it was rather intense." He kissed her eyes.

She knew he tasted salt.

"It was one of the most difficult hours I've ever spent. I read my story to her. I brought you a copy." She handed it to him and looked away. "Read it whenever you want."

"I want to read it now to be on the same page as you." He smiled at his own page joke.

"Okay?"

"Sure. I'm going to walk across the way. I'll give you space. Maybe give me space, too." She sat on a bench opposite his, and down the path.

After he finished, she saw Giles staring into the distance. *What would he think? Say?* He got up, crossed over to the bench where Jemma sat, and wrapped his arms around her. Her face was a delta of tiny rivers, hers and his. He brushed her hair aside and held her face. "Jemma, look at me. I love you. You'll never be in the grey hell again. I won't leave you. We are in this together: the past, the now, and our future."

"You love me, Giles?" She took his hands away and held them more tightly than ever. Her cobalt eyes bored into his onyx ones, searching with a small expectation of rejection.

"Yes, baby, I love you. I've loved you since the bookstore when I saw you crying because of my singing and your heart response to my song. Now I know why."

"Why I cried then? Or why you love me now?"

"Both. And more."

They faced each other as their hearts merged, beating together. Their souls met, sinking into vulnerability, strength, and the unknown.

CHAPTER THIRTY
SISTER MICHAEL, BERNICE, AND TOM: CHICAGO, 1992

The Rosemont bells rang strong at six o'clock amidst the increasing wind and tumultuous skies. Blue-black clouds conquered the morning sun. The Mother Superior had awakened early to go to morning prayers. She knelt and bowed her head.

"Oh, Mother Mary. What am I to do? How am I to give up confidentiality now? Thirty-eight years ago, I made a choice to keep my information to myself. Now I must break my vow and give up secrets. I must do it for Suzanne, for her husband, her mother, and somehow, her son. You know about sons, mothers, and husbands. You know about suffering in the service of freedom. I know Bernice will suffer more because of me but I also know she will gain freedom. Amen."

Michael crossed herself and walked out of the chapel strengthened and committed to resolution. She returned to her office to page through the old file containing her conflict, feeling a little sick.

After a soft knock, Bernice walked into the office. Tom shortly followed and returned the folded blanket to the couch. Sister Michael offered them croissants and pastries, coffee and tea.

"I know it's my turn," began the Sister. "I'm committed to the truth as we all are." Michael looked to Bernice and Tom, one holding coffee, the other tea. They looked as rested as they could after yesterday. "After Suzanne started seeing me and began to trust me, I wrote notes after each session. Suzanne did also. At the end of her senior year, I suggested we read our notes to each other. She replied with a far more creative idea. 'Why don't we put them together? Each of us will keep a copy. I trust you to show no one. It'll be like making a quilt or weaving a tapestry.' I liked the idea. The creative parts come from her. You'll be able to tell."

"Wait!" Tom interrupted, eyes big, one hand up as a stop sign. "It just came to me. I saw the notes, the papers!"

Bernice turned quickly, eyes afire. "You read them? You know already?" Quick anger mixed with the hurt of being left out.

"No. No, of course not. I would've told you." He sounded defensive, nerves on edge, matching Bernice's. "I saw them being burned." Both women stared at him. "It was the night we signed our adoption application. Suzanne was in the backyard, a small fire going. I went out with my usual questing intrusion. 'Paul, it's a ritual I do sometimes. I burn what I've written. It's my way of letting go. I'm burning a story I wrote at Rosemont. It's a part of my past I want gone forever. I want to be free of my past for our new baby.' I asked to join her. 'No, not yet. It's my past. In a while, bring something of yours to burn. We'll have a new beginning for our baby.' I haven't thought of that evening until right now." He explained reflectively. "I went inside and watched through the window. She burnt page after page. I did not go out as I had nothing of my own written yet. The words were still buried too deep."

"I've wondered about her copy," mused Sister Michael.

Bernice shook her head slowly. "She carried so much alone."

"Now you'll both hear her memories. Remember it's thirty-six, thirty-seven years ago." The nun began to read Suzanne's words.

I yearned for my mother. I had no father, just a Robe that stood in front of the people every Sunday morning. Sometimes it prayed. Mostly it hung on a hanger in the church study. My mother called it my father. She didn't see much of the Robe either, husband and father both hidden inside its dark folds. So, what? It gave me and my mother more time together.

Often, we went to stay with my grandparents in Chicago. I love those grandparents. Not the ones near Smotelyville. My mom took me to shops, museums,

dances, concerts, bookstores, and all the magical things in Chicago. Even Mom felt
magical, alive and smiling.

Until we got home and the Robe covered everything.

I remember loving my mother so much. Until the severed part of my life that
happened on the worst night ever.

Bernice closed her eyes. Tom was riveted to the Mother Superior's voice as she
continued reading.

The Thursday twilight called to me, drawing me to the rising full moon. I was
restless. I had already written my valedictorian speech for my eighth-grade
graduation. My mom was sewing my dress. I decided to wander around the lot
between home and the church. It was attached to the school. How could the deacons
have a meeting every Thursday night with hardly any lights on in the church? I
stepped between Mom's gardens. Tomatoes, peppers, melons. Hostas, roses, forget-
me-nots.

I softly moved closer to the church and school, seeing a tiny slant of light at the
bottom of one of the pulled shades in the church basement. There were two sets of
stairs, one to the church proper and a smaller set to the basement. The children used
the basement stairs after recess and lunch if they went outside. I drew closer to the
sliver of light in the middle window, halfway down the steps. All of the other
windows had shades drawn tightly to the bottoms.

I remember creeping down the stairs, hearing their voices. Singing? Talking?
No, they were chanting like in my Chicago grandparents' Catholic church. I peeked
in the first four inches of the slanted light and was surprised to see flickering black
candles. I had never seen a black candle. There were so many. Was this the gym I
played in? Ate lunch in? My insides told me something was wrong. I counted
thirteen men. I saw my father and grandfather immediately even though the black

robes had hoods attached and nearly covered their faces. Why was my father there? Who was my father anyhow? I never really knew my grandfather. He was scary.

The frightened feeling kept creeping into every part of me. My father was there. No, he's not there. I'm wrong. The twisting inside me said I was right. It was his robe in the room of black candles. I closed my eyes.

When I opened them, my stomach tightened and I felt like I had to go to the bathroom. I didn't think the men could see me, but what if I was wrong? They were facing away from me, chanting and making signs in the air. I was hypnotized by the sounds and moving hands. Then my heart started to beat faster. None of this was as it should be. I shivered and noticed the twilight had turned to dark. The flickering candles were now glowing. I got more scared.

One of the men walked forward, carrying something close to his robe. Was that Grandfather Adolf? I moved another four inches into the opening, believing they couldn't see me in the dark. He was carrying a knife, its blade long and shining. It sparkled. My head began to pound. But I couldn't look away, watching a church meeting turn into a horror movie. He walked to the front, blade raised high. What was on the altar? Something white. A bundle of clothes?

The man put the communion chalice on the little table next to it. My throat caught. It was a baby goat! Or it was a baby lamb? I couldn't move. Blood drained into the chalice. I tasted vomit.

I held my hand over my mouth and ran away so I wouldn't scream. Or faint. Or die. I reached the house and lay on the grass, retching and gagging and gulping. I crept into a prison deep within. It was safe, dark, no movement, no pictures, no chanting. Through a foggy mist, I knew Mom was holding me, rocking me, and dripping salty tears all over my head. Baptism.

Both looked at Bernice hugging herself. She said in a cold voice, "No talking. Go on, Michael. Don't stop now."

The nun hesitated. She felt a need to pause as she put the old pages on her desk. "My story is next. No notes." She took a deep breath and released it. She looked directly at Bernice. "I'm deeply sorry. My choice to keep Suzanne's secret was, I believe, the worst mistake of my life."

Bernice returned an unblinking stare, her eyes glazed over with cold anger. "You knew. You knew that I did not know, and you never told me. I came up for breaks, for summers. You even joined my parents, Suzanne, and me for holidays. And all these years you knew?" The temperature in the room dropped.

"It's no excuse, but I only knew for one year. Suzanne began to remember in the middle of her junior year."

"That's two years, plus thirty-five. Go on." Icicles were forming in the office.

Tom turned from one to the other. He had a sick feeling. His face was grey with shadows from the gathering storm. Thunder began in the distance. He sat back with his arms crossed over his chest.

Sister Michael sat down. Her face showed more tiny lines as her spirit deflated. She began. "Suzanne began to see the horror movie replay itself at night. Then she saw it during the day. I told her to come to me whenever it happened. If I was teaching, she could go to my office and get a pass. She was unraveling. That year was very difficult. I held her, listened, and told her she wasn't wrong. Her father and the deacons were wrong. After each session, she made me promise never to tell. If I told, she would deny it all. She asked if I believed in evil. I told her yes and these things were from the pit of hell."

Bernice interrupted "What did she say about me?" Silence. "Tell me the truth, Michael. Thirty-six years later, finally tell me the truth!"

"Suzanne began to remember the time you spent together before that Thursday night. The wonderful memories, your love."

"Cut it, Michael. What did she say about that Thursday night? Did she think I knew about her father? The meetings?"

Silence. Michael nodded. "She was angry. 'How could my mother not know! She did nothing.'"

"But she made me promise the same thing!" Bernice shot back. "She begged me to tell no one. I was paralyzed. There were no therapists in Smotelyville. I tried to get her to go to one in Chicago. I kept urging her. Finally, she turned to you and away from me. You were her therapist, Michael. Or were you her mother?"

Michael felt knife points in her stomach. *Tiny, tiny cuts. Acid burning each one. Jesus in Gethsemane, drops of sweat as he prayed, "O Heavenly Father, take this cup from me." God didn't then. He wouldn't now. God did not work that way.*

Bernice continued, "How old were you? Thirty-nine? Early forties? Your childbearing years ending? Were you happy with your vows? Did you covet my child? More so, did you take her from me? Did you, Michael?" The frost in the air multiplied in spite of her heated tones.

Tom got up and walked straight to the armoire, bringing the brandy and the glasses. He sat down again, the only one drinking. "Bernice, I've got to hear more. I have to know if she told Sister Michael why she could not have children. When I asked her to marry me, she first refused, saying she could never get pregnant. Michael, did you know? Did she tell you? She told me her father told her in her senior year never to have children. Another thing I forgot." His face reddened.

Bernice glared at him but softened. She turned to Michael. "You clearly have more information than Tom or me. Go on." She sat up even straighter in her armchair.

The Mother Superior spoke quietly. "Her periods got heavier, more painful. The bleeding goat and the chalice appeared in her mind during every period. She was terrified of having children. I convinced her to meet with Rosemont's consulting gynecologist, Dr. Rudolf Mueller."

"From Smotelyville?" Bernice escalated as she got up and paced. "Rudolf Mueller who left Smotelyville as a child and never returned? That Rudolf Mueller, Michael? Did you know he and his mother moved to Chicago after his brother

161

Helmut committed suicide? Helmut was a young deacon at the time. How much Smotelyville history do you know? Oscar told me about the suicide one day when he was so upset after one of his breakdowns. He rarely told me anything about the men in the church. Rudolf is your consult? How in the world did you choose him? This is unbelievable. You would've needed my consent, Michael. How did you manage that without me knowing?"

Brittle silence. "I would prefer you sit, Bernice. I'll tell you everything I know, which is clearly not everything."

"I prefer to stand. I need to be by the window. I need the cool glass. I need the space from the unbelievable." She rested her forehead on the pane. The room was quiet. After a moment, Bernice turned around, her face set. "Go ahead."

"I'll cut to the chase. Suzanne and I met with Dr. Mueller. He was adamant something needed to be done. The heavy periods were damaging to her. He asked if her father could come up." The nun nearly whispered the last words.

Bernice paled. "Her father?"

"Reverend Schmidt came. We returned to Dr. Mueller's. The Reverend spent a long time with him while Suzanne and I waited outside the office. We agreed her father was odd. Almost lifeless. Yet, Suzanne said she felt some sad love coming from his eyes. Her father came out and went into another consulting room with Suzanne while I met with Dr. Mueller who explained the most successful treatment, even at her age, would be a hysterectomy. Suzanne reaffirmed she wanted never to have children."

Bernice began to pull a side chair over to the window. Tom got up to help her. She sat down. "A hysterectomy. Sterilized, at seventeen, not even a woman. Without me knowing. My daughter." Tears ran down her flushed face, reflecting the rain falling outside.

Sister Michael hurried on, "She was hospitalized for a week. Her recovery was quick because she was young."

"She told me about not having children also, the summer before her senior year. I told her she was too young to know what she wanted later. She denied it. 'No, mom. I do know. But don't worry. That's in the future.' Sterilized, Michael. Go on. Go on with your murderous story."

The nun was taken aback but continued. "Her father signed. At the car, he brushed Suzanne's cheek and told her it was for her own good. She waved goodbye and as far as I know, never saw him again."

"I don't understand. What did her father tell her? Didn't she tell you? Her therapist and her new mom? What's the truth, Michael? Good or evil, what is it?"

Sister Michael aged a few more years. *Why not? Empty it all out. It can't get worse. Maybe my sins will be forgiven.* "Suzanne said her father told her that having children would not be safe for her. In Dr. Mueller's consulting room, he underlined his deep concern for her life. When she was born, her father made a promise to protect her life and he knew part of that meant no children. He could not explain more, but she had to trust him. She did. The men in hooded robes, the goat, the blood, her periods, and her father's plea formed a kaleidoscope pattern that made sense to her. Somehow it gave her peace."

"That's enough of your poetry, Michael. Enough of your smoke and mirrors. I entrusted Suzanne to you. You broke that trust and took my daughter. I'll never forgive you. Never. You and I shared so much these past three years. When were you going to tell me about my daughter? When were you going to tell me her father, my husband, was in a cult? Would you ever have told me if Tom hadn't come here? Of course not. Right now, I hate you, Michael. Who are you? Who are you really?"

The leaded glass in the door trembled in her wake.

CHAPTER THIRTY-ONE
PETER, DEREK, AND MR. K: SEATTLE, 1992

Derek was hesitant as he walked into Peter's office. They rarely met at the university, yet Derek wanted to see Peter on Wednesday before the ritual. "I'm really anxious, Peter. I don't know if I can come tomorrow."

Peter whipped his head around. "Tomorrow? The Ritual? Why not?"

"Peter, when you spin your head around like that, it reminds me of *The Exorcist*. Not a pleasant memory. "

Peter watched Derek lose color, knowing when Derek paled, he was shaken and scared. It was exactly how Peter liked him. "What do you mean?" Peter's eyes narrowed.

"Easy, Peter. I'm just telling you my thoughts. I'm scared."

"Scared is a feeling, not a thought. Again, what are you talking about? Scared of what?" His pupils were pinpricks.

"You, for one. When you go icy and angry like you are now. You're supposed to help me, not get cold and yell. Your eyes go all lizard-like. It's creepy. Where did you learn that?"

Peter opened his eyes wider. "I'm sorry. Derek. You caught me unawares. I haven't seen you here in my office since we met. Of course, it's fine to be here. It simply startled me." He exhaled and pointed Derek to a chair. "What's going on about tomorrow?" *Jesus Christ, not now. Mr. K is arriving tonight. He's going to lead the meeting and size up Derek. Think quickly.*

"I remember feeling scared my first meeting. I was thirteen." *So untrue! I loved it and my time with your mother, Derek. Hah! If only you knew, which you never will.*

"Peter, I know nothing. Tell me something. What's it about? I feel like Lennie in *Of Mice and Men*. 'Tell about how it's gonna be.'"

This was the Derek that aroused Peter. Scared and vulnerable. Pitiful. Delicious. *The desk would work so well. I could lock the door. There's enough time.*

"Derek, you're okay. Really. They aren't determining if you can join or not. You won't even be participating, just watching. They'll be wearing robes with hoods. It's just what we do. You'll get a robe and silently stand next to me." He looked at his watch. *Is there enough time? God, I want him. Now.*

"I thought you were the leader."

"I am the leader of the Northwest Sector. For this meeting, however, I've invited the leader of the Southwest Sector. Mr. Wolfgang K. I don't think my father, Martin, is coming. He's tending to his best friend, a former leader who is in a nursing home. Mr. K. will lead the meeting and talk with you afterwards."

"What happens during the meeting?" Derek's color began to return.

"We chant, wear robes, light candles: perform the ritual. Did I tell you the name of our group, Derek?" Derek shook his head, eyes trusting Peter.

"You'll hear it tomorrow. Well, if you promise to tell no one you knew beforehand, I'll tell you. It is strictly up to Mr. K to tell you when he invites you to the next meeting in Sedona for your initiation."

Derek continued to reach softly into Peter's eyes.

He's all mine to relish and command. Whatever I do gives him pleasure. I have to be sure to keep my walls though. Hah! My heart is so walled it would take a nuclear explosion to knock it down. Stonewall. Me, Peter Stonewall. No more heart, just a stone.

"Peter, where are you? You were going to tell me the name. Unless. Unless something else has come up?" He looked expectantly with curiosity as he recognized Peter's look. "Here? In your office? What if someone comes?"

Peter broke the spell. "No, Derek. Not now. I must get to the airport." *If he thinks he is going to direct this...*

"Weren't you going to tell me the name?" Derek started to get up.

"We are called Maharba. We began in Germany centuries ago."

"For what? What's the purpose of Maharba's meetings?"

"To draw power. You know how much love you felt at Unconditional Love, Inc.? Well, here you will feel power from the depths. It's a different kind of power. Because there are thirteen of us, there's more power. I can't tell you anymore. Never tell anyone what I just told you. And, of course, tell no one anything you will see and hear tomorrow night. I've got to go, Derek. Mr. K comes in shortly. I'll pick you up at seven tomorrow evening. Wear dark clothing. No jeans."

Peter did some quick calculating on his way to the airport. Derek was not ready for the sacrifice ritual. Not at all. He had miscalculated. *Damn. Was Derek getting past the stone walls? The ones I erected around my heart? Never. That vegetarian crap. The fear in his eyes earlier. Think, Peter, think! Mr. K is coming with the expectation that Derek is ready to join and participate in the blood ritual before his initiation on the full moon. Not a chance. Not yet. I've got to prepare him more. Slow him down. Derek needs me to be patient, secure, and strong. No surprises. What was I thinking? It's Martin's fault. Pushing me. Me still wanting to please that old bastard. Maybe when I become the Grand Kapitan, I'll sacrifice him! Watch out, Abraham.*

Peter arrived at Sea-Tac and saw Mr. K walk towards the curb in the pick-up lane. Perfect timing. He got out of the Porsche and opened the trunk. "Mr. K!" They shook hands, small fingers interlocked.

"What's it been, Peter, a year since we met? A year since I told you no more 'Mr. K?' It's Wolfgang. Co-Kapitans. It's great to see you."

"Likewise, Wolfgang. Likewise."

They drove back to the city. The first ten minutes of the trip were soundless in the evening twilight. Peter really did like Wolfgang and always had. They could talk openly and Peter's stress dissolved. "I'd like to offer a change of plans, Wolfgang. I suspect you are the only one of the Quadrant Leaders that will understand my strategy."

"Sure, Peter, go ahead. Tell me."

"It's Derek, our key man for all the years. He's simply not ready. I made a poor judgement call. Martin was pressuring me. No, it's not Martin's fault. I should've stood up to him."

"Ah, Peter. Martin's not easy. He's rarely, if ever, open to another's ideas. I've known him for decades. I get it. It must be very challenging to be his son."

"Thank you, Wolfgang. I knew I could count on you. I do feel terrible about the last-minute change, especially as you flew in for the Ritual. But, Wolfgang, he's just not ready. It was only this afternoon I saw his fear. And I discovered he is vegetarian because loves animals. I was too lax. I should have asked him earlier."

"Peter, ease up on yourself. The prize is too precious to lose. In the first place, how smart of you to ask! I never would've thought of it. You mentioned a strategy. What are you thinking?"

"I say let's still meet tomorrow. I'll bring him. But let's meet earlier with the men and discuss one of the lesser rituals, not a Blood Ritual. We'll hold the Blood Ritual to initiate him in a little over a week at the November full moon. Tomorrow, we'll still robe, chant, invoke the power. Now I'm getting excited. I knew you would understand. I knew you would make it better. 'The prize is too precious.' I love it."

"Peter, let's use the Seven Windings Ritual. We can really raise the power so he can feel it. He will want to be one with the power. Maybe he can see he has power over animals!"

"Wolfgang, you're a genius. Of course, the Seven Windings! Why didn't I think of it? Your idea is so much better. I just wasn't thinking. It's the perfect pre-initiation experience, especially as we use no animals."

"Oh, you were thinking, Peter. I always watch you. You never miss a beat. You found him. You groomed him. He will attend his first Ritual. It will simply be a different one than planned. To have Suzanne's son being initiated into Maharba in Sedona during Scorpio is the manifestation of our hopes, Peter. You found him. We have him. We have time. Patience."

"What about the head pain? Should we give him E?"

"No, let him experience the pain. Then he will know firsthand the true experience of power. So, we have a plan, Peter. The Seven Windings here. Then both of you fly to Sedona for the initiation. It couldn't be better. Use the ecstasy then. You'll have a little over a week to prepare him. Is that enough time?"

"I think so. I have another idea. Let's invite him for a drink with us tonight after dinner. I want you to meet him before the others to get your input. Okay?"

"Excellent, Peter." Wolfgang smiled. Peter detected pride. It warmed his ego.

He punched in Derek's number. "Derek, how are you? I just picked up Mr. K and he would love to meet you tonight, if, of course, you aren't busy?" Peter guarded his excitement. "That would be great. Meet us after dinner at the Spiderweb. Let's say nine. Yes, certainly." Peter hung up and beamed at Wolfgang. "He's in. At nine tonight, you'll meet Suzanne's son. No Maharba Promise goes unfulfilled. They didn't know that her blood sacrifice would make Derek the generational blood we demand. Wolfgang, I've always wanted to know. You were there. You wrote on the parchment with her blood. How was it, Wolfgang?"

"One of the best, Peter. The power reigned. We put her blood in Derek's mouth. He is now ours. How was it for you, Peter? At your thirteen-year initiation? How was it for you?"

"Wolfgang. The best. I became a man. I drank the power from the chalice and became the power. We have never parted."

CHAPTER THIRTY-TWO
JEMMA AND GILES: WICHITA, 1992

The plane rose in the crystal clear blue sky and Jemma's anxiety increased with its ascent. "I mean, really, Giles, what and why? So futile."

"We're going to discover if we can get some information about your baby. Is the baby a boy or girl? Where did the baby go? Step one. Actually, step two. First Moms was step one." Giles took her hand. "It's okay, Jemma. It's a journey right now, not a destination. The worst that can happen is that there are no records. I doubt we will run into that problem."

Fortunately, they had little luggage, found the car rental quickly, and were soon driving into Wichita. "Please, Giles, can we go right to the building?" Jemma unfolded the city map. "I remember the address so well." She grimaced. "607 Fourteenth Street. Sisters of Compassion."

Her voice started to quaver. "They have to show us the records, right?"

"I trust your research is accurate. You've got your birth certificate and driver's license. 'Open birth records' has to mean open to you. I suspect it also means open to your baby as an adult." He reached over and took her sweaty hand. "Soon."

"All these years, I fought to say it didn't matter. But it does, Giles, it matters more than ever that I find the truth. The more possible truth becomes, the more it matters." Her hand clutched the map as if it would blow away, although the windows were closed.

"You say Bromler ends on Fourteenth? What about this ramp ahead? I have to take it. Is the ramp on the map? The interstate?"

The lines between her eyebrows deepened as she studied the map. "No ramp, no interstate. How old is this map? The rental woman had to rummage around to find it." She unfolded more of the map. "Oh, Giles! It's a really old map!" She crushed it and tossed it in the back seat. "I told you it was futile." She set her mouth in a grimace.

"Let me stop and ask. Sisters of Compassion on Fourteenth Street, yes?" He went into the gas station. He came out and leaned into her open window. "A delay, Jemma. Not a dead end, just a delay. The Sisters of Compassion Asylum was razed in 1965 to build the highway."

"Giles, no!"

"Wait, Jemma." He brushed the hair from her face. "They have to store the records elsewhere. There has to be a central Catholic Services Agency. It's most likely downtown. We're going to find it. We really are, Jemma. For now, I suggest dinner. Then we'll check into the hotel and check the Yellow Pages for Catholic agencies. Are you game for that?"

She nodded, without smiling. "We have no other choice, do we?"

After passing several restaurants, they found one that looked friendly, cozy, and had a booth. They ordered wine and dinner. Jemma muttered, "So long ago. Why did I ever think it would still be here after decades?"

"Don't be so hard on yourself, Jemma. It's been a long day. We had to be at the airport early and pick up the rental car, and the map wasn't updated. Finding our way to the asylum is a challenge."

"And we did not find it. Instead we discovered an elaborate highway system." Her eyes clouded.

"This is true. Tomorrow we'll check the main office of the Catholic Services Agency. We'll be fresh. I know we'll get some information."

"Yeah, well, the information will probably be 'There is no information.'"

"Sweetheart, I know this has got to be rough on you, being in Wichita again. Remembering the streets, going back in time. Did your parents bring you?"

Jemma stopped eating and pushed her plate away. "No, they didn't. I came on a train, the Sunflower. I was totally alone. I went home on the Missouri Pacific Railroad. I traveled alone again, a mom without a baby. After I returned, I had six weeks to get ready for my senior year. I jumped into school and studied most of the time, which is why I was awarded the Smith scholarship. Giles, I'm sorry. I should've been done with this by the time I met you. I thought I was. Then you sang *Motherless Child* and I clearly wasn't done with anything." She took his hand. She loved seeing the contrasting skin tones that brought such warmth to her heart. "I'm not really sorry. I'm so grateful for you being here." She kissed his hand. A loud sigh of exasperation and throat clearing broke their mood, clearly directed towards them. Jemma opened her eyes wide, anger rising. "Is that because…"

He interrupted her outburst before it could happen. "Easy, girl. You're not in Seattle anymore. Do you see any other person of color in here, much less a mixed-race couple? Don't turn around; just keep talking. Don't ever stop looking at me with those eyes of love."

She took a deep breath., keeping her hand on his. "And we're supposed to go into a Catholic agency and ask about the asylum? What if they treat us that way at the agency?" Her eyes narrowed.

"We'll be cool from the get-go. We'll get arrogant. We'll use our Dr. titles." He winked.

"Dr. and Dr. Cool."

The hotel was elegant. Giles planned the whole trip on the spur of the moment, all two nights of it. No one at the hotel was less than polite and proper. The bellman opened the penthouse suite with a flourish as soft lights brightened the room. He left with a large tip. The king-sized bed was turned down, chocolates on each pillow, jacuzzi tub for two, champagne chilling, and plush robes awaiting them. Giles toasted in the tub, "To the first of many hotels together. To success tomorrow. I love you, my Jemma." He sang to her *This is the Time to Remember*. She received all of it, all of him.

Their lovemaking was as luxurious as their surroundings, building slowly, ceaseless caressing, *Bolero* playing in the background. They were timeless. City lights flickered as Jemma's cries shattered the barrier around her heart. Sleep wrapped the lovers in deeper unity.

The sunlight awakened and welcomed them to live their love. "You are so beautiful, Giles. Your head, your eyes, your nose, your mouth," kissing each body part as she spoke. She continued, creating more love in the bright sunlight.

Giles whispered, "Ah, my love, we must get up. We've places to go, things to accomplish, the past to unearth, questions to resolve. How about if I scour the Yellow Pages while you scour the breakfast menu?"

Her pessimism and disappointment of the previous day were clearly dissipated. "Perfect." She placed the order and left for the shower. After a few moments, Giles called the kitchen, delayed the delivery by thirty minutes, and followed Jemma into the shower.

After the rather long shower, breakfast arrived. Giles spoke after eating his omelet. "I suggest we go to the main Catholic Services Agency. It's not far; we can walk. Do you think we should call?"

Jemma shook her head. "No, that will set them up to tell us nothing. I'd rather walk in unannounced. The surprise factor will work to our advantage, Dr. Cool." She got up, took her jacket off the hanger, and asked "Ready?" They descended to the lobby and he opened the door to late morning sunshine and busy streets.

"I asked the bellman and the destination is closer than I thought. We can walk." After five minutes, Giles stopped. "Here it is." He looked through the window. "Seems to be one of those forgotten-about agencies." They entered the less-than-welcoming reception area.

"I believe we're in the right place." Jemma questioned the young woman behind the fairly messy desk. "This is Catholic Services? The Main Office?" A nod of affirmation. "I'm Dr. Jemma Gran. I'm from the Adoption Project at the university in Seattle. This is my colleague, Dr. Giles Wright. I apologize for not scheduling an appointment. We're in Wichita for a different study, but seeing your agency reminded us we could add to our research. So, here we are, taking a chance that we might speak with your director now. Do you think you could help us?"

"Of course, Dr. Gran. Let me check with him."

Josiah McCormick was engaging and welcoming. Jemma explained the bare bones of the Project, involving adoptees, adopters, and the moms who were unable to raise their infants. She continued, "Our research showed that Kansas was one of the first two states with open birth records. It seemed Catholic Services served these young moms for many decades, is that correct?"

"Oh, yes, Dr. Gran. We did all we could to help and serve the poor, unfortunate girls."

Jemma took a deep breath. "Is that right? Could we look at some records of these moms? Of course, I assume the records are coded for confidentiality."

"Well, Dr. Gran, I'm happy to help you. What do you expect to find?" he questioned in a slow deferential tone.

"We're comparing ages of the moms within twenty chosen states with the genders of the babies. We are then comparing those genders with the final locations of the adopted babies. It may seem irrelevant, but we are following the research of the best studies in Switzerland, Germany, and Ireland. I can send you the results after the study is published. Of course, we'll give you and your agency an acknowledgment of your help. Do you prefer Josiah McCormick, Director of Catholic Services on the footnote, or something different?" Jemma smiled at her confused fabrication. She knew he thought the smile for him.

"That's perfect," he beamed. "Thank you. I don't exactly understand the study, but I do know we have boxes of records from the Home on Fourteenth Street that operated from the late 1800's until 1965. Would that be helpful? Yes, all are coded for confidentiality. I'll phone Mrs. Barrett in the archive department: lower level, room five. She'll be expecting you." After much hand shaking, they descended to the archives.

"Lovely job, Dr. Gran. Very quick thinking. You'll have to update me on that particular international study. I'm not familiar with it. Nor did it make one iota of sense." His eyes twinkled in delight. Jemma's butterflies quadrupled in her stomach.

Giles charmed Mrs. Barrett, helped her carry the boxes, and soon they were seated at a large walnut library table with over a dozen dusty bankers' boxes. "Will you be okay if I go back to my work? Just come to my desk if you need anything. I'm sorry the space is so small. Or the desk too big. The basement has become a kind of storage room." Giles thanked her with his engaging smile.

"Are you ready for this, Jemma? Whatever you see may change your life. Most likely will change your life." He paged through several folders. "They are extremely brief. We only need 1963. They did not deliver many babies, according to these slim files. There are no live birth certificates."

"Of course, they are brief and tell as little as possible. God, I hope mine is there! No birth certificates? Could they have removed them?" Her eyes reflected a sudden wild fear. She swallowed audibly. "I'm readier than I thought possible. I want to know. I want to know for Step Three, finding the truth about my baby. Where do we begin? All these boxes." Dismay crept into Jemma.

"With these nearly empty files, it won't take long. Well, then, here is 1963." He handed the box to her. "Do you want me to open it? Look for it?"

"No. I can do it. I just need a few minutes. It's like I am going to meet my daughter for real, even though it's totally not true." She got up and paced.

"I can't believe how anxious I am. My stomach is a roller coaster." She opened the box, flipped several files, reaching one labeled June. She rubbed her neck. She opened the June file and turned two or three pages. She found the one she wanted and closed her eyes for a second.

Opening them, Jemma read aloud:

"June 30 1963. Live birth to 16-year-old girl." Deep breath.

"Baby boy. Sent to Chicago, Illinois." She put her head down on crossed arms over the paper. The few minutes seemed like hours to Giles. He waited, his hand on her back.

Jemma lifted her head and reread the single page. "All those years, Giles. All those stories I created. All wrong. A boy. I feel numb. Empty. Lost." Tears filled her eyes, unbeknownst to her. "I don't know what I need."

"What about plane reservations to Chicago?" questioned Giles softly. "Tomorrow afternoon?"

Jemma's eyes lit up, as much as they could. "Plane reservations. Yes, Giles. Exactly."

CHAPTER THIRTY-THREE
TOM, MAGGIE, AND BRUNO: MINNEAPOLIS, 1992

After the door stopped shaking from Bernice's exit, the Mother Superior excused herself and left for the restroom, closing the door quietly. Tom wrote a brief goodbye note, took the yellowed file off her desk, and hurried out to catch up with Bernice. "Bernice!" He yelled as she was pulling away. He ran and yelled again. She stopped and opened the window, her rage still with her. "Please, give me your phone number. I don't want to lose you."

Bernice stopped, wrote quickly, and got out of the car. She handed the note to him, then grabbed and held him tightly. "You won't lose me, Tom. I promise. Give me some time, then call." She returned to her car and left. Tom walked to his car.

The nun went back to her office, feeling unbalanced and nauseous. She watched through the window. The world began to spiral downwards as she lost her balance and reached for her chair. Her vision blurred. Her arm and leg weakened. Trembling, she slid into unconsciousness, pulling the heavy chair on top of her.

Tom called Maggie from the rest stop, forcing Chicago back into the past. "My journey's almost over. I can't wait to see you and Bruno. I've found so much information. I'm about two hours out of Chicago, staying overnight along the way. I'm way too exhausted to drive it in one stretch. Are you free tomorrow?" Tom shifted feet, beginning to feel the weariness permeate his body. "Thank you, Maggie. I love you."

Where did that come from?! I've never told Maggie I loved her, even though she's my only relative and knows everything about me. We only talk once or twice a year, yet she and Bruno saved our lives. I suppose I'm pretty raw and exposed, and it is too painful. Plus, there is an overwhelming amount of information. I met

Bernice! Secrets are tumbling out all over: mine, theirs, all coming out of hiding. I suspect there are many more secrets. Did the Mother Superior really take Suzanne from her mom?

He found a roadside hotel, went out for a quick dinner, and sighed as he packed the stolen file on the bottom of his suitcase. He had no energy to read it now, and besides, Sister Michael had just read it to them. Showered and relaxed, Tom called Terese to assure her he would most likely be home within the week. "You've been so great, Terese, not asking questions or demanding updates and trusting I'll share it all when I get home. Thank you from the depths of my heart." He stopped to swallow. "No, I don't suppose I have spoken exactly like that before. Burdens are being lifted. The emotional cost is overwhelming. It's been a life-changing trip. Right now, I'm fading and suspect I'll sleep better than I have for days. I love you."

Next morning, Tom found himself talking aloud while driving and reviewing the past week. "There are several things I know for sure. There was a cult." He stopped, disbelief still predominant. "I mean, I think I'm pretty sure it's real. Suzanne saw a sacrifice. The deacons in the church met on Thursdays." The memory of Derek and Thursday meetings flashed into his mind. He would deal with it later. He gripped the steering wheel a bit tighter.

"I know they murdered Suzanne." He gulped and stopped speaking. *How can I just be stating this so matter-of-factly? She was murdered. They were never caught, never charged. Yet, I saw them. Would I even recognize them after all these years? I've got to hear everything from Bruno. The pledge of silence that I made him take, to tell me nothing when we changed our identities is over. All these years, he honored it. Now I'm ready to hear. I must hear. I have no other choice. Derek's life is based on the truth of what actually happened.*

Tom decided to take his mind off the remaining mystery and calculate what he knew to be true.

"I know Bernice and I have a connection, not only through Suzanne, but between us as we are now. I really like her.

"I know something wasn't quite right in the Mother Superior's relationship with Suzanne. That's for later.

"I know Suzanne couldn't have children, but I don't know why. I don't know what her father told her before the hysterectomy. Will I ever? How could I find out?

"I highly suspect Derek is getting deeply involved in some group. Is it a cult? It meets on Thursdays. It can't be the same one. The old one ended in Smotelyville in 1975 when the church burnt. Are Thursdays just when cults meet? No, that's ridiculous. A mere coincidence." He felt his intestinal walls deny it.

"Most of all, I know I must tell Derek the truth of his birth. I have to tell him he is fully adopted, not just by Terese. I must tell him I am not his biological father. Do I have to tell of Suzanne's murder? Later. At least I can tell him he has a grandmother."

Tom stopped, gripping the steering wheel more tightly and taking deep breaths. He nearly shouted. "I will no longer live my life as I have been living it. I've got to be honest. Totally honest. Here I was getting so upset about Unconditional Love, Inc. spelling you lie. U.L.I. I lie!" He banged the steering wheel. "Oh, my God! I'm so deep in lies!"

He got out of the car and walked to a grassy place on the side of the highway. He sat on the ground with his head in his hands for ten minutes. Fortunately, no one stopped. He walked back to the car, got in, and merged with the traffic. He was less agitated and more grounded.

Tom inhaled the lakes, the green, the organic beauty of Minnesota. The vast differences in the Midwestern geography gave him a sense of wonder and peace. He remembered driving here thirty years ago in shock with infant Aron, running for their lives. *Is this trip a repeat? It sure feels like it. Except I'm more in charge. Am I? What have I done? What have I not done? That doesn't matter anymore.*

What matters now is what I AM doing. It matters to get all the information I can and act on it, no matter what.

He found the house easily, remembering his two-month stay. The evergreens were stately and so much taller. The stones on the house were more worn by the elements. He couldn't help but smile as he saw them sitting on the stairs, waving with enthusiasm.

Their hugs were aloe on Tom's raw soul. Would the spigot in his eyes ever shut off? "I'm sorry. It's been a long journey to get here, on all levels. And I almost forgot to congratulate you on your marriage! May it be as happy as your long, long courtship!"

Maggie hugged him again. "You're really apologizing? For tears? Tom, you're reliving the horrors of the past visit. You're in a safe space. Once again, our haven is yours. Thank you for the good wishes. We did think living together for over thirty-five years was enough of a trial period." She grinned at both of them.

Bruno took Tom's suitcase. "Well, I'm glad you're finally here as well." His intelligent warm brown eyes seemed to reflect the unspoken words, "on all levels." Tom did not think he was imagining it; Bruno seemed to be happy that Tom could be here mentally and emotionally as well as physically, unlike thirty years ago. At least Tom was smiling. "I'll take your bag up to your room. It's a different one than before; we've rearranged. I'll meet you on the patio with drinks. Scotch? G and T?"

"Gin and tonic sounds great. Thank you, Bruno, for everything: then and now."

They settled on the patio to watch the boaters on the lake, feeling peace for the moment. Tom remembered the last time he sat here, seemingly forever ago, writing in his journal, trying to make sense out of horror. Going over and over those moments seeing Suzanne's body drained of blood and the four men carrying her away. The murderers. He would write and write, then tear the writing into tiny pieces and place them in the lake. Letting go, letting go. Two months of therapy, three days a week. Paul and Aron becoming Tom and Derek. He looked at his cousins. "You know, I never could've continued without the two of you, never. Sitting here, I'm feeling and remembering my sense of safety, beginning the healing. The razor pain has softened, reduced, and rarely visits, except for these past several days. You gave me a new life. You gave Derek his life. I can never repay you."

"There is no debt. Never was." Bruno made a circle with his thumb and forefinger. "But we need to know where you have been this past week, weeks. What did you find? What do you want to know? Why now? First though, how is Derek? Terese? The girls? Your new grandson?" Bruno's assessing gaze was never intrusive, just this side of penetrating. The stare, like Bruno, was always steady, with additions as needed. Right now, the additive was gentleness, despite the rapid questions.

Maggie refilled his drink. "Let's eat first, catch up when we want. We have time, right, Tom?" Tom nodded.

Bruno stood up. "To the steaks. Oops, Tom. You're not vegetarian, are you?"

"No, I'm not, although Derek is very much so. He has been for most of his life. No blood for him." He pressed his hand to his forehead. "O my God, I don't know why I said that!"

"You've been living nothing else but blood and Suzanne's murder for the past week. Plus, you are back here." Maggie touched his arm tenderly. "It's okay, Tom. Be kind to yourself."

They took a walk around part of the lake after dinner, Tom filling them in on his journey and his driving review of the past day. "I don't suppose I have any new information for you, Bruno. Your agency did a pretty thorough investigation. Ferdie in Smotelyville told me of the FBI and the fire in 1975."

Bruno replied, "Some is new, Tom. I wasn't aware of the relationship between Bernice and Sister Michael. Neither mentioned it when we were interviewing decades ago. Bernice clearly knew of no cult, although she mentioned the

Thursday night meetings. Sister Michael, told us of Suzanne's memories, although very reluctantly, I must add. She kept speaking of confidentiality and 'her' Suzanne. We thought it odd, but she finally broke and gave us the information we needed."

"And it ended in 1975, right?" Tom implored Bruno.

Bruno slowly shook his head. "No, Tom, it did not."

Tom's face drained. "Can we hold off for ten minutes? I can't hear this without sitting down. I don't know why your information is so threatening to me, especially after Bernice and the Sister have told me nearly everything. But it is."

"Sure. Of course. I suspect you see my information, FBI information, as more of the truth that's been hidden for too long. I get it, Tom." Bruno walked a bit slower. "I admire your willingness to know it all. With Derek being older, I can see why you are concerned." Tom stopped breathing for a minute. *Concerned? I didn't say concerned.*

"I'll go start the coffee," Maggie threw over her shoulder as she jogged ahead. "Besides, I need the exercise."

Bruno's eyes followed his wife with appreciative love. Tom really missed Terese at that moment.

"One question, Bruno, before we get there. Do all cults meet on Thursday nights?"

Bruno looked surprised. "No, Tom, not at all. What a strange question. Why do you ask?"

"Ummm. Because of Derek and the new group he's joined. More because of another group he may join."

"They meet on Thursdays?" Bruno's voice was clipped, suddenly intense.

"Well, no. The Unconditional Love, Inc., group meets on Wednesdays. But he's been asked to join a subgroup. They meet on Thursdays. It's exactly why I had to make this journey now. I felt a terrible fear for Derek. I know it's crazy, maybe. I feel more fear now. But..." His voice trailed off.

Bruno inserted quietly, "You don't know the name of the leader, do you?"

"The leader? Oh, I do. His name is Peter."

"Peter." Silence. "You're one hundred percent certain?"

"Could not be more certain. Why?"

"Tom, there's so much to tell you. I know you won't say anything to Derek unless we agree. You have the right, morally and legally to know. It's a very long story. I'm glad you are at a point to hear all of it. Let's check on the coffee."

Tom did not like the change in Bruno's eyes nor did he like the set of his jaw, and he chafed at the harsh tone in Bruno's voice. He especially did not like the worm of dread burrowing in his own stomach.

CHAPTER THIRTY-FOUR
AZURE AND CHARLES: SEATTLE, 1992

Charles Dirgence sat in his university office experiencing a moment of joy as he placed the phone in the receiver with a smile that came from deep into his heart. He began to realign the already even edges of the three stacks of reports in front of him. The square walnut table in the corner of his office held seven more piles. Giles Wright, his co-researcher, had planned the Adoption Project well. Charles leaned back in his desk chair and watched the sun break through the gathered clouds as it often did, a prelude to the evening twilight. It's what he loved about Seattle. Even if clouds and rain seized the day, he could often count on the sun making its late-day appearance, especially during El Niño. He focused on Mt. Rainier coming out.

His smile met the sun break and he chuckled. Azure Manjursi – tonight – for dinner.

Thank the God of synchronicity for both of their schedules being open at the last-minute notice. He checked on the name Azure gave to him, finding his application: Peter Gehman, one of the collators in the Project. He remembered Peter as a strong dynamic personality.

Glancing through the file, he saw nothing extraordinary: IT background, Ph.D. in Computer Science from UCSF, developed and led positive thinking groups, great recommendations, on sabbatical and researching group dynamics based on everyone's need for love. Peter told Charles he would like permission to do a piece of his own research with the adoptees. Charles told him that was not possible nor ethical. He remembered Peter flashing a smile and apologizing. Now Charles wondered about the response. He would check with Giles to be certain Peter understood. *He looks sound on paper. What could Azure be up to?* Whatever it was, he knew it wouldn't be simple. In their days together, he often called her his matrix.

Rainier began to dissolve in the gloaming. It was his favorite time of day. The day was easing into the night and all her mysteries. Mysteries always held possibilities, and tonight's featured Azure, whom he loved.

Maximilien at Pike Place Market never failed. Charles asked for a secluded table on the bay with views of Puget Sound, the islands where he hoped to live one day, the Olympic Mountains, and the starlit sky. The window next to their table was open to the sounds of the moorings, seagulls keening, and people moving quietly on their boats.

Charles stood as Azure walked towards him, their greeting always the same. They embraced longer than most couples, drank in each other's eyes, and touched cheeks with their fingertips. There was no rush or words.

"You always choose the perfect table, Charles, especially this one. It's ours."

"It is. You look beautiful, Azure. I am graced by your presence."

"You are the biggest romantic I know, Charles, or have ever known. Even though our true and complete path is still ahead of us, you'll remember that we agreed on some distance to protect our hearts." Azure's smile was disarming.

"We sort of agreed, as I recall. My heart has never been so open. Who needs protection around love? Weren't there some exceptions to the norm? Like renting a houseboat for the night?"

"Charles. No." Her eyes betrayed the disingenuous 'no.' But the no took its place at the table and was very quiet.

"I know, Azure, I know. We can always discuss it later, another time. I'm simply grateful to be with you tonight." He saluted with a wink.

"As am I." She opened the menu, looked up with a raised eyebrow, and asked, "Did you check on Peter?"

"Of course, my dear. Better yet, I brought his file. Do you really want him with us at our dinner? I don't. Perhaps we can put him on the dessert tray."

"Good idea. Let's catch up, as they say. Or, let's not and just be where we want to be. How are you, Charles?"

A fter two hours and a bottle of French Cabernet, Charles brought out Peter's file. "Check it out. Then I want to know your interest."

Azure looked up after several moments of perusal. "Well, he reads well on paper. Did you check his references?"

"My assistant did. Two were stunning. The other three were unavailable: moved, no forwarding address."

"Hmm. Is that standard? 40% of the references?"

"No. We usually go for 60%. But as it's a research study and since the collators are practically volunteering, in the financial sense, we let it go. Why do you ask? Do you know him? I sense you don't have a good feeling about him."

"I'm working with two people involved in the Project. They both brought up Peter. My impression is that he is very charismatic and... seductive. I get a bad vibe on his honesty."

"I can see the charisma part now, although I didn't until a few weeks into the Project. Very recently, Giles casually mentioned we needed to talk about Peter as he had some concerns. Giles is currently on a trip with one of the collators, Jemma." Conspiratorial smile. "I've never seen him so happy in a relationship; it does my heart good. I'll make a point to talk with him when he returns. Clearly you have questions, so out with them."

"I'll give you the facts I know, which you can confirm anywhere. Then I'll tell you my thoughts. Peter runs a New Age Love group once a week. I dropped in once. Really, it felt like a traditional tent revival sporting New Age clothing. Guitars played songs of love. Peter implored love. I didn't see any Kool-Aid, though."

Charles felt the seriousness of Azure's story as he felt caution stir inside her. "Go on."

"I saw Peter's charisma and influence, as well as his effect on some vulnerable adoptees from the Project. He has a swooping energy. The other day I was walking and saw an eagle devouring a young rabbit. I know it's a balance of nature, yet I could not help but think of Peter. One person I know is already in his talons. I suspect there are more."

"What does he do with his followers? What's his purpose?"

"I'm not entirely sure. I do know he has targeted one follower for an additional group, its purpose unknown. Peter has also completely sexually seduced this person who is now in love with him. Charles, it doesn't feel good."

His face was a study in tension and alertness. "Doesn't sound good either, Azure. And I'm responsible for hiring him. Can you tell me more?"

"No, Charles, I can't. We're feeling the same danger alert, however. Let me see if I can get a release to share more with you if my client agrees."

"Are you scared, Azure? For this adoptee? For others?"

"On the verge of it. I didn't get a good feeling from reading his file. It felt like it was written by an unreliable lobbyist. It's clearly designed to be impressive, but has big gaps and lacks authenticity."

"You can trust I will follow up on Peter, his meetings and purposes, and especially his use," he hesitated. "Yes, use, of the adoptees. I'll get back with you as soon as I can. What are you going to do?"

"I'm going to talk with my client and see how willing he is to share information. I may tell him my concerns and feel out if he is open to talking with you. I fear he is too enthralled right now. He's in love."

Charles did not drop his gaze. "And well we remember falling in love, my dear."

"I've never forgotten." She touched his fingers and leapt into his eyes.

"You know I'm still in love with you, Azure."

She nodded slowly, smiled mysteriously, and held his hand tighter.

They got up, took each other's hand, and walked together out to the Sound.

CHAPTER THIRTY-FIVE
THE SEVEN WINDINGS: SEATTLE, 1992

"So what did he think of me?"

Still sweaty and ruddy, Derek lay confidently with his hands laced under his head, eyes alert and hunger sated.

"You mean about the last thirty minutes?"

"Yeah, right, Peter. Now you have hidden cameras for Mr. K. to see?" Derek smirked, snorted, and languidly waited.

O, my God, my boy toy is growing up. Peter felt a few seconds of sadness? Pride? Fear? Never did Peter feel fear. "Derek, you please me. I trust you will continue to do so in all areas: bed, Maharba, rituals, everything. When you please me, you please Mr. K. Come here."

The night passed into dawn and Derek kissed Peter before he left to return to the mundane world of booksellers. "See you tonight, Peter. I love you."

"I lo...I'll pick you up at 6:00. Be ready. No jeans." *What! Did I almost say "I love you?" Never. Stone walls don't love. They don't crack. My stone wall doesn't. My walls are secure and immutable, a fortress for my heart. Actually, what heart?* A small line that Peter could not see appeared in the fortress.

"Just do what I do," commanded Peter in the black Porsche on the way to the meeting. "Mr. K. will lead. You don't need to understand any of it. Just let yourself flow with the energies. Feel the power. Do not speak."

Derek nodded as anticipation filled his body.

Thirteen white pillar candles wavered on the wrought iron floor candlesticks forged in Germany centuries ago. Over fifty votives created an outer circle. In between the dancing flames were thirteen robed and hooded men, including Derek, whose innards were in chaos. He stood next to Peter, silent as the men chanted. The melodious deep cadence seemed to soothe him even though he knew calm often preceded a storm.

The brown robe was heavy. *Why did I wear corduroy pants?* The heat and the incense were cloying. Derek wanted to rip the robe off and get the hell out of Dodge. *I must please Peter.*

The circle seemed to tighten, though it stayed the same. His chest was filled with lead, his palms clammy. His ears began to close. A shrouded and obscured man held both hands up, presumably Mr. K.

"Seat yourselves, my brothers. We begin our most Sacred Power Ritual, the Seven Windings. We are reminded with each winding of Abraham leading his son, circling the serpentine path to the altar of life, of death, of power. He seeks the way to his deeper Power. We find the way to our Power tonight, reactivating our vows to Maharba, strengthening our brother bonds, and receiving once again the sacred power. Thus, we begin."

The men sat, palms turned upward resting on their thighs, breathing evenly. Derek felt cloudy, unstable. He deepened his breath, slowed it as Peter taught him, and watched.

Mr. K. spoke slowly. Derek could not understand his words although had studied several languages. He gave into the rhythm, quieting his inner tremors. Derek's shoulders loosened, his stomach less tense as he watched Mr. K. move around the circle in geometric patterns. He stopped in front of each man, continuing his flow of mystical words. Each man nodded briefly, ever so slightly. When he stopped in front of Derek, the words reduced in rapidity, like an engine slowing before the bend. Derek shivered as he felt his soul being invaded. After the first pattern, the men chanted in unison, confusing Derek with the mystical sounds.

Mr. K. spoke English once more. "We have completed the First Winding. We now enter the realm of the Second Winding." He walked in new directions, creating geometric patterns with his hands and fingers. His language seemed to change again. Derek felt his heart beating hard. Peter must have sensed the shift in Derek as he put his hand on Derek's just for a moment. He heard Peter hiss something Derek could not understand.

The series of movements, patterns, and chanting grew more complicated as each Winding commenced. Derek was astounded by the changes in his body and mind. Tense and relaxed. Groggy and clear. He wished for a blanket. A sense of flying over it all brought him a peace he had never felt. Then he was plunged into what felt like the core of the Earth, into piercing heat. He spun as a plane crashing. His head began to pound, concrete blocks crushing his skull, moving to a millimeter of squeezing his brain out of his head. Derek pressed his hands to his head inside the hood. Suddenly the pounding stopped.

Mr. K. spoke loudly, clearly, and slowly, once again in a language Derek knew. "As we begin our Seventh Winding, we remember our commitment to receiving the height and depth of the ancient power. Our father Abraham and our brother Isaac, and the Garden Serpent transmit to us in our final Winding." Derek heard more unintelligible words. Suddenly, Mr. K. moved quickly, like a dervish spinning, stopping, staring, starting again all over.

Derek's brain was being pulverized by an invisible vise. He pressed harder on his temples trying to quell the ferocity of the growing pain. He could hear the sound of a train gathering speed inside his head. *I'm going to die. I can't make it. I want to die. Kill me. Kill me!*

Mr. K stopped circling and the men stopped chanting. The only sounds were Derek's thoughts as they made their way out of his pained mouth. "Kill me. Please kill me." He could not see the men pushing back their hoods, smiling, and locking wrists. Derek was crouched in agony unable to hear the men whispering, "The Serpent reigns. The Serpent gives. The Serpent gives to us the power. We are the Power forever and always."

Derek fell to his side, clutching, weeping, and rasping, "Kill me. Kill me." He thought he heard Peter's hiss, "He's ours..." Mercifully, blackness obliterated the pain.

CHAPTER THIRTY-SIX
JEMMA AND GILES: CHICAGO, 1992

"I'm not even Catholic and never was, yet all I seem to do is visit Catholic agencies in the Midwest." Jemma remarked in the taxi from O'Hare to Michigan Avenue. "Um, Giles, how is it that you choose such luxurious hotels?" as the taxi pulled up to the front of the Drake Hotel.

She smiled quizzically.

"You're really wondering how I can afford them." Giles mirrored her smile.

She blushed. "You're right, but how rude to ask. Being on sabbatical, I can't contribute and it's all for me and my search. Plus, I know you would never accept money from me. It's hard to receive so much."

"Exquisitely accurate conclusions. My goal is to open your beautiful heart, Jemma, in every way I can. It's all rather selfish, you know. I only benefit. Back to your initial question, though. My parents did very well for themselves and believe my sister and I should not have to wait until their death to be able to enjoy their good fortune. They teach me as I learn how to receive. Now we best get out of this taxi before we owe a fortune in meter fees!" He grinned. "We've places to go, Dr. Gran."

Jemma sat in the lobby while Giles leaned on the registration counter, charming his way into excellent service. She reflected on her whirlwind world of the past weeks and last few days in particular. She found it so easy to be with Giles before she discovered he was wealthy. Now she found herself distancing a little. Jemma's ex-husband was wealthy and her history gave rise to her caution.

Of course, not all wealthy men were Lotharios. Still...

Meeting Giles as a musician, then as a college professor made it easier to love him. He fit her image of her partner, her lover. *He's still trustworthy,* she told her suspicious self. *There's no talk of a shared future. Just stay in the moment. Receiving is purported to be a good thing. It's said to be enlightening. Azure has brought it up several times.* Jemma was reminded of the framed quote by Anaïs Nin in her office at Macalester. "The day came when the risk to remain tight in the bud was more painful than the risk it took to blossom." *I affirm my commitment to be a risk-taker.* Jemma vowed she would believe in Giles's love until proven otherwise. Perhaps trust her heart? Trust her joy? She got up to meet her beautiful man as he walked toward her. "Thank you, Giles." She kissed him on the cheek.

They unpacked, went down to lunch and planned their strategy. "We'll save time by going to the Central Office first. Do you think we should have had Josiah call ahead? Introduce us? A Catholic Services connection?"

Giles held her eyes. "Not with the faux research story, Jemma. You need to be the mom this time. Step Three is you, the grown-up mom, seeking the identity of your son."

They silently stirred their cappuccinos. "What if Illinois is not an open birth records state? We don't know. We rushed here so quickly."

"Did you learn about other states at First Moms?"

"No. But I can call the leader. Or we can simply risk it and go to the Central Office," stated Jemma with her newfound courage. She grabbed the check before Giles, as the waiter laid it down on its silver tray. She left a fifty-dollar bill on the tray and said, "Let's go, my friend. There are risks to be taken." Giles smiled, kissed her cheek, and followed her out as she hailed a taxi.

"We certainly aren't in Kansas anymore," noted Giles as he held the door for her to enter a streamlined glass and metal reception area. Jemma walked over to the receptionist and requested a meeting with someone who knew about adoption records in 1963.

"You know Illinois is a closed adoption records state," the receptionist intoned robotically. "But, I'll see if Ms. Feighan is busy." She rang an extension.

Jemma's face splotched and her eyes shifted. She looked at Giles with the beginnings of anger, rage, fear, despair happening all at once.

"Of course, Lucy. They'll be right down." The robot pointed to her left. "Room 117." She returned to her typing, dismissing them.

"Forget risk-taking," Jemma seethed.

"It's a bump, Jemma. You know that I'm here with you. Let's see what we can find out. It's a process," reminded Giles.

Jemma glowered at him, but saved her breath as she mentally spewed, *Screw the process.*

Lucy Feighan did not look happy. Jemma thought she could show a little compassion or interest. "I apologize for the law. You cannot know how many times I have delivered this sentence. It hurts me every time." Lucy seemed to have adopted the receptionist's robotic style.

Jemma could see Giles willing her to remain calm. He knew her that well.

"I see," substituted Jemma for what could have been a stinging retort, glaring at both of them.

"How did you end up here? One of the self-appointed adoption circles that have been springing up? I've seen more disappointments than success from such groups." *Lucy has to be blood relative to the robot,* thought Jemma.

Lucy riffled though some papers clearly not related to Jemma's quest. "Illinois does not have open birth records nor open adoption records. I would've thought someone in your group knew that."

"I did not deliver in Illinois, Lucy. I delivered in Wichita, Kansas in a Catholic Home for Unwed Mothers. The birth records are open there and I found that my son was sent to Chicago to your agency." Jemma spoke in a quiet and steady voice, while defending herself.

"That is highly irregular, even illegal." Lucy's voice rose. "You should not have that information. Are you sure it was Catholic Services?"

Jemma thought her tongue would soon be shredded from biting it. "Yes, Lucy. It was two days ago."

"Well, I don't see how I can help you."

Jemma knew she was clearly not making any friends in Room 117.

"Jemma, would you be okay if I told Lucy what we know so far? I'm sure she can help us if we can give her a more complete picture." Giles's even tones prevailed.

Jemma had no more energy. "Sure." She returned to her chair.

He began. "Jemma gave birth to her son on June 30 in 1963 in Kansas at the Sisters of Compassion Home. She was told she delivered a girl and was forbidden to hold her, only seeing her from a distance held in a nun's arms." Lucy's eyes widened. "Jemma and I are running a research study for moms who have adopted or adopted out, as well as adoptees. We are based in Seattle. Our personal findings brought us here to find out what we can about Jemma's baby."

Jemma continued the story. "I'm on sabbatical from Macalester College in Minnesota while working in the study. It awakened my own loss. Having discovered the First Moms' Group in Seattle – and yes, it's home-grown but not rabid – I went to Kansas for more information. There at Catholic Services, we discovered I had really given birth to a son. The nuns lied. The Magdalene Laundries were not only in Ireland." Jemma's increasing confidence and composure gave her a strength that seemed to affect Lucy.

"I've heard stories of the Laundries but have never met anyone who lived in one. I thought they were only in Ireland if they even existed at all. The supervisors here told us the whole thing was made up to discredit the Catholic Church. I see they lied to us as well. Jemma, my heart goes out to you."

"Thank you." Jemma felt appeased and continued. "I've dealt with those pain-filled days. I only want my son to know I love him and had no other choice. Could you put a letter in his file to let him know if he ever checks where he can find me? That I would certainly want to meet him?"

"I cannot put the letter in his file. I cannot give any information concerning his adoption, Jemma." The robot returned.

Giles interrupted. "Lucy, could you at least confirm what the Kansas agency has already told us?" Jemma shot him a look of gratitude.

"I can see if he really ended up here. June 30, when? How do you spell your last name?"

"Gran. G-r-a-n. Jemma. J-e-m-m-a. 1963."

"I'll be back in fifteen minutes. Do you want coffee?" Giles and Jemma politely refused.

Lucy left.

"Good recovery."

"I can be very professional, Giles." Jemma's tone was cool.

Lucy returned in ten minutes. "I can verify that a baby boy was received here on July 12 from The Sisters of Compassion in Wichita."

Jemma's hope sprung up like an opened jack-in-the-box.

"I can only tell you because he was not born in Illinois. Also, because we have absolutely no more information. His file has been, for all intents and purposes, purged. Even the copy of his birth certificate is missing, as are his adoption papers."

"Oh, my God, did he die?" Alarm shot through Jemma and the room.

"No. We would have that listed, although I am not supposed to tell you that either. I've never seen anything like it. One sheet of paper. Baby Boy. His date of arrival. His birth date and place. Your name. I shouldn't give you all this information. I could lose my job and be prosecuted. I'm sorry, Jemma. I need my job to raise my two children."

"No birth certificate copy? Nothing else? No name or family of adoption?" pleaded Jemma.

"If there was, I could tell you nothing. I am only letting you know there is nothing. I don't understand and I cannot ask. Again, my job. The laws." Fear and annoyance began to gather in Lucy's eyes.

"Lucy, I appreciate all you have done for me. You have my word, as a mother, my silence is solid. Thank you." Jemma shook her hand, then patted it.

"And I as well, Lucy. I know you went above and beyond but there are no answers. Have a blessed day." Giles shook her hand as they walked out of the office and found a taxi. Soon they were at the Drake.

Once they were in their room, Jemma's professional stance transformed into tears she couldn't blink away. "Dead. The search is dead. Over. Nowhere else to go. I want to go home, Giles. Not to Seattle yet. I want to go to St. Paul. I want to be in *my* house, with you. It feels so close to here. Can we?"

"Sure, Jemma. We'll rent a car and leave late morning. Why not?" He held her.

"Oh, Giles, we're going to need another hotel in St. Paul. I have a house sitter. We can't stay there. But I just need to see my home again. I want to be with you in my home. I'll ask her to go out for the evening. I need to be home. Right now, I must have a glass of wine and lie down."

CHAPTER THIRTY-SEVEN
TOM AND BRUNO: MINNEAPOLIS, 1992

After the patio was cleared of food, Bruno's clipped tone continued. "Tom, you've avoided the topic all day. Now it's evening. I may have misunderstood. What's your reason for coming at this time, on this trip? Maggie said you were ready for my information. Tom, it's now or never. Do you want the follow-up to Suzanne's murder? The cult? Its influence and leaders? I appreciate what you found out. It's not a closed case, Tom. It's cold, but still alive. What's your answer?"

Tom's Adam's apple moved up and down slowly, as did his eyes. He stared out to the lake, quiet now in the evening. Bruno waited, his eyes not leaving Tom's. Tom sat up straighter, took a deep breath, jutted his chin, and nodded. "Okay, tell me."

Bruno sipped his bourbon. "It's like this, Tom. You came here with your infant son four days after Suzanne's murder. You became Tom and Derek. Paul and Aron disappeared completely. You told me everything you could remember: the four men, the parchment that ended with a threat to your son. You asked that I pursue every avenue, whatever I needed to do, to find justice for Suzanne's murder, with one prohibition. I was never to tell you anything about it until you asked. Do you remember any of that?"

Tom shook his head. "Nothing except the don't tell me part. Everything else is a blur. Don't worry about repeating."

"Well then, here it is. I couldn't lead the case because of the family connection, but I could be part of the team. The team would find out about the four men and determine if there was a cult, if they killed Suzanne, and bring the murderers to trial. All we knew was the Rev. Schmidts, the deacons, and Smotelyville. Easy-peasy, right? Wrong. We got nada for over ten years. Every smooth-talking effort to 'help' us was a red herring." Bruno grimaced, swallowed, and put the glass down.

"The younger Rev. Schmidt wasn't helpful at all. He was in and out of mental hospitals after Suzanne died. The older Rev. Schmidt, Adolf, was tight as a drum. Bernice Schmidt, Oscar's wife, could tell us nothing. The deacons met every Thursday night, come rain or shine.

"She reported a terrifying incident one Thursday night. Bernice could get no details from Suzanne, who saw something horrible. Whatever happened sent Suzanne to Rosemont for her high school years to protect her from any recurrence. But we still had no details we could use. Bernice told us about her daughter severing all ties at graduation, never bringing up the meetings, her father, the church, or Smotelyville. Are you with me, Tom? I know you know most of this part, but it's important to start at the beginning for this one."

"Yes, it all matches with what Bernice and the Mother Superior told me. But..."

"Hold on, Tom. I'll get your story later and answer what I can. Let me continue."

"Of course," submitted Tom. "I'm listening."

"We knew one of our men was a Maharba member before we hired him, planning someday he could be of use to us. His name was Reinholdt; he was one of the deacons who seemed less loyal. He worked with us as a mole and was excellent with details, the sacrifices of animals, the secrecy, the whole set-up of the organization. It goes back many generations to Germany, always with a Rev. Schmidt in charge. Talk about the sins of the fathers."

Tom blinked, startled, and widened his eyes. *My sins...*

Bruno continued. "Reinholdt purported to know nothing about Suzanne's death. He was reluctant, but our thinly-veiled options were too enticing. He gave us the names of the five lead men. One was the older Rev. Adolf Schmidt, grandfather to Suzanne, who is still alive. Reinholdt named the four men who carried her out and told us Martin was the new leader, Grand Kapitan, as they call him. Rev. Oscar Schmidt was too weak, too mentally ill to carry on the Schmidt name as leader. He also told us about Martin's son, who was a key man in their organization: young and committed to the cult, growing it, and expanding it. His name is Hans Peter."

Tom knew everyone at the table could hear his stomach roiling. "Peter?" he asked incredulously as sweat broke out on his forehead. His denial about Peter was shattering like a tossed crystal champagne flute.

"He went by Peter, after moving to Montana. He was the Crown Prince and Reinholdt hated him, called him a chameleon, a cold snake in the grass. It was quite an indictment coming from one of their deacons. Reinholdt told us he knew who the murderer was and would testify when the man was charged. The day we were to come in, arrest them, and get the records was a Thursday night in May of 1975. When we arrived, the church had been burned to the ground, nothing left but scorched rocks and smoke still coming out of the charred remains. The four men and the elder Schmidt? Gone. The younger, Oscar, had previously moved to an adjoining town. We had no license plates, no anything. Names, yes. Grounds? No. Reinholdt was gone as well, after feeding them everything, it appeared. He happened to be in a fatal accident that month, although I doubt that was a coincidence. We lost our opportunity and our witness, not to mention they were operating out of two locations. The case was left to go cold."

"Are they dead? The others? Peter?" Tom's voice quavered, knowing it was his last stab at denial.

"It certainly doesn't seem they are dead. They successfully stay under the radar in four different cities, quadrants, as they call them. It's a very clean operation. None of the men even have a driving ticket, and certainly no reported murders. As for their rituals, nothing is illegal."

"Peter's still in Montana?" Tom asked with what looked like hope in his eyes.

Bruno took a deep breath. "No, Tom. Wake up! Peter is in Seattle. He is extremely well-schooled in cults, organizations, and computers. He is known to be educated and very charismatic."

Tom stood up. "I'm sick. I have to get Derek. I know it's the same Peter who's hooked my son. I've got to go to Seattle, now."

"Hold on, Tom. Sit down. Keep listening. I have some ideas."

Tom sat down, face flushed, tremors in his hands, and with a new look in his eyes. Bruno thought it looked like determination.

"We're going to get this group, Tom, the cult who murdered Suzanne. We'll at least find the man who murdered her. It depends on you."

"On me?" Tom's voice rose in disbelief and anger. "The FBI has had information for thirty years! And the murderers are still free? The Crown Prince is luring my son into the cult that killed his mother! What if he wants to kill Derek? I'm supposed to do something *now* where you failed? Why is it years later and they are still free and clean? How could it depend on me?"

"Funds, Tom. Budget cuts. When the 1975 mission failed, the people above me delegated the case to the back burner. They had bigger fish to fry. It wasn't closed, but no money and no manpower would go to it. I've kept following Peter on my own. I'm not a great hacker but do know how to obtain computer information for my benefit. If I can get all the information, develop a plan, and be certain, I think I can get a small amount of funding to find and charge the murderer. I don't think we can get all four for murder, but maybe the one if we could find proof. Can we disband the cult? Don't count on that. No reason. Freedom of religion, you know." Bruno grimaced.

"You see, Tom, cults weren't that important in the seventies and eighties or even now. Most cults don't murder like this one. They don't do anything illegal. You may know there's a Church of Satan - all legal and not tax-exempt by their choice. The reason I bring it up is that Peter joined with and literally bought into the Church. He lives by its beliefs, so he has more power than just in Maharba, the

Smotelyville cult. Peter studied cults for seven years in Montana. Then he studied with Anton LaVey, the founder of the Church of Satan, for seven more years in San Francisco before he moved to Seattle. Maharba may be a small part of Peter's activities. But, to you and me, it is the important part."

Tom put his head in his hands, elbows on the table and shook his head. "Church of Satan. An official church. Do they worship Satan? My God."

"No, Tom, they are mainly atheists who believe in pride, freedom, individualism, fame, and wealth. One of their goals is material gains at whatever cost. They know the right people: those with power and lots of money, Tom. Deceit and manipulation are the tools of their trade. You see, Tom, there is no wrong. There is only gain." Bruno combed his hair back with his fingers. "Their organization and far-reaching influence are incredible: government agencies, politics, newspapers, Hollywood. But, enough on that."

"I'm lost and overwhelmed. I have to get to Derek. Why does Peter want my son?" The life had gone out of Tom. Bruno saw a dejected, scared father.

"Think about it, Tom. To have the son of the mother they murdered join Maharba? What a coup for them. I didn't know Peter had found Derek. Tom, they won't hurt him. They want him to join their cause. We'll get him out and hopefully the FBI will give us some resources to close the case. We need to get the facts on Suzanne's murderers and their activities. Are there more murders? What about the mole? Tonight, we'll make a plan. You and I will work together to save Derek and discover what we can about Suzanne's death. You hear me, Tom? Derek'll be okay." He pressed his hand on Tom's forearm.

"Okay... What about his mind? He's one of the most open-minded people I know. It's how we raised him. Now I regret it. Despite his three decades of living, he is naive and confused. He walked out of my life two weeks ago after he told me about the Love group and a sub-group, which scares me now more than ever. He mentioned Peter. What if he's mentally trapped?"

Bruno interrupted. "We're going to stop it as soon as possible. Derek will have to lead us to Peter. Peter leads us to Maharba. Justice could prevail."

"Bruno, what if, once again, he walks away from me?"

"Then Tom, you'll think of something to make him see the truth that they killed his mother. Only he can do something about it."

Tom stared at the dark lake, the flickering lights, the lake that gave Tom what healing he could get for eight weeks after the murder. Tom spoke to no one in particular, "I remember baby Aron smiling at the dancing bears, totally trusting his father who lied to him and continued to do so. No more. Okay, Bruno. What's the plan? I'm leaving early tomorrow morning. I'm going to Derek with the truth: his truth, my truth, all of it." He stood up. "Are you sure they are after Derek's life and not his death?"

Bruno stood up and looked Tom in the eye. "I'm pretty sure, Tom. That's all I have."

CHAPTER THIRTY-EIGHT
DEREK AND TOM: SEATTLE, 1992

Tom sped west while speaking into a tape recorder. At first, he felt a little foolish, but got over it quickly as his thoughts rushed in.

Maggie was concerned about my driving while I'm so shocked, angry, afraid, and unsure of what's next for us. She gave me this tape recorder when I told her I do my best thinking while driving. She wanted me not to be distracted and disturbed about forgetting important details. So here we are, tape recorder and me. Bless Maggie. Of course, I'm not going to talk the whole two days, but I appreciate her concern. Bruno, too. He does tell it like it is, in spite of my denial and protests. Decades later, he tells.

Now it's nearing the end of 1992. Can't end too soon! Yet I have some time to finish. Forever ago, I drove the same route with my son Derek, less than three months old. How did I do it? Most of it is foggy in my mind. Both of us grieving for my wife and his mommy. They say babies adopted out have no emotional memory of their birth mom and her absence. I don't for one second believe 'they.' Derek experienced it twice through his birth mom and Suzanne; sometimes he was inconsolable, unlike his sisters. He often stared in his crib at the dancing bears with no expression. To me it was a mournful stare. Terese said maybe yes, maybe no. Maybe he was picking up my sadness. I don't think so. He did seem to love Terese the minute she first held him. How could I really know this? Truth or wishful thinking? Her love could not take away all his sadness, nor could mine. These are all my thoughts. They may not be true.

My job now is one of - no, it's the hardest job of my life. I have to confess to Derek every lie I ever told him. Every one. I feel like I have to stop the car to throw up. Or I may have to swerve into an oncoming semi. End it. Of course, I won't. But I cannot take the easy way out anymore because it isn't easy for those I love. I've loved Derek the longest of all of them. How do I tell him I'm not his birth father and that I don't know who his biological parents are? No one knew then. There's a ping pong game in my brain between, "Yes. I did the right thing," and, "No. I screwed up totally." I loved him. I damaged him. I love him. I lie to him. It's going to be okay.

It's totally chaos. Put music on. Stop talking. The back and forth of everything never stops.

I'm on the road again and slept later than I wanted to. Terese said not to set the alarm. I will be getting in very late tonight unless I stop to sleep closer to home. I still don't know if I am going straightaway to Seattle or home to Terese. She said not to decide yet. The answer will come to me. To be honest, I can't wait to hold Terese, to be in her arms and feel whole again.

Will a wife do that for Derek, too? I so want that for him. He can't keep long-term relationships. Because of the past? Losing two mommies? Because of my lies? What are they? What do I have to tell him?

One: I'm not his birth father.

Two: Suzanne or what's her name on the fake birth certificate? Elizabeth? She's not his birth mom. Okay. Get through that.

Three: The new identities. "What?!" he's going to ask. "You're joking. Although it doesn't feel very funny. Identities?"

Four: There's more. I can't tell him everything at once! The cult. The murder. The threat.

Our flight. Of course, start there. Bruno's plan. Derek's involvement.

Five: My journey back East. One of the men who killed his mother has a son named Peter Gehman who wants Derek to join the cult in order to complete the ugly circle planned over decades. That Unconditional Love, Inc. is a joke, a front. That the sub-group is dangerous and it's the very cult that killed his mom. That cults do exist, and thrive, and look like regular people.

There's even an official church.

Six: The biggie. He has to lead the FBI to Peter's cult.

The car swerved. Horns blared. One a semi. Tom stopped on the berm.

How can I save Derek if I can't even save myself? Right here, with cars and trucks causing my car to tremble, I make the biggest resolution of my life, to tell all. Tom took a deep breath, started the car, and continued his journey to Seattle, of course.

T om counted on Terese calling ahead. He beeped under Derek's apartment and turned off the ignition. Derek charged out of the front door in pajama bottoms, eyes like lightning and hair askew. "Dad! Get out of the car!" He did not need to say it as Tom already embraced his son with eyes dripping all over Derek's t-shirt. "Dad, why are you crying? I left you with so much anger. I was confused. I'm sorry. I missed you. I love you."

"Oh, Derek. I love you too. More than you will ever know. Ever, ever know."

"C'mon in." He grabbed Tom's backpack. "What's up? How was the trip? Why did you go? Why did you come here before Terese? I'm sorry I couldn't get off work today. I'm nearing the end of my vacation days and need to leave soon again. But I don't need to go in until three today. I'll tell you all about my last few weeks. And more! And listen to your story."

They sat on Derek's small balcony, watching the ferries and houseboats in Elliott Bay. The sun warmed them enough to wear sweatshirts. Tom smiled. "You look happy, Derek." His unspoken thoughts: *You are alive. Maybe Bruno is right. They don't want to kill you. You are so happy. I'm going to ruin it all.*

"I am, Dad. Happier than I have ever been. I've discovered something very deep and hidden about myself. Dad, I'm gay. And I'm so at peace, more than ever before!"

Tom's eyes transform to saucers. "Gay? Gay. Okay. Gay."

Derek laughed. "Some people live in that closet longer than others, not knowing there's a new and better world. All I had to do was see the door, turn its handle, and walk out. The hole in me is now Whole. A W in front of the H. Nothing missing." He looked off to the distant islands.

"Are you okay with it, Dad?" implored Derek, seeing Tom's eyes wide as saucers.

"Of course, Derek. You must imagine my shock. Or surprise. I didn't know, although it kind of makes sense given the women in your life not working out and your love of dancing." He stopped abruptly. "Oh, my God. I'm so stupid. You'll have to tell me if I am stereotyping. I mean, I know all male dancers are not gay." He stumbled and stopped, shaking his head.

Derek laughed again. "Ease up, Dad. It's all okay. I'm okay. You're okay. Right? So that's the first news. We can talk about it more later. But listen."

"I'm listening." Tom had never seen his son so animated. He was anxiety-free and laughing from his belly. *Damn. And I'm going to ruin it.* He knew he would.

Derek stopped laughing. "What's wrong?" Parentheses formed between his eyebrows.

"What happened?"

"Nothing. I'm sorry. Nothing's wrong at all. I love to see your joy. Really...I don't know. We'll talk about it later. I'm happy to see you. To see you so happy! Honest."

Tom's words did not match his expression, but Derek let it go. "Hold on. I forgot. I have some pastries to go with our coffee. I'll get them. More coffee?"

"Sure. More coffee. It's been a long three days. A longer ten days!"

"I want to hear all about your trip. Why so sudden? Where'd you go?" His voice faded as he went out to the kitchen. "God, I hope the B&O never closes," mumbled Derek as he ate a raspberry scone. "Isn't this the best?" Without waiting for a response, he went on, "I know you remember the Love group I was going to," he smiled, "because you weren't so happy with it as I recall." Derek's mouth twitched.

"I remember. ULI? And a sub-group was next? You're right. It struck me wrong. Actually, it was the reason for my trip. Derek, I have so much to tell you."

Derek continued eating. "That's great, Dad. I want to hear all about it. But first, I want you to hear my story and a big source of my joy. I'm in love, Dad, SO in love!"

Please, not with a cult member. Tom almost spoke out loud but caught himself.

"His name is Peter. I mentioned him before as the leader of Unconditional Love, Inc. He's also a researcher for the Adoption Project I'm in."

"Peter. Adoption Project?" Tom blinked.

"Dad, I told you about it. At the university. Because I am half-adopted."

"Half." Tom muted the rest of his thoughts.

"Sure, by Terese. I joined the Project thinking it would solve some of my confusion and anxiety. It didn't, but meeting Peter sure did. I want you to meet him, even though this week is really busy. The Adoption Project is not so important. But Peter. Me. Special groups. Meetings. Rituals."

"Are you in love with Peter as leader? Or..."

"Oh, yes! As my lover. He's beautiful, smart, funny, highly educated, wealthy, mature. He's older than me, but younger than you." Derek smiled as his eyes drifted to the Sound.

It's a miracle I continue to sit here, thought Tom. *My heart is going to stop; my insides are going to explode from absolutely every opening possible.* "Derek, Peter is one of the things we must talk about."

"Should I call and see if he can stop over?" sparkled Derek.

"No, Derek, that's fine. Later. There's just so much you need to know." *Damn Peter. Derek believes his first lover is real. He could never comprehend it's a lie to get him to join the cult. I have to be careful.* Tom realized he was tipping toward more concern about being in the cult than Derek being murdered by the cult. Trust Bruno?

"Real quick, Dad. I told you I was invited to a sub-group. If I tell you its name, will you double, triple, promise to tell no one? Not even Terese?" Tom nodded, waiting to hear Maharba.

Derek whispered, "Maharba. It's centuries old and began in Germany in medieval times. It's even connected with a church and ministers."

Tom tried to look interested and nonjudgmental as his hope fragmented into the smallest of pieces. He feared it was irreparable. "Tell me more. Have you gone to any of their meetings?"

"Oh, yes. I was invited to a ritual called The Seven Windings. It didn't turn out so well, but it was an out-of-this-world trip. No drugs, but a real trip. I went places in my mind I have never been. My head was in so much pain that I fainted."

"Derek! Are you okay?!" That fear for Derek's life sprang up again.

"Oh sure, Dad. Peter and Mr. K helped me out. Also, I've been invited to join Maharba. Tomorrow night I fly with Peter to Sedona. It's my initiation. All on my own, Dad. My life is falling into place all on my own."

Tom got up to hug Derek. "It certainly is, son. It certainly is."

CHAPTER THIRTY-NINE
TOM AND DEREK: SEATTLE, 1992

Tom returned from the bathroom, sat on the balcony chair, and began nervously, "What time do you need to be at work?"

"Three, Dad. We've plenty of time. I really want to hear your story. You're sure you don't want to meet Peter today?"

"Derek, I'm positive. Perhaps you may not want to meet him today either, after I tell you what I learned on my trip back East."

His son's eyes narrowed. Their intensity increased. "Are you upset he's my lover? That I'm gay?"

"You know I'm fine with you being gay! Honest. You know me well enough to know that. My thoughts about Peter and Maharba are a completely separate issue."

"Go ahead then. I'm listening. But just to let you know, I'm pretty committed to both." He stood up, leaned against the balcony railing, and crossed his arms.

"Is there more coffee? Another pastry?" Tom needed time for more quick thinking. *What do I reveal? What do I hold back? How can I get the Bruno plan going? I have to keep remembering they want Derek alive to lead, not dead. Too bad God died with my parents, or I would ask him for help.*

Tom got up to take the pastry plate and Derek put the insulated mugs on the small table. He sat down and crossed his arms again, then his legs.

Triage, thought Tom. *The cult information is most important. Telling him the dangers of the cult and the murder are directly related to Derek's life. The murder is the most important at this moment.* "I went on my trip to discover more about your mother's death."

"Mother? Mom? Terese dead? What are you talking about?" Puzzlement led to fear. He stood up.

Tom stared at him, incredulously. How old was this son of his?

Derek sat back down, a little embarrassed. "Oh, my birth mother. I'm sorry. She's really out of my mind. I used to ask about her, but we just stopped talking about her. I was so young and remember nothing you told me. She died shortly after I was born, right? Complications?" He reaffirmed before crossing his arms once again.

"Yes, your birth mother." Tom's heart winced at the continuing lie. "Derek, she didn't die from birth complications. She was murdered."

"Dad!" Derek rapidly stood up, eyes wide. "Murdered. By whom? How? Why? Is he in prison? I don't get it." Sadness, shock, and confusion filled his eyes. Tom thought his son was feeling the loss of long ago, yet how could he know? It was possible Derek didn't know what he was feeling. Certainly, Tom could not begin to know.

"I know. It took me a long time to get it also. I found her. You were asleep in your crib."

"How do you know she was murdered? Maybe she died in her sleep." His voice got louder. His accusing eyes wouldn't leave Tom's. "Why didn't you tell me? I'm nearly thirty, hardly a kid anymore. You never told me."

Tom could hear disbelief, anger, and disappointment. "I kept this from you because the murderers left a note on her blood-drained body." Tom stopped, his throat closing. He cleared it, "They told me to tell no one, especially not the police, or your life would be taken next."

Derek moved to the corner of the balcony and looked to the Sound. He turned around and met Tom's eyes. "Did you ever find out who wrote the note? Who killed her? Why? Is that what your trip was about? You have to tell me." He held the rolled cuffs of his sweatshirt to his eyes. He pushed his hair back and said more loudly, "I need to know, Dad. She was my mother." He glared at Tom.

Tom stood up and leaned against the balcony railing stating, "I know, I know, she was your mother." *Liar! Liar!* "You need to keep this between us." He acknowledged Derek's imperceptible nod. *Please, please, join the dots...* "Your mother..."

"Elizabeth."

"Yes." His mind shouted, *No! Suzanne!* "Elizabeth was the daughter of a small-town minister in Indiana who was in a cult that demanded her life upon the birth of her first child. They said she would have a son on her twenty-fourth birthday."

"Me."

"Yes, you. You're still not to blame for her death." Derek nodded. "The day after you came home from the hospital..." *The last time I lie!*

"I went out for thirty minutes to get a new mommy gift. You were asleep in your room, and she was resting on our bed. I came home, went upstairs, and saw her body and the note. I ran to your room to see that you were okay and closed your door. I ripped the note into tiny pieces and flushed it down the toilet. Soon, four men in black suits came up the stairs. They never went to your room. I suspect they had already looked at you. I was terrified. They said nothing, looked down the entire time, put her body on a stretcher, carried her into a van, and drove away. I ran to your room again and saw you were still asleep and safe under the dancing bears." Tom's voice trailed off.

"I remember them. The bears. But, Dad. Really? Never caught? Did you see their faces? Couldn't you identify them?"

"No to your last two questions. I was in shock and they kept their faces away. They were only there for a few minutes. I'm sorry, Derek, to be telling you now. I realized on my trip I had to tell you everything. The FBI is re-opening the case."

"The FBI? Re-opening? Now?"

"They worked on it for twelve years and came to a standstill. The discoveries on my trip sparked their interest once again. "

"I don't understand. They came all the way to Minneapolis to murder her? That's why we moved to Portland?"

The color rose in Tom's face. "You were born in Chicago. Then we, you and I, fled to my cousins' in Minneapolis to get my thoughts, actually my life and yours together. My feelings. My fears. Yes, then get as far away as possible. Portland."

"I thought my birth certificate said Minneapolis." Derek shook his head.

"It does. I'll explain that later. There's more."

Derek exhaled. "Go ahead." He sat down and searched his coffee mug.

"My cousin is Maggie. Her husband is Bruno. He's in the FBI. I told him I wanted to know nothing until I asked because I feared for your life. That was thirty years ago."

"That's the reason for your trip. You asked. Dad. I can't really hear any more of my mother being murdered the day after we came home from the hospital. I mean she was my mother! She gave birth to me!"

"I hate telling you, Derek. But I am fearing for your life again. You have to know one more thing." Tom saw Derek's guard go up. He saw his son was protected by shock. "Su - Elizabeth, your mother, was murdered by four members of the cult from her father's church. Her father was fourth or fifth generation. All were ministers. It began in Germany." Tom waited for the penny to drop.

Derek's eyebrows shot up. His eyes widened, then glazed. He caught himself. "Probably a common denominator for groups. Germany. European countries. Of course." He looked out to the Sound.

"The name of the cult was Maharba."

Derek's guarded attention returned to cool composure. "That's pretty far-fetched, Dad. It's not the same as my group, Peter's group. I know I promised not to tell anyone, but I really want to check it out with Peter. I'm getting initiated tomorrow night in Sedona. It's not the same group that killed my mother. Maharba is not a group like you are talking about. It's especially not a cult. It does not kill."

Silence. *Do I continue to speak to a strongly defended brick wall?* Tom saw the alliance with Peter was far too strong to influence Derek at this point. *I have to* trust Bruno is right. Besides, I can't ground him. I can't undo the secrets of thirty years. I have to dampen my fear.

"Sure, Derek, check it out with Peter. I'd rest easier if I knew it wasn't." *Sedona could be the lead Bruno is looking for, even though twenty-four hours is not enough time now. It's a start. Derek has to see it on his own. I'll bring Bruno up to speed and we'll figure out something. A plan. Any plan.*

Derek was unruffled in his response. "Okay, I appreciate the information. You obviously have no idea what hearing that my mother was murdered does to me. I'll get some answers. Peter will help me. We'll find my mother's killers. Maybe Peter knows about this old cult who has our same name."

Tom ignored the use of "our" and said, "That's a good plan, Derek. Will you get back to me as soon as you know? The next morning? Oh, and for my comfort, take my credit card just in case you need to fly out earlier or later or whatever. I am sickened to tell you all of this."

Derek reluctantly put the plastic card into his wallet. "Okay." He hesitated, then asked, "Can you at least wish me well in my initiation? Especially after dropping a murder bombshell on the eve of my sacred path?"

No, I can't. I can't wish you well as you enter the cult that killed Suzanne.

"Sure. May you find your truth and meaning in life through your spiritual path." Tom hugged him fiercely.

"Never forget I love you." He walked out.

Soon, Tom stopped for gas and phoned Bruno. "Bruno. I told him about the murder, not the adoption. He reacted more deeply than I would have thought. I know it's his mother! Consequently, he's looking to Peter to help him, not me. You are sure Maharba isn't going to kill him? He's going to his initiation in Sedona with Peter tonight. The initiation is tomorrow. You're sure? Yes. I told him about the FBI, so Peter will know. Are you sure it will bring them out? Yes. I'll call you Wednesday morning when I hear from him. Why can't we go tonight? Okay. More information. Good-bye, Bruno."

Tom got in the car and drove to Terese. He reflected on his call with Bruno. *How could Bruno be so certain Maharba was not after Derek's life? To be another sacrifice? A repeat of Suzanne?* His blood ran cold. He knew and trusted Bruno. He remembered the trust he once had in the God of his youth before his parents were killed.

CHAPTER FORTY
JEMMA AND AZURE: SEATTLE, 1992

zure's office was cozy in contrast to the cold rain and the dwindling daylight outside. The fireplace was on and she could hear the music from the waiting room. Azure opened the waiting room door, looking forward to hearing from her next client. "Come in, Jemma."

Jemma settled into her purple chair and managed something between a smile and a grimace. "Hello, Azure." She took a deep breath. "To cut to the chase...it's over. Uncle. Finis. Done. Accepted."

"Well, that certainly is cutting to the chase. Stop for two minutes?" The chime toned. Azure began, "What's over? Surrendered to what? Accepted what? What are you done with?" The puzzlement on Azure's face underlined her words.

"I gave birth to a son and, for some reason, his birth records are completely gone. I suppose knowing and becoming okay with not finding out is just what's meant to be. I don't know if I'm even upset anymore. I'm so tired of being sad. That's what I've accepted in addition to knowing that one of my life missions is unsuccessful but done. It's a loss of hope but maybe a gain of energy."

Azure was silent and alert. "Go on."

"As crazy as it sounds, I was so attached to my perceived daughter that now I find it easier to accept her death. She was so alive in my imagination. I watched her grow in my lifelong story, which wasn't anywhere near true or real. She isn't real either."

"She was real to you, for a long time." Silence. "You found out you gave birth to a son. The nuns lied. I'm angry you were deceived and that you had to create the fantasy you now are grieving. It was all so wrong. Deception always is."

"The son? My son? I know nothing about him. I searched as much as I could. Wichita. Chicago. All dead ends. No story."

"Really? Historically or in the future?"

Jemma continued, "Historically and in the future. There will be no story ever for the baby boy. He has an empty file; there's no information. It was so painful during and after her story that I am vowing not to do it again. I want to live my own life - not hers, not his. She never existed." She stopped.

"Wait. He did or does exist. Here's his story in one sentence: 'He was given to a good family, has no hang-ups, and loves his life and his genes.' I gave him life, a gift that has no price. That's my story for now." Her face tensed.

Azure half-smiled and lifted one eyebrow, knowing they would pick the story up later. Set jaws were set jaws. "Actually, it ends a little like a fairy tale: 'and he lived happily ever after.' Paradoxical." *One more try at therapy.*

"Azure, I'm forty-five and have lived long enough and read way too many great novels to recognize that Walt Disney wrote stories about stories. There are no happily-ever-afters. I'm in a 'happily right now.' That's all I know." Jemma shook her head in mock scolding.

"I imagine it's a deep relief to put down a burden you have carried for much of your life. I applaud your commitment to discover and resolve it." She was certain Jemma was finished with discussing the unknown child for today. "Wasn't there another journey on the table? Your travel companion? Giles?"

Jemma blushed. "My travel companion." She smiled. "Yes. He was there with me the whole time. I wouldn't have done it without him. I'm learning to trust him. It's a huge challenge. There haven't been people in my life I could trust, with whom I could let go and be understood, supported, and seen as wonderful." She looked down as she spoke more quietly. "I want a real relationship, not just an infatuation." She switched her position, sat on her hands, and looked up.

Azure sat up straighter, glanced at the fireplace's glow, and thought of Charles. "Nothing's wrong with infatuation, Jemma. It's a powerful beginning for a relationship. It cements other positive factors into a base for a good connection. The infatuated feelings can continue and reappear throughout the love. They can last for years. Of course, they will be joined by many other feelings and thoughts, not excluding thoughts of murder." Her eyes twinkled and she smiled. "If you can see him somewhat realistically early on, if you can truly be more of yourself than not, and celebrate the infatuation, I foresee a good relationship. This is, of course, providing you both have an open mind and are honest with your inner selves and each other in the moment, as opposed to weeks later."

Jemma nodded thoughtfully. "That's a perfect topic for tonight's dinner, along with one other thing. I have to talk to Giles about Peter. I've been putting it off. It's a complicated discussion for me." She blushed again.

"When I think of Peter, his Love group, and the vulnerable Project subjects, I feel sick, especially after I noticed he has put more flyers around the Social Work Research area. They're now meeting twice a week. I've heard several students talking it up with excited tones and bedazzled eyes." She looked out the window for a moment at the descending night. "Azure, it's really disturbing."

"It's an excellent idea to talk with Giles. It is his research project so he has the means to investigate. But, what's the complication?" She asked, knowing the answer.

"Azure. You know the complication. My date with Peter. I actually went out with the creep. I slept with him!"

"You didn't know he was a creep at the time, as I recall. Are you going to share everything with Giles?"

"Not if I can help it. It was one of my worst decisions ever." Jemma's face was one of complete despair.

"I agree. Very difficult. Do you want to say more?"

"No. It's gross, embarrassing, and shameful." She looked down, sighed, got up, and took out her calendar. "I can't make it two weeks; would next Wednesday be okay?"

Azure checked her book. "It'll have to be in the evening. Does seven work for you?"

"Perfect. Thank you." Jemma closed the door quietly.

zure felt time was of the essence, although she could not state why. She dialed and put the phone on speaker when he answered. "Hello, Charles. Do you have a minute?"

"For you? Always. How are you?"

"Charles. It's about Peter. Did you find more?" She knew he was smiling. "It's urgent."

"Actually, Giles just left my office and I was about to call. We did a more detailed background check. Your concern is right on. He's moved from Indiana to Montana to San Francisco to Seattle. He told us he was born in California and had been teaching computer science at UCLA. He lied about his Ph.D. and doesn't even have a Master's degree. The deception is intolerable. Giles is as adamant as I am that he needs to be confronted and fired. We're going to the next Wednesday night ULI meeting because we want to see him in action. He'll be fired the next morning."

"I'm so glad to hear that. But can't you do it immediately?"

"I apologize for not getting on this sooner, Azure. And no, for various reasons, we have to do this right. Human Resources will be on my back if I don't. Your intuition was accurate. Do you want to come with us to the meeting?"

"No, Charles. I've no interest in his performance."

Silence. Charles questioned softly, "Dinner? Tonight?"

"Sure. After your nursing home visit? I don't want to cut into her time. You know that."

"Of course, I do. You know I have always appreciated your understanding about my marriage. It's one of myriad reasons why I love you."

"I'll be ready at seven. Can you pick me up?"

"With pleasure…"

They hung up wistfully, at the same time.

CHAPTER FORTY-ONE
BERNICE: CHICAGO, 1992

Bernice drove back down the familiar driveway that circled Rosemont School for Girls, knowing it would be the last time. Michael was gone. She intended to come to terms with Michael, although she knew those terms would be bitter and angry. Still, Bernice had looked forward to her mission.

Upon learning from a young novice at Rosemont that the retired Mother Superior had suffered a severe stroke in the past few weeks, Bernice replied with an "Oh, no!" suspecting it was mistaken for compassion by the young nun. In reality, Bernice was deeply disappointed.

"You can see her though, at the St. Joseph Home. She's not responsive, although the Little Sisters of the Poor are excellent caregivers, even healers." The eyes of the novice glowed in admiration of the Mother Superior. "Maybe she'll respond to you," she added hopefully.

"Well, I wouldn't count on that, but I am a former student and friend." *Former friend for certain, but I don't need to say that.* "Are there visiting hours? It's not too far from here, correct?" Bernice softened to allow a slight smile for the energetic young nun. It had nothing to do with her.

"They have twenty-four-hour visiting. You know, in that part of the home, visitors aren't common. Sister Michael is so highly respected, though, she may have more visitors. Just drive over and walk in. It's not more than twenty minutes from here. I know the Mother Superior will appreciate seeing you."

Bernice drove into the city, parked the car, and took a few minutes to gather her thoughts. She sat on the iron bench outside of the St. Joseph Home and wondered how long the sun would continue to shine, opposing her mood of disappointment mixed with increasing anger. *So, this is what you've come to, Michael. The nursing home. Comatose.*

She thought of what the young nun had said about Sister Michael appreciating the visit. *Not really, dear novice. I very much doubt she will appreciate my visit. What an appalling turn of events! I get it together and she's not there to tell. Well, her body's still here. Let's go in, get it all out, and perhaps get the closure I need.*

The Sister at the front desk was delighted Michael had a visitor. She walked Bernice down the long side hallway to a corner room, door opened to streaming sunlight. "She hasn't opened her eyes since the stroke. It was very bad and complicated by a fall. We do our best to keep her comfortable," whispered the nun. "Stay as long as you want; I won't disturb you. Would you like coffee or tea?"

"No, thank you. Perhaps later. But I do need privacy." She dismissed the nun. The door closed and Bernice stared at the inert figure in the bed. Several minutes passed. "Michael. It's Bernice." There was no movement or no change in breathing.

"I have a few things to say and I will say them. I'm saying them for me. If you can hear, then for both of us: but, mainly, for me. Before you get all grateful and clergy-phony, I'm not here to ask for, nor give, anything anywhere near forgiveness. You won't receive those gifts from me. First, you've never asked for forgiveness. Second, from what I can see, you'll never have that chance. Third, I'm here to begin to forgive myself for trusting you with my daughter and for being blind to most everything."

Bernice paced a few times and brought the visitor's chair closer to the bed. She draped her coat over the back and sat down, focused on Michael. The fine lines in her face were smoothed out in a restful pose that angered Bernice, whose breathing was rapidly increasing. She watched the still nun while her memories ignited emotions with gathering force and fire.

"Michael. We met when you came to Rosemont as your first calling. You were twenty-three and I was eighteen, a senior. We connected immediately and I felt my heart turn over. I've not since felt that response for anyone else. I don't believe those intense feelings happen in a vacuum. We never acknowledged our feelings with words. We became very close during my last year. I adored you. You gave me special time. On graduation day, you hugged me longer than anyone else. Oh, yes, I watched. We both had tears. Now, as a seasoned woman, I do know there was more, though it was unspoken. I left, became Lutheran, got married to a minister, and had Suzanne two years later.

"I was a perfect pastor's wife with no training and a very empty marriage. It was far more noticeable after Suzanne was born. My husband never attached to her and detached from me. But I had Suzanne and loved, no, love her deeply for fourteen years only. Then I gave her to your keeping, trusting you to keep her safe. Within that time, you discovered raw, tragic events in her life. Her father was involved in a cult and Suzanne had experience with it. You helped Suzanne rip out her life-giving organs while only seventeen, only discussing the hysterectomy with her father, who was never a part of Suzanne's life. He was not even part of my marriage. What else did you discuss with him? How much of the cult did you actually know about? Perhaps even before you met Suzanne? You never told me! A hysterectomy at seventeen? Why, in God's name? Why?"

Bernice's eyes flashed. She got up and walked to the other side of the bed. Her voice became dangerously low as she leaned closer to Michael's ear. "You betrayed me, Michael. And especially Suzanne. You unnamable cursed..." Bernice's tears were hot with impotent rage.

"You cursed power of evil!" The quiet tones were louder than screaming.

Bernice moved to the end of the bed, took a deep breath, and looked for any signs of movement. None. Her anger abated. "What am I doing here?" she asked out loud. "What in God's name am I doing here!" Bernice continued.

"You lie there, for all purposes, dead: deaf, blind, dumb, with your silent conscience holding your lies. You knew a cult was active in my husband's church and in his life. It entered Suzanne's life. For decades you have known. You kept silent. What about your moral fiber, your clerical responsibilities to report suspected evil?

"Even more so, you didn't tell me about my daughter. Maybe I could have saved her, Michael. Maybe I could have done what you couldn't do. If I had only known what you knew about the cult, I would've taken her very far away. I would have called the police. Maybe you were involved in the cult. Is that why you kept your sacred secrets? Why did you purposely and blatantly take my daughter's love from me? You betrayed your God, my daughter unto her death, and me. You... cruel heartless bitch. You'll lie there and you'll die there, with your bloodless heart and stone cold-conscience."

There was still no movement. Bernice was spent. She moved the chair to the window and stared unseeing, at the slowly disappearing sun. Her thoughts were racing. *I needed to say that at another nursing home, to another clergy, to another betrayer. Of my... of our daughter, of me. Of the God he preached. Lutheran God. Catholic God. Do either of them care? Clearly not. They let evil continue unobstructed, and worst of all aided by clergy, deacons, church members. All of them.*

I don't know why I feel a little easier toward Oscar. Maybe because he did try to protect her, to save her. Maybe because he was so broken by his father, so weak, and he was aware of it. Because he began to lose his mind paying the price? Small justice. Not that I forgive him either. Oscar was weak and Michael so strong. Did they both knowingly work with and give into evil? Why? Why?

Her anger spent and exhaustion flooding in, Bernice got up, put on her coat, and moved next to Michael. "Goodbye, Michael. I must go. I must let you go."

She opened the door and walked out of the room, the room of advancing death. Bernice saw a sign a few doors down that read Chapel, with its door ajar. She walked in and sat in one of the dark pews, focusing on Mother Mary who held her child on her lap.

"Did you ever forgive yourself, Mary? For not protecting him from the cross? The betrayers? The power of evil? Did you forgive God? Can I forgive myself for Suzanne's father's sins, all on my watch? Can I forgive that dying nun down the hall for taking my daughter's affection and making Suzanne a keeper of secrets? Could I forgive Michael for betraying me by not telling me about the cult, not reporting it? In some way, leading Suzanne to her murder." Her eyes flooded warm tears, no longer hot.

"I don't know if I forgive myself, but I do hold Oscar and Michael accountable. In my head, I will always hold them accountable. They have already left my heart. Do I hold God accountable? Maybe it's not a 'God thing.' It's the duality concept I struggle to understand. Good and Evil. Light and Dark. I don't understand. But, you know what, Mary? I'm going to work at letting it go. Letting my anger with Michael go will be the challenge. Letting my anger and pity for Oscar go is easier. I know it's a lifetime practice to let of my pain and anger. Over and over and over. But maybe eventually, I can begin to forgive myself."

Bernice wept.

CHAPTER FORTY-TWO
DEREK AND PETER: SEDONA, 1992

Peter and Derek were on the flight to Sedona. Stretching in first class, bourbon in hand, Peter found himself quite satisfied he could provide such luxury for his young lover. He thought the words, *All the better to eat you with, my dear,* and he chuckled. "How's the bourbon, my friend?"

"Excellent, Peter, everything is excellent. Except..." He stopped.

"Except what?" demanded Peter, turning his head and narrowing his eyes, sensing Derek apparently had something difficult he needed to say. "Out with it!"

"I can't believe we're landing at eleven and having the meeting at midnight," parried Derek.

"Believe it. All initiations are at midnight under a full moon. Black robes this time. Silk, not the heavy brown ones like the Seven Windings. Boxers and a t-shirt are all you wear. Better flow for the silk. Back to your hesitancy before..."

"Hold on. Why use all this flight time to go to Sedona? Why the rush? We just did the Seven Windings in Seattle."

Peter was pleased, even though annoyed at the interruption. "I'm glad to see your interest, Derek. Mr. K. flew in from Sedona to be part of the Seven Windings and to meet you to see if you were the right choice for Maharba." He placed his hand on Derek's thigh, always a hot spot.

"And you are. The other eleven men were from the Seattle Quadrant, the Northwest Quadrant. We meet most Thursdays right in Seattle. The other Quadrants are in Sedona, Montpelier, and Selma. My father Martin is the current leader of Maharba and Mr. K. the leader of the Southwest Quadrant. Both live in Sedona. The older former leader also lives in Sedona. So, it became the center of the centers or Quadrants. Because yours is a very significant initiation, three men are coming from each center, and you'll make thirteen. My father will be here tonight. He is very interested in you. Afterwards, you will meet all the men. It's really a big deal, Derek, a great big deal.

"Why the rush? All initiations are under the full moon, which is tonight. It's especially auspicious as we are in the sign of Scorpio, sign of mysticism and the depths. You really don't know how fortunate you are tonight. Even the stars smile upon you!" He tightened his grip on Derek's leg.

"Now, back to your father. What's going on? Is it about seeing your father this morning? How was his trip? What did he say about it?" He massaged Derek's thigh.

"We talked. He found out about another Maharba group back East. Is that a common name for a group? He called that group a cult." Derek waited.

Don't move your hand. Don't react. Peter swallowed more bourbon. "That's odd. I don't know of any other group using our name. But, back East? Who knows? I'll check on it and let you know. Did he say anything else about it?"

"Well, they murdered my mother."

Peter blanched and nearly dropped his drink. He was extremely grateful for the dark plane. "What! Are you okay? How horrible."

"About my mother? I mean, my birth mother. I'm okay. I never knew her, but it feels... well, kind of sad. I'm still digesting it. Actually, it's the biggest shock I've ever had. Her father was a minister and the cult is from his church in Indiana. Do you think there a Maharba in Indiana?"

"I have no idea. I've never been farther east than Montana. I doubt it. Do you know if it's spelled the same as ours?"

"No. That's probably the difference. I just wanted you to know because I'm not good at keeping things from you."

"So, there's nothing else you think I should know?" Peter softly demanded.

"Oh, I almost forgot! His cousin or someone is in the FBI and they're going to look into my mother's murder. They looked into it when it happened but gave up twelve years later. Jeez, Peter, I hope they find my mother's killers. Can you do anything?"

Peter's mind was spinning. *Damn, damn, damn! The FBI again! Why? They must have found new evidence about the murder. It was three decades ago! Tom must know. I've got to send Derek back to the hotel after the initiation and we all have to meet. We need a plan and quickly.*

"I've always appreciated your honesty, Derek. Especially about your mom, your birth mom, being murdered. I feel really badly for you and want to do whatever I can to help you." He began to move his fingers slowly and carefully.

Derek smiled and pulled the blanket over himself.

The landing was perfect. The taxi took them right to the Sedona Center. After spiraling downwards into the basement of the building and punching in security codes, Peter led him to a small anteroom.

"Leave your carryall here. It's safe. Here are our robes. Just wear your boxers and tee. We better hurry, it's close to midnight. Remember, follow me and do what I do. We finish with a small glass of wine. It's doctored so you won't feel any pain in your head like the Seven Windings." *And you won't notice the magic alchemy or the lamb's blood mixed with the wine.*

"I will make a small cut in your little finger for a blood brother thing like you probably did in high school," he tried to be casual.

"I didn't, but I've read about it. You know I'm squeamish about germs. I can do it, though. I trust you. You seem awfully nervous, Peter."

"No. No, not at all. Just excited that my lover is becoming my blood brother. You look good. Follow me."

I follow Peter. The silk robe feels cool and soft. We enter a room very different than the one in Seattle, probably because Sedona is the center, a kind of home office. I quickly scan the room and notice rich leather chairs and sofas along the side of the room with tables and nooks, all clearly shouting expensive and luxurious.

So many candles! All are black with some red ones. Maybe thirteen? I've no time to count. Besides the candlelight, there are dim violet lights wavering over the altar.

It's so beautifully carved. Such deep, rich polished wood. I bet I could see my face in it. What's it called? Black walnut? Mahogany? A shiny white cloth reflects the dancing purple lights. It must be satin. There seems to be something under it. Next to the altar is a matching chest with two doors and a top drawer. On top are many silver goblets and an exquisite pitcher. They look so old.

The men are chanting just like the twelve who were at the Seven Windings. I make thirteen, which seems to be their number. Their deep tones, the flickering candles, and incense, all for my initiation. I'm mesmerized and feel unsteady. I've got to sit down or I'll fall over. Peter must have noticed. He takes my arm, steadies me. I love him so much. The circle opens to welcome us. We walk through the opening to the altar. Peter turns me to face the men, the altar behind us.

They keep chanting and moving in an almost dance, slowly and sensually. Peter holds up his hand and the chanting stops. He speaks in low tones, "I offer my brother, Derek Freborne, as a willing initiate seeking to join Maharba, the only Maharba." The men softly intone, "Maharba. Maharba. Ancient past and now present. Centuries of Maharba." Peter continues in his deep voice, "Derek wishes to follow all of our precepts, rituals, and doctrine. He asks to become our blood brother tonight." I stagger slightly but Peter takes my hand and raises it high.

"Derek offers his blood to join with ours."

He drops my hand and steps to the chest, opens the drawer, and removes a large silver blade with diamonds and rubies embedded in the handle. The bolster must be pure gold. The violet lights enhance its rare beauty. Peter walks back to me, takes my left hand in his, squeezes my small finger, and looks at me with the unspoken question. I nod yes, knowing the blood brother ritual he told me about is beginning. The blade barely touches me. My finger oozes red. Peter cuts his finger and mingles his blood with mine, looking into my eyes with deep love.

We move to each man in turn, joining our blood, becoming one. I forget about the germs. I've never felt such bonding, such joy. Peter gives me all of this. When people speak of coming home, this is what they mean. It is the third time I have this sense of coming home. The first was with Peter at Unconditional Love, Inc., then again at The Seven Windings. I clearly belong with Maharba.

He turns me to face the altar. I need the wine to stop my tremors. Please let that be next! The men are chanting and making odd symbols in the air with their fingers. I see blood on their hands. I don't understand any of their movements, but hear the words, "Abraham, Isaac, Father, Son," over and over with building volume and intensity.

We walk closer to the front and Peter moves me away from the head of the altar. Turning his back to me, I think I see the fabric move slightly. I must be imagining it. The lights are creating illusions.

Peter puts the ornate pitcher on the floor next to him at the head of the altar. He angles the bundle close to the edge, right over the pitcher. My temples begin to pound. What's in the bundle? It's clearly moving. Peter raises the blade. I can't help myself. I grab his arm and move forward without thinking. In my gut I know it's alive. An animal. With my other hand, the one with the blood stains, I rip off the satin sheet.

O, my God, it's a lamb! A small lamb with bound feet, a muzzle on her short snout. Her ears are down, her eyes pleading.

Peter looks at me in shock, then anger. He grabs my arm, raises the blade high in the other. "What the fuck are you doing?" He screams. I push him away and pick up the lamb. "No, Peter, no!" He falls against the altar and screams again, "Derek! Stop!"

The men stop chanting and stare at me, aghast. I run towards the door carrying her. One of the men steps in front of me. Adrenaline flowing, I push him aside and keep going. I hear another shout, "Let him go! Weakling!" I run out of the door, slam it, and hear a man yelling, "He's weak like you! Asshole! You're not my son anymore!"

I don't know what to do as I run to find the room with my clothes and carryall. I put the lamb in the bag, rip off my robe, pull on my jeans and sweatshirt, and zip the carryall halfway. I race outside and down the street. "Find a cab," I tell myself. Two blocks away, finally a cab stops. I quickly close the zipper most of the way and open the back door. "Airport!" I wheeze to the driver.

He looks at me, "Are you okay, son?" Luckily, he must not think I'm a thief. "I'm really okay. I'm afraid I'll miss my plane!" What plane, I ask myself. Lamb on a plane? Then what? I try to think.

It's one-thirty when we arrive at the airport. I give the driver the credit card and ask him to write down the address of where he picked me up on the back of the receipt. He shakes his head and hands me the card and the receipt. I run to the ticket counter knowing there are no flights so late. The woman tells me, "You're in luck, there's a delayed plane to Portland leaving in ten minutes." I take two minutes to call my dad. "Get me at your airport. Six o'clock. In four hours. Flight 349. Southwest." I manage between breaths.

I jog down the jetway as the doors prepare to close. I find an empty row in the back, sit and turn to the window, exhale, and start to cry. I unzip the bag an inch more, touch the face of the lamb, put my face to hers and weep, waving the stewardess away.

CHAPTER FORTY-THREE
JEMMA AND GILES: SEATTLE, 1992

Jemma arrived early at the Ristorante Machiavelli on the edge of Capitol Hill. It was their favorite for Italian fare. She inhaled the rich scent of garlic, onions, spices, and simmering tomatoes. She called ahead for the most secluded booth and slid into it, facing the entrance.

Damn. How am I to negotiate this dreaded discussion? How could I have slept with such a slime? His sweet talk? Too much wine? Too long being celibate? Whatever, I was seduced and live to regret it. Especially now. Maybe Giles is too much of a gentleman to ask. But she knew she was being unrealistic. Giles was the most intuitive and direct man she had ever met. *It is a blessing and a curse*, she realized.

"Hey, sweetheart. You look so deep in thought. Room for me?" Giles kissed her on the cheek. "Next to you or across?"

Ah, the solution! We'll have less direct eye contact. Perfect! "I think next to each other would be cozier." She moved over and made room for the man she loved most in the world. He got out his lighter to light the candle and rose to get another from the next table.

"I love that you always carry a lighter to be sure we have the candle glow!" Jemma kissed his hand.

"Ah, that's my impatience for romance."

They both read the menu for a moment before Giles asked why they bothered because they always ordered the same thing. Shaking his head, he moved the menus to the other side of the table. "The Puttanesca for you? Me, the Spinach Ravioli. Tapenade and Pinot Grigio? What's new?"

Jemma laughed. "Are we really that predictable?"

"We are and I love it. How was your day? I think it was your Azure day?" He put his arm around her shoulder and kissed her lips. "You do know how much I love you?" His still-waters-run-deep black eyes met hers with fervor.

"I do, Giles. As much as I love you." *Oh my God. I'm starting to get a migraine. I have to get it over with.* "Yes, it was an Azure day, which reminds me. Have I ever mentioned a fellow researcher to you named Peter?"

Giles's expression altered slightly. "No. Should you have?" He looked at her quizzically.

"What's wrong? Your expression changed. What?" Jemma turned to face him fully. Now she kept their eyes locked. It felt empowering to her.

"I just sense something different from you, something I haven't experienced before. I don't know what's going on, but I'm very curious. Go on."

Meanwhile the wine and tapenade arrived. They both toasted and drank to the evening, Jemma with trepidation.

I have to continue this. Get it in the past. "Do you know Peter?"

"Not as well as I should have. His presence must be in the air today. Charles and I had a long and revealing discussion about him this afternoon. But I want to hear your thoughts first, since you brought him up."

Damn. I could have avoided the whole thing! He would have mentioned Peter and I'd be home free. Saved. "I recently saw one of the fliers for the meetings he holds called Unconditional Love, Inc. He has added another, making two a week. I'm concerned he's enticing our research subjects as well as others to attend. In fact, I fear they are his target."

"Target? That's a serious image. Scary. Why did you use it?" probed Giles.

"Well, the subjects I've been working with are pretty vulnerable. It's dangerous."

"Dangerous? How? Have you been to one?"

"Actually, I have, at the beginning of the Project."

"And?"

"Giles, he's like a televangelist, singing about love. He gets louder as the meeting goes on. He gets them chanting and swaying. It really reminds me of Jonestown. I saw some of the adoptees just drinking it in. It felt dangerous for them and unethical for Peter."

"I see your concerns. We'll go back to that in a minute. I'm really interested in what made you go. Do you know Peter well?"

The food arrived hot and steaming. They moved the appetizer out of the way and settled the plates the way they always did, making it easier to share.

And a rest from the eye connection, thought Jemma. *Why is he so focused on me? I don't like it one bit! His questioning is just a little too... pointed, like he's on the scent of something. I'm NOT afraid anymore. It's my life, my past. I wonder about all of HIS women! I need a strategy. The best defense is a good offense.*

They exchanged murmurings about the excellent food and Jemma poured more wine into their goblets. She began, "Of course I know Peter. We're both collators. In the first week, we met to discuss the procedures manual and agreed it was terribly confusing to me, an English professor, and him, a computer programmer. It really does need rewriting, Giles. When the Project is over, I wouldn't mind working on it." How much more could she distract?

"That's very generous of you, Sweet. I'm making a note of it. Go on."

"Well, after our discussion we decided to get coffee. That led to dinner where he told me about the meetings and invited me to one. I went, got concerned, and talked with Azure about it. She suggested talking to Charles about it, which I never did. Today I brought it up after seeing the fliers, and she suggested bringing it up to you. What did you and Charles discuss about Peter?" Now her stomach rebelled against the puttanesca. *Change the subject.*

Giles stopped eating and turned his whole body to face her. "I'll get to that. But I have a strange feeling you want off the subject. What's going on?"

"Nothing is going on. He just feels creepy to me and I worry about the people he's influencing."

"Did he feel creepy at dinner?"

"No. Yes. Not exactly. I saw it more at the meeting." She stopped eating.

"Did you date him?"

She turned to face him. "Giles. We have both dated many people before we met. We were both married. We dated. It's no big deal. And, no we never went out after that." Her voice got a little crisper. She turned to face him.

"What's this all about? I feel like I am being emotionally stalked by you." Her eyes did not leave his.

"Because it's the first time I felt something different in you. Discomfort? I could be wrong, but your voice is staccato. You're clearly restless, avoiding topics, and now you're holding your stomach."

By now their tones were less than warm. She moved her hand. "It's just discomfort from your questions, that's all. I know where you're going, Giles and you better change your direction." Her voice got stronger.

"Did you sleep with him?"

If he weren't in the way, I would leave. Stupid idea to sit next to each other on the same side of the table. "I don't know if I'm going to answer that question. Ever." Her eyes were sparking in anger.

He continued his probing gaze, not responding.

"And, you know what else? I'm beginning to feel like a possession. You're checking on your property because I may have been with someone you know. This is a side of you I never suspected and I don't like it."

"You know I don't feel that way, Jemma. You'll always be a free woman and choose whatever you want to do, however you want to be, especially when we are together. I'm merely asking the question. One date and he's a creep?" He kept the gaze. "Did he hurt you?"

He pressed the right button. Tears began to gather. "I questioned my judgement the next morning and have continued to question it. I went to the meeting to prove he was seductive. I've never... had sex on a first date. I don't know how it happened. He did not hurt me. Anyhow, it's none of your damn business!"

Giles rubbed his forehead. "Jemma. Forgive me. I'm coming off like such a jealous jackass. You're right. It is none of my business. I am sorry you went through all of that with Peter. To quell your self-judgement, he *is* deceptive and seductive. Charles was seduced into hiring him without a complete background check, which we discovered this afternoon. He lied about everything. Wednesday we're going to one of his meetings. Thursday we're firing him. Yes, my envious possessive self stepped up, the most unloving part of me. Please be patient, I'm working on it. I'm sorry, Jem, really." His eyes glistened.

She hesitated but her heart gave into his apologies.

The waiter retreated, seeing their embrace.

CHAPTER FORTY-FOUR
PETER AND WOLFGANG: SEDONA, 1992

The cult members were still in shock. Several looked at the slammed door as if it would open again to Derek and the lamb returning. Martin was still sputtering. Peter looked like he was ready to plunge the blade into his father. Wolfgang moved closer and caught his eye, shaking his head slightly. Peter took a breath and put the knife down.

Martin continued bellowing at his son. "You stupid idiot! I trusted you to bring Suzanne's son to complete our thirty-year plan. You failed! Did you seduce her son? Did that blind you to his weakness? Was that it, faggot?"

Murder seeped back into Peter's eyes.

Martin continued in a red rage. "Turn on all the lights! Extinguish the candles! Take down your hoods and look at the betrayer of Maharba. Look at the son I now publicly disown." Several men hurried to comply.

"Even though we wanted Derek to drink the blood tonight as an adult, he did not. He is not true blood in Adolf's line. He was adopted. His adoptive grandfather Oscar was a weak demented failure. We need to be free of his family. Now Peter is a failure. He has wasted and dishonored the deepest full moon in Scorpio. Peter has failed at everything."

Wolfgang stepped in. "Wait. Maybe it was a good idea. We were so determined to have Derek in Maharba that we never considered his character. Personally, I think he's too weak to be with us. Our plan of thirty years ago has to change. We need our members to have the strength to operate without inner conflict or conscience. We need to resolve outer conflict with courage and dignity. We need another leader to succeed Martin when he is finished." Wolfgang focused on Martin for several seconds, then Peter. Dead silence.

Peter began to feel a tentative movement within the group, begun by Wolfgang's words. He saw that Martin also noticed. He saw his father was caught off guard, a flash of fear reigniting Martin's rage. "What are you saying? Peter made a stupid insane decision to bring Derek here. He should have known from The Seven Windings we were dealing with a wimp! Wimp attracts wimp. Faggot attracts faggot. We have no leader in the wings!" Rage contorted his face into an ugly sneer.

Peter began to visualize killing his father in earnest without conflict, with building resolve and commitment. No longer would Maharba be based on Abraham's plans to murder his son to appease the sky God. There would be a tectonic shift. Isaac would no longer let himself be bound and laid on an altar to wait for his death. He would take the blade and murder his father, to appease the power.

Wolfgang nodded imperceptibly as if reading Peter's revelation and knew he had chosen correctly. The seeds he had sown in Peter during their talk after the Seven Windings were now sprouting long green shoots. *Let Martin be done. More than done, gone!* Find Martin's buddy, Adolf Schmidt, who was already in a nursing home and give him the death drug. Derek was clearly not Maharba material, much less leader material. Wolfgang did not want to be the leader.

Wolfgang's desire had always been to own the leader, and Martin would not be owned, save by Adolf.

Peter was the perfect choice. He valued and trusted Wolfgang, who had few outer ego needs. Peter would be the showman, the leader with seductive charisma, unlike Martin who evoked fear. Finally, Wolfgang would achieve what he wanted his whole life: the role Adolf took from him decades ago and gave to Martin. Now Wolfgang had Martin's son, who Wolfgang respected, admired, and now owned. Peter would never know. It was unnecessary. He saw Derek as a very useful pesky fly. He couldn't wait to talk with Peter, but first he had to end this debacle.

"Martin, you've expressed yourself clearly. We'll now finish and meet again tomorrow to plan our future. We will use our full moon to initiate our New Maharba." He knew Martin would run and prattle to Adolf at the nursing home. Wolfgang continued to take charge. The men were dismissed and reminded to return tomorrow at 10:00 in the evening. He nodded at Peter, raising his eyes to indicate their meeting would be upstairs in Peter's room.

Wolfgang knocked on Peter's hotel room. Peter opened the door with a warm smile. "Come in, my brother. We have work to do. Bourbon? Scotch?"

"Always scotch, my friend. Single malt, if you have it." They settled into the comfortable chairs, moving them to face each other. "How are you feeling?"

"Better, thank you. I could have killed him. But my visions led to a brilliant idea. First, I've got to tell you that Derek told me the FBI is back in the picture. I suspect we can come up with something tonight. Everything's moving so fast. Let me tell you what I'm thinking." Peter shared his thoughts about the new Maharba.

"The past and current Maharba has very small parameters. Meet every Thursday. Use Lutheran churches. The pastor is the leader. Sacrifices are animals in the Lesser Rituals, humans in the Greater. The reenactment of the Abraham story of walking up the mountain and terrifying his son. In each thirteen-year old initiation, the terror the boy feels as his father ties him to the altar and raised the blade. Those who make it through are asked to stay in Maharba with their fathers, then given the old 'one score and four' promise, though it's actually a threat. Of course, they are never chosen to be a sacrifice. Someone else is, or a daughter. Generation after generation, terror reigns in the name of God."

"What do you see for the new Maharba, Peter? How do we get there?" Wolfgang's voice was inviting.

"First, we have to increase our membership. Joining with the Church of Satan brought with it great opportunities. Martin has never agreed to letting its influence be part of Maharba. He is wasting a powerful connection. I think you are aware the Church is based in wealth, power, and influence. Martin doesn't understand any of this. Every time I have tried to incorporate their practices with Maharba, he silenced me. My patience is at an end. There are so many opportunities, but he can't see it. He has one of the smallest minds I know. The FBI would've been off our radar long ago if we had used the influence of the Church. We must expand the Quadrants exponentially. No longer will we use some church basement enclave.

"Second, we'll do so with Unconditional Love, Inc. as the front-end feeder. We will increase the meetings of Love, Inc. Our clear intent is to increase our membership through our merger with the Church of Satan. The New Maharba. We'll closely observe the Alabama and Vermont Quadrants to determine if we need more dynamic leaders."

"If, Peter? Those old men must step down."

Peter smiled as he sipped his drink. "We'll need new leaders – men and women – to draw in the younger crowd. Then, like we did with Derek, offer a sub-group invite to our new Maharba. You and I can discuss which rituals, sacrifices, and initiations to keep, and which to let go. We are the developers.

"Third, we have to get Martin out. He is closed to all new changes. Plus, we hate each other."

Wolfgang listened with obvious enjoyment. "Peter, I concur with your thinking. Centuries and generations can no longer determine Maharba. You and I will create a Maharba more in line with our thinking. We'll have plenty of time to develop a plan that works for our new brother and sisterhood."

Peter jumped up, unable to sit still in his high excitement. "Oh, Wolfgang, the possibilities are endless. The Church is our biggest safety net. Their membership is influential in high government offices. Truly a new Maharba! But, for right now, what about the FBI? Which, incidentally, we'll never need to worry about again."

Wolfgang got up and spoke with passion. "I figured Derek's father would learn of the FBI's dabbling in 1975. He is determined to get justice for Suzanne's death. It will work completely into our plan. I'll tell you in a minute. I knew we were on the same wavelength. I agree with your thoughts. I've thought of the future of Maharba as well. Organizationally, we'll no longer be divided into quadrants. We had to do it in 1975 when the FBI descended in Smotelyville. Washington, Arizona, Vermont, and Alabama have kept us alive, but with little growth. You and I will join our forces, our leadership. Sedona and Seattle will dissolve. We choose not to stay in either of those cities after tomorrow night.

"We'll form a triad, keeping Vermont and Alabama. The new city, picked by you and me, will be the headquarters, forming a trinity with the other two. I like trinity better than triad. We'll base our plan on it. We'll allow Maharba members who are afraid of the word Satan to continue their traditional sacrifices and magic. Our new union with the Church will merge into a powerful organization maintaining the mystical with the new."

Peter nodded with a smile. "Quadrants gone. Three cities are much more in keeping with the unholy trinity. The wording is important, Wolfgang. There will be no more sacrifices to the sky God. Now we make offerings to the inferno God. It's so much better. We make human or animal sacrifices as we wish or need. You know the Church of Satan is the fastest growing church in America, so no more worries with the FBI. Once they get Martin, they could not care less. They have no idea of the infiltration of the Church. Bruno is simply aiding Tom to finish his past.

"No more does the serpentine path lead up to the altar. It now leads down from the altar without Abraham. The deed will be done: not what the sky God requested, the sacrifice of the son, but rather what our God asks, the sacrifice of the father."

"It's truly a beautiful plan, Peter. We work very well together. I've known we would for a long time, in fact, since you were very young. Your cult studies have strengthened who you are, who we are, and more so, who we are becoming now, tonight. The details will work themselves out. I see us having plenty of time to develop our New Maharba. I'm so proud of you. I don't even need to ask if we are on the same page, do I? I see the fire dancing in your eyes."

Peter sat down, his eyes gleaming. "Oh yes, my brother. I'm in. I didn't know it would be so soon. What's your plan?"

"Let's craft it together. Time is paramount. First, I know Derek is in love with you. He most likely still is, even after tonight's debacle. Are you in love with him?"

"No, Wolfgang. I think I could've been. He's so adoring and has all the unflagging sexual zest of a young man newly released from the closet. But, no, I don't need him anymore. I found him, I seduced him, I enjoyed him: for me and for the old Maharba. I always complete my tasks. He doesn't have it. The circle won't be completed as the old-timers wanted it. Now I take him to the trash."

Wolfgang sat back down after adding to his scotch. "Hold on with the trash, Peter. First, we do not kill him. Peter, you must know Maharba murder is sacred murder. It's never an impulsive or wasted move. We plan. We think. We execute, all with sacred purpose. In the New Maharba, we have no revenge needs, no fears with Derek. We'll use him to finish our work with Martin, then let him go. He's served several purposes. Because of him, we have the new organization with you as leader. You sacrificed your ego to that humiliating rant from your father. That's another key to our future."

"My ego? I sacrificed it?"

"Actually, Peter, you offered it. You will never lose your enhanced dynamic self, or your leadership. It was a moment of offering. It had to be, to concretize the transition from Martin to you. Do you see?"

Peter got up, stretched and walked to get more scotch and bourbon. He spoke as he returned. "I think so. By the way, it should have been humiliating, but I

241

didn't feel it. By his censure he wanted to make me small and a failure. Yet, I felt neither. Even if others may have seen me that way, I didn't."

"Only his followers would have," Wolfgang interrupted. "There are very few who respect Martin."

"In reality, he looked like a raging lunatic. He has no dignity. In losing his shit, he lost the leadership. Now we will take it. How, Wolfgang?"

"Tomorrow at our meeting, you'll tell the others you have discovered the FBI are back on our trail. You can tell them what you've surmised from Derek's conversation with his dad and you. You'll draw them into your plan."

"I understand. But what about Martin the lunatic? He will rail again."

"No, he won't. I'll stop him. No problem. Listen."

Peter listened.

"First, fly to Seattle tomorrow and back before the meeting. Schedule the jet. Find Derek and tell him there is another meeting Thursday night and we want him there.

"Second, tell him you are sorry for what happened. That it was the first and last time any animal would ever be sacrificed. Ask him to try once more. We really want him. Seduce him, whatever it takes. We want him here Thursday night. You won't have much time.

"Third, tell him Maharba is no longer a secret. We are joining with Unconditional Love, Inc. We are trading in love only."

Peter laughed in glee. "Trading in love! With the inferno God! How rich!"

"Fourth, to prove there are no secrets, he can tell his dad everything, even bring his dad on Thursday."

"His dad? Here?" Peter looked genuinely puzzled.

"Because, Peter, his dad is most likely onto us. He won't come alone. He was back East, in Minnesota probably with the FBI guy Bruno. Tom will call him immediately with news of the meeting. The FBI will come. They are still smarting over their 1975 failure. But we won't be here. Most of us will be gone. We're all leaving Sedona by the next morning or going underground: except one of us. All the records will be gone just like in 1975. Close your office and Unconditional Love, Inc. I'll see you tomorrow night." Wolfgang got up and walked around the room.

Peter's eyes shone, gathering the plan. "Except one of us? When they come for the Thursday night meeting, only Martin will be there?"

Wolfgang stopped in front of Peter with a fierce concentration. "Precisely. You have two choices. You can let the FBI take him alive. Or you can let the FBI take him dead."

Peter took a deep breath. "Wolfgang, what a gift: The New Maharba." He was astounded, a rarity for Peter. "In twenty-four hours, so many of my dreams will be realized. Where will we go Thursday morning? To the new center?"

"Not yet, Peter. That takes planning. We'll do that together in luxury."

Wolfgang showed Peter two tickets to Argentina. First class, of course.

CHAPTER FORTY-FIVE
DEREK, TOM, and TERESE: PORTLAND, 1992

Tom pulled up at PDX arrivals, relieved to see his son. Derek was alive.

Derek opened the passenger door and got in. He looked drawn and pale and could hardly speak.

"Derek. What happened? You look terrible. I'm so glad you called."

"I can't talk about it now. I'll tell you and mom later. One of the things? There's a lamb in this bag." He opened the carryall's zipper and removed her muzzle.

"Lamb. Derek?"

"And, yes, you may have been right about Peter. I don't know about everything, but he changed with me. He got so angry. Worse, he was going to kill this lamb. I don't understand anything anymore. Maybe they are a cult."

Tom pulled out of PDX and braked suddenly. He chose to focus on the lamb, while being thrilled Derek was questioning Peter. *At last!* "A lamb, Derek. You brought it home? How did you get it on the plane?" Cars started to beep softly, Portland style. He began to drive, waving thanks to the car behind him. He was reminded of all the lost and forlorn animals Derek brought home when he lived there, although Derek had never brought home a lamb. "Derek, do rescue centers take lambs?"

"I'll check as soon as they open. I know I'm not keeping the lamb but I couldn't leave her to be killed."

"Of course not. You know I want to hear everything. It's a good idea to wait until we get home, have some coffee, and settle in."

They drove the short distance with Derek calming the bleating lamb. As soon as he walked into the kitchen, Derek unbound the lamb who had difficulty standing for a while, but amazingly got her balance. Then he hugged Terese. "I'm not keeping her, Mom. I just couldn't let her die."

"Of course not, Derek. What will she eat? Will she drink cow's milk?"

"We can only try. She probably hasn't eaten in two days." Derek put the milk in a bowl. "I still can't believe it," he muttered.

The starving lamb drank the milk and wouldn't leave Derek's side. After settling in with coffee and breakfast food, he poured out his story of the midnight ritual to Tom and Terese. He only stopped once to use the bathroom. They could hear him retching. He kept his little finger in a small glass of peroxide.

Tom was reeling but grateful to have his son home. "Derek, I don't know what to say. It's gruesome. I agree, evil. You've been to hell and back. Right now, you need sleep. Your bed's made up. Sleep 'til you wake. You're safe. I'll put the lamb in the mud room with newspapers on the floor, with a blanket. I'll call the farm animal rescue place and keep an eye on her. After you get up we can talk about your next step. What about Peter? It's gotta be hard right now."

Derek did not respond, but on his way up the stairs to the bedroom, he threw out, "Yeah, Dad? Peter said there is only one Maharba group. None back East. I knew it was a different Maharba that you were talking about." He closed the bedroom door.

Within seconds, he bounded back down the stairs. "Mom! Did Dad tell you I'm gay? Sorry to just mention it in passing, but I needed you to know."

Terese went to the landing and embraced him. "Derek, he did! I am so happy for you. To know who you truly are is a rare blessing. I love you. Now, please get some sleep? You're beyond exhausted."

"Thanks, Mom. I knew you'd say that." He kissed her and wearily climbed the stairs once again. The bedroom door closed.

Terese and Tom shook their heads, smiling about their son. Tom's look of exasperation soon followed.

"How can he even speak of Peter? What's he doing with all that horror?" demanded Tom.

They spoke of Derek's chaos and what they thought could be a crossroads in his life. Tom asked, "Does it feel like he's done? With Peter? The cult? It doesn't feel like it. I don't get it. How can he not connect live sacrifice, the cult, and Peter?"

"I agree. I don't know. The cult is pretty powerful, all those generations. And Peter? He's Derek's first love as a gay man. It would be hard to give that up. Plus, Peter sounds completely seductive and powerful on his own. I hate to say it, but don't count on him being done. You heard him still defending Peter's group in spite of the horror he witnessed. It seems like he blames the cult more than Peter."

Tom sighed, dejected. "You're right. We're not at the finish line. And we don't know Peter's next move, either. He did mumble some conflict about Peter in the car." Tom got up to check on the lamb. Fifteen minutes passed.

Derek interrupted them, walking in a daze. "Dad, I had the taxi driver write the address where he picked me up in case you want to tell your FBI guy." He handed the receipt to Tom and weaved back to his room.

"That's my boy!" cheered Tom, pumping his fist in the air. "In the midst of chaos, he was thinking! He's not sold on Peter. He told me to call Bruno."

"Hold on, Tom. True, he was thinking in Sedona amidst chaos. But I'm not sure he's completely ready to turn against Peter, if at all. It's his exhaustion talking. See where he is when he wakes up."

"You've got to be kidding. We have the address of the meeting center, Peter, and the cult that killed Suzanne and wants my son. You say wait? Bruno could get them tomorrow."

"For what? A good old boys club? An almost-sacrificed lamb, now sleeping in the mudroom? Secret handshakes?" Her voice was gentle, her words were not. Tom winced. Damn her logic. "We can't let them get away. Again."

"What if Derek wakes up more centered, further from the event, still in love with Peter? What if he asks if you've called 'your FBI guy'? If you say 'Yep, sure did,' he gets no choice. It might be better if you could tell him, 'I wasn't sure that's what you would want after you slept, so I didn't call. Here's your address.' There's time, not much, but enough."

"I'm not going to lose that address!" He stormed.

"Tom. Copy it down, sweetheart."

"Oh, yeah," as he sheepishly wrote it down.

"You know you're as exhausted as Derek. You just got home last evening, not even twenty-four hours from a long and hard trip that changed your life. You haven't even unpacked yet. So unlike you. Go lie down. I'll be here. Derek won't leave. Neither will the lamb. Please?"

Tom got up, rubbed her shoulders, and said, "You're right. Thanks, babe," and left. Terese smiled as she watched him tread the stairs, somewhat laboriously. "Home safe. Derek too. I can breathe. Later I'll unpack for Tom. Poor guy."

Before he took his glasses off, Tom called Bruno, briefed him, and told him he had an address. "Give it to me."

"No, Bruno. We've got to keep Derek in on the plan. Empower him to leave Peter and the cult. I'll call you soon." He barely hung up the phone before he was snoring.

They were all eating a late lunch after returning from the Farm Animals Rescue when the phone rang. Terese picked it up. "Hello? Yes, Derek is here. May I tell him who's calling?" Her face flushed. "Thank you." She took a breath. "Derek, it's your friend Peter." Tom put down his sandwich. His heart was racing.

"Thanks, Mom. I'll take it upstairs." Derek took the phone and they heard his bedroom door close.

He was out of breath from leaping up the stairs. "How did you get this number? I did? I don't remember. Hey, I'm sorry I freaked out. What was going on?! I thought you were going to kill her! Were you? You know I love animals. You apparently know nothing about me!" He listened. "You knew I'm vegetarian. Why did you...Okay, okay, I'll listen." Twenty minutes later, he joined his parents in front of the fire, espresso in hand. Stretching out on the rug, he said, "God, it's good to be home. Mom, how much did Dad tell you about me being gay? Did he tell you Peter is my lover?"

Terese hesitated. "He did. It must be difficult right now with the crises in Sedona."

Tom was jiggling his foot. "What did Peter want?"

Derek's eyes lit up. "Wait 'til you hear this! I knew I fell in love with the right guy." He looked at Tom pointedly. "You need to trust me, Dad." He wasn't smiling. Tom's face moved not a muscle although he noticed his jaw hardening.

Terese encouraged him. "What, Derek?"

"Peter apologized over and over. He said everyone there was upset. It was the first time they tried to use an animal for the sacrifice. They all hated it and are dropping the name Maharba. They're joining with Unconditional Love, Inc. and trading only in love." Derek's eyes were dreamy.

"Do you really believe him?" Tom kept his expletives inside.

"Of course, I do. I could hear it in his voice. He was so sorry to upset me and...listen to this! He said to invite you, Dad, to the next meeting so you can see what Unconditional Love, Inc. is all about. He didn't say you, Mom, but I'm sure you could come."

"No, Derek. Thanks for asking. You go with your dad. I'll go next time."

Tom managed a quiet, "When's the meeting? Where?"

"Well, that's the thing. It's Thursday, this Thursday. Tomorrow. Please come, you'll meet all of the men, especially Peter."

"In Seattle?"

"No, Sedona. They want to totally redo last night's meeting by officially changing it to Love, Inc. It's in the same place. You still have the address?"

"Yes." Tom felt saved. Grateful.

"Did you call your FBI guy?"

"Yes, but I didn't give him the address. I wasn't sure when you woke up if you would want me to." He glanced a look of gratitude to Terese.

"Well, at this point, it really doesn't matter. Our group was not connected with that other one. And after Thursday, there won't be any Maharba. I'm sure you could tell your FBI man. He'd probably like to hear that."

He got up and stood in front of Tom. "Dad, we have to finish your trip story. Didn't you say there was more? To be honest, I'm feeling pretty surrounded by secrets that involve me. My mother murdered, for instance. You don't seem to realize what that did to me."

Tom started to interrupt. "Derek, I..."

Derek interrupted. "No, Dad, you don't. Let me finish. I'm tired of being an outsider to my own life. Of course, you had nothing to do with me not knowing I'm gay. That's mine. I sense there is more. More for me to know. Is that right? Monday you said 'that's for later.' Well, later is here. I need to know everything about me that I clearly was never told." He glared at Tom, a mixture of strength and anger.

"Derek..."

"Tonight, I have an appointment with my therapist in Seattle. I want you to come with me and spill it all. It feels pretty big and I want her there for support. I want a witness. Our meeting is at 6:00. I'm going to call and ask for another thirty minutes. We need to leave soon. My car is at home, so I'll have to ride with you. No talking, however. I'm talked out. I'll be down in twenty."

Tom's head was whirling. *Who was this new Derek?*

"By the way, I won't be coming back with you tonight. I have a dinner engagement with Peter. You can let me know the flight arrangements for tomorrow night. We won't need to leave until later in the afternoon. I'll drive back down tomorrow. I still want you to be there at the initiation for Love, Inc. It's incredibly important to me." He went upstairs.

Tom looked to Terese. She held her hands out, arms open, with an expression of incredulity. "You best get ready, love. You've another journey ahead of you, added to the one tomorrow and on top of the one you just took." She reminded him softly, "I love you."

CHAPTER FORTY-SIX
TOM, DEREK, AZURE: SEATTLE, 1992

Tom and Derek arrived in Azure's waiting room around 5:45. "This is a unique office in a great mansion, Derek. How did you find her?"

Derek answered tersely. "From one of the researchers at the Adoption Project. I appreciate you coming here without notice and going to Sedona. I just cannot abide the secrets and the scent of secrets any longer from anyone." He grimaced, thinking about the drive up from Portland and being unwilling to live with lies.

"I understand. I have to tell you... things about your birth that you don't know, things I lied about." Tom studied the eyes of his son staring into his own.

Derek couldn't believe his father had just brought up lies as he was vowing to live in the truth. "Like the murder? You already told me that. That's why we're here. Do you mean more lies?"

"Yes, Derek. Another one."

Derek stood up. "I have a dinner appointment tonight at 7:45 and I'm not changing it."

Tom hesitated. "Did you ask for the extra half-hour?"

He stared at his father. "I told you I would, didn't I? She even moved the next person to 7:30. You really don't trust me, do you? Even when it's my plan. Actually, even when it's my life." His voice rose.

Azure opened the door. She smiled and commented, "It sounds like the session has already begun." Both stopped talking as Tom stood up. Still smiling, Azure reached out to Tom. "I'm Azure. It's good to meet you. Derek assured me he's comfortable with you being here."

Derek corrected her. "Not comfortable. Okay with him being here." He walked into the office. The other two followed.

Father and son sat in the deep purple chairs. Azure settled into her rocker. Both turned to the gas heater with its glow. "I don't know if Derek told you, Tom, that I start with a chime." Tom shook his head. Azure explained the process and chimed.

Tom sighed as he opened his eyes. "That was a bit calming: a good way to start. Thank you for seeing me and us and for the extra thirty minutes. I know you've rearranged your schedule."

"It worked out well. You're welcome. Who wants to start?"

"I do. My initiation with Maharba never happened." Derek proceeded to tell the story.

Azure and Tom listened.

He finished with, "So Maharba is joining with Unconditional Love, Inc. No more black candles, darkness, and especially no more secrets. Now we are all about love. I know I had an influence on Peter and feel stronger. I'm going back tomorrow night to redo my initiation, only it will be into Love, Inc. and no sacrifices. My dad's coming with me. He can meet Peter and experience the group."

Tom's jaw ached from his effort to keep it shut. He began to rub it.

"I can't imagine what you went through, Derek." Azure responded with compassion and surprise in her voice. "Or, that you're willing to return and open yourself up to it again." Silence. "I'm not sure what you've told your dad, so I'm omitting names." She looked to Derek questioningly.

"He knows I am gay. He knows about Peter being my lover, the Seven Windings, and Sedona. I've kept no secrets from him. Apparently, he's kept several from me. In fact, I'm really sick of secrets. Now it turns out there are lies too. So you can say whatever you want."

"Thank you, then I'll continue. Did the unfinished initiation shake your trust in Peter?" Tom sighed inside with gratitude.

"Well, no. He called to explain and apologized and, well, he loves me. We all make mistakes."

"Didn't he say the cult was generations old? Now they're changing?" She cocked her head.

"Azure. It's not a cult. I never called Maharba a cult. He never called it a cult. And, yes, groups do change. I haven't said this to anyone and I know everything here is confidential." He turned to Tom. "Even you, Dad. No FBI guy." Tom nodded, waiting.

"Peter told me they're considering asking me to be their new leader after I train with him for several years. My decision to save the lamb had an impact on him. I wouldn't join a cult. From what I have read, cults kill. We are about love." He looked out the window.

Tom felt better hearing about Peter's plan. For now. *Maybe Bruno was right about them never wanting to kill Derek, although I'm still sickened at the thought of Derek joining the group. But tomorrow night, the threat will be gone. The murderers would be in jail, or at least one of them would be. The FBI will take the names of everyone there as witnesses. I still have a hard time believing they are interested in a thirty-year-old-murder. It has to be Bruno doing me a favor. I'll call Bruno on my way back to Portland.* He brought himself back to the office and his purpose.

Azure continued. "Okay, Derek, we'll get back to your news. Is this a good time for your dad to talk? Tell us why he's here?"

Derek appeared nonchalant. "Sure. Dad, go ahead. I don't know what could top your news about my mother being murdered."

Azure gasped. "Your mother was murdered?" She looked at both of them. "Derek?"

Derek responded. "Yes. My dad told me yesterday that my birth mother was murdered by men from a cult in her father's church, right after I was born. The name of that cult seems to be similar to the name of Peter's group. Peter told me there's no relationship and now our group is changing names anyhow to Love, Inc. to avoid any more confusion."

Azure clearly looked troubled. "Let's go back to your mother's death. What are you doing with that? What are you feeling? You also said the group was going to kill a lamb. Is there a connection?" She looked to Derek, to Tom.

"Of course not, Azure. And about my birth mother? I have some waves of loss, but it seems so strange to say that, even stranger to feel it. I never knew her. I do want justice and her murderers caught. Peter is going to check into it. He is brilliant with computers. Right now, I'm fine and just want to hear what my dad has to tell me." He sat back, crossed his legs, and looked at Tom pointedly.

"Do you want me to start, Derek?" He looked for permission and possible cooperation. Also, he did not want to shortchange his son's feelings.

"Go ahead. I'm fine. For now." He put his legs over the arm of the chair and kept his eyes on Tom. Then he turned to Azure. "Know, Azure, that was the first time they even thought of sacrificing an animal. I think it was a Bible thing, some Abrahamic ritual. All of them decided it would never happen again. Peter asked about the lamb and was happy to hear she was going to a farm and doing well. As horrible as it could have been, she didn't die. I saved her. Plus, I was the catalyst for a major shift in the group to become a Love group. I'm proud of my impact."

Azure pushed her hair behind her ears and withheld an expression of exasperation. Tom screamed inside. *Can't you SEE it, Derek! All lies! How can you not see an obvious lie?* He blanched. *Because you grew up with lies about who you are, about who you were. God, how did I do this?* He spoke out loud. "Derek, I need to tell you so many things."

A slow nod from the man draped into the purple chair. "So, tell me."

Tom exhaled. "I'm going to tell you the true story of who you are. There are many falsehoods, lies that I told you and others. I thought it was to protect you from death, fear, despair, and from any more confusion. I apologize. I was wrong. I now know I should've told you much earlier. I was complacent. I was a coward."

"Dad, start. I'm listening." His voice was infused with impatience.

"First, your mother's... name was not Elizabeth. It was Suzanne. Her father was a minister who promised her life to the cult in his church in Smotelyville, Indiana, on her twenty-fourth birthday, predicting she would give birth to a boy. The cult was named Maharba."

"Not the same. Go on, Dad, I'm listening. And getting confused." His voice softened and he sat up straight, still facing Tom.

Azure was astounded. *I've never heard anything like it. Yes, I've read of cults, but not experienced any clients with a connection to one. Hearing Peter's name and cult in the same story makes my heart skip and my stomach tighten.* "Go on, Tom."

"When Suzanne was at the end of her eighth-grade year, she snuck down to the church during one of their meetings. They met every Thursday night. She was curious and peeped through a shard of open space that a window shade did not completely block. She saw thirteen men in robes, and a baby goat on an altar with blood pouring out of its neck into the communion chalice. She fled to her mother in shock. She couldn't talk." Tom thought this would get Derek to see the similarity, but no luck.

"Dad. Who is Suzanne?"

"The woman who was murdered. My wife. I'll explain that later. Can I continue?"

Derek nodded, shaking his head. "My mother."

Tom took a deep breath. He felt like Judas. "Her mother, Bernice, made the decision to get her away from the church and her father, though she didn't know any details of that night. Suzanne went to her mother's alma mater in Chicago. With counseling, she put the event behind her. I knew nothing of it until my trip back East. There, I discovered Suzanne's father arranged for her to have a hysterectomy in her senior year. He thought it would save her life from the cult's promise. If she could not give birth, she would not die. He was wrong."

"My birth mother had a hysterectomy at seventeen? I don't understand." He moved the chair to face Tom. "How is that possible?"

"Derek. Suzanne, who you know as Elizabeth, is not your birth mother. I am not your biological father." He stopped speaking, choking down emotion. "We adopted you the day before Suzanne was murdered."

Derek narrowed his eyes, brushed his hair back, and glared at Tom. He grabbed his stomach and exhaled as the tears came. "I can't do it. A lie, dad. My whole life. A huge lie. No wonder I was confused and depressed much of my life. It wasn't all about being gay, was it?" He turned to Azure. "Help me." A simple plea, wiping his tears on his sleeve.

"What do you need, Derek?" Her eyes wrapped him in compassion.

"Tell me it's not true. That it couldn't have happened. That fathers don't do this to their children."

Tom's heart was breaking. "Derek." He leaned towards his son.

Azure shot him a look that seemed to say, "Wait." Tom stopped himself. The pain in his heart was excruciating. His tears were hot.

"Derek, I believe it's true. We don't yet know the whole story. I can't imagine the hurt and betrayal you feel right now. There's more we have to hear. I do see your father loves you very much and I believe he always has, but I don't think you can feel it right now. I wouldn't be able to feel much about love right now."

"I feel it a little. Mostly, I feel... lost somehow. No me. Nowhere. Dark. Cold. Lonely. Scared. So alone."

Tom whispered, "Derek, I've loved you from the minute I saw you. I've never stopped." He wanted to embrace his son, but knew it wasn't time. "I have to continue, if you're okay with it. I want you to know everything."

"Now. A little late." muttered Derek. "Why now?"

"I made a big mistake. I have to be honest, for your life."

"Yeah, for my life." Derek rubbed his eyes and stared at the fireplace.

"Derek, I had no choice but to do what I did. I had to save your life. Yes, I should have told you when you became an adult. That was my mistake. Protecting you was not a mistake."

"Do you have other questions for your dad?"

He shook his head. "Not yet. Wait. Is Terese my real adopted mother?"

Tom quickly affirmed, "Yes! Why would you ask that?"

Derek rolled his eyes. "Why would I ask if you are telling the truth? You've got to be kidding, except it's nowhere near funny. So it's true my adoptive mom is my adoptive mom."

"Yes, that's true. Can I continue?"

"Sure. Why not?" He wrapped the blanket from the back of the chair around him.

"Suzanne never told me anything except that her father said something very bad would happen if she ever gave birth. So we chose to adopt you. Suzanne couldn't stop crying as she took you from the agency woman's arms. She kept saying, 'He's so beautiful. How can I instantly love him so much?' I felt the same. Those twenty-four hours were the most joy I have ever experienced."

"Until you came home to her bloodless body twenty-four hours later, on her twenty-fourth birthday, with me sleeping in my room." Woodenly spoken.

"Yes."

Derek kept talking, "The four men carried her body out. They were never found. We moved to Portland." He spoke to the floor, head in his hands.

"Yes. There's more. Another lie. You were born in Chicago. It's where the murder happened. Then we fled to Minneapolis, where you and I received new identities, birth certificates and all. Suzanne did as well."

"Like in the movies?"

"Yes. Like in the movies."

"The FBI guy?"

"Yes. Bruno. Before the new identities, we named you Aron. Aron Miller. I was Paul Miller. She was Suzanne Miller." Tom could almost hear shards of broken glass fall to the floor as truth broke through the container that secured the truth, or was it the lies? For so many years, he had too many glass containers to break with a lie in each one.

Derek nodded. "Nothing's real anymore. Do you have my real birth certificate?"

"No. I had to turn in your birth certificate, your adoption certificate, our birth certificates and wedding license, drivers' licenses. The FBI obliterated the records. There are no traces of those three names or their existence after 1963 for that matter."

"Was I really born in Chicago? Can I find my real birth certificate?"

"They told us you were born in Chicago. The adoption agency gave us a certificate of live birth with our names on it. Your original birth certificate was sealed."

Azure made a note. One word. Tom wondered what she wrote. She clearly wasn't a therapist who took notes during a session. Derek stared at Tom for a whole minute. Tom waited, his eyes never leaving his son's.

"Any other lies, Dad?" He spoke without sarcasm, just quiet curiosity. Defeated.

"No, son. There's nothing else."

"What do you know about my real birth mother?"

"I'm sorry. Nothing. If there was anything in your file, it was destroyed with the old identities."

Azure wrote another word. She looked to Derek. "Where are you now? What do you need?" Her words were soft, comforting.

"I don't have a clue." His tears spilled again. "I know I feel so lost. So alone. I feel totally abandoned. They aren't unfamiliar feelings. I've felt them my entire life. Yet now they feel new and overwhelming."

Tom couldn't stand it anymore. He went to Derek's chair, knelt on the floor, and hugged him fiercely. After a few seconds, Derek tentatively returned his embrace.

Azure looked at the two words she had written, hoping her tears would not fall free. She very quietly said, "Our time is nearly up. I'm sorry. Do you want another appointment?"

"Yes," both of them said together. They smiled ruefully at each other.

"Next week? Same time?" asked Derek.

"Perfect. See you then." She silently hugged both of them on the way out.

They walked through the waiting room, oblivious to the woman reading a magazine. At the bottom of the outside stairs, Tom turned to Derek again. "Until tomorrow? I know you have a dinner date tonight. Our flight leaves at four tomorrow, gets in at six-thirty, seven-thirty Sedona time. Are you sure it's enough time?"

"It's fine, dad. I told you we don't start until ten that evening. Stop second-guessing me. I'll be at your house by three."

They looked at each other awkwardly. "Dad, I know that was hard. Thank you. But you have to know it tilts my whole world. Everything is out of balance, out of control. There's a lot we need to talk about: not now but over time. I still can't believe you lied to me for nearly three decades." He turned away.

Tom started, "I'm sor..."

Derek interrupted. "Enough with the sorries, I know that. I just need time and answers. In my time. See you tomorrow." He couldn't wait to see Peter, lie in his arms, and weep.

They walked in opposite directions to their cars.

Tom stopped at the B&O to phone Bruno, while he ordered a large espresso. "What's the plan? I just told Derek everything. His adoption, new identities. He's not happy with me right now. He's crushed, angry, and betrayed. Yes. We're still going to the meeting tomorrow night in Sedona. I know Peter will be there. Martin? Of course. Derek said Peter's father is one of the leaders and another is Mr. K. They have to be the men from thirty years ago. Bruno, I cannot meet Suzanne's killer and not end his life. Damn, I am slowing down. What's the plan? You don't get it, Bruno.

"Oh, okay. You'll meet us there. Wait! You can't do that! Derek will flip out. He's adamant about the 'FBI guy' knowing nothing. Well, yes, he did say it was okay to tell you. He clearly did not mean to invite you to the meeting! We'll manage it. I know you can't arrest anyone without proof. You never did find any, did you? That was the reason for stopping? I know. You've been doing your job forty years. Okay. Just tell me what to do. Got it. Go to the center with Derek. Watch the ceremony. Forget the rest. Got it. Of course, I'll keep a lid on it. G'nite."

Tom walked out of the coffee shop, espresso in hand, and drove to Portland. *I'll focus on justice. Derek. Trusting Bruno. How can I go through the ceremony without killing the murderers of my wife? I'm exhausted.*

Derek listened to the answering machine in disbelief. "Sorry, Derek, I can't meet for dinner. I've got way too much to do. I really do feel badly and will make it up to you. In fact, I'll make it up tomorrow night, after the meeting and your initiation to Love, Inc. We will be spending lots of time together at the leadership training too. Mmmmmmm. We'll spend two whole nights and two whole days, just the two of us: my dear boyfriend and me. Two nights to please you, over and over and over. See you tomorrow at ten bells. No robes, all that is over! Kiss kiss!"

Derek listened again, choking down the lump in his throat. *He's never called me his boyfriend.* He smiled in the midst of his whole evening of disappointment. *Disappointed is hardly the word. Devastated? Ravaged? I'm not staying here alone. As much as I don't like my dad right now, who isn't really my dad... I'd rather be home and sleep in 'til two in the afternoon, until I can fly to Peter. Actually, the drive down to Portland will be good for me, thinking time.* He stopped at the B&O

and thought he saw his father's car driving away as he walked up to the door. *Possible? Maybe. Doesn't matter.*

"Large latte and three Russian tea biscuits, please. To go."

CHAPTER FORTY-SEVEN
AZURE AND JEMMA: SEATTLE, 1992

Jemma couldn't help but notice the two men coming from Azure's office. Their eyes were red. She felt immediate compassion well up. Wasn't that the young man from the Adoption Project who she saw at Peter's meeting? He looked different, but she still recognized him. Was the older man his father? They both seemed wiped out and grim. She glanced back to her magazine, feeling very intrusive. The door closed, but she felt the pain linger.

Azure's door opened. "Come in, Jemma. I'm sorry that I'm a few minutes late. Thank you for adjusting your appointment time. I appreciate it." She held the door open.

Jemma sat and noticed the incense in addition to the candle burning. "Incense?"

"The appointments were so close, I didn't have time to let the energy clear."

"I saw them. I can see why you're burning incense."

"Let's chime." The deeply pitched tone slowly dissipated. Azure nodded to Jemma to begin.

"I'm not sure where to start. I wanted to talk about Giles and me, but there really is not much more to say than we had our come-to-Jesus talk and resolved our first major disagreement. While I did not explicitly confirm it, he knows I slept with Peter. We moved to another level of trust. Both of us learned more about ourselves and each other. I feel stronger. So that's good.

"He talked with Charles Dirgence. They found that Peter lied about almost everything on his resume. They're going to the Unconditional Love, Inc. meeting tonight and told him to meet with them tomorrow to fire him. God, I get so skeeved thinking of him! I have to let it go. It'll be easier when I don't see him around the campus." Jemma stared at the gleaming hardwood floor for almost a minute.

Azure was silent and listening intently.

"Well, this is totally weird and unexpected. I haven't thought of him in ages." Jemma looked out the window.

"Haven't thought of whom, Jemma?" puzzled Azure.

"The boy who got me pregnant at my first sexual experience. Maybe it's talking about men I've been intimate with, but the memory of him just leapt into my head. The one I slept with to 'get it over with?' The one who couldn't manage putting a condom on successfully? Then, the baby."

"Of course. Your baby. I forgot when she, I mean he, was born? June of sixty-three?"

"Yes. June twenty-ninth."

"I think you said the father never knew? You never saw him again?" She wrote the date down.

"No. I mean, yes, he never knew. We weren't in a relationship. Maybe that's why I'm remembering him? I wasn't in a relationship with Peter either." She watched the mesmerizing grate in the fireplace. "Is that it?"

"I don't know. Say more about the high school boyfriend. Does he have a first name?" Azure's mouth twitched.

"Richard. There's not much to say: basketball captain, smart, popular, nice-looking. I heard he went on to become a physician. My father's a physician. Was. Did I tell you that? Damn, I never thought of it. Richard even reminded me of my dad physically. Maybe it was seeing that father and son walking out before me that brought it back. I haven't thought of him in so long."

Azure looked at her notepad. *No. Of course not. Way too Hollywood.* "How did you choose him to be the one to 'get it over with?'"

"Good question. Shallow, perhaps, but all the reasons I described about him. We were at a party with beer and no parents. The kids were using the bedrooms. I wasn't drunk, nor was he. It just happened. Sounds so lame, I know. I don't see why I'm reminded of him. No big deal, maybe it'll come back to me."

"It will or it won't." smiled Azure.

"New topic. I went back to First Moms to tell them about my trip and the lack of results after I found out it's a boy. The meeting reminded me of how desperate I was to find my daughter. They listened to my story. I told them I would not be returning. There was no reason." She stopped and thought. "I have found such peace in being freed of my daughter myth. Thank you."

"It was your idea, Jemma. You did the work. It's impressive! Most don't do the work, you know."

"Why would someone go to therapy, pay for it, and not do the work?" She asked in surprise.

"There are lots of reasons, but back to you. Your life seems very much at peace, especially compared to when we met. Your baby quest is resolved at this point. You and Giles seem to be building a real relationship. What do you want to do now about therapy?"

"I'd like to come back in a month to check in and be sure I'm on the right track with Giles. Will that work?"

"Certainly. I have some clients who come in for a check-up every three or six months. Four weeks? Wednesday the sixth at 4:00?"

"Perfect. And Azure?"

"Yes?"

"Thank you so much. For everything."

"Thank you, Jemma, for being open and persistent and for doggedly pursuing your inner self."

They said goodnight together as Azure opened the door. She closed it thoughtfully after Jemma left.

Azure sat at her desk, making notes from both sessions. *Jemma's therapy is pretty much finished for now; Derek's is just beginning. Jemma is at peace, while*

Derek is at a loss, his world turned upside down. Why did Jemma think of Richard now? She only brought him up when she spoke of her pregnancy. She did not even mention his name until now. Time will tell. Or not. It's Jemma's story, not mine, she mused.

Azure knew she was being a romantic when she looked at the words she had written from both sessions. The first two set her mind imagining. The third brought butterflies to her heart. 1) Chicago. 2) Files destroyed for new identities. 3) June 29, 1963. Well, she best dissolve that fantasy and free those butterflies. "It's impossible," she murmured as she went to the beginning of Derek's file. *See! August 10, 1963. Well, Silly, that's that,* she admonished herself, as the butterflies began to leave.

There's plenty of work with Derek. His initiation tomorrow night. He just found out he is totally adopted, not half and that he has two adoptive moms, one murdered. Plus, Peter getting fired. She felt a frisson of sorrow in her heart. She felt like crying. "Tears always come unbidden when I'm tired. Which I am, a very long day." She spoke to herself as she sighed in weariness with loneliness added to her heavy spirit.

Azure straightened her desk, turned off the heater, the lights, and was startled and surprised to find Charles in the waiting room. He stood, took her into his arms, and held her. The weary and lonely feelings faded in an instant.

CHAPTER FORTY-EIGHT
TOM: PORTLAND, 1992

Tom came home late that evening, looking forward to finally having a good night's sleep. He was worn out from the session with Azure, but relieved to have gotten it all out. He closed the garage door and came into the kitchen, surprised to see Terese still awake.

"How was it? How are you? Derek? How are the both of you? I'm sorry; you look beyond exhausted. You can tell me more tomorrow if you want."

"It was perhaps the most difficult thing I have had to do. Actually, there are way too many difficult tasks lately. I told him everything. He was shocked, angry, betrayed, and he said he felt so alone. My heart was breaking. I don't know when our relationship will come back. Actually, I know it won't, can't. I can only pray for a new and better one. But that won't be for a while. He still wants me to go to Sedona with him tomorrow. I am glad of that, so I can see and be with him. We were both wrung dry."

"Oh, Tom, how difficult and painful. It is for the best for both of you." She held him for a long time. "I stayed up to tell you something that might be important. I unpacked for you. There was an old and yellowed folder in the bottom of your suitcase. I didn't read it, but the label on the front is Suzanne Schmidt. If it's important, I didn't want you to miss it, fall asleep, and be annoyed in the morning."

"Thank you, sweetheart. I forgot all about it. It's the folder the Mother Superior was sharing with us during the tell-all. I actually stole it from her desk." He held out his arms and raised his eyebrows in the universal gesture of puzzlement. "I'll glance at it but read it tomorrow."

om awakened Terese with, "Holy shit! I've got to call Bruno." Terese commented that it was 2:00 AM.

"He needs to know that he may have to do some quick planning if he wants to arrest Suzanne's murderer tomorrow night!" He left their room.

"Sorry, Bruno, it's Tom. I took a folder from the Mother Superior's desk but neglected to read it on the trip. Yes, I know that was a mistake. Can I go on? It was the one she was reading from about her time with Suzanne. Terese unpacked it and Bruno! She did not read everything to us. She states in there that Martin was the killer! She spent an hour with Oscar, Suzanne's dad, when Suzanne decided to have the hysterectomy. He told her the whole history of his experience in the cult. That under the influence of alcohol and his father's and the deacons' pressure, when Suzanne was born, he promised to give her to them on her twenty-fourth birthday. They told him she would give birth on her twenty-fourth birthday to a son who would become the leader of the cult in Oscar's church. She would be sacrificed. Murdered. He told Sister Michael everything! She did nothing and let Suzanne be murdered! Okay, I'll slow down." He took a deep breath.

"Meanwhile Oscar was so sick and worried they would take her firstborn child that he urged her to have a hysterectomy at seventeen, believing she would die at twenty-four if she got pregnant. The surgery was done in Chicago by a younger brother of one of the cult's members who committed suicide. I'm sorry I'm all over the place. I just can't believe it." He took some time to gather himself.

"I know it sounds crazy, Bruno. He even named the leader his father Adolf had chosen to be the killer: Martin Gehman, Peter's father! Oscar began to have lapses in memory and bouts of depression after Suzanne's birth. For sixteen years, he went downhill. Then when he met the Mother Superior, he was heading into another depression. He trusted her confidentiality, clergy to clergy. He knew the deacons could not be stopped. He called the nun to tell her after the murder. She knew all of this and said nothing! I can't believe it. You can arrest Martin now, can't you? What about the Mother Superior? Was she involved with the cult?"

"Okay, call me as soon as you know what we are going to do. G'nite."

Tom thought he would not sleep that night, but he slept very deeply, not knowing he was crying in the night with tears wetting the pillow. Terese held him tightly, disbelieving such a thing could actually happen. She heard Tom's side of the phone call.

Was clerical confidentiality beyond the law and protection of someone's life? Was the nun an accomplice? Knowingly? Unknowingly? Does murder go unpunished if it's done by a cult? The same one both of my men were going to meet tomorrow? Not without FBI protection, she determined to announce to Tom when they awakened.

M orning brought light rain which matched Tom's mood. He sighed.

Terese felt him stir. She turned on her side. "How are you doing, Tom? I heard some of your call. What was in there? Do you want coffee first?"

"No, we can go downstairs in a minute. In the file was incredibly important information that might have saved Suzanne's life. While Bernice and I shared what we each knew about Suzanne, the Mother Superior, lied through her teeth. Terese. A high-ranking clergy lied." He swore disgustedly.

"What crimes are glorified in the name of God, in service of confidentiality? You heard most of my call? I don't want to repeat myself. Oh, yeah, you only heard my side of it! I need to tell you the whole unbelievable story. Let's go make the coffee."

On their way down, Tom was surprised to see Derek's door shut with a note on the outside. "Came home. Don't wake me until two-thirty. Thanks, D." He must not have spent the night with Peter. One positive.

They settled into the breakfast nook, buttered a croissant, inhaled the aroma of Sumatran coffee, and breathed deeply. Terese invited, "Whenever you are ready, sweetheart."

Tom looked out to the garden and back to Terese. "I'm ready. I know you heard some of this, but I have to tell the whole story at once. Before Suzanne's father left Chicago after the consent for her hysterectomy, he met with Sister Michael for an hour to pour out everything. Suzanne would die – murdered – on her twenty-fourth birthday as a sacrifice for the cult. Oscar agreed to it the day she was born. Four of the deacons would come to Chicago and bring her lifeless body back to Smotelyville. He even gave her the name of the chosen murderer: Martin Gehman, Peter's father. She knew about the murder seven years before it happened. God almighty!"

"Tom, can't she be charged with being an accessory? Something?"

"Bruno will let me know the next time we talk. She also lied to us about not seeing Suzanne after her high school graduation. They did see each other after we fell in love and planned to marry. On top of it, Michael gave Suzanne the name of the Catholic Agency where we adopted Derek! There's so much. I feel betrayed by Suzanne that she never told me." His voice faltered.

Terese took his hand. "Tom, it's nearly over. Really over. Some kind of justice will prevail. It could've been avoided if the police were involved earlier. If you had known, you could have told Bruno before her death. Will Martin be at the meeting tonight? What did Bruno say? What's his plan?"

"He didn't exactly say what it is but told me the same thing, that he wished he had known or done something and that it's nearly over."

"Does Bernice know any of this information?"

"No. I'll call her tomorrow after the arrest. It has to be before Derek's initiation. He cannot join that cult! I'll call her when we get home with the last chapter."

"You're sure Bruno will be there tonight? With back-up? A gun? What will this do to Derek?"

"Yes, love. We'll be safe. Derek will have to see Peter's father handcuffed and led away. The rest? I don't know. Most likely, he'll still see Peter as innocent.

269

Because now they are 'all about love,' as he says, Derek may remain blinded by love. I don't know, but I'll be there with him." He added, "In truth."

CHAPTER FORTY-NINE
PETER, WOLFGANG, AND MARTIN: SEDONA, 1992

On Wednesday at seven in the evening, it was dark outside the center. Inside, incandescent lamps at the various teak tables glowed a soft light. There were no candles and no robes. It's a business meeting for Maharba. The men sat in various groupings on couches, chairs, and settees. Most had a drink in hand, some cigars. Martin sat with two of the men, the compliant ones. Occasionally he glared at Peter, mouth twisted in scorn.

Wolfgang and Peter quietly exchanged a few words on the side. "Did you close everything up?"

"Yes, I emptied my apartment of anything personal, my university office as well, and even put a sign up for Love, Inc. stating the center would be closed until further notice."

"Derek?"

"I didn't see him but left a voice message apologizing and promising the next two nights together. I hate to cause him distress since he's done so much for us. However, it's just one life. There will be other Dereks for me, but never another Peter for him." Peter's tone was clearly sardonic, his full lips curving. "Everything else on schedule?"

"It certainly is. Good work, Peter." Wolfgang looked around at the plush setting commenting on how well it has served them. "Hate to leave the Eames chairs. We'll get new ones." He put his feet on the brass and glass coffee table. "Anything else before we get on with the meeting?"

Peter wondered aloud, "What happens to all this elegant furniture? My apartment things?"

"We don't look back, Peter. Once we have learned what we need from history, we take it forward into a whole new day. Are you ready for this meeting and for what comes afterward?"

"I am. I'm so ready. Proceed." He checked the supplies in the far corner and was pleased.

Wolfgang stood up and a hush entered the room. He walked to the altar and looked at each member, connecting with them individually. "This is the last night that we meet as the Southwest Quadrant of Maharba."

Martin rose quickly. "What the hell are you talking about?" His large booming voice, matched his ferocious look and his oversized body.

Wolfgang simply gripped Martin's eyes with his clear gaze until Martin looked away reluctantly. "Martin, it's all working out. I called you several times this afternoon. You never picked up. I found Peter and we devised a plan. No intent to leave you out."

"I was with Adolf. He's being transferred to a different nursing home. Why Peter? Why was he involved?" He grumbled and sat back down.

"Because Peter has some information regarding the FBI from a very reliable source. I would think is of prime importance to you, considering 1963." Martin blinked. His face went empty.

"As you know, Derek's father's trip to Smotelyville has stirred things up for us." He looked around the circle. "I highly suspect the FBI will be here tomorrow night because Derek, and most likely his father, believe it's the New Maharba or Love, Inc. meeting. They will be here; we will not."

Several of the men looked puzzled. One questioned, "Love, Inc.?"

"It is a ploy for Derek to return tomorrow night. We will always be Maharba. Martin, you best get Adolf to another state, soon. Everyone else must leave or stay low until we tell you the location of the new center in a few months. The center will create the Maharba Trinity, our new organizational configuration. There really is no need for the rest of you to worry about the FBI. I believe they are only interested in one of us. Cults are not illegal, as we know."

"Ha! The unholy trinity!" laughed one of the men. "Perfect!"

Martin stood up again, his face a contorted mash of anger gathering into rage. "Why was I not in on these discussions, these major decisions!"

Peter said nothing, not wanting to incite him more. Not yet.

Very calmly, Wolfgang explained the plan was devised quickly. He counted on Martin staying after the meeting to revise and firm things up. With the FBI close on their heels, the members needed to choose to leave or live under the radar until they heard from the leaders.

"In fact, I propose we restate our vows of loyalty before we bid farewell, knowing we'll meet next as a stronger Maharba to continue the work of our forefathers. We'll see no more of the lurking FBI who wants to finish old business." He looked pointedly at Martin, who flushed.

During the next hour, the men repeated their vows, chanting, and making the geometric configurations in the air. They did their special handshake and left the room in solidarity.

The atmosphere subtly changed and it seemed that time moved slower. Martin, Wolfgang, and Peter arranged a small setting for their meeting. Peter locked the door and Wolfgang began. "Do you want to know the whole plan, Martin? Or just live it?"

Something in Wolfgang's voice and manner checked Martin's rage. "What plan? I make the plans, not you and certainly not Peter, who's been censured. Derek's a wimp and out of Maharba. I decree it. Both are ousted faggots. We need to find some new members. Who do you think would be good, Wolfgang?" He took out a cigar, licked it, and pulled out his gold guillotine cigar cutter.

Wolfgang repeated in slow deliberate tones, "Do you want to hear the plan, Martin, or live it?"

Martin stopped his cigar ritual, put down the cutter, and asked, "Live it? What the hell are you talking about?"

For the first time ever, they saw a fleeting glimpse of fear in Martin. "Well, you see, Martin, we can tell or we can show the plan," Wolfgang responded, never leaving Martin's eyes.

"Great little tool, that cutter. Don't you think so, Peter?"

Martin looked from one to the other. "I don't like what I see." He tried to speak loudly, but his words came out quieter than he intended. He began coughing.

Peter got up and walked to the altar, removed the satin covering, and folded it neatly on the right side of the altar.

"What are you doing?" Martin demanded. "Answer me, Peter! Now!"

"Just getting the altar ready for the last Sedona sacrifice, Father. It's our offering." Peter moved with purpose, as he realized he had not called Martin "Father" since he was a boy. He looked at Martin and saw fear for the second time. His father's fear began to dismantle the dam built around Peter's heart in childhood. *Yes. For this moment, the dam could slowly come down.* His heart remained stone-strong.

"What's the story, Father? Abraham takes Isaac up the mountain and lays him on the altar? Binds him? Raises the knife to kill his son? Maybe he is a member of Maharba? Oh, of course not, we are named after him. We still can reenact the scene. Maybe change it a little? What do you think?" Peter turned to look at his father and saw his face drained of color.

"I see no need for that." What began in bluster ended in a garble. Clearing his throat, he repeated, "No need."

Peter opened the deeply polished teak chest and removed the silver chalice, placing it on the left side of the altar. He stopped, rethinking, and placed it on the chest instead. Noticing a piece of dust, he removed the polishing cloth, working to sanctify the chalice. "Important to remove every mote, right Father? I

274

remember you telling me you had to remove every mote of impurity from my soul."

Martin was silent, determined to repress his rising terror and get out from under what felt like a clear reversal of power. He looked to the door.

Peter suddenly glanced at his father. "Father, you don't look so good. Is anything wrong? Did you maybe want to apologize for 'faggot?'" After opening the top drawer with felt covering on the inside, Peter took out the blade and began to polish it. He polished slowly and sensually as his memories of childhood continued their deluge into full consciousness.

Wolfgang was fascinated by the slow-motion scene unfolding before him. "Peter, you know I didn't mean it. I was angry. Our thirty-year plan went wrong."

Peter repeated the question, while polishing every facet, every jewel in the blade. "Do you want to apologize?"

"Yes. Yes. I'm sorry. Now I need to go to Adolf."

Wolfgang broke in. "You needn't worry about Adolf anymore, Martin. He's dead," and he picked up the cutter. "I never understood why men use this type of cutter. It reminds me of a circumcision. What do you think, Martin?" Peter's eyes gleamed at Wolfgang's words.

Martin began to sweat. Something was terribly, terribly wrong. "Adolf dead?"

"Yes, we wanted to be sure he wasn't left in the nursing home with no visitors. That wouldn't be kind." Wolfgang sat back in the Eames chair and put his feet on the table in front of him.

"So, Father, do you know Wolfgang and I are initiating a new Maharba tonight?" He continued stroking the blade.

"Yes. I know. Triangle, not Quadrant."

Peter looked up and raised his voice. "Trinity, not triangle! You don't ever listen to me, do you? You don't know. You don't know a fucking thing!"

Martin pulled back, desperate as his fear entwined itself with terror. "Yes. Trinity. I'm sorry."

"Come on up here, Father. We're going to play our parts in the new Maharba. I'll give you a clue. Isaac is no longer the bound one. He has the knife, a beautifully jeweled, polished, and sharpened blade like this one." He showed it to Martin. "Yes. The one we used for the goats, lambs, Suzanne, the mole, and others. Remember the mole? 1975? Remember Suzanne, Father? 1963? You used this same blade to sever her life, drain her blood, and bring her to me. Remember, Father?"

"Peter, something's all wrong. I'm afraid, Peter. Put the blade down."

Peter laughed. "Put the blade down, Peter," he mocked. "No, Martin, no blade down. Take your pants down. Your shirt off. All your clothes." Martin gasped.

"Quickly, my man. Or I shall cut them off. Swiftly." He brandished the blade and took a step forward, smiling.

The terror became horror. Martin began to remove his pants but stumbled.

"Faster, Father. Or do you need help?"

Martin struggled out of his trousers, unbuttoned his shirt, and trembled.

"All of your clothes, Martin. Shoes, socks, shorts. Quicker." Peter moved the blade slowly like a metronome. "Now, get up on the altar. You can do it, old man. Or should I help you?" He used the knife as a pointer. "See, I knew you could do it. Lie still. If you can, quit shaking. Very wimpy of you, don't you think?"

"Wolfgang, bring the leather. Bind him, please." Martin sobbed as Wolfgang tightened the leather bonds. "Turn the lights low, except for the violet one that shines upon our altar. Keep that one trained on the man I have grown to hate most in the entire world. Then you can return to your seat, Wolfgang, thank you."

Peter placed the silver chalice beneath the head of the altar. "Oh, Father, look. You have wet yourself on our sacred altar. Do you remember what you did to me when I wet the bed just once? You wrapped the wet sheets around me, around my head, tied me to the bed with your leather belt after you struck me over and over. Do you remember that?

"Let's remember the times you taught me to rip the legs off insects, kill dogs and cats? Do you remember knocking me down, punching me, beating me and knowing how not to leave bruises? What, you fool! Did you think I would forget? Cower? Honor you? Do you remember the time I was five and so proud that I cut my own toenails for the first time? You scorned me, told me I did it all wrong, and made me pick up the nails with my teeth?

"Do you remember showing me pornography and telling me, demanding that I masturbate in front of you? Was I nine, ten? You did all that to your son. To me. The man who touched me as a child, over and over. Telling me it was God's will and I must obey.

"Shine the light on him. That man. So he can see his son during his final moments. Like this..." Peter smiled as he drew a fine line across his father's neck. Martin and Peter watched as the ornate, antique silver chalice of Maharba slowly filled.

"It is finished." Peter wiped the blade clean with his own linen handkerchief, returning both to his leather case.

Wolfgang placed the chalice filled with blood on the chest and rearranged the satin around the bloodless naked man. After washing his hands, Peter wrote and carefully laid a note on the body.

They turned up the lights, closed, and locked the door. The two men walked to the Porsche, drive to the airport, and wordlessly settled into first class. The plane began to climb to the welcoming night skies, with Argentina calling to them.

It was finished.

CHAPTER FIFTY
DEREK, TOM, MARTIN, AND BRUNO: SEDONA, 1992

D erek came down to the kitchen around two-fifteen, Thursday afternoon. Drowsy and hungry, he checked the refrigerator. Terese came in, gave him a hug, and announced she would fix him a proper breakfast, or lunch, as it may be. He said he would make the coffee – as strong as possible – and then sat down. She couldn't read his mood.

"How are you doing after your appointment last night? Your dad told me much of it. I can't imagine what it is like for you right now."

"Terese, I love you and always will. I'm not able to talk about the fact that my dad is not my dad right now. Okay? Maybe down the road. Right now, I'm going to focus on my new life with Peter and Maharba."

Terese took a deep breath. "Of course, Derek. I am here whenever you need me. You know that. You know I love you." Derek nodded.

She continued, "Do you know what's going to happen tonight? How do you feel about it?"

"After my coffee, I'll feel pretty excited. A whole new group and no animal sacrifices: we will just be practicing love. I am going to need it after yesterday's news of you being my second adoptive mother and he being my adoptive father."

"I'm sorry he never told you. He felt he needed to protect you. As you grew, it kept getting harder. He didn't even tell me until right before his trip back East. I'm really sorry. It's not easy for you." She reached her hand to his.

He put his hands over hers. "I know you're sorry, but Terese, I'm really sick of hearing 'sorries.' They don't make it any easier. I feel like then I'm supposed to make you feel better when I'm the one who has been deeply hurt for my whole life."

"You're right. You're absolutely right. Is there anything I can do?"

278

"No, but thanks for asking. Well, I guess there are a couple of things. I'm staying in Sedona over the weekend. For another thing, I'm going to be out of contact for a while. I need to work this my-entire-life-being-a-lie thing through on my own. I'll call now and then, but please do not contact me. Tell Dad the same thing. I can't go over anything anymore, too exhausting."

Terese held back reacting. "Okay, Derek, whatever you need. Know we are here. Breakfast?" She placed pancakes, bacon, eggs, and a croissant in front of him. She would convince Tom to let him alone for a bit after the meeting tonight. What a story! She sat down and casually picked up the afternoon mail.

Tom walked into the breakfast room and wondered why Terese gave him the eye immediately. "Hi, Derek. Good plan to come down here and get some sleep." He almost asked about his dinner plans last night with Peter, then quickly decided to back off. "We'll leave around three. We don't have checked bags, so there's plenty of time." He checked his watch.

Derek nodded, finished, and announced he'd be in the shower and down at three. "Thanks, Terese, it was perfect."

"What's that all about?" Tom asked when they heard the shower turn on. "Pretty grim in here."

"Wouldn't you be pretty grim if you found out at thirty that your father lied to you about your whole life?"

He saw her anger. "You're right. It's the biggest mistake of my life."

She asked, "Did Bruno call?"

"Yes, but he was terse. He told me to go to Sedona with Derek and he would take care of the rest. It's certainly going to be a big night."

"Are you going to be okay, Tom? I mean, as far as you know?"

"Well, if I'm not okay with two members of the FBI covering us, I don't imagine I'll ever be okay. I'll call as soon as I can. Terese, I regret getting you into this whole mess."

"It's part of the better or worse. Please don't probe Derek. He needs some time off from family. It's the best we can do for him right now, especially after tonight."

"Okay, I know. I'll curb it on the way down there and let him decide afterwards what he wants." He made a zipping motion over his mouth.

She smiled and turned to get more coffee.

The plane ride to Sedona was very quiet in seats 25 A and B. They both read and had one drink each. They caught a taxi to take them to the Maharba center. The taxi driver squinted at Derek in the rearview mirror.

"Didn't I just pick you up, young man? Late Tuesday night? Rushing to the airport? Wasn't your name Tom?"

"I'm not Tom, and yes, you are correct," Derek said in a tone that shut down further conversation. He paid in cash in front of the center.

"There're no lights, Derek."

"Because the center is in the middle of the building, on the bottom floor, no windows. Just follow me. I have the code for the door."

Tom watched him press 666 twice. He shook his head in dismay but kept quiet. The door unlocked.

Derek wound around a sinuous passage that seemed to go down forever. Tom followed, his heartbeat increasing in rapidity. Only their shoes made sounds. He reminded himself that Bruno and his colleague were somewhere nearby.

"Here's the center." Derek put in the same code and the door unlocked. They entered the room with the purple spotlight on the altar. Derek shut the door after him. "This is strange. The meeting's at ten. It's nine-forty-five and no one is here but the lights are on. There is no phone in the building. I can't call anyone. Something's wrong."

Tom was the first to see what was wrong. "Oh, my God!" he couldn't help shouting.

"Derek, don't look."

Of course, Derek looked. He ran up to the altar shouting, "No! No! No!" He saw the scarlet-filled chalice. He staggered.

Tom followed him to the stark white, bound, naked body with a perfect slit in its throat. He saw the note and streaks of dark blood. He had an immediate flashback to Suzanne with parchment on her chest and knew he would not touch this paper. He felt sick and weak. "Who is it?"

"It's Martin, Peter's dad. I don't know what to do!" Derek saw his name on the note, written on parchment. He felt his body quaver.

Derek grabbed the note and sat heavily on a chair facing away from the altar. Tom continued to stare at Suzanne's killer, murdered. He thought it almost looked like one of the four men. No, he couldn't remember. He sat down and covered his face with his hands. He was beginning to lose consciousness. He had to stay alive for Aron. He put his head between his knees.

Derek read to himself.

Sorry, Derek.

I know I lied.

It's who I am.

You'll never see me again.

Believe me.

You'll be fine.

Thanks for the memories.

Take this key to my apartment.

Take whatever you want.

It's yours.

A gift of our time together.

Ciao. Peter.

erek stayed sitting, too broken to weep. His anger was as a machine gun. "Fuck it all! Everyone. Everyone lies. Everyone betrays. I'm getting out of here!" He started to get up, but fell back into the chair, filled with weakness.

Tom was in his own emotional flashback, shocked and helpless. Again, a bloodless cold body, again the parchment of the past. He felt the horror as if for the first time.

The door opened. Bruno and his colleague walked in, immediately took in the scene, and went to the men. Bruno nodded to the other man to make the ambulance call. Bruno sat down in front of Tom and Derek.

"I'm sorry you had to see this, Derek, Tom."

"Sorries! Everyone has their sorries all the time. But nobody fucking does anything! Where were you when this murder happened?" Derek turned to Bruno. "Why didn't you solve it thirty years ago and none of this would've happened. Who killed him?" Derek seemed to forget Peter wrote the note.

Bruno couldn't believe what he was hearing, but then realized Derek was in shock.

"You're right, Derek. It should have been solved and it wasn't. Now it is. The murderer of Suzanne has received justice. Thirty years too late, I agree. We don't know who killed him. I have a sense no one is going to report him missing. Do you want justice for him?" Bruno pointed to the bloodless body. "Do you really want us to look for Martin's killer? I suspect that person is en route out of our jurisdiction."

"Are you sure it's him, Bruno?" Tom needed to be undeniably certain.

"Is that Martin, Derek?"

"Yes, it's Martin." He dropped his head onto his chest, motionless.

Tom tried to get up and sat back down. "I'm done looking for killers, Bruno. Derek?"

Derek shot an undecipherable look at Tom, put the folded parchment in his pocket, and moved his head from side to side. "Don't look."

"I'll take care of his body with the local police. Stay there, Tom. The ambulance is coming. You and Derek aren't in any condition to leave on your own. The shock will take a while to go away. I'll see you in the ER." Bruno put his hand on Tom's shoulder. "It's finished, Tom. Case closed."

D erek and Tom rode in the ambulance together. The ER put father and son in adjoining rooms. "I've got to leave tonight. I have to get out of here," repeated Derek over and over.

"There's no flights tonight, son. You'll be out of here tomorrow," the nurse assured him.

"Not even the late one with all the connections? The one I took Tuesday?"

"No flights. Easy."

After a full exam, they were sent upstairs to the same room with medication to ease the shock and tension and make them sleep deeply. Neither spoke. The next morning Bruno walked in and quietly told them he found flights leaving in three or four hours.

"Are you going to Portland or Seattle, Derek?" he gently asked.

"Seattle, as soon as I can. My car's in Portland and I'm not returning there for a while." He looked to Bruno to solve it.

"We'll get it to you as quickly as possible, two days at the most. Jake, my colleague, will ride with you on your flight, Derek. He has to go to Seattle as well. He'll fill you in, if you want, if that's okay? We'll get someone to drive your car to Seattle."

"Sure. Fine. What's not okay keeps happening over and over. Why ask?" He turned on his side.

While Bruno was finishing flight arrangements, the nurse came in to tell them both to take some time off to recuperate: doctor's orders.

"I'm fine," retorted Tom.

"I'll fly with you, Tom. You're not in very good shape. I called Terese last night. She knows you both are o... I mean safe."

Tom half-smiled, his shock reduced considerably. He saw Derek looked worse than ever. He didn't want to see Derek leave, yet knew there was no other choice. He was grateful Jake would be with him.

O n the flight to Seattle, Derek slept most of the way, unable to face the contradictions and conflict that only mushroomed with each passing thought. At one point, Jake asked if he would mind if Jake shared a small part of his life. Derek nodded.

"I lost my first boyfriend. He was killed in a motorcycle accident. So was the man he was with. I never knew he was seeing someone. It's not like your loss, I know, but the feelings of betrayal with the loss are similar. It takes time, Derek. It takes time."

Derek looked at him. "Thanks."

T om arrived home with Bruno, introduced him to Terese, and showed him the guest room. Bruno thanked them. He knew all three of them needed to talk. There were decades of questions of murder, justice, and cults.

Later that day, Tom said he had to call Bernice and tell her the final story. It seemed so long since he had seen her, although it wasn't very long at all.

"Bernice, it's Tom. Is this a good time for me to call? Thanks. Yes, I'm fine, but there is an incredible story you have to hear. I hate to do it on the phone. What? You would come here?! That's wonderful. When? Of course, call me with the flight info. I'll be there. Of course, you'll stay here; Terese can't wait to meet you. Derek lives in Seattle. I can't promise you'll meet him this visit, but I know you will. I do have a gift for you. It's been wrapped for thirty years. And Bernice? It's finished. There is justice. Occasionally, there is justice."

CHAPTER FIFTY-ONE
JEMMA AND DEREK: SEATTLE, 1992

J emma knew she had to go to Peter's office. She needed some kind of closure. Giles told her on Friday that Peter was gone, had cleared his office of personal things and, well, just vanished. Somehow, she didn't feel like she imagined she would feel. Monday brought her to the darkened hallway leading to Peter's office. She walked closer and saw someone sitting on the bench in front of the dark door. The name plate was gone. What should she do?

She sat down and recognized the young man from Azure's waiting room. His sunken chest, thinner face, and forlorn look opened her heart. "Do you mind if I sit here?"

He lifted his head. "No, of course not. There's nothing much I mind anymore. I minded too much. Doesn't matter if I do mind, either. The bench is long enough. I can always leave if I want to. That much I have control of in my life, if nothing else." He looked at her momentarily, then returned to his vigil of staring at the dark door.

Jemma risked one more question. "Were you looking for Peter, too?"

"Not anymore. He's gone."

"I did hear he left abruptly. I think I had to come here to be certain. I also heard he said goodbye to no one." She softened her voice. "Not to you, either, it looks like. By the way, I'm Jemma. I worked with Peter in the Adoption Project. You look familiar." She offered her hand.

He took it. "I'm Derek. Yes, I'm in the Project. An adoptee. Three times."

"Three times? Adopted by three families?" She was thoroughly confused. "I am being intrusive. We can stop talking if you are uncomfortable."

"No, for some reason, it's okay with me. The first time anything has been okay in a long time. I haven't talked with anyone all weekend. The people I thought were my real parents, until less than a week ago, adopted me when I was two weeks old. Then my adoptive mother was murdered the next day. My adoptive father fled with me to Minneapolis, fearing for our lives. Then we moved to Portland. He married Terese a year later and she adopted me. For thirty years, I believed he was my biological dad and that the murdered woman was my biological mom.

"Last week my father told me most of that story wasn't true. I'm not going into it, but I'm taking a break from him. Then, the next day, I had a horrific experience and I lost Peter." He gave a deep sigh. "Did you know him?"

Jemma was trying to sort out Derek's tale. "Oh, yes, Peter. I knew him slightly. We were both collators on the research team. I'm on sabbatical from St. Paul. It's a small world with you being from there also, well, Minneapolis. What do you mean you 'lost' him?"

Derek turned to look at her. "He was my lover, my boyfriend. He was my first boyfriend. I had no idea he was leaving. No idea he was leaving *me*. Now I don't think I can believe anything he ever said to me. He was in something deeper and eviler than I ever knew. He was pulling me into it. I believed him that it was about love. It wasn't. It was decidedly about evil. How can I still feel love for him while I begin to hate him at the same time?"

Jemma felt so much for him. She had instant compassion, sadness, a deep desire to help. She remembered feeling the same in Azure's waiting room. "It must be terrible for you. First the family truths..."

He interrupted. "Lies."

"Yes, the family lies. Then your lover abandoning you. Now seeing a totally different side of him. Then there are the horror and circumstances that I don't know and can't even imagine."

"No, you can't." Derek sat with his elbows on his knees and head in his hands. He turned to her. "Thank you for not saying you're sorry. I cannot hear another 'I'm sorry' without vomiting or screaming."

She smiled. "Well, I am glad I avoided both of those reactions."

"I won't ever get over him. He helped me to recognize that I'm gay. It was very recent." Tears welled up. He showed her the name plate he removed before she sat down. "'Peter Gehman, Ph.D.' I'm taking it as a keepsake. Some souvenir," he said bitterly.

Jemma saw the pain in Derek's whole body. She felt his broken heart and felt hers. What now? She couldn't walk away after he had poured out his sad story. "Are you sure you're okay with telling me all this? I can leave if you want to be alone."

"Apparently I am okay with it. Don't go. Alone and sad are too overwhelming right now." He wiped his eyes with his sleeve. "I'm not even sorry for crying. I have no choice." He met her eyes for a few seconds before looking away.

"You're right. Pretty wise for you to see that," she encouraged him.

"Sometimes. Sometimes I have a choice, but not now."

"Derek, we can stay here and keep talking, although in front of this dark office is pretty desolate. We can also go to my office down the hall, which is much lighter, or if you're hungry, we can get a bite to eat. I know of a good coffee shop."

"The B&O?"

"No, but I do love that one. It's close to my apartment. This one's called Paradox. It was started by two doctors." She waited.

He half-smiled. "Ha! Generally, I enjoy a good pun. It's good, but I don't know if I'll ever appreciate anything again. Enjoyment seems to have gone underground."

"Did hunger go with it?" She asked.

"I don't know. I haven't eaten much since Friday." He took a minute, continuing to stare at the dark door. "Yes, I would like that. My car's not here. It's in Portland."

"No problem. Mine is out front. Let's go." Jemma stood up, suddenly anxious to be away from Peter's office. She was uncomfortable with Peter's name plate going with them.

Derek stood up, put the plate on the bench, and explained, "I really don't need a stupid stolen sign. It seems I have his apartment full of things. Weird, I know."

"Yes, it is," she agreed. She thought to find out more at Paradox. Derek and his story clearly intrigued her.

She pulled into Paradox, remembering it was where Peter took her many months ago. She thought of it as a redo. Meeting Derek would supplant Peter's memory. She did not know Derek carried much more of Peter than she could imagine.

They walked in and found the only open booth close to the back of the restaurant. "I'm an introvert. I hate being in the middle of a restaurant in the mix. I hope this booth is okay with you?"

Derek smiled. "Sure. Me, too, although I never would have known why I picked an obscure booth."

They sat across from each other, studied the menu and ordered. He looked up at her.

Jemma was startled and almost shot straight up. His eyes. Who? Whose? She remembered Richard had very similar eyes. Richard? Twice in one week? She began to notice her heart beating. "So, you were born in Minneapolis?"

"Not born there. I was born in Chicago. Well, now I don't even know if that's true, seeing as everything else is not true about me. All of it is coming out and I suspect more lies will be revealed. I was adopted in Chicago. But when we fled to Minneapolis, my dad and I, and even my murdered mother, got new identities like in the movies."

"When were you born?" Jemma tentatively questioned. She took a silent breath.

"Again, that's another lie I've discovered. I thought that the August 10, 1963 on my birth certificate was when I was born. But my dad said all the original records were destroyed and my real birthday is June 29, 1963."

288

Jemma knew. His eyes were Richard's. Chicago. Destroyed records. The awakened memory of Richard in Azure's office. She knew why she had remembered her father. She could see the likeness to him as well. A tsunami of tears threatened. "One moment, Derek, I'll be right back."

She leaned against the bathroom wall and could not stop crying. She took deep breaths, splashed cold water on her face, and reapplied some of the deluged makeup. She began her longest walk ever back to their table. "Excuse me, Derek. I'm fine, just had a wave of memory." She sat down and picked up the menu.

She held back her tears, the urge to hug him and never let him go. Jemma thought deeply and knew she had to proceed very slowly. Now was not the time. She knew she needed more validation. Maybe a DNA test down the road. She didn't mind because there were years ahead of them. He did not need one more trauma. She had the rest of her life to know her son now that she knew. Deep in her heart, she knew.

WITH DEEPEST GRATITUDE

I have been blessed with many encouragers, readers, and supporters throughout the development of *Blood Draw*. I know I would not have written, much less finished, my book without the biweekly input of the Mac's Backs Writers' Group! Thank you, Suzanne and Rosa, for your generosity and warmth providing the space and welcome. Thank you, Writers' Group: Ben Langhinrichs, Brad Zuercher, Chris Garson, Doug Guth, Eileen Beal, Robert Sheeley, & Quinn Hull.

I am deeply grateful to my dedicated Alpha readers who plowed through a terribly formatted first draft and provided encouragement and excellent suggestions: Chris Garson, Cynthia Nodland, Debbi Mayo, Dee Shedlow, Glenn Lyons, Jim Oathout, Keli Zehnder, Lou Freborne, and my dear first-grade friend Ron Schwartz. Thank you! Thank you! Thank you!

Thank you, family and friends, for your four-year-long interest and support, especially Cindi Lee, Howard Davis, LouLeary Dennis, and Marie Conder.

Several singer-songwriters have been Muses to me. I thank Joni Mitchell for *The Magdalene Laundries*, in addition to her other songs. I thank the late Leonard Cohen for *Anthem* and all of his songs. I thank K.D. Lang for her powerful rendition of Cohen's *Hallelujah*, and Ann Mortifee for the songs of her journey.

Bethany Beams, my book birthing doula, you are the miracle who truly brought *Blood Draw* into life, this very life we are holding as we read. Your exacting editing skills, your unique creativity, and so much more – especially your investment in me and my writing – are truly a gift. Thank you...

GABRIELLE JARRETT, 2018

PERMISSIONS

Motherless Child. Negro Spiritual circa 1870's by The Fisk Jubilee Singers. Score written 1899 by William E. Barton D.D.C.

I've Got the Green Light. Song written and recorded by Brian Lee. Cleveland, Ohio.

96820064R00167

Made in the USA
Lexington, KY
24 August 2018